Extinction Machine

Also by Jonathan Maberry

Novels
Assassin's Code
King of Plagues
The Dragon Factory
Patient Zero
Dead of Night
The Wolfman
Flesh & Bone
Dust & Decay
Rot & Ruin
Bad Moon Rising
Dead Man's Song
Ghost Road Blues
V-Wars (editor)

Nonfiction
Wanted Undead or Alive
They Bite
Zombie CSU
The Cryptopedia
Vampire Universe
Vampire Slayer's Field Guide to the Undead (as Shane MacDougall)
Ultimate Jujutsu
Ultimate Sparring
The Martial Arts Student Logbook
Judo and You

Graphic Novels
Marvel Universe vs. Wolverine
Marvel Universe vs. The Punisher
Marvel Universe vs. The Avengers
Captain America: Hail Hydra
Klaws of the Panther
Doomwar
Black Panther: Power
Marvel Zombies Return

Jonathan Maberry

Extinction Machine

St. Martin's Griffin
New York

EXTINCTION MACHINE. Copyright © 2013 by Jonathan Maberry. All rights reserved. Printed in the United States of America. For information, address St. Martin's Press, 175 Fifth Avenue, New York, N.Y. 10010.

www.stmartins.com

ISBN 978-0-312-55221-3 (trade paperback)
ISBN 978-1-250-02661-3 (e-book)

St. Martin's Griffin books may be purchased for educational, business, or promotional use. For information on bulk purchases, please contact Macmillan Corporate and Premium Sales Department at 1-800-221-7945 extension 5442 or write special-markets@macmillan.com.

First Edition: March 2013

10 9 8 7 6 5 4 3 2 1

This one is for Geoff, Donna, and Brandon Strauss.

And, as always, for Sara Jo.

Acknowledgments

Thanks to Bill Birnes, publisher of *UFO Magazine*; Stanton Friedman; Richard Dolan; Peter Robbins; George Noory, host of *Coast to Coast AM*; Tom Danheiser; Jeff Strauss, national technical director for MUFON (Mutual Unidentified Flying Object Network); Eunyoung Jo; Kyle S. Johnson; Ric Frane; Brian Bird; Bobby and Robin Cooper; Jared Frane; Hollie Johani Snider; Christina Kristofic; Suzanne Robb; Michael Sicilia of California Homeland Security; Nancy Keim-Comley; and Sam West-Mensch.

And, of course, my literary agents, Sara Crowe and Harvey Klinger; all the good folks at St. Martin's Griffin: Michael Homler, Joe Goldschein, Rob Grom; and my film agent, Jon Cassir of Creative Artists Agency.

Part One
Conspiracy Theories

The U.S. must carry out some act somewhere in the world
which shows its determination to continue to be a world power.

—HENRY KISSINGER, *as quoted in* The Washington Post, *April 1975*

The individual is handicapped by coming face to face
with a conspiracy so monstrous he cannot believe it exists.

—J. EDGAR HOOVER

Chapter One

The word "impossible" used to mean something. It was a line that couldn't be crossed. It was the outer edge of the safe zone.

I can't find that line anymore.

Chapter Two

Shelton Aeronautics

Wolf Trap, Virginia

Thursday, October 17, 10:36 a.m.

It started with a door knock.

It was the last time it would be knuckles on wood. Next time I'd pound with my fist.

"Nobody's home," said Bunny. Not for the first time.

"Parking lot's full of cars," said Top.

"They're here," I grumbled.

Master Sergeant Harvey "Bunny" Rabbit popped his chewing gum. "Then how come they're not answering the door?"

I gave him a withering stare. He's six seven, so I had to look up to do it. "Do I look like Carnac the Magnificent?"

"Who?"

"Cap'n's telling you that he's not psychic, Farmboy," said Top. Full name was First Sergeant Bradley Sims. He currently held my old spot as leader of Echo Team. "And I believe he's saying something to the effect that if you keep telling him no one's here he's going to kneecap you."

"Words to that effect," I said.

I knocked again. Louder. With the side of my fist.

This was not how I planned to spend my vacation. Sure, I love my country and yes I would die to protect her . . . but this was my first vacation since dinosaurs ruled the earth.

I had today planned out, too. It was a very well-constructed plan, starting with lots of sleep, followed by the kind of diner breakfast that would keep my arteries nice and hard. Then take Ghost, my white shepherd, for a long walk in the park where he would help me appear irresistible to pretty women. Then I'd catch the first part of an Orioles doubleheader in the afternoon, ideally to see them make the Phillies weep and gnash their teeth. Then back to planning the greatest bachelor party in the history of personal excess.

My best friend and occasional shrink, Rudy Sanchez, was getting hitched in two months. His fiancée, Circe O'Tree, was away on a book tour, and Saturday night was the party. I already had Sunday set aside for whatever was required after the party: medical attention, psychological counseling, or bail hearings.

Instead, where was I at ten in the morning on a glorious Thursday?

Stuffed into a suit, not flirting with girls in the park, standing outside of Shelton Aeronautics with Top and Bunny who were every bit as disgruntled as I was.

And nobody was answering the goddamn door.

We were out on one of those busybody projects that are often immense time wasters. We were out doing legwork to try and track down some cyber-terrorists. Yeah, I know—that battlefield is online so why were first-team shooters knocking on doors?

Like everything else in my life, it's complicated.

The short version is that over the last few months there have been some significant attacks on the computer systems of several of the most important defense contractors. These were all private corporations who used intranet rather than the Internet for all the important stuff, so Web access to their research records was supposed to be impossible.

Well, virtually impossible. *We* could do it. By "we" I mean my team, the Department of Military Sciences. The DMS has the MindReader computer system and MindReader is to other computers what Superman is to the spandex crowd. MindReader can intrude into any other system, read and copy its data, and exit without a trace. Its superintrusion software package is unique and it rewrites the target system's software to erase all tracks. Other invader systems leave some kind of detectable scarring, no matter how subtle. MindReader doesn't.

The attacks began small. Some cute little viruses that were more nuisance than threat. Like jabs a boxer throws when he's trying to get the measure of his opponent's timing and reflexes. You're not really trying to score with the jab, but by learning how the opponent reacts you set yourself for the hard right.

The hard right came around the first of the month.

Someone hacked the security computers at a Lockheed Martin plant in New Jersey and accessed the fire control system. The virus told the system there was a major fire in the labs and that tripped the halon fire retardant. Without a single warning bell, the security doors autolocked and massive white clouds of toxic gas began jetting into the labs. The fully staffed labs. Thirty-eight people wound up in the hospital.

Two days later a missile in a test silo in Kansas tried to launch itself. Luckily the warhead was a dummy and there was only residual fuel in the tanks, so the damage was minor. The implications, however, sent shock waves throughout the Department of Defense and Homeland.

The attacks escalated. A tapeworm tunneled through the mainframe at an Aurora Flight Sciences plant at the Manassas Regional Airport in Virginia, destroying all files associated with a new unmanned aerial vehicle, and then self-deleted. Sure, there were backups to all the files concerned with the UAV, but there was a scramble to pull them off any hard drive even remotely attached to an Internet connection.

The big play had been the triggering of an autodestruct protocol at a testing facility in Poker Flat, Alaska. The autodestruct wasn't something as dramatic as a nuclear core going into the red zone. There was no automated female voice warning everyone to get to minimum safe distance. Nothing like that. This was a small series of thermite charges connected to the mainframes of the lab's supercomputers. In the case of a physical intrusion, the crucial information was supposed to be flash transmitted to a satellite uplink right before the charges blew. Only it happened the other way around—the charges blew without warning and without uploading the files. The price tag was eleven million. Supercomputers ain't cheap.

So, the industrialists called their contacts on the congressional oversight committee, who called the brass at the DoD, who called the president, who called my boss who pulled me in despite my being on vacation. Suddenly I was attached to the Cyber Crimes Task Force.

Everybody had a theory about what was happening and who was behind it. The Chinese Ghost Net got a lot of play, of course. Lot of people in Washington agreed it was exactly the sort of thing they'd do. Not only was it a cyber-attack that was so cleverly managed that it couldn't be tracked back to anyone, it also did a lot of damage to our efforts to bring the next generation of stealth and unmanned aircraft to fruition.

Of course the Russians, Iranians, and North Koreans were put on the Cyber Crimes Task Force watch list. Even some of our allies—the Israelis, the Brits, the French, the everybody else—got some play because when you're the biggest, toughest, richest kid in school nobody really likes you.

I had to admit that I wasn't in the mood to buy Uncle Sam a beer either. How the hell were the Orioles supposed to win without me watching?

Chapter Three

Shelton Aeronautics
Wolf Trap, Virginia
Thursday, October 17, 10:37 a.m.

"Let me knock," suggested Bunny.

He knocked really hard. The door rattled, the building shook.

It was an overcast morning and every light in the place was on. No one had answered any of the phone lines and no one was answering the door.

Top cupped his hands and tried to peer through the frosted glass of the big double doors. "Lights are on, but no movement that I can see."

Shelton Aeronautics was a sixty-person firm—twelve engineers, two metallurgists, a handful of physicists, and various support staff. Owned by Howard Shelton—yes, that Howard Shelton, the one who was on the cover of *Time, Newsweek,* and every talk show from *Hannity* to *Colbert.* The guy who was putting gaudy chunks of money into commercial space programs to mine raw materials from asteroids. The Sheltons were very old money, having made their consecutive fortunes from growing tobacco, importing slaves, coal and iron mining, B-52 bombers, and more recently stealth fighters and missiles. Interesting karma.

It was a four-story block building, functional rather than decorative, with big windows on the upper stories and lots of sculpted greenery. Parking lot had a bunch of cars, one motorcycle, and a late-model ten-speed bicycle chained to a rack.

Bunny ticked his head toward the camera. "Maybe they think we're the IRS."

It was a running joke with us, because when we do plainclothes scut work like this the DMS policy recommended that we wear dark navy blue or black suits, white shirts, plain ties. The outfit marked us as feds, which was an intentional move, but at a glance we could be FBI, Secret Service, NSA, or any of the many investigative arms of the Department of Justice, Homeland, or the Department of Defense. It was a way of hiding within the nondescript federal motif. Most people, when confronted by big men in dark suits and sunglasses didn't get smart-mouthed. Not since 9/11 and the Patriot Act. And, although I thought the Patriot Act was a hastily written and poorly considered rag that I wouldn't clean my dog's ass with, the fear of its nebulous but ominous powers worked magic on tight lips.

I tapped my earbud. "Bug, where are we with that eye in the sky?"

"Getting the thermal scans now," said Bug, our computer guy. "Wow. Looks like a party in there. Massed heat signatures, all in the same room. Clustered too tight to count individuals, but there's a lot of them. Maybe the whole staff. We must be getting some interference from the structure, though. Signal's weak."

"Which room?"

"Top floor, toward the rear. Most are stationary, two are in motion on the ground floor."

"Bunny," I said, "take a walk around back."

The big young man nodded and turned to the left, heading across the manicured lawn toward the east corner of the building. Harvey "Bunny" Rabbit looks like a Southern California beach volleyball player—which he used to be—and comes off as a harmless goof—which he never was.

In a quiet voice Top said, "Not a big fan of surprises most days, Cap'n. Maybe less so on days like today."

"Hooah," I said under my breath. It's a general Ranger response that could mean anything from "yes sir" to "fuck you." Occasionally both.

I stepped directly into view of the door camera and held up my leather identification case to show the NSA credentials. Again. Then I pocketed the ID, gave the camera a look that was a carefully constructed blend of annoyance, disappointment, and a threatened ass-kicking from Uncle Sam, and stepped to the right, out of video range.

"Call it," said Top.

"Stay on the front door," I said. "I'll circle around the other way and meet Bunny."

"What do we do if no one opens a door for us? We're not here with a warrant."

I shrugged. "We'll improvise."

He grinned at that.

Behind us, the main street was mostly empty except for a few cars. No one was looking at this building, so I eased around the corner. There was nothing on the side of the building but hedges, beyond that was a narrow side street. As I passed the end of the building I saw that there was a rear entrance to the Shelton campus that spilled into a small parking lot intended for deliveries. Instead of a proper loading bay there was a walk-in entrance with a metal roll-down door. I paused. That door was up, and there was a car parked at a crooked angle in front of it.

A black SUV.

I tapped my earbud. "Cowboy to Green Giant, what's your twenty?"

"Cowboy," said Bunny, "I'm on the far side by the back corner. I can see a black—"

"I see it but I don't see you." I said quietly. There was a subtle movement to my right and I saw a muscular shoulder move into and back out of my line of sight. Bunny was at the far corner of the building, in a shaded cleft between the wall and a row of trees.

"I see you," I said. "Any movement?"

"Nothing. You?"

I drew my weapon and moved away from the tree, cutting through the hedges to the side street to put them between me and anyone who might be in the car. I bent low and ran fast along the pavement until I reached the driveway, then stopped for a moment to study the scene from this new angle. The windows of the SUV were smoked to opacity. Both front doors were open. I lingered at the corner of the building, searching the scene with narrowed eyes.

Bunny spoke quietly in his ear. "I can see the plate. Federal tags. Running it now."

"Copy that. I'm going to the car," I said. "Watch me."

I rose from cover and ran in a diagonal line to come up on the driver's side blind spot. I reached the car in two seconds.

"Empty," I said. "Nothing inside. Bug—what do you have on the plate?"

"Uh-oh," said Bug, "MindReader's kicking back a 'no-such-number.' These guys are either phony or deep, deep cover."

"We're not the only gunslingers investigating this thing," I said.

"I'll keep looking," said Bug.

Bunny said, "You're thinking these guys have cover that goes deeper than MindReader? Is that even possible?"

I hurried over to meet Bunny near the open back door. The big man had his gun out, too. We nodded to each other and then wheeled around the edge of the open door, bringing our weapons up in two-handed grips.

All we saw was a storeroom filled with boxes. No people.

There was an inner door at the back off the storeroom. It was closed.

We moved inside, each of us moving along one wall so our field of fire could cover a large portion of the room and offer crossfire backup. Very quietly I murmured, "Cowboy to Sergeant Rock, hold your position. We're going inside."

"Call and I'll come running," he said.

At the back Bunny and I faded to either side of the door.

"You open and cover," I said. "I'll go through."

Bunny nodded and reached for the handle. But before he could even touch it the door opened and two men stepped through into the storeroom.

Two big men. Dressed exactly like us. Black suits, white shirts, dark ties. Wires behind their ears.

The newcomers stared at Bunny and me.

Bunny and I raised our guns.

"Federal agents," we barked. "Turn and face the wall. Hands on the wall. Do it now."

The strangers did not move. If the license plates hadn't popped up as phony we might have handled this different, but my spider-sense was tingling.

"You're making a mistake," said the taller of the two. His voice was calm, his pronunciation of each word very precise.

"And you are pissing me off," I said. "I told you to face the wall."

"We're federal agents," said the shorter of the strangers. "We have identification."

"Nice to know. But the man said to assume the position, chief," said Bunny, getting close enough to fill the man's line of sight with a lot of chest. "Don't make a mistake here."

The two men looked at each other. There was no change in their expressions, no obvious exchange of signals, however without another word they turned and placed their palms against the cinder-block wall of the storeroom. They spread their feet and waited.

Bunny nodded to me and I took up a shooting position, feet wide and braced, hands holding my Beretta rock steady. Bunny holstered his piece and used both hands to do a quick but very thorough pat down of each man. He wasn't rough about it, but it wasn't a Swedish massage either.

"Gun," he announced as he pulled the first man's jacket back to reveal what looked to be a Taser in a shoulder holster. "I think."

Bunny took the gun and showed it to me. It wasn't a Taser but I didn't know what it was. It had a chunky frame with a slightly elongated square barrel. At each of the four corners of the barrel were curved metal prongs. There was no opening to the barrel, so whatever this gun did, firing bullets was not part of its function. That didn't mean it was a toy. There were a lot of variations of Tasers out there and some of them were quite nasty. A few of them were even lethal. Bunny dropped the gun into his jacket pocket, then took the man's wallet and ID case. He continued with the pat down and paused again, feeling along the agent's arms. Then he grabbed the back of the man's jacket collar and yanked the sports coat down and off.

"What?" I asked.

"He's wearing something under his shirt."

The agent said, "Don't ruin your career with a bad choice."

Bunny showed him a lot of white teeth. "How about you pour yourself a nice big cup of shut the fuck up?"

Then he hooked his fingers between the folds of the man's shirt and yanked. Fabric tore, buttons flew everywhere and Bunny stepped back to let me see. Beneath the crisp white shirt was what looked like a gray leotard. It was very thin and formfitting, and it was crisscrossed with a mesh of thin wires.

"The hell is that?" I asked.

"Thermal underwear," said the agent.

Bunny pinched some of the fabric between his fingers and rubbed it. "I think it's some kind of Kevlar. Like that new spider-silk stuff, but thinner." He gave the agent an uptick of the chin. "What's with the wires?"

"Insulation for duty in cold weather."

"Uh-huh," murmured Bunny. He repeated the pat-down procedure with the second man, found another four-prong gun, and confirmed that the man wore the same micro-thin Kevlar. He took their ID cases and flipped them open. "FBI. Agent Henckhouser and Special Agent Spinlicker."

I glanced at the pictures on the IDs Bunny held up, but I didn't lower my gun.

"May we turn around?" asked the shorter man, Spinlicker.

"Turn around," I said, "but stand right there."

The agents turned slowly. Their faces were bland, their eyes dark and calm. Spinlicker asked, "Are you with the Cyber Crimes Task Force?"

"Are you?" I countered.

"You're required to show us your identification," said Henckhouser.

"Blow me," I said.

Bunny backed six feet away and drew his gun. With his other hand he tapped his earbud and read the ID info to Bug.

I lowered my pistol, letting it hang by my side. "Okay, gents, you want to tell me who you are and why you're here?"

Henckhouser said, "How about returning our weapons and possessions?"

"How about I don't and you answer my questions?"

The agents said nothing.

"Where's the staff?" I asked.

Henckhouser and Spinlicker exchanged a look, but said nothing.

Top buzzed me. "You need backup, Cowboy?"

"Negative, we got this," I said. "Let me know if you see anyone else."

"Copy."

Then Bug was on the line. "Got something for you. The names and descriptions match active agents, but I have a couple red flags. The first is that they are currently assigned to the Alaska bureau. They're not supposed to be all the way down here."

"That's interesting," said Bunny. "Maybe they're allergic to moose."

It was a joke but it was also a code for Bug's ears. Alaska was where the Poker Flat testing range was. One of the first sites of the cyber-terrorism campaign.

"Give me something better."

"That's the second red flag. MindReader kind of burped while running these guys down. At first we got a message saying that they were inactive, with a pop-up screen providing details of how they were both KIA while on that white supremacist terrorist thing in Pine Deep, Pennsylvania, ten years ago. But then the system did an autocorrect and replaced that with an error message. Now I have data saying that they are on active status."

"So—is that a computer error or what?"

"I'd go with 'what,'" said Bug. "Doesn't feel good, Cowboy. We're contacting the FBI deputy director to the lowdown."

"Keep me posted," I said. "In the meantime I think we'll take these jackasses into custody. Maybe they'll enjoy sitting in a holding cell for the rest of the month."

Agent Henckhouser said, "You're making an unfortunate mistake, Captain Ledger."

That froze the moment.

I took a half step forward and pointed my gun at Henckhouser's face. "Now how in the wide blue fuck do you know my name?"

Henckhouser continued to smile. "We're working toward the same goal, Captain. We both want to know who is behind the sabotage."

"Not liking this, boss," murmured Bunny.

I sucked my teeth. "Okay, I want both of you ass-clowns facedown on the ground, hands on your heads, fingers laced."

Bunny produced a fistful of plastic flexcuffs and reached a hand out to turn Spinlicker.

Then without a word or a change of expression, Agent Spinlicker lunged at Bunny.

It just happened.

There was no tensing of muscles, no sign at all. Spinlicker went from bland immobility into a full-speed attack that was so blindingly fast—so improbably fast—that Bunny was caught totally off guard.

Before I could even react, Henckhouser's left hand whipped out and knocked my gun arm aside and he chopped at my throat with the stiffened edge of one callused hand.

Chapter Four

Shelton Aeronautics

Wolf Trap, Virginia

Thursday, October 17, 10:41 a.m.

I turned, sloppy but fast, and took the blow on my shoulder. Spinlicker pivoted and did his level best to bury his fist in my kidney. I twisted away and the punch hit at the wrong angle, skittering up my spine. Even so there was enough solid force behind the blow to knock me forward.

Out of the corner of my eye I saw Bunny stagger backward into a stack of boxed computer paper. The whole stack canted and fell, hammering Bunny down to the floor. Reams of paper flew everywhere, sliding like bulky hockey pucks across the concrete floor.

Then I was too busy to look. Henckhouser drove straight at me, throwing rather conventional karate-style kicks and punches at me, but throwing them with insane force and speed. He was like Chuck Norris in his prime, and then fed a shovel full of uncut coke. I blocked, evaded, and parried as fast as I could.

Son of a bitch was dishearteningly good.

Then I saw an opening and changed the game on him. He tried to smash my nose with a back fist but I ducked directly into it so that he crunched his knuckles against my forehead. It hurt me, but it had to have done damage to him. The backfist isn't intended as a bone breaker. He hissed in pain—the most human reaction he'd had so far—and yanked back his hand like it had been scalded. I dove into that, following the hand back, making the long reach to slap his elbow up, and then drove one mother of a straight right hand into his short ribs.

It knocked air out of him with a whoosh and he fell back in a sideways series of tiny overlapping steps. He kept his balance, though, and when I closed on him he tried to kneecap me with a low side-thrust kick.

I dropped into a crouch and used the sudden dip in weight to drive a pile-driver fist into the hard meat on the outside of his thigh. That's usually a deal closer. You put 80 percent of your body weight into a downward punch that concentrates all that speed and mass into the surface area of two knuckles and the other guy sits down and cries for mommy. If he's lucky, and if he has friends to help him, in two hours he'll be able to limp out to the car. That was the basic plan, and I hit him a doozy. I think the inventor of the side-thrust kick suddenly rose from the dead and yelled ouch.

Agent Henckhouser winced.

Didn't fall down. Didn't burst into girlish tears.

He winced.

Balls.

And I remembered the thin Kevlar he was wearing. There are all sorts of new experimental body armor materials out there, and some of them could stop more than a bullet. Some were designed to slough off the foot pounds of impact. I had a bad feeling that Henckhouser's longjohns were making my attacks feel like baby taps.

Shit.

He abruptly dropped, spun, caught up one of the fallen reams of computer paper and, while still moving, twisted and flung it at me with all the skill and precision of a competitive Frisbee player.

I got my arms up to block it.

The second one he threw caught me right in the gut and knocked all the air out of my lungs. I went *whooooof* and fell backward into the stacked boxes of office supplies—which tore apart as they toppled over, showering me with packs of Post-it notes, plastic boxes of pushpins, packages of pens, and rolls of toilet paper.

I was buried up to my teeth. As I began to thrash and flounder my way out, I saw that Bunny was on his knees and he had his weapon. Then there was the thunder of gunfire as he opened up on the agents. His first round went wide, but he kept firing. Henckhouser started for the open loading door, but that was Bunny's best line of fire; so the agent shoved some stacks of boxes at him and made for the inner door. Bunny corrected his aim, but then Agent Spinlicker plowed right into him, driving him all the way across the loading bay. Bunny clubbed the agent with the gun and twisted his massive body and they were halfway into a turn when they crunched into another stack of boxes. Whatever was in the boxes was too fragile to withstand the impact and the two men collapsed into a deep, ragged hole. More cartons rained down, smashing Bunny and Spinlicker to their knees.

I was in the middle of a comedy act. The more I tried to fight my way free of the office supplies, the more of it rained down on me.

Looking dazed and hurt, Bunny still managed to swing the gun around, but Spinlicker swatted it out of his hand. The agent punched Bunny in the chest.

Bunny was six and a half feet of lean muscle and brute strength, but even so the punch half lifted him off his knees. He exhaled with a mighty *whooof* that was identical to my own.

That Kevlar underwear had to be more than protection. Those wires must be part of a muscle enhancement system. I'd read reports on those but no one had perfected the science yet. Or, so I thought.

I hate it when I'm wrong about stuff like that.

The only upside was that these guys were bozos with high-tech Underoos. Not vampires, not genetically enhanced supersoldiers. Though, at the moment that "upside" sucked ass.

Even with all the power of that blow, Bunny did not go down, and Spinlicker gaped at him. People often underestimate Bunny. Few things short of a cruise missile can put him down for the count.

With a roar, Bunny swung a roundhouse left that caught Spinlicker in the stomach and lifted the man all the way off the floor and sent him crashing against the wall. The agent's mirrored sunglasses flew off and shattered against the cinderblock. It should have ended the fight right there, but all it did was send the agent sprawling.

"You're making a mistake," Spinlicker wheezed as he struggled to his feet. Blood trickled from his ear. "You have no idea what you're dealing with."

"Yeah, well kiss my ass," said Bunny and threw himself at the agent, hooking a big right into his stomach and a left across his chin. Spinlicker canted sideways, but he still did not fall. Had to give the guy points for that because he didn't have fancy superhero underwear to protect his jaw.

With a growl, Spinlicker whipped around and drove a backward heel kick into Bunny's midsection that folded the big man in half and put him back down on his knees.

I finally kicked loose of the office junk. My own gun was buried, but I had the Tasers we'd taken from the agents and I pulled one out of my pocket and pointed it at them.

"Freeze!" I bellowed.

They did. For about a second. They stared in horror at the gun in my hand.

Then they whirled and ran for the inner door.

I pulled the trigger.

There was no blast. The gun didn't launch any flachettes.

Instead it made a hollow and rather disappointing *tok* sound.

Suddenly a stack of boxes beside the inner door exploded in a fireball that showered everything in the room with melting packages of staples that hit us like hot bricks.

I gaped at the pistol. The tiny sound and the power of that explosion seemed to be part of two separate events rather than cause and effect. I was actually flummoxed for a moment. Not sure I've ever actually been flummoxed before. Thought it was just an expression.

The agents jerked open the door. "Go!" yelled Henckhouser, as he pushed Spinlicker before him.

Bunny was on his knees and he had my Beretta in his hand. "Freeze or I will kill you."

They leaped toward the doorway.

Bunny opened fire. His first bullet hit the metal handrail, the second struck the wall, but the third punched Henckhouser between the shoulder blades and slammed him into the doorjamb.

"I said freeze!" yelled Bunny.

Top must have heard the shots because his voice was suddenly bellowing in my ear.

"Top!" I yelled. "Two hostiles coming your way. Put 'em down."

"Hooah," was Top's growl of a reply.

Bunny staggered to his feet, firing, filling the room with new thunder. Rounds punched into the agents as they disappeared. I saw the impacts slew them around, stagger them.

I pulled the trigger on the clunky pistol. It *tok*ked again.

Whatever it was firing hit the metal security door as the agents dove inside the building. The door was instantly wrenched off its hinges and flung against the wall. Big pieces of it flew everywhere. One chunk struck Bunny in the chest and sent him sprawling backward.

I raced over to him, but he moaned and waved me away. "Get the fuckers," he said with a wet groan.

Clutching the weird gun, I ran toward the open door. The frame was smeared with blood, and there was a large pool of it on the floor. Either Bunny or the flying debris had tagged one of the bastards. I quick-looked through the doorway, but the hall was empty.

"Top—talk to me," I breathed.

No answer.

I ran down the hall, pistol held up and out. There was plenty of blood. Red footprints on the carpet. Red handprints on the wall. A long smear as if one of them had leaned against the wall for support while he ran.

"Top," I called again.

There was a sound. A groan. I slowed to a careful walk a few yards from where the corridor opened out into a small lobby. The lobby was empty, the doors open and smeared with blood. I slammed through the door and there was Top, flat on his back outside, eyes open and blinking, mouth working like a beached trout. An impact injury, not a gunshot wound. Thank God.

He had his pistol in his hand and waved it toward the side of the building.

"Go . . . ," he wheezed.

In my ear I heard Bunny say, "Out back!" at the same instant I heard gunfire.

Shit.

I spun around, reentered the building, ran down the hall, jumped through the open doorway to the loading dock, barrel coming up and out, seeking a target. Bunny was on his knees, firing at the black SUV.

As I ran past him into the parking lot I squeezed the trigger over and over again, hearing that silly little *tok* sound each time, seeing bushes explode into fire and a masonry wall detonate into a cloud of dust. I got one good shot at the SUV and the rear window exploded, but the wheels spun on the blacktop; plumes of rubber smoke rose in oily columns behind the SUV as it lurched forward.

Bunny limped out and a moment later a winded Top staggered around the side of the building.

The car vanished around a corner and was gone.

Bunny said, "Jesus Christ, boss . . . we just got our asses handed to us."

Chapter Five

Shelton Aeronautics
Wolf Trap, Virginia
Thursday, October 17, 10:45 a.m.

Then we turned and looked at the building. At the lights, the open door. The utter silence. The thermal scans had told us that there was a mass of heat signatures on the top floor. Bug had thought there was interference from the structure because the signatures were fading.

But that wasn't it and as we stared up at lights we all knew what it was.

The thermals were fading because body heat diminishes after death.

Bunny said, "Oh, man . . ."

We didn't want to go inside. We knew what we'd see.

We went in anyway.

I wish I could say that there were no surprises, but . . .

Chapter Six

Shelton Aeronautics

Wolf Trap, Virginia

Thursday, October 17, 2:19 p.m.

We called it in. Police, FBI, Homeland, the coroner's office.

As each new team of professionals arrived on the scene, we had to flash our NSA IDs and retell the same sanitized version of the story. Then we had to take the poor bastards up and let them visit the horror show.

That's what it was, too.

There were sixty employees at this particular Shelton Aeronautics lab. Twelve top engineers and a lot of support staff. Everyone showed up for work that day. No one was lucky enough to have the flu or a broken leg or a sick child. Sixty people clocked in.

And then Henckhouser and Spinlicker showed up and destroyed them.

There's really no other word for it.

Destroyed.

I stood next to the Fairfax County deputy coroner for almost five minutes, neither of us speaking, both of us staring at what lay inside the big conference room. If you caught it out of the corner of your eye you'd think it was splashed with red paint. Walls, floor, ceiling.

Then, when you took a closer look, you'd understand. When you smelled the stink of copper and feces and the thousand other odors released when a body is burst apart, you'd understand.

But, like the coroner and the rest of the people there, you would not understand how.

I thought I did. The clunky little gun—the one that looked like a Taser but wasn't—was snugged into the back of my waistband, under my coat. Bunny had the other. They were mentioned in no official report that anyone outside of the DMS would ever read. I called in a full description to Mr. Church.

An EMT looked us over, put Band-Aids on minor cuts, gave us chemical ice packs for the bruises, and made sure not to look us in the eyes. He'd been upstairs already. He was dealing with that.

The only thing the coroner said to me the whole time was, "Jesus H. Christ."

Top, Bunny, and I got out of there four hours later. We got into my Explorer, buckled up for safety, and made our way to I-95. Church called and I put him on speaker.

"What's the status of your team?" he asked.

"Dented and dissatisfied," I said.

"I passed along your description of the pistols you obtained and your account of the damage done. Dr. Hu tells me that they fit the profile of a microwave pulse pistol, an MPP."

"How come I never heard of it?"

"Because until today it was a hypothetical weapon. Dr. Hu says that it's never been practical because the energy output would require a battery approximately the size of a Subaru. His words."

Top currently had one of the pistols, turning it over very gingerly in his hands. "Can't weigh more than a pound."

"Someone cracked the science then," said Church. "I'm sure Dr. Hu will be delighted to study them."

Dr. William Hu was the DMS's pet mad scientist. He was way past brilliant and he had a pop culture sensibility that almost made him likable. But then you got to know him and it turns out he's an asshole of legendary proportions. He'd have probably gotten a chubby looking at the damage the clunky little gun had caused. He was like that. He'd be sorry it hadn't been used on me. Neither of us broke a heavy sweat worrying about the other guy's health.

"What about the computer systems and research materials at the lab?" asked Church.

"Slag," I said. "The computer room looks like melted candles, and the file cabinets are full of ash. This was a very nasty and very thorough hit."

"That is unfortunate."

"You talk to Shelton?" I asked.

"Briefly," he said, "but remember we're not running this show. There are, at last count, eleven separate investigative agencies working on this case. The president asked us to provide some extra boots on the ground."

That was not entirely true, but the real reason wasn't something generally shared among the overall task force. Yes, Church had put some assets—like Top, Bunny, and me—on the ground, but what the president really wanted was MindReader. Church had obliged, with reservations. All the task force's data was being run through MindReader in hopes that its pattern recognition software would find something. A fingerprint, a lead, anything. Those requests were funneled through Bug and his geek squad. Church declined, however, to allow anyone from outside the DMS to even look at MindReader, let alone play with it. That's no joke—MindReader was Church's personal property and he guarded it with the ferocity of a dragon. We all knew what kind of damage someone could do with that system. As it was, only Bug had total access.

I said, "After today, are we going to be cut a bigger slice of this?"

"Is that what you want?" asked Church.

"Not sure," I admitted. I could feel Top and Bunny studying me. "Part of me does. Part of me wants to have a more meaningful discussion with agents Henckhouser and Spinlicker."

"I believe Dr. Sanchez has frequently spoken out against the need for revenge."

"It's not revenge," I lied. "There are some, um . . . technical questions I'd like answered."

"Such as?"

"They shook off a lot of damage. Physical blows, hard falls, gunshots."

"That's right," said Bunny, speaking up for the first time. "When I patted them down I didn't feel any heavy body armor, found microthin stuff. Those guys took hits they shouldn't have been able to. *We* need that stuff, and we need to know where they got it."

"Maybe we're looking at a new generation of body armor," I said. "The Canadians have been playing with some ultralight stuff."

Church grunted. "Let me make a few calls to some friends I have in the industry."

We all smiled at one another. Church always seems to have a "friend in the industry," no matter what industry happens to be involved in our investigations. He can make a call and suddenly we have whatever we need. Circus tent to use as a field biohazard containment command center? No problem. Special effects experts from Industrial Light and Magic? Sure. Next year's prototype deep-water submersible? Pick your color. Church never explains how he happens to know so many people in so many critical industries, but as long as he's one degree of separation away from whatever helps us do our jobs, then it's all cool with me.

"What else?"

"They were strong," said Top. "Even with gunshot wounds they were fast and strong. Maybe we can hijack the lab results on the blood work, see what kind of pills these boys are popping."

"I'd like to see a DNA report, too," I said. "Wouldn't be the first time we've run into freaky-deaky gene therapy."

"Noted," said Church. "So, am I to infer that your only reasons for wanting to encounter these agents again is for the opportunity to take a full set of forensic samples?"

His voice was as dry as desert sand.

"Sure," I said. "If anything else occurs to me, I'll let you know."

Church didn't respond to that.

"So, again, I ask," I said, "are we going to take a bigger role or not?"

There was a long silence. So long, in fact that I thought the call had dropped.

Finally Church said, "Actually, as of now we are off the case."

"What? Why?"

Another pause. "There are two answers to that, Captain. The official answer is that now that Congress has doubled the task force budget they will be able to pay overtime for more FBI and NSA agents to participate in the investigation."

"That sounds like bureaucratic bullshit. What's the real reason?"

"No one will come out and say it," murmured Church, "but some off-the-record sources have informed me that the task force has concluded that cyber-attacks of this level of sophistication could only be accomplished by a computer with MindReader's capabilities."

I nearly drove my Explorer into the oncoming lanes.

"What?"

"The report stopped short of accusing us of criminal activity, but there is language in there suggesting criminal negligence in—and I'm quoting from a report I am not supposed to have—'mishandling security for the MindReader system resulting in person or persons unknown to use it for the purposes of cyber-terrorism.' "

I looked at Top, who closed his eyes and lightly banged his head on the side window. In the backseat, Bunny very quietly said, "Jesus fucking Christ."

"Whose name is on that report?"

"Ah," said Church, "that's the other new development. The vice president has personally taken charge of the Cyber Crimes Task Force."

"Well isn't that just peachy," I said sourly.

"I thought you'd find it amusing."

Vice President Bill Collins was no friend to me, the DMS, or Mr. Church. A while back, when the president was having bypass surgery, Collins—in his role as acting president—tried to use the NSA to dismantle the DMS. We could never prove that he was doing so in order to help some crooked colleagues. Collins is a master at keeping shit off his shoes, but ever since that incident we've kept a wary eye on him. This task force nonsense was exactly his sort of thing.

"Are they going to file charges?" I asked.

Church gave us one more pause. "They are welcome to try," he said.

"So—what's the game plan?" I asked.

"No game plan," he said. "Go back to the Warehouse, send those guns up to Dr. Hu at the Hangar, write your reports, and try to enjoy the rest of your vacation."

I thought about what I'd seen at the lab. The red walls. The destroyed people.

"Yeah," I said. "Sure."

I disconnected the call. The three of us lapsed into individual brooding silences all the way back to Baltimore.

We thought it was over.

We thought we'd seen the worst of it.

We were out of it.

Sometimes you can be so totally wrong about something.

Chapter Seven

VanMeer Castle

Near Pittsburgh, Pennsylvania

Thursday, October 17, 7:22 p.m.

Howard Shelton loved to blow things up.

Everyone needs a hobby, a passion, and that was his.

When he was eight he did it the wrong way. Firecrackers duct-taped to the butler's cat earns you a beating. A rather savage beating, in point of fact. When his mother was not in diamonds and a ten-thousand-dollar Dior gown she was a heavy-handed witch who knew where to hit and how to make it last without leaving visible bruises. And, thereafter, Howard was fairly sure that the cook—who rather fancied the butler—spit in his food.

So, Howard did not blow up any more cats.

Not unless he was traveling. Then, for recreation, to let off a little steam, sure. *Fuck it, it's a cat.*

In high school they gave him awards for blowing things up. Science fair judges loved that sort of thing. People stood and applauded, they gave him trophies. Mom kept her hands to herself.

In college it was hit or miss. A lot of it depended on what he blew up, how controlled the explosion was, and who was in the lab when it happened. If it was Bryce Crandall—the math stud who was putting it to Howard's girlfriend, then that was bad. That was a police report, black armbands around campus, and a bad breakup with Mindy who, Howard guessed, never quite believed that it was all an accident.

On the other hand, if the explosion was in the firing vault and the people in the lab were those cold-eyed men from the Department of Defense . . . well that was a whole different picture. That was pats on the back, job offers, and grant money. That was *egregia cum laude,* a level of graduation honors rarely seen even at MIT.

Mom actually hugged him that day.

The people from the DoD brought along a couple of stiffs from DARPA—the Defense Advanced Research Projects Agency. Lots of handshakes, more serious job offers, and doors blown completely open.

Not that Howard Shelton needed to work. Dad was two years dead by the time Howard got his Ph.D., and Mom was one shove down the stairs away from leaving Howard six hundred and twenty-two million dollars.

Shame about those steps, that loose bit of carpeting.

All things considered, though, Howard would have preferred to blow her up.

But . . . you can't have everything.

On Thursday evening, Howard Shelton sat on an exercise bike in his personal gym, pedaling and sweating and watching the TV news coverage of the massacre at his laboratory in Wolf Trap, Virginia. There was different coverage on each of the four big screens mounted on the wall. Howard watched the news for two solid hours.

"Perfect," he said aloud.

He never stopped smiling once.

Interlude One

New Technologies Development Site #18

One Mile Below Tangshan, Hebei

People's Republic of China

July 28, 1976, 3:38 a.m. local time

General Lo peered through the foot-thick glass, his lips pursed, eyes narrowed to suspicious slits.

"What guarantees do we have this time?" he asked. "I would be disappointed with another failure."

Lo deliberately pitched his voice to be cold and uncompromising. That made these scientists jump. It reminded them that they worked for him and he was the face of the Party here. Just because they were afforded more personal freedom and greater comforts because of this project did not mean that they were untethered from the chain of command. If they were as smart as they were supposed to be, then they would realize and accept that their comforts were the equivalent of clean straw and fresh water in a pet rabbit's cage.

The scientists straightened respectfully even though Lo was not looking at them. But he saw it in the reflective surface of the window.

Good, he thought.

The chief scientist, an ugly fat man named Zhao, said, "Everything is working normally, General Lo."

"You said that last time," said Lo, continuing to study the machine that squatted in the stone chamber on the other side of the glass. It was a bulky device, awkward in appearance, looking more like a haphazard collection of disparate pieces rather than one integrated machine. And, to a great degree this was true. Only six of the machine's ten components were original. The others were copies made from pieces or from schematics bought from the Russians or stolen from the Americans. The last of the ten pieces, which was one of the very best recovered components, was held suspended over the device by chains. It was the master circuit, a metal slab eight inches long and four inches wide; slender as a wafer but improbably heavy. Once that piece was fully inserted the machine would become active. It would growl to life.

The Dragon Engine.

Lo privately scoffed at the name. Dragons were part of the old China mentality. Hard to shake from the more practical and far less romantic communist way of thinking. But his superiors had liked the name. Ah well.

Ice crystals glittered like diamond dust on the Dragon Engine's metal skin. Lo glanced at the thermometer mounted on the inside of the glass. Minus 160 degrees.

"Yesterday's pretest was a—" began Zhao, but Lo cut him off.

"Yesterday was very nearly a disaster." Lo turned to face Zhao and the other members of the science team. They flinched under his stare. "During each of the three calibration tests the well water in the local villages visibly rose and fell."

"Yes, General Lo," agreed Zhao nervously, "but it was not at all like what happened before."

That was true enough, and even Lo had to admit it to himself. On the twelfth of last month superheated gasses suddenly shot from wells in two other villages. On the twenty-fifth and twenty-sixth gas erupted from another dozen wells during tests of the power couplings connecting the device to the gigantic batteries built to store the discharge. Five civilians had been seriously burned and one killed.

That was when the dragonflies fled into the forest. Although Lo would never admit it to anyone else, he personally believed that the sight of thousands of dragonflies fleeing the towns was a bad omen. That happened with earthquakes and the worst storms. The dragonflies knew.

They always knew.

And they had not yet returned from their leafy sanctuary.

Lo glowered. "What assurances can you give me, Scientist Zhao, that turning the complete device on won't set the countryside on fire?"

"No, no, General Lo," insisted the scientist, "we have solved those problems. We have reinforced and triple insulated every coupling. We have coated the seals with nonporous clay, and the temperature in the chamber has been lowered to well below the safety level. We've added nonconductive baffles to soak up any resulting static discharge. We have learned so much from each of those tests and we are confident that the Dragon Engine will work perfectly this time."

Lo stepped close to Zhao. He was a very tall man, so the closeness forced the scientist to crane his neck in order to look up at the general. That created a position of weakness and subservience that Lo found very useful.

"You will be held personally responsible for any further delays or accidents," he said quietly.

The fat scientist's body trembled as if he wanted to shift from foot to foot, but discipline required that he stand and endure. Sweat beaded Zhao's face.

"Are we in agreement on this?" asked Lo.

"Y-yes, General Lo. I will not fail you."

"Then, for the prosperity of the Party and the enrichment of the people, you may continue."

With that General Lo turned and walked back to his spot in front of the glass. He ignored the bustle of technicians moving to their places and the low chatter as orders were given and information shared. If the Dragon Engine worked, then so much would change. The world itself would change. That thought made Lo feel like a giant. It made him feel like all the potential energy promised by that machine coursed through him. Lo imagined that America and its many allies were already trembling, aware on some deep spiritual level that their political, military and economic domination of the earth was a button push away from ending.

"We are ready, General Lo," said Zhao. "All indicators are green. Dampeners and buffers are functioning at one hundred and fifteen percent. We have a wide safety margin."

"Very well," said General Lo. "Turn it on."

Zhao exchanged a quick, excited smile with his colleagues.

He touched the button that would lower the final component into place. That was all it took. No bolts or screws. The machine's parts adhered to each other using a unique form of magnetic assembly.

The master circuit descended on its slender chains, pulled into its proper place.

Sparks danced along its bottom edge. Tiny arcs of electricity leaped between the circuit and the rim of the slot. General Lo bent forward, suddenly fascinated by the process. Until today the entire Dragon Engine had never been fully assembled. The disruptions of the last few weeks had all occurred at this point, with the board not quite in place.

"All readings are still in the green," said Zhao. "We are already past the disruption point."

The board slid down, vanishing millimeter by millimeter into the slot. Snakes of electricity writhed along the whole machine now. Then the master circuit clicked into place within the heart of the engine. There was a moment—a millionth of a second—where the machine seemed to freeze in place, the arcs of electricity vanishing.

"Scientist Zhao . . . ?" murmured Lo.

"The readings are still in the green. Dampeners and buffers are functioning at ninety-two percent. That is more than enough to—"

General Lo did not hear the rest of Zhao's sentence.

The Dragon Engine exploded.

General Lo saw a shimmering bubble of energy balloon outward from the device, and on the other side of that millisecond, he was vaporized.

The lab—all thirty-two rooms that comprised the New Technologies Development Site #18—became extensions of the blast.

The force punched like a fist down into the heart of the bedrock, smashing along the twenty-five-mile Tangshan Fault, causing the Okhotsk Plate to grate against the great Eurasian Plate. The whole earth recoiled from that blow, shuddering from the impact. Waves of trembling power shot through the entire region.

Some seismographs metered it as 7.8 on the Richter magnitude scale; on other machines it was measured at 8.2. The unbridled ferocity of it shot upward through the earth, tearing apart thousands of buildings. There were no foreshocks to warn people. There was no hint at all that this was coming. It was incredibly fast and without mercy. Virtually none of the structures in this part of China had been designed to withstand such fury. Hundreds of thousands of buildings were destroyed. Tremors were felt as far away as Xi'an, nearly five hundred miles from the blast. Closer cities—Qinhuangdao and Tianjin, and even Beijing—shivered as the shock waves hit, shattering glass, cracking walls, tearing up the streets.

So many people were asleep when it happened. Nestled in bed, unaware that hell had come to their part of the world. Houses and buildings crumbled to become tombs for more than half a million.

The New Technologies lab had been built there because Tangshan was a region with a relatively low risk of earthquakes.

And yet this was the worst earthquake of the twentieth century, and the third deadliest in all recorded history.

Nearly seven hundred thousand people died.

Within a month teams of diggers had burrowed beneath the rubble of houses and the bones of the dead and were inching their way down into the troubled earth. Not in hopes of finding survivors. Not in hopes of recovering General Lo or Scientist Zhao.

However, if there was a chance—a single chance—to recover even a piece of the Dragon Engine, then nothing could be allowed to interfere.

That excavation continues to this day.

Part Two
Taken

Stars, hide your fires; Let not light see my black and deep desires.

—WILLIAM SHAKESPEARE, *Macbeth*

Look at how a single candle can both defy and define the darkness.

—ANNE FRANK

Chapter Eight

Nothing was happening. That's how Duty Officer Lyle Ames liked it. The ideal day for the Secret Service Presidential Detail was one in which the president did nothing, shook no hands, saw none of the public, and basically stayed indoors, out of sight, and safe.

The press hated days like this.

Ames loved them.

According to the duty log on his desk, nothing much had happened all day. It was slow. Boring.

Perfect.

He sipped coffee from a ceramic mug with the presidential seal on it and flipped the duty log over to the last page. Nothing there, either. Nice.

The office was nearly empty. His agents were at their posts, and Ames's only company was Regina Smallwood at the ops desk. Smallwood sat in front of a row of computer monitors that displayed real-time feeds of security cameras. Each monitor screen was divided into many smaller windows that displayed telemetric feeds, coded to correspond with the heartbeat of an individual. Green lights pulsed for the president, the first lady, their family, the vice president, and the key members of government who formed the line of succession—the speaker of the House, the president pro tempore of the Senate, secretary of the Senate, all the way down to the secretary of Homeland Security. Most of the green lights pulsed with the slow, rhythmic beating of sleeping hearts. A few were more rapid, indicating that these people were night owls or in different time zones.

The signals were sent by RFID chips—radio frequency identification chips the size of rice grains. Each VIP had one surgically implanted in the fatty tissue under their triceps. Unlike the passive chips used to store medical information, these were true telemetric locators. The chips were late-generation models manufactured by Digital Angel, and as long as GPS tracking satellites circled the earth the chips would locate the wearer and send a continuous feed to establish location and proof of life. It was one of the technologies that allowed agents like Ames to dial down his Maalox consumption.

Ames set down the duty log, stood, stretched, yawned, and took his cup over to the Mr. Coffee to pour some hot into it. As he raised the carafe he heard a *bong-bong* sound. An alarm from the telemetry board. A soft, unthreatening sound; more of a notification than a crisis shout.

Smallwood snapped her fingers at him. "Got a transponder failure," she said. "POTUS just went dark."

"Balls," growled Ames. He set his cup down and hurried over. "Is it the panel or the transponder?"

"Unknown, but the other signals are strong and steady." She looked up. "You'd better call it. Gil stayed over tonight."

Ames was already hitting the speed dial for Gilbert Shannon, the president's body man.

A sleepy voice answered, "Shannon."

"Gil, this is Lyle. Are you with the president?"

"No, I'm in my room down the hall."

"Okay, I need you to go put eyes on the president. Have the agent at the door accompany you in."

All the sleepiness vanished from Shannon's voice. "Is there a problem?"

"Probably not, but the boss's transponder stopped transmitting."

"Oh, okay. I'll call you in one minute."

Ames set down his phone and made a second call to alert the agents outside the president's bedroom door. That done, he bent over Smallwood's shoulder to study the telemetry feeds. The small pulsing green light had been replaced by two words in red LED letters: SIGNAL LOST.

Ames did not yet feel panic. There was only a tingle.

"Could have happened at Camp David," suggested Smallwood.

"Hm?" asked Ames.

"The transponder. The president was all over the place. Basketball, jogging, that softball game at the barbecue. He could have banged his arm when he tried to steal second base in the third inning. Remember, he dove in headfirst? Brierly tagged him pretty hard and I think that was on the upper arm."

Ames shook his head. "He reached for the base with his left arm."

"Sure, but he was tagged on his right. The ball could have hit the transponder."

"Maybe," said Ames.

"Or, it could have been——"

The phone rang.

Ames snatched it up. "Talk to me."

It wasn't Gil Shannon. It was Sam Holly, the senior agent on shift at the residence. His voice was ratcheted tight with tension.

"Sir, we have a situation . . ."

Chapter Nine

The Rose Garden
The White House
Sunday, October 20, 3:25 a.m.

Agent Jeremy Nunzio had his weapon in a two-handed grip as he ran along the row of hedges outside the Oval Office. The radio in his ear was a crazed jumble of yells, commands, contradictory orders, questions, and desperate demands for fresh intel.

"We've got movement," cried one of the other agents. Sziemesko. "We've got movement."

Sziemesko shouted the location and everyone was in motion, a fist closing around a specific point outside the White House. Nunzio was the closest, he got there first, rounding a corner, bringing his weapon up, finger laid along the trigger guard, all his years of training bringing him to this moment. He saw Sziemesko standing a few yards away, his back to the building, staring into the darkened lawn. Suddenly a dozen additional security lights flared on.

"On your six," Nunzio called, as he caught up with Sziemesko. The other agent's gun was also raised, pointing to a specific spot within the darkness. Nunzio sighted down the barrel of his own piece.

And saw nothing.

Just darkness and security lights and . . .

He and Sziemesko moved at the same time, their guns jerking left as one of the lights moved.

"Freeze!" bellowed Nunzio.

"Step into the light with your hands raised," yelled Sziemesko. "Do it now."

But no one stepped out of the darkness and into the glow of the lights. The light itself moved. It looked like a lightbulb, but there was no flashlight attached to it; it projected no beam. It was simply a light. Simply there.

Drifting slowly from left to right in front of them. Unattached, unsupported.

Just a light.

"Freeze!" Nunzio repeated.

The light continued to move. It was forty feet away from them.

"The fuck—?" murmured Sziemesko.

The two agents edged forward, weapons ready. Voices in their earbuds told them that the White House was now in full crash mode. Doors and windows were locked. Every agent on duty was involved in a search for the president.

Nunzio felt panic exploding in his chest.

The president was gone. Missing from his room.

And what the hell was this thing?

The light stopped moving for a moment, then it dropped down to the grass and hovered inches above the lawn.

"Go," said Sziemesko, "I've got your back."

Nunzio edged tentatively forward.

The light suddenly rose from the lawn and began moving away. Nunzio broke into a run, yelling at it to stop. Yelling at a person to stop, even though he could not see anyone out here. The light moved faster and faster and Nunzio almost—almost—took the shot.

Two things happened to prevent that. Two things that made him almost forget he was even holding a gun.

The other five security lights, the ones that had switched on when he'd run to this part of the lawn, also began to move. The movement was abrupt, without warning, and they accelerated until they caught up with the first light. They moved across the lawn in a straight line of retreat from Nunzio, then they slowed and formed a circle of lights that seemed for a moment to be frozen against the night. Then the circle rose.

Straight upward.

Very fast.

Too fast.

As Nunzio watched, the circle of lights tightened until there was only one large light.

It pulsed once.

Twice.

And shot away into the eastern sky so fast that it was gone before Nunzio was aware that it was in motion.

Nunzio stood there, gaping up at the sky. The dark and empty sky.

"Nunzio!"

He whirled at the sounds of Sziemesko's shrill yell. Nunzio ran back to the other agent and skidded to a stop, remembering his gun, fanning it right and left.

Sziemesko stood with his pistol hanging limply from his right hand, his slack face staring in total confusion at the lawn. Nunzio realized that there was something wrong with the grass. The lawn had been trampled as if a hundred people had run through here.

He thought that, but even as that idea formed the rest of him rebelled at the assessment. The lawn was not trampled. No one else had been out here. No one had been out here since Nunzio had come on shift.

He glanced at Sziemesko and their eyes held for a moment. Then slowly, wordlessly, they began backing away from the trammeled grass. They backed up almost to the White House itself, then they stopped. Nunzio heard Sziemesko say something under his breath. A denial, maybe. A curse. A prayer. He wasn't sure.

For his own part, Nunzio had no idea what to say. What words would really fit?

The grass was not haphazardly smashed down. The blades looked folded. Nunzio knew that there was a name for something like this, but his mind did not want to think it. That name was connected to something that had nothing at all to do with the White House, and the president, or anything in Nunzio's world.

Except that maybe it did.

The name, those two words, despite all his denials, whispered inside his head anyway.

This was a crop circle.

Chapter Ten

Aboard the *Secret Escape*
Chesapeake Bay, off the coast of Virginia
Sunday, October 20, 3:28 a.m.

Linden Brierly was still awake. He lay in his bunk, staring up through the skylight at the infinite starfield that was spread like a jeweler's display above the Chesapeake. His boat, a thirty-six-foot custom Beneteau, rocked gently, keeping him at the edge of sleep but not yet tumbling him over. His wife lay curled against him, soft and warm and beautiful. Her hair was still tangled from lovemaking, and the cabin smelled of her expensive perfume, superb wine, and sex.

Brierly stroked her hair, careful not to coax her to the surface of her dreams. By starlight her naked body was alabaster perfection. After nine years of marriage he still marveled at her, lost in the graceful lines and curves that only he knew with such intimate familiarity.

He glanced at the luminous face of the bedside clock and watched it turn from 3:29 to 3:30. He and Barbara were three and a half hours into the tenth year of their marriage.

Nice.

The boat rocked on a series of small, slow rollers.

And then Brierly's cell phone rang.

His hand snaked out and snatched it off the night table, his thumb hitting the ringer mute halfway through the first jangle. He cut a look at Barbara, but she was still down deep. Then Brierly looked at the screen display and his heart lurched in his chest.

No name. Instead there was a coded symbol: ***!!!***

Jesus Christ, he thought. *No, no, no . . .*

He answered the call.

"Brierly."

"Sir," said Lyle Ames, "we have a *Jackhammer* situation. Please verify that confidential protocols are in active play."

Brierly's heart was thundering now.

Jackhammer.

God almighty.

He punched in the three-digit code that activated the scrambler.

"The blanket is down," said Brierly.

"Verified."

"What's happening?"

"Linden," said Ames in a voice that was strained to the breaking point, "the president is missing."

Beside him, deep inside a dream, Barbara Brierly groaned as if in pain.

Chapter Eleven

The White House
Sunday, October 20, 5:12 a.m.

Two hours later, Linden Brierly ran up the stairs of the White House. A phalanx of agents followed him, and even with everything that was going on, Brierly wondered how many of them were eyeing his back and wondering if they would fall with the director? Brierly was the youngest man ever to hold the position as director of the Secret Service. There had been a lot of controversy over his appointment. Too young, they said. Not enough experience.

God.

He fitted a speaker-bud into his ear and adjusted the gain to a restricted channel. It was abuzz with chatter but no one was saying anything he wanted to hear. Talking about finding Jackhammer.

Jackhammer.

Each president has two code names assigned by the Secret Service. At all other times, this president was Spider-man. But now, with him missing and the chance that someone could possibly hack the team radio channel, a crisis code name was employed. Jackhammer. An appropriate name, thought Brierly. Something that would break everything apart and turn it all to rubble.

The president has been kidnapped.

God almighty.

Every light in the building was on. People were shouting, running. Brierly knew that not all of them were aware of the *exact* nature of the calamity. The agents who didn't know were giving fierce looks because they wanted top marks in what they'd been told was a high-profile surprise drill. The ones who suspected that this was something real were scared and, as they'd been taught, they fine-tuned their fear to bring them to a deadly level of alert preparedness. Brierly could spot the ones who knew, though. They had a different look in their eyes. They were scared—for their own careers as much as for the president—but more than that they were angry. It was their job to protect the president. Something had happened, someone had made them fail at that job. The cold fury in their eyes promised awful things to whoever was behind this. Brierly knew that it wasn't bravado. He felt it, too. The rest of the staff—anyone who was not part of the security detail—was under armed guard. Interrogations were already underway. The entire White House had been crashed and locked down so hard that a fly couldn't slip through without a body cavity search.

But the president was still missing.

No, Brierly corrected himself. *Not "missing." Taken.*

His cell rang and Brierly glanced at the screen display. He slowed to a stop, wincing, steeling himself to take this call.

He said, "Yes, Mr. President?" Addressing the man who had been vice president less than two hours ago. William Collins. A man Brierly personally and professionally despised.

"Where do we stand?" demanded Collins.

"I just arrived on-site and—"

"I didn't ask that," Collins snapped. "I asked for a status report."

Brierly was young for his directorship but he was a very experienced agent. He never let his personal feelings color his words or flavor his tone.

"At this time we have not located the POTUS," he said crisply. "The first lady is being interviewed by one of my best men along with a staff psychologist. Ditto for the president's body man and the team who were on duty outside the room."

There was a heavy pause in which Brierly knew he was supposed to appreciate the full weight and scope of the acting president's imperial disdain.

"Have you searched the building?"

No, asshole, Brierly thought, *that never occurred to us. So glad you called.*

"Yes, sir. Every room, every closet, under every desk."

"And the transponder? Still no signal?"

"That is correct, sir."

"Have you considered that the surveillance systems and computers may have been compromised?"

"Yes, sir. We have teams—"

"I've requested specialists from my Cyber Crimes Task Force," Collins said briskly, emphasizing the word "my," as if he was anything more than a nominal head of the investigation. "They'll be there within the hour. You are to give them full access and total cooperation."

Brierly frowned. "Sir, surely you appreciate the necessity of keeping this matter restricted to as few people as—"

"A great number of those *few* people are suspects."

"I understand, sir, however we have protocols for this kind of an investigation and—"

"Protocols? For this kind of thing? Really? Tell, me, Brierly, when have you ever even heard of this kind of thing? This is outside of the scope of your experience," said Collins, leaning on the word "experience," making a point with a sledgehammer. "And surely even you have to realize that this is connected with the terror campaign being waged against our country. Get your head out of your ass. Expect my team within the hour."

"Yes, sir," said Brierly in as flat a monotone as possible. "Thank you, sir."

"Brierly . . . this happened on your watch."

"Thank you, Mr. President, I am fully aware of my responsibilities in this matter."

And fuck you, you arrogant little shit.

"We are going to have to discuss your handling of things," warned Collins.

"Yes, sir."

"And one more thing," said Collins. "I don't want to hear about you running to Church or the DMS with this."

"May I ask why not? Something like this could not have been accomplished without advanced technology and the DMS is—"

"The DMS is on my list, Brierly. Don't think they're not."

"What exactly do you mean, Mr. President?"

"Surely it's occurred to you, Brierly, that only a system as sophisticated as MindReader could have accomplished the intrusions and done the damage we've seen. Either Church is involved or he's bungled his own security so badly that someone else has accessed MindReader and is using it to systematically attack some of this nation's most highly classified projects."

"Mr. President, are you accusing Mr. Church of—"

"I'm not accusing anyone of anything yet. When I do it will be spelled out on a federal warrant. In the meantime, you might want to decide where your loyalties lie."

"Sir, I—"

The line went dead.

Brierly looked down at the cell phone. He took a moment to compose his face and then hurried down the hall to the president's bedroom. Lyle Ames met him at the door.

"Talk to me," said Brierly, and he could hear the edge of pleading in his own voice.

Ames, an old friend, touched his arm. "There's nothing here, Linden. I mean nothing. No signs of a struggle, no forced entry. Video of the hallway verifies the report of the agents on the door. If the president was abducted by force there is no sign of it. Nothing."

Brierly lowered his voice to a sharp, confidential tone. "That's not acceptable, Lyle. I just had my ass handed to me by our new president. He's sending some agents from his Cyber Crimes Task Force and he expects us to cooperate with them. If there's anything to find I want us to find it, not them."

Ames grunted. "The only thing we have is something two agents found on the lawn. They found it during the first sweep of the groups, so the timing fits, but we have no idea what it is or what it means." He produced a high-res color print and handed it to Brierly. "It's about ten feet across, so to get a clear picture I had to put a guy in a helicopter."

Brierly frowned at the image. "This was on the lawn?"

"Pressed into it, yes."

The pattern was odd but orderly; a strange ratcheted pattern, radiating out clockwise from a smaller circle at its center. On the top arc of the circle were three smaller circles in descending size.

"What is it?"

"I don't know. It's not the symbol of any terrorist organization I've ever heard of. We're running it through the symbols and logos database."

"Are you sure this was left by whoever abducted the president?" asked Brierly.

"Not sure of any damn thing," confessed Ames. "It was on the lawn and the agents walking the grounds say that it wasn't there before the alert."

"I want to see the surveillance cameras for this part of the lawn."

Ames cleared his throat. "Those cameras have a four-minute window where all they show is static. The pattern is not there before the static and *is* there afterward."

"Shit."

"Yeah."

"Collins is going to call that a cyber-attack and he'll use it to take this whole thing away from us."

"I know."

"Besides—it's bullshit," snapped Brierly as he slapped the picture against Ames's chest. "You can't make something this big and complicated in four minutes. Come on, Lyle, I don't need fucking fairy stories right now. Give me some actual goddamn evidence."

Ames colored. "Linden, I'm giving you what we have and aside from this thing on the lawn we have nothing. We're working everything. We have the first lady downstairs. I spoke with her already, but she said she slept through it and didn't wake up at all until Gil and the door team entered the room."

Brierly searched his face and took Ames by the elbow, pulling him out of earshot of the other agents. "And—?"

"And I believe her. We can ask her to take a polygraph, but I know what it will say."

"Will she consent to a blood test?"

Ames nodded. "Already has. She insisted we do it, and she wants those results as badly as we do. We're also running tests on the glass of water beside the president's bed, his toothpaste, pills in all of the bottles in the medicine cabinet . . ."

"He doesn't take a lot of pills."

"I know, most of them are vitamin supplements, but we don't know if he took anything tonight. Or if the first lady took anything. She says that she doesn't even remember lying down."

"What does that mean?"

"It's what she said. She and the president came into the residence, changed into pajamas, and that's it. That's all she remembers before the agents opened the door and woke her up."

"How was she when she woke up?"

"Borderline hysterical, but that was a reaction to the events. She didn't appear logy or dazed. None of the reactions you'd expect from a chemical sedative. Even so, there might have been something in her system, maybe slipped into something she ate or drank. We'll look for contact substances, too—something that could have been placed on a surface they might have touched."

Brierly nodded. "What about Gil Shannon?"

"Same thing. I have two men with him now—both top interrogators—and they're working him pretty hard. I spoke with the agents who were at the POTUS's door and I laid it on pretty thick, too. Promise of immunity if they had anything to do with this and could provide actionable information."

Brierly grunted. "You get approval from the attorney general?"

"No, the AG's in Florida. I lied. I figured, fuck it."

"What'd you get?"

"I got some very angry, very outraged agents who I think will pass a polygraph. But . . . they also know that they're done as far as the Service goes."

Brierly said nothing.

Ames sighed. "I guess we're all done. I know I am. POTUS goes missing while I'm shift supervisor? I won't be able to get a job guarding a landfill after this."

"If you do, put in a good word for me, 'cause I'll be the first one out on my ass."

Brierly knew that he would be in the crosshairs because some people were going to try and use this to build or protect their own careers by making sure they were seen as executioners of the guilty. Brierly would go down as the Secret Service director who had managed to lose the president. You don't recover from a career stumble like that. Even if this turned out to be something completely beyond Brierly's control, he would take the bullet. A head must always fall, otherwise the system looks like it's driving on a bad tire.

They traded small, grim smiles, then turned to survey the bedroom.

There were a dozen people in there. Forensics techs dusting and collecting. Photographers. Agents looking everywhere in hopes that they'd be the ones to find the first thread. Every single person in the room looked frightened, even the techs who had no reason to be.

He stared down at the empty bed, and its emptiness seemed to mock him. The heavy covers, the rumpled sheets, the dented pillow. The absence of sense.

"Let me see that goddamn photo again."

Ames handed it over. Brierly scowled at it. It was bullshit. Total bullshit. No way it could be connected.

"God . . . we need the Deacon and his geek squad. We need the DMS."

"It'd be your ass, Linden. The president said not to call him."

Brierly bared his teeth. "*My* president didn't give that order."

Chapter Twelve

VanMeer Castle
Near Pittsburgh, Pennsylvania
Sunday, October 20, 6:07 a.m.

Mr. Bones was Howard Shelton's minion. It was not how it was supposed to be, but it played out that way. It was an arrangement that developed over time and it settled into a relationship that worked for them both. Bones—whose real name was Alfred Bonetti—knew that he was never going to be the alpha of their little pack. Howard was, and that was clear from the first time they met.

"Minion" was, perhaps, an inexact word, but after nine years Mr. Bones did not know which would be a better fit. Ostensibly he and

Shelton were colleagues, two of the three governors of Majestic Three. In practice, Howard was the mastermind and Mr. Bones was . . . ? What? Assistant was the wrong context. Lackey was too weak. Henchman was a bit old-fashioned. Enabler was too New Age. Number two sounded scatological.

He liked "minion." Minion had a strangely appealing ring to it. It made Mr. Bones feel like he was an acolyte in some secret cult of immortals.

Fun stuff.

There were even sacrifices. Last week it was the entire staff at the Wolf Trap lab. Some good people, too, including that redheaded secretary. Yum. A body in a box now, of course, but yum once upon a time.

He and Howard were in the big kitchen at Shelton's estate in Pennsylvania. The kitchen was enormous and the estate was positively obscene. Howard had the entire VanMeer Castle disassembled and brought over from Europe, then rebuilt with a few alterations. Howard and Mr. Bones referred to it as their "secret lair."

They were mad scientists, after all, and that was a hoot.

Howard poked at half a grapefruit. "How the fuck am I supposed to feed my brain with this shit?"

Mr. Bones peered at him over the glasses that were halfway down his nose. "You're not. The protein drinks and the vitamins and the flower essences are for your brain. This is to keep your waistline and your IQ from reaching parity."

"Tastes like sour piss."

"And you'd recognize that taste how?"

"Oh, very funny." Howard speared a chunk of fruit, shoved it in his mouth, winced, and chewed.

Bones poured himself a fresh cup of coffee, added some hot to Howard's, and went back to studying the data flow on his laptop. It was an odd-looking computer, known within M3 circles as a Ghost Box, and it was unlike anything on the market. There were two wings that folded out from the screen to form a three-sided box above the keyboard. This allowed for some very nice holographic imaging. There was also a unit attached to the back that looked like an extended-use battery, but wasn't. This was an encryption-intrusion drive that allowed the Ghost Box to operate in almost the same way as the MindReader system. It was a much newer technology than MindReader, and it combined elements of the Chinese GhostNet along with a few radical design jumps drawn from technology sources particular to M3.

"What's happening in the world?" asked Howard.

It was not a general question. The information that flowed across the laptop was a very private news feed comprised of information, updates, and intelligence from hundreds of sources within the M3 network, including quite a lot of it that came from sources that had no idea they were reporting to senior members of a secret cabal hidden within the U.S. government. Some of those people would have rebelled at the idea and they would begin inconvenient witch hunts. As neither Mr. Bones nor Howard Shelton fancied having their heads on poles, they kept such information on a need-to-know basis.

"It's been a busy night."

"Give me the highlights," said Shelton. "Don't tell me stuff I don't need to know about."

"Okay . . . well, the air show is still on track, though two more exhibitors have dropped. Belmann-Kruas and Mitsubishi are out."

"Good. That's what—eight gone?"

"Seven, GE decided to stay in. Apparently they were able to transfer their entire project to Houston, so all they really lost is four days."

"Hm. Should we hit them again?"

"Oh, I think we have to."

"Do it."

Mr. Bones nodded. For seven weeks now they had been running a very carefully crafted series of cyber-attacks. Ghost Box's intrusion technology allowed them to sneak into virtually any company's computer and, once in, introduce viruses of all kinds. Some were tapeworms with very specific agendas, some were what Howard called "romper-stomper programs" that just randomly destroyed things. So far every major private contractor working with the Department of Defense had been hit, and the DoD itself had taken a few punches below the belt. Even Shelton Aeronautics had been attacked, though this self-immolation had been carefully planned to give a very realistic appearance of maximum damage to their new Specter 101 ultra-high-speed stealth aircraft program. As far as anyone in the upper echelon of the industry was concerned, Specter 101 promised to be the first of a brand-new generation of stealth craft. A Mach 20 masterpiece that was a ghost to everybody's radar.

It was the lamb that Howard was placing on the altar that was the Project.

The *real* Project.

The Project that M3 had been working on for a very long time.

Everything else—even the quite lovely Specter 101, mattered so much less. Just like the sixty employees at Wolf Trap mattered so much less.

"If you want to hide in plain sight," Bones had said when he'd suggested the slaughter to Howard, "and even get some sympathy from people who would ordinarily love to see your spleen on a platter—namely the boards at Boeing, Lockheed, and all the rest—then become a victim. Let them console you, Howard. Hell, let them pity you. God knows they will. So will everybody who reads a newspaper or logs on to a news feed. You'll be the heroic Howard Shelton, publically mourning at funerals, donating gaudy amounts of money to trust funds that provide for the offspring of whoever works at Wolf Trap. You'll embody the tragedy so much that you'll receive more sympathy cards than all the families together."

Howard Shelton had stared at Mr. Bones for nearly a full minute before he said, "You are an actual evil genius."

"This I know."

"If you had a twin sister I'd bang her silly."

"That is the most disgusting thing I've ever heard," laughed Mr. Bones.

That discussion was two months ago. The slaughter was a little over two days ago. The offices of Shelton Aeronautics were so crammed with sympathy bouquets that it looked like a tropical rain forest. The president had called. The CEOs of every major defense contractor called. Celebrities had called. It was delicious.

"How would you like to hit GE this time? Cyber or something more physical?"

Howard thought about it as he winced his way through another chunk of grapefruit.

"Let's up the game. I think a fire in the corporate offices might do it."

"Done," said Mr. Bones and sent a coded e-mail to someone who loved to play with matches. Then he wired a third of the payment to a Cayman Island account. Good faith money for a useful contractor.

"What else?" asked Howard.

"Well . . . if we're going to keep this up, then we're going to have to give the feds someone to look at. Too much blame is being directed at China, and they're starting to complain to us."

"Pussies."

"Agreed, but they do have a point."

Howard pushed the grapefruit aside. "God, I'd rather eat a dead rat than another piece of that shit."

"Lose forty pounds and we can discuss pancakes."

Howard sipped his coffee. "So, you want to throw someone to the wolves. Good call. But who?"

"I still want to point them at Mr. Church."

"Good luck."

"Oh, come on. He's mysterious, he's devious, and people don't even know his real name. He's perfect."

"He's a Boy Scout," said Howard. "The only reason you think he looks good for it is because he has MindReader, but it's a bad fit."

Mr. Bones scraped butter onto a cold piece of toast. "Has to be one of his people, then. That nerd who runs their computer department, what do they call him? Bug?"

"No. He's too small fry. He looks like a puppy. No one would buy him for it."

"Aunt Sallie?"

"Not a chance. Besides, she scares me more than Church."

They thought about it through toast and coffee refills.

Then Howard snapped his fingers. "Christ, I know . . . and it's been staring us right in the face."

"Who?"

"Church's pet psychopath. I mean, he was right there at Wolf Trap for fuck's sake. He found the bodies. He's perfect. People will think it's like an arsonist calling in a fire."

It took no time at all for Mr. Bones to recall the name. "Ledger?"

"Ledger."

Mr. Bones nodded. "Oooh—I like it."

He sent some e-mails to get that process going and at high gear. The phone rang as he was finishing. There were three cell phones laid side by side on the kitchen table. This was a gray one. The coded one. Mr. Bones picked it up and listened.

After fifteen seconds of listening, he said, "Jesus Christ."

"What?" demanded Howard, but Mr. Bones held up a hand.

"Bullshit. Don't tell me that there's no information, goddamn it. You fucking well find out, and get back to me right away."

He closed the phone with a sharp snap. His hand was trembling as he set the phone down.

"What the hell was—" began Howard, but the look on Mr. Bones face stopped him.

Mr. Bones said, "The president of the United States has been abducted. He was taken from his bedroom at three twenty this morning. There was no intrusion, no attack. The Secret Service agent at the door heard and saw nothing. There is no physical evidence, no trace. He is simply . . . gone."

"What? Who did it? How did they do it?"

After a dreadful silence, Mr. Bones said, "If it's true that he simply vanished from his bedroom without a trace of physical evidence . . . Well, Howard, there's only one way to do it that I know of."

Howard Shelton stared at him.

"Oh . . . shit," he said.

Part Three
The Majestic Black Book

The best weapon of a dictatorship is secrecy, but the best
weapon of a democracy should be the weapon of openness.

——NIELS BOHR

As the bomb fell over Hiroshima and exploded, we saw an entire city
disappear.
I wrote in my log the words: "My God, what have we done?"

——CAPTAIN ROBERT LEWIS

Chapter Thirteen

Camden Court Apartments, Camden and Lombard Streets
Baltimore, Maryland
Sunday, October 20, 6:09 a.m.

Really bad time for the phone to ring.

The naked woman in my bed picked my phone up and, without looking at it, threw it across the room.

"Wrong number," she said. The phone landed under the dresser and rang through to voice mail.

I peered at the lady from between eyelids that had been welded shut a moment before. What was left of my brain was still deep in a dream that was a sweaty replay of the party last night. The dream wasn't specific because my brain was too deeply pickled for that. Instead there were flash images. The slideshow started off with an R-rating for content. The guys from Echo Team serenading Rudy Sanchez with a song from *Mamma Mia!*, with a few significant modifications of the lyrics. Our version of the lyrics would have been too extreme for the letters page of *Penthouse* magazine.

We didn't go as low as hiring hookers, but there were strippers.

Lots of strippers.

Rudy had asked for something small and tasteful, but let's face it, he asked the wrong guy. Me. No way was I sending my best friend down the aisle with anything less than a blowout of epic proportions. Creating an international incident was a real likelihood at one point, no joke. I believe the police were involved for some of it, but I'm pretty sure we wound up cuffing some of them to the toilets in the ladies' room.

It was that kind of a party.

For what it's worth, even though I may have kissed several people— and I pray that most or all of them were women—I did manage to go home with the woman I came with.

Violin.

A luscious Italian shooter-for-hire who had a psychotic mother who frequently wanted me dead. Violin had warrants on her from several countries that had extradition agreements with the U.S. She also had a set of curves that made me not care about any of that, and more importantly, she was one of "my" people. That's a small group of folks who I trust completely. Violin and I had history, we'd been through fire together, which meant that if anyone ever took a run at her they'd have to go through me. That would get very expensive in ways most people don't want to pay.

Were we a couple?

Not really. Not in any way you could write a romance novel about.

When she was in this part of the world, and if neither of us was otherwise involved, we tended to attack each other in hot and creative ways. There were no strings, no obligations, and that was an arrangement that worked just fine for both of us.

Violin lay sprawled in a tangle of sheets in my Baltimore apartment. I think she'd gone back to sleep before the phone stopped ringing. She had pale skin with just the slightest hint of a Mediterranean olive in her complexion. No trace of a tan or even the ghost of a tan line—she's definitely not the beach type. Round where it mattered, but lean and strong. Really, really strong. Some might say freakishly so, but she didn't look it. She lay on her stomach, her face turned toward me, eyes closed, emitting a soft, purring snore. My middle-aged marmalade tabby, Cobbler, was snugged up against her, almost nose to nose with her, and they breathed with exactly the same feline rhythm.

The phone began ringing again.

My cell.

And then the house landline.

My dog, Ghost, started barking on the other side of the bedroom door. *Balls*.

"Don't," mumbled Violin as I started to get up. It was somewhere between a plea and a threat.

"It's probably my office."

"Let someone else save the world for once. It's Sunday, you're hungover and more importantly I'm hungover. If you don't let me go back to sleep I'll kneecap you." She said all this without opening her eyes, her voice a soft mumble of credible threat.

"I'll risk it," I said.

"Your funeral."

I sat up and the motion set the room to spinning. Violin wasn't joking about a hangover. I remember swearing to God while on my knees that I would never—*ever*—drink again if He'd just let me stop throwing up. Next time I was in church I was going to have to take a look at the fine print on that contract.

Right now, though, I watched the room do a tilt-a-whirl around the bed.

"Oh God," I mumbled.

Both phones stopped ringing right before they would have gone to voice mail.

"Thank you, Jesus."

And started up again.

I lunged for the cell phone, missed it by ten feet and crawled like a sick tree sloth across the carpet, grabbed the cell, pushed the little green button.

"What?" I snarled belligerently.

"Good morning, Captain Ledger," said Mr. Church.

"Ah . . . shit."

"Although it pains me to interrupt your Sunday morning meditations, I would appreciate your attention on a matter of some importance."

Church hadn't been at the bachelor party. I'd invited him but even though he didn't say so I believe he would rather have been eaten by rats. Partly because, let's face it, a bachelor party wasn't his scene, and partly because Circe was his daughter. A precious few people on earth knew that fact, and I don't want to know what Church would do to someone who let that fact leak. I'm a scary guy, but Church scares the kind of people who scare me.

"I'm off today," I said with bad grace. "The duty officer is—"

"Joe," said Church, "you need to get into the office now."

Church never calls me Joe. Never.

I sat bolt upright.

"What's happening?"

"Are you alone?" he asked.

I looked at Violin. She'd caught the urgency in my voice and propped herself up on one elbow. Alert and cautious. Cobbler crouched on the sheets next to her with wide, wary eyes.

"No," I said.

"Then call me from your car. I'll expect to hear from you in two minutes."

He hung up.

I've been working for Church for a couple of years now, I'd seen him in the middle of some of the most terrible catastrophes this country has faced. Stuff that doesn't make the newspapers, which is why my fellow Americans can still sleep at night. I've seen Church in situations where everyone and everything is falling apart and he's always as cool as a cucumber.

But now there was something in his voice. Raw emotion held down by his iron control.

Fear.

Or maybe . . . panic.

Chapter Fourteen

VanMeer Castle
Near Pittsburgh, Pennsylvania
Sunday, October 20, 6:10 a.m.

Mr. Bones opened the wings of his Ghost Box and engaged the encryption. When it finished running through a system check, he waved to Howard, who was pouring cups of coffee into a pair of tall ceramic mugs. Howard's mug had Doctor Doom on it, Mr. Bones had Lex Luthor. They had matching workout shirts. Christmas was weird last year.

"She on the line?" asked Howard. He hooked a wheeled chair with one bare foot and pulled it over to the desk. They were no longer in the kitchen. The incident in Washington had sent them running for Howard's big office, where they each made a series of phone calls to try and get the latest information. In almost every case the people they called had no idea that anything was happening in Washington. Only the vice president,

Bill Collins, knew anything, but the extent of his knowledge was the same as what they knew. It was maddening.

Now they settled down to call Yuina Hoshino, the third of the three governors who ran Majestic Three. Hoshino was a naturalized American whose family had moved from Japan when she was one. Like her parents, she was a physicist. Unlike them, she was a laconic and introverted hermit who seldom spoke to anyone except her lab staff and the other governors. She was not a mouse, as Mr. Bones viewed it, but more like a burrowing tick—relentless, solitary, and bloodthirsty.

The space between the wings of the Ghost Box glowed and Yuina Hoshino's head and shoulders appeared. She had straight black hair streaked with gray, glasses hanging around her neck on a chain, and a face that might have been pretty had she spent any time at all in sunlight and fresh air rather than inside a lab. At sixty-one she was five years younger than Shelton and looked ten years older.

"What do we know?" asked Hoshino in a voice that was creaky with disuse.

"Only what we've told you," answered Mr. Bones.

"What's the problem with our intelligence sources? Are we out of the loop?"

"No," said Mr. Bones, "that's all there is. Linden Brierly arrived to take charge. Ghost Box has taps on all cellular and landline calls, we're inside the Secret Service intranet, and we have bugs on every important wall. If there was more to know, we'd know it."

Hoshino frowned. "That's disturbing. This is not a good time for mysteries. The air show is so close . . ."

The Third Annual American Advanced Aeronautics Convention—informally known as "the air show"—was held at a fairground in Ohio. It was the highlight of the year for all defense contractors invested in fixed-wing aircraft, and particularly those who were rolling out new prototypes like old money families trotting out this season's debutantes. M3 planned to steal the show with the Specter 101. The air show was not open to the public, of course, but everyone even tangentially associated with the DoD, Homeland, and the crucial arms sales to foreign markets would be there. It was the best opportunity to impress the brass and the congressional bean counters, and it was equally fine for showing up the competition.

Last week the security systems at the Ohio fairground were hit by the cyber-attacks, so Howard offered to host it at VanMeer Castle, where he had his own private airfield and grounds well screened by mountains and trees. Howard offered to augment security with a hundred operatives from Blue Diamond Security, a company in which he owned a sizable interest. The other exhibitors were reluctant at first, but the promise of security by the fierce Blue Diamond private contractors helped smooth things out. That, and there was a lot of sympathy for Howard after the tragic events at Wolf Trap.

"This won't stop the air show," assured Howard.

Hoshino snorted. "Of course it will. I'm surprised the show hasn't already been canceled. And, frankly, Howard, it surprises me that you even want the show to go on. After Wolf Trap and the others events, it's clear that whoever's behind these cyber-attacks wants that show stopped and they want Shelton Aeronautics crippled."

Howard hoisted a suitably morose expression into place. "My security people tell me that the new upgrades will assure a safe event."

"Maybe," grudged Hoshino, "but even the air show is secondary to this thing in Washington. And . . . let's face it, gentlemen, we've all known that this could happen."

"What exactly is it you think *has* happened?" asked Mr. Bones.

"Isn't it obvious? Someone else has developed a working device before us."

"Who?"

"It could be anyone," said Hoshino. "It could be the Chinese. They've acquired most of the D-type components that were on the black market recently, and they've had an army of agents out there looking for more."

"No," said Howard. "If they had a complete device we'd know it by now."

"Maybe we *do* know," said Hoshino. "Maybe that's what we're seeing now. This could be their opening move."

Howard constructed a brooding and contemplative face. "If they had a device," he said dubiously, "they'd have to test it first before they did anything like this."

"If you ever bothered to read my reports," said Hoshino, "you'd see that there's some indication of that. Sightings are up all over the world."

"Oh, hell," barked Howard, "we're seeding most of that crap into the press. And a lot of it's faked by morons hoping to get onto one of those stupid specials. They spray a Frisbee with silver paint and get one of their asshole friends to throw it over the house so they can take a picture of it with a cell phone."

"Some of it," agreed Hoshino. "Not all."

"What are you saying?" asked Mr. Bones.

"I'm saying that there's something up there and it's not us," said Hoshino. "It could very well be the Chinese. Maybe they've finished testing their device and this abduction is the opening move in something bigger."

Mr. Bones grunted. "Maybe . . . but having a device and being willing to use it in such an outrageous way is a big jump. Attacking us like this?"

"It might not be the opening salvo of a war," said Hoshino. "It could be an attempt to send a message."

"You mean a threat?" asked Howard.

"Of a kind," she conceded. "Something that only certain people would be able to recognize for what it is. People like us."

"Are you saying they're behind the sabotage of our computer systems, too?" asked Howard.

"We're not the only ones being attacked," said Hoshino.

"That's not the point. Someone is waging a war . . . but I don't buy China for any of this. Maybe the attack on us, if they had the tools, which they don't, but not taking the president. That's just too risky for them. They'd have to know that if we got wind of who was behind something like this, even if the president is returned unharmed, we'd retaliate. China's tough, but they're not as tough as the press paints them. They're not ready for a nuclear exchange or even an air war. The Seventh Fleet would love any opportunity to prove that they aren't patrolling those waters for show."

"What about the Russians?" asked Hoshino. "They're working on something—"

"They *were* working on something," corrected Mr. Bones, "until Pietrovich woke up dead."

"Wait . . . what? Pietrovich is dead? When did that happen?" demanded Hoshino.

Mr. Bones cleared his throat. "End of September."

"Why wasn't I told?"

Another pause. "Guess it was an oversight. Sorry, Yuina. Didn't mean to cut you out of the loop."

"Loop?" Yuina Hoshino turned to Howard. "Did you know about this?"

"Well, yes," he said blandly. "I'm shocked Bones didn't tell you."

"Sorry we didn't tell you," said Howard. "It was one of Erasmus Tull's quiet little magic tricks."

"Tull?" said Hoshino with distaste. "I thought he retired."

Howard snorted. "He's only as retired as we want him to be."

"And you didn't think it was important to tell me any of this?"

"I said I was sorry, but it's done and Pietrovich is in the ground. What matters is that it closed down a line of research that could have hurt us. If you want me to go whip myself later, Yuina, then fine. Mea culpa, mea culpa, mea fuck me culpa. Correct me if I'm wrong, but that's yesterday's box score and we have something a lot more important right here, right now."

"Fine, fine," said Hoshino in a totally artificial tone of concession, "let me know next time. Especially if you're going to activate an agent like Tull. He was erratic at the best of times."

"They're all erratic," said Howard. "Bunch of test-tube freaks."

"They're our children," chided Hoshino.

"The fuck they are. They're meat by-products. And, even though I use Tull because he gets the job done, that cat gives me the creeps. All of them do, so let's not romanticize them, okay? There's not going to be a Hallmark Christmas special at the end of this. Either they serve their purpose or we put a shiny new bullet into each of them. End of story."

Mr. Bones cleared his throat to clear the air. "If it's not the Russians and it's not the Chinese, what are the chances that the North Koreans rebuilt their lab?"

"'Rebuilt'?" repeated Howard. "Rebuilt what? That lab is a hole in the goddamn ocean. No, the Koreans only ever had two genuine D-type components, and they lost those when the lab blew. And maybe—maybe—they've acquired one or two more parts since then, but that's a long way from having a device. Besides, if it was them, and they could take the president out of the White House, then we'd have found his body hanging from a tree in the Rose Garden. I'm not saying they'd sign their handiwork, but they wouldn't risk holding him hostage or waste time with a catch-and-release."

"They might," said Hoshino. "If they were able to take him, imagine what kind of threat they could make. Instead of the usual saber rattling with their missile program, they would be able to whisper right into the president's ear: 'Look what we can do!' Think about it. Think about how that would impact every decision the president made."

"Maybe, but I don't buy it."

"Who does that leave? Brazil? Israel?" asked Mr. Bones. "Do we start looking at our allies now? We knew that there was always a possibility they'd turn on us if they got a working device, but I can't see it this soon. It's way ahead of any projection."

"Actually," said Hoshino slowly, "I think you're wrong about that. There is one more possibility we're overlooking. It skews everything, but the more I think about it, the more I'm beginning to believe that all of this fits one of our earliest projections."

"Which one?" demanded Howard Shelton.

Yuina Hoshino looked from one to the other.

"The Truman Projection," she said.

The silence was as fragile as spun glass and it lasted a long time.

"Oh my God," said Mr. Bones.

Chapter Fifteen

Camden Court Apartments, Camden and Lombard Streets
Baltimore, Maryland
Sunday, October 20, 6:12 a.m.

It took me three minutes to dress, grab my gun, yell a goodbye to Violin, hustle Ghost into my car, and start the engine. I called Church as I backed out of my parking slot.

He told me what was happening.

That sobered me right up.

"Jesus Christ," I said.

I put the pedal all the way down.

And broke every speed law in the state of Maryland.

Chapter Sixteen

The White House
Sunday, October 20, 6:13 a.m.

As Lyle Ames ran interference for him, Linden Brierly slipped into a quiet corner where he could make a discreet call to Mr. Church. His cell phone had a built-in code scrambler based on a design originally used by Hugo Vox and the Seven Kings, but which Church had reconfigured for the DMS. And friends.

"Linden," said Church, "has there been any change of status?"

"Nothing good."

"Better tell me anyway."

"First, there's nothing new on the president, and per your suggestion I've put a lid on that crop circle we found. It's a needless complication. I put two agents on it, but I've also isolated the agents who found it and the helicopter crew that took aerial photos of it. They're not talking to anyone right now."

"Good."

"But I just heard from a friend in the AG's office—a former agent now with the DoJ. The acting president has requested that the attorney general meet him right away."

"Why?"

"Don't know for sure, but my friend said that he heard the president use two names. Yours and Joe Ledger's. My guess is that Collins is going to try and get a warrant to allow him access to MindReader."

"The cyber-attacks thing," said Church.

"What else can it be?"

"Thank you for the heads-up, Linden."

"Deacon . . . if the president doesn't come back . . . If he's hurt or dead . . . then Collins will well and truly be our president."

"I know," said Church. "And won't that be interesting?"

He disconnected.

Chapter Seventeen

On the road

Baltimore, Maryland

Sunday, October 20, 6:17 a.m.

I took a corner on two wheels and as my Explorer thumped down onto the side street I tried to kick the gas pedal through the floor. Ghost yelped and dove for the footwell. He was trained to be passive during high-speed driving, but I think he had doubts about my skills while hung-over. Fair enough.

Church put me on hold to take a call from Washington. While he did that I switched from cell phone to the tactical communicator—a tiny earbud for a speaker and a high-fidelity mike that looked like a freckle next to my mouth. One of the guys at the Bose lab makes these special for Mr. Church.

He came back on the line, but before he could say anything I yelled, "How in the wide blue fuck does the President of the United States go missing from the goddamn White House?"

"We don't have answers," said Church. "The vice president has assumed temporary power—"

"That shithead shouldn't be allowed to manage a Taco Bell."

Church agreed with a sour grunt. He related his recent call with Brierly. It did nothing to improve my view of our temporary commander-in-chief. Vice President Bill Collins was, at best, an opportunistic dickhead who had a hard-on for the whole DMS and once used the NSA to try and tear us down. At worst, he was a closet traitor who may have been in bed with the Jakoby organization, one of the worst cabals the DMS ever tackled. Or he could just be a total damn fool. Whichever way, Collins was a wizard when it came to keeping shit off his own shoes. Even Church hadn't been able to prove that Collins was bent. Knowing that Collins was now in power, however conditionally, made my nuts want to climb up inside my chest cavity.

"So," I asked, "what's our official involvement?"

"Official? None. Linden Brierly has been expressly ordered to keep us out of this. Apparently President Collins believes that we may be tied in some way to the cyber-attacks. No, Captain, don't try to make sense of that, you'll hurt yourself."

I didn't. Instead I cursed a lot, in several languages. Church rode it out; he neither stopped nor contradicted me. I did some weaving in and out of traffic. Lot of horns blared; lot of people flipped me the bird. I spread love and peace everywhere I go.

"What's the alert status?"

"The military is bulking up at all the appropriate hotspots, notably the Middle East and the Taiwan Strait. The official word is that this is an unscheduled preparedness exercise, so nobody is launching missiles," said Church, "but we're not far enough back from the brink. Everyone is suspicious of 'exercises' because they can be used to hide just this sort of emergency protocol."

In the White House there are protocols for everything. Presidents have been assassinated, they've died in office. There have been shots fired at the White House, there have been bomb scares. There's even a protocol for an armed invasion of the capital by enemy troops, crazy as that sounds. Depending on the scale of the crisis, phones ring throughout the city, causing the pillars of government to shudder.

"However," Church said, "the base commanders have not been told the nature of the alert."

I could understand that. Ever since 9/11 and the subsequent wars, we've gone to high-alert status way too many times. Homeland and the Department of Defense don't always share the "why" of this, even with base commanders. The Joint Chiefs have become very cagey—you could use the word "paranoid" without too much exaggeration, and for good reason. Sure, most of those alerts were false alarms, but there have been a number of times when something very big and very bad was looming and everyone had to be ready—just in case. Often it was the DMS who put the monster back in its box.

"We need to keep this totally away from the public," I said.

"No doubt. A whiff of this would cause panic and likely crash several of the world markets."

The yellow light ahead was about to turn. I did something fast and irresponsible, and as I shot through the intersection a pedestrian threw a bottle of Coke at me.

"Hey, the sky is falling, jackass," I yelled out the window.

"Captain?" said Church mildly.

"Almost there."

I laid on the horn as I blew through another intersection. My Ford had lights and sirens, and if the local cops ran my plates they'd get a message that basically said "fuck off and leave him alone." But this was my town and I knew most of the cops anyway. Didn't hurt at all that my dad, former chief of police, was mayor of the fine town of Baltimore.

Ghost barked continually, his nerves jangling in rough harmony with mine.

To Church I said, "How does someone kidnap the president out of the White House? Isn't that supposed to be impossible? I mean actually impossible?"

"Yes," said Church, and disconnected.

Chapter Eighteen

Little Palm Island Resort
Little Torch Key, Florida
Sunday, October 20, 6:21 a.m.

Erasmus Tull stood by the slatted wooden rail of the deck and watched the woman walk from the surf wearing a scuba tank and a bikini bottom that was barely more than a swatch of colored cloth. The ocean was a soft blue, shades lighter than the sky, and it was unseasonably warm for October. Water streamed down the woman's tanned legs and beaded on the undersides of her small breasts. Her nipples were bright pink after her exertions and they looked somehow more sensual and more vulnerable that way. Tull felt a heavy throb deep in his loins.

He sipped his Scotch and smiled.

The woman called herself Berenice, but that was as false as the name he'd used when they had booked this vacation.

Berenice stopped by the chaise lounges on their private stretch of beach, hit the release on the tank harness, and slid it off. Tull watched her, appreciating the care she took as she lowered the tank to the sand rather than letting it drop. That kind of consideration went a long way with him. He despised the casual arrogance of so many of the scions of the super-rich. The ones whose access to wealth encouraged them to value nothing, and to even show contempt for property—anyone's property, even their own—merely because it had no true value in their minds.

This one was different, even though she was the daughter of the billionaire Dutch owners of Donderbus Elektronica, the second largest military weapons manufacturer in Europe. Berenice stayed out of the tabloids as often as possible, and gave the paparazzi nothing to sell beyond the occasional long-distance topless photo. And who cared a damn about that? Not when the Internet was rife with celebrity sex tapes pedaled by disgruntled exes of lower income or station. Not her, though. Not this lovely woman with the long legs and liquid green eyes. Berenice was quiet—boring by media standards—preferring to linger inside her own head, to explore her thoughts with as much diligence and receptive interest as she maintained for the seas in which she swam. She and Tull had snorkeled and dived in the ocean, sometimes swimming naked under star fields scattered with ten billion diamonds.

Tull wondered if he was falling in love with her.

He wasn't sure if he could. Some of the others in his family seemed to manage it; others did not. So far, he hadn't.

It troubled him, as it often did when he wondered at the big empty places inside his head and heart. He took another brooding sip. The rich Balvenie 191 burned its way down his throat with such elegance that he closed his eyes for a moment to explore the complex subtleties of the whiskey. This, he decided, was what love probably felt like. So—was that what he felt for Berenice?

After weeks with her he still wasn't sure.

The cool breeze off the ocean ruffled his blond curls.

Berenice picked up her sunglasses from the table between the lounges and put them on, then she stood for a long minute looking off toward the swaying trees that grew lush and dense here on Little Palm Island. Tull followed the line of her gaze and saw a small key deer step daintily out from between the trunks of two torchwood trees. It was a young doe whose coat was still splashed with faint spots and was only now growing into the gray brown of adulthood. The deer seemed unaware of the woman as it poked around on the ground for fallen thatch pine berries.

Tull knew that Berenice was as unaware of being watched as was the deer, and her unguarded smile was lovely. Peaceful and uncomplicated in a way that lent her face a look of profound serenity.

Yes, thought Tull, *you are falling in love, old sport*.

The cell phone on the porch railing began to ring. It was a soft sound, not enough to startle deer or woman. A very specific ringtone. Tull picked it up and clicked the button with a thumbnail.

"Go," he said.

Berenice heard him and she turned, still smiling, and gave him a small wave. Tull blew her a kiss.

The caller said, "There is a fire in heaven."

Tull sighed and parked a haunch on the rail. He frowned into the amber depths of his drink as he swirled the Scotch around and around.

"Are you sure you have the right number?" he asked. It wasn't the agreed-upon response code, but he was annoyed at having the moment spoiled. There were so few moments like this in his life.

There was a slight pause at the other end. "There is a fire in—"

"Yes, I heard you," sighed Tull.

Down below Berenice was trying to approach the deer with the bread and lettuce from the sandwich she'd left unfinished before going diving. The doe peered at her with a blend of innocence and natural wariness, her muscles tensed for flight.

The silence on the other end of the line was ponderous.

Tull shook his head and wondered if it wouldn't be better to simply chuck the phone out into the salt water. He didn't need to work anymore—he had enough money squirrelled away to live in sybaritic comfort for the rest of his life. Granted, he enjoyed the work, but today he was in a different head space.

Berenice crept closer to the deer, and the animal still had not fled. The princess moved like a tai chi practitioner, keeping her weight on her back leg, letting the other move out slowly to find its place, and then using a controlled shift of her body to empty her weight from one leg and fill it onto the other leg. It was so smooth it was as if she glided across the sand. No jerky steps. Lots of pauses to allow the deer to find its trust and its courage. Tull found it both fascinating and very sexy. Not because of the similarity to tai chi, but because a beautiful woman wearing only a

skimpy bikini bottom stalking like a hunter pushed a lot of the right buttons in Tull's libido.

The caller tried it one more time. "There is a fire in heaven."

Tull really wanted to drop the phone and stomp on it. Instead he gave
the counter-code. "Where are the angels?"

"In the east," said the caller.

"Hello, Mr. Bones."

"Hello, Mr. Tull. I trust you are well."

"I was better before the phone rang."

"Ah. Then, on behalf of the governors, please accept my apologies.
However, your services are needed."

"Send someone else," said Tull.

"We can't," said Bones, and Tull heard a note of alarm in his voice.
"There are complications."

The doe spooked and bolted, vanishing into the woods. Berenice
stood, the sandwich in her hands, her disappointment written in the lines
of her body. Even so, the day remained beautiful. Bees and dragonflies
flitted from flower to flower and far away a few white clouds floated like
sleeping giants on the bed of the horizon.

"What complications?"

"*Religious* complications."

It took a moment for Tull to grasp the meaning from the obtuse language. His pulse quickened. Religious complications.

Religion.

Church.

God almighty.

"Tell me," he said. Mr. Bones told him.

With each word the colors seemed to drain out of the day. The music
of the waves turned to noise; the sound of the songbirds became the dis-
cordant chatter of pests. It was how it always happened. It was how it
usually was for him. Sadness crept into his heart as he felt the magic that
defined this day, this place, this moment, slip like oiled flesh through his
fingers.

Below, the princess turned and began walking along the beach toward
their bungalow. Sunlight reached for her through the trees and dappled

her breasts and shoulders. Tull sighed, and the sound of it, even to his own ears, was filled with weariness and sadness.

"Very well," said Tull.

"You'll accept the assignment?"

"Yes." His voice was a soft croak. "Send me any intel you have. I've got a little travel time ahead of me, but I can be there soon. Have my jet fueled and the airport cleared. Call Aldo—I'll need him. In the meantime, make sure there are some good people on this guy Ledger. See if you can put him in a box until I can get there."

"Thank you, Mr. Tull. We have assets in play as we speak."

The line went dead.

Tull finished his Scotch and set the glass down and leaned on the rail with both hands. It would be so hard to leave this place. To leave this woman. To leave this chance at being like other people. At being normal.

At being human.

Tull sighed again, and went inside to pack.

Chapter Nineteen

The White House
Sunday, October 20, 6:22 a.m.

Linden Brierly and a dozen agents moved in an armed wave to intercept the president from entering the White House. Before Brierly could say a word, William Collins pointed a finger at him.

"Don't," he barked.

"Mr. President," said Brierly in a tight whisper, "this is extremely ill advised."

The president stopped and looked around. His motorcade sat in the underground entrance, lights swirling, armed men and women everywhere. Security cameras were mounted on the walls, guards at the gated entrances.

He closed on Brierly, getting right up in the director's face, and his whisper was every bit as fierce. "You told me you swept the building."

"Yes, sir—"

"Top to bottom, every room, every possible hiding place."

"Yes, Mr. President."

"You ran scanners over every inch of wall space. There are no listening devices and no hidden compartments where the entire Al-Qaeda could be lurking."

Brierly said nothing.

Collins had enough courtesy to lower his voice so that only Brierly could hear him. "Whatever happened this morning is over. Your own team has deemed the building safe."

"Sir, I approved a memo saying that there were no detectable threats. That's hardly the same—"

"I am the president, Linden. I know it pains you to accept that fact, but there it is. Now get the fuck out of my way while you still have a job."

Collins glowered until Brierly reluctantly stepped back and to one side.

With his entourage in tow and agents fore and aft, the president went into the White House to lay claim to the Oval Office. Linden Brierly, defeated, followed in his wake.

Chapter Twenty

Camden Court Apartments, Camden and Lombard Streets
Baltimore, Maryland
Sunday, October 20, 6:23 a.m.

The two men in the black Crown Victoria watched the huge red-brick apartment building. The driver chewed gum slowly and methodically as he studied the building through dark sunglasses. The man next to him was hunched over a small laptop whose split screen showed him the feeds from several camera drones that perched as fake pigeons on power lines, light poles, and window ledges. From ten feet the drones looked entirely real. At close range their tiny black bird eyes were too dark, too lifeless, too unnatural to sell them as real. But they did not need to pass close inspection, and no one looks twice at a pigeon in Baltimore.

"Okay," said the man with the small laptop. "The woman's leaving, too."

A tall and lovely young woman stepped out through the main doors and raised her arm for a cab. Both men paused to admire her legs and the way her clothes clung to her ripe lines.

"Ledger's pumping that?" said the driver. "Lucky bastard."

"Yeah, well his luck just ran out," said the passenger. "Hope he got laid this morning, 'cause it's going to be a long time before he sees a pair of tits again."

"Ah, well," said the driver. "Life's a bitch."

The other man laughed, then he tapped his Bluetooth. "The apartment's empty. Send in the team."

Chapter Twenty-one

On the road
Baltimore, Maryland
Sunday, October 20, 6:24 a.m.

As I drove I tried to make sense of things. On one hand, abducting the president made every kind of political sense—if you were a terrorist. If you were willing to die to make a point, this would be the biggest play of the game. Short of detonating a nuke on U.S. soil there's no real way to top something like that.

On the other hand, abducting the president made no sense. It was on a par with kicking a grizzly bear in the nutsack. Yeah, you can brag about it if you live long enough, but how much do you like your odds? You'd have to know that once guys like me—and the thousands of other agents, lawmen, soldiers, and shooters who would be in this hunt—were on your trail, you were done, cooked. Dead, if you were lucky; in custody if your luck turned to shit. There are worse things that can happen to an enemy of the state than Gitmo. Hate to say it, hate it to be the truth, but there it is.

Who was the bad guy here? Who had either that much balls or was that crazy?

The U.S. of A has a lot of enemies, and some of them are supposed to be friends and allies. Friendship is every bit as illusory as the concept of alliance—it's all really a balancing of mutual interest, mutual greed, fear, and barely concealed exploitation. And that math is skewed even more when you factor in that everyone hates the guy at the top. So, who among our bitter enemies or supposed friends would risk abducting the president? Who would think the rewards would outweigh the risks? Moreover, who was dumb enough to believe that a hostage, even one of such importance, is a genuine shield? In the short term, sure . . . but that kind of protection goes toxic faster than macaroni salad at a hot August picnic.

Hold a hostage too long and that person's political relevance diminishes. There would be a change of power in the White House—hell, the veep was already the de facto president. All the useful codes were already being changed. Pretty soon the hostage has symbolic value only, and I wouldn't want to live on those terms.

Maybe this was political from a different camp. I mean, the loss of the president would tear down a lot of partisan structures. The president's party would lose face and would likely be overwhelmed in the next round of congressional elections. The people most loyal to the missing president would be held up to scrutiny in case there was any possible chance that they were complicit in action or derelict in duty, and that stain of doubt would never wash off. Gradually everyone upon whom the president relied for swift, decisive action would be diminished, replaced, or otherwise disempowered.

And, of course, there was the issue of retaliation.

I couldn't believe that any government was directly responsible for the abduction because this was an undeniable act of war. It was also a violation of our apparent strength and security. Once this was out we would lose face with the other superpowers; and the stock market would go right into the crapper. Our only response would have to be one of overwhelming military force. We would need to identify the culprits and utterly destroy them. If this was the work of a nonnuclear state, then they would be invaded and steamrolled flat. I'm not saying I agree with that, but I'm practical enough to understand the political philosophy of it. If you want to maintain the reputation as the absolute strongest, then when someone slaps you, you don't slap them back. Instead you run them down with your car and make sure all four wheels bump over their bones. Barbaric? Sure. Spiritual? Of course not, because it is the exact opposite of the lessons of the enlightened teachers. But practical for a corrupt, illogical, and fiercely violent world? Sadly, cynically, yes.

I was nudged out of those gloomy thoughts when a black car shifted into my lane two cars in front of me. It was a Crown Victoria of the kind often used by government agencies. It caught my eye because there was one just like it behind me. We reached a light and the four of us sat there—the first Crown Vic, then a red Honda with a woman with two small kids, then me, and then the second Crown Vic. On another day I might have missed the cars, or noticed them but dismissed them. Today was not another day. Today was today and weird things were already happening.

The light turned green and we moved forward in a line to the next corner. The green light was about to turn and the lead car had just enough time to hurry through the yellow. He didn't. The driver slowed and allowed the light to go all the way to red.

I punched a button on my cell and called Church.

"Boss, did you send an escort?"

"No," he said, "what are you seeing?"

I told him and gave the tag numbers from the one behind me, transposing them from the reverse image in my rearview. "Can't see the numbers on the lead car though."

"Hold on," he said.

The light turned green and we moved forward. The red Honda peeled left and went down a side street. That left my Explorer sandwiched between the two government cars. I gave Church the plates of the lead car, which I could now see.

Church came back on the line. "Both plates belong to cars in the general FBI fleet. Do you need to know who checked them out?"

The light turned green, but the lead car did not move. I was in a box. I had six feet between my front bumper and the lead car, but the follow car had crept up so close he was crowding my taillights. Some wiggle room if this got weird.

"I have a feeling this is about to go south on me, boss."

"I'll roll backup," said Church. "Be careful, Captain."

"Always am," I said.

Doors opened in both cars. Front doors, both sides. Four men got out. All of them tall, all of them in black suits with crisp white shirts, nondescript ties, sunglasses. Their jackets were unbuttoned and there was a slight breeze, however each man used one hand to keep the jacket flaps closed.

"Uh-oh," I said to Ghost. Actually I said, "Rut-roh," in my best Scooby-Doo voice.

Ghost straightened and looked out of the windows, turning to look in front and behind us.

The agents closed in on my Explorer. Two on the passenger side, two on the driver side. The point man removed his identification wallet and held it out as he approached my window. Ghost growled softly, the ridge of hair on his spine standing as straight as a wire brush. He bared his teeth, four of which were made of gleaming titanium—replacements for the ones he'd lost on the Red Order gig in Iran. Ghost loves biting things with those chompers. He's never hugely friendly with strangers at the best of times and right now he was picking up my tension. This car stop had "wrong" written all over it. It was weird, it was unexpected, it was improper and today wasn't the day for that shit. I gave Ghost a couple of get-ready-but-wait commands.

I rolled my window down one quarter of an inch. Enough for sound, not enough for any hanky-panky. The glass is bullet-resistant. I'm not.

"Federal agents," said the point man. He was a medium-size guy with a beaky nose and hardly any lips. All I could read on the ID were the three big letters that my boss insists do not stand for "Fart, Barf, and Itch."

I slapped my ID against the glass. I'd dug a set of NSA credentials out of the glove box. Since these guys were FBI, I wanted to both trump them and also play home-court advantage—and the NSA is based in Fort Meade here in Maryland. The DMS doesn't have ID cards or badges being one of those "we're so secret we don't officially exist" things.

Beaky Nose barely looked at my credentials. "Federal agents," he repeated. Which, in the circumstances, was kind of a silly thing to say.

"Me, too, friend," I said coldly. "I am responding to a matter of national security. Please move your car."

He did not acknowledge my statement in any way. Instead he said, "Please step out of your vehicle."

"Sorry, did you miss the part where I said that I'm with the National Security Agency? Perhaps you've heard of us? Bunch of officious pricks with way too much authority? Including the authority to tell you to back the fuck off and let me go about my business." Just to be pissy I gave him a toothy smile and added, "Please."

Beaky Nose opened his jacket and laid his hand on the butt of the pistol clipped to his belt. "Please step out of your vehicle, sir. Don't make me ask you again."

"You just did," I said. "You made yourself say it again."

Beaky Nose didn't seem to know how to answer that. While he was sorting it out I opened the door and stepped out. He stepped back, his hand still on his pistol. I was wearing jeans and an unbuttoned Orioles shirt over a thermal undershirt. My Beretta was in a quick-draw shoulder rig, out of sight but in easy reach. The second agent, a beefy man with black hair and an Italian face came around from the far side of the car and stood a few feet behind me and to my right. My car door was still open, and it formed a nice barricade between us. The guys from the follow car, a scarecrow with sallow skin and a black guy with a precisely trimmed mustache and a gleaming bald head, stood behind me and to the left. Maybe six feet behind me. Almost but not quite the right distance to stay out of my range. Ghost stood up on the seat, but I kept him in place with a small hand sign. I left the door open, though, just in case things got creative out here. Ghost makes a great party crasher.

"We need you to come with us," said Beaky Nose.

"Why?" I asked.

"We need you to come with us."

He repeated the comment with exactly the same deadness of voice. No emotion, no inflection.

"What's your name?" I asked him.

He didn't answer.

"Let me see that ID again."

Beaky Nose didn't answer. He stared through the black lenses of his sunglasses. I couldn't see his eyes at all, not even the outline of them through the opaque lenses. It was a sunny morning, but the street we were on was shadowed by the tall buildings on either side. I was surprised he could see with such dark glasses.

"We need you to come with us," repeated Beaky Nose. It was almost robotic. Lifeless.

Yeah, it was a little bit scary.

The whole setup was scary.

And it was all wrong.

"Listen to me," I said, "I'm a federal agent and I've been called in on a matter of national security. Unless you have a warrant, then detaining me is a federal crime. Now, you're going to get into your cars and I'll get into mine. You're going to move your cars so I can get around you. Are we understanding each other here?"

Beaky Nose looked at the Italian, then over to the Scarecrow and

Baldy. Then he looked at me again. There was no flicker of expression on his face. He did not repeat his favorite catchphrase. He did not, in fact, say a goddamn word.

Instead he went for his gun.

Up till that moment I'd hoped that this encounter wasn't as weird and threatening as it seemed. And, up till that moment Beaky Nose had a chance of ending the day without severe physical discomfort.

That moment passed.

I kicked Beaky Nose in the nuts with the tip of my shoe. Very, very hard. I have big feet and my shoes have steel toes. This is never good news for the sorry son of a bitch whose balls get in the way of my rage issues.

He screamed loud enough to crack glass.

"Ghost—*hit*!" He launched himself out of the car like a snarling white torpedo as Scarecrow moved in on me. They went down hard and messy.

I slammed the half-open car door into the Italian, jolting him to a sudden stop, I whipped the door shut and jumped at him with a short-range front kick, crunching the flat of my foot onto the front of his thigh. It knocked his leg way too straight and way too hard and the leverage bent him in half and sat him forcefully down on his ass. Even as his tailbone tried to drill a hole in the asphalt, I pivoted my hips, cocked my leg and gave him a flat-of-the-heel side thrust right above the eyebrows. I'm pretty sure he was in happy land before the back of his head hit the blacktop.

Then I whirled to see the bald guy caught in a moment of indecision—help Scarecrow or go for me. He spun and went for the dog. Wrong choice. I reached him in two fast strides, grabbed his collar and jerked him backward off his feet. His gun went flying straight up into the air. I twisted my hip and dropped into a crouch, using the torque and downward weight shift to slam Baldy's back against the ground with a meaty thud. Air burst from his open mouth, and before he could take the next breath I leaned over and drove a two-knuckle punch into his solar plexus. He made a strangled screech and lay there, gasping and twitching like a gaffed marlin.

"Off!" I called, and Ghost released Scarecrow's bleeding arm. Ghost's metal teeth had done impressive damage. The man screamed in pain. I knotted my fingers in Scarecrow's hair, half lifted him and used my other hand to punch him in the face twice, breaking nose and mashing lips. He went out like a light and I let him drop.

I spun, crouched, ready for more.

But there was no more.

The Italian and Scarecrow were out; Baldy was trying to figure out that whole breathing thing, and it was going to take him a while to remember the rules. That left Beaky Nose, who was curled into a fetal ball. As I approached him he tried to wriggle away, but we both knew that wasn't going to happen. I felt something give when I'd kicked him. Probably his pelvis.

I'm a nice guy most of the time.

I'm a really nice guy some of the time. Last night at Rudy's bachelor party I was everybody's pal.

When it comes to ambushes, however, I find it hard to be affable.

Chapter Twenty-two

VanMeer Castle

Near Pittsburgh, Pennsylvania

Sunday, October 20, 6:26 a.m.

Once the call was ended, Mr. Bones closed the Ghost Box and turned to Howard Shelton. The old man was leaning heavily on the desk, head low, eyes staring fixedly into the wood grain. His color was bad and he was sweating.

"This is scary as hell," said Mr. Bones.

Howard merely grunted.

"I mean," continued Bones, "on one hand we should be happy that she's still clueless about the cyber-attacks and—"

"Fuck the cyber-attacks," snarled Howard. "We've got that safeguarded seven ways from Sunday. What about this thing in D.C.? What the hell is happening?"

"It's definitely not the Chinese."

Howard's lip curled back from his dentures. "Yeah? And how do we know those slippery bastards aren't screwing us?"

"We know because they can't. Remember the last time they tried? That entire lab complex in Tangshan became the epicenter of a very,

very big earthquake. Worst of the twentieth century, am I right? You really think they're going to risk that again?"

"How the fuck should I know?" growled Howard, his face becoming livid. "*We* keep risking it. Any risk is worth it. Mount St. Helen's, Haiti . . . even if someone ever puts two and two together, they'll see how everything we've had to do is all for the ultimate good. That's easy math. Besides, if we hadn't gotten lucky with the organic component we'd be in the same boat as them." He shook his head. "But it's not the damn Chinese I'm worried about. Or the Russians or the frigging North Koreans or anyone."

"Then what?"

"What Yuina said . . . about the Truman Projection. Christ, Bones, what if she's right?"

"Oh God, you're worried about that? You think we're being invaded by aliens?" Mr. Bones burst out laughing. "Yuina is a very brilliant, very dedicated, very crazy lady and she's been in the lab far too long."

"Yeah, but what if she's right?"

"She's *not* right. ET's gone home, Howard. We have junk and burned bodies and nothing else. This is all past tense and you know this."

"What if she's right?" Howard insisted.

"Not a chance in hell," said Mr. Bones with absolute certainty.

Howard merely grunted, but sweat continued to boil from his pores. It ran in lines down his cheeks.

"Jesus Christ, Howard," yelped Mr. Bones, "what's wrong?"

"I . . . I think you'd better get my nitro," said Howard very carefully. "I feel like shit."

Chapter Twenty-three

Baltimore, Maryland
Sunday, October 20, 6:33 a.m.

We were starting to draw a crowd. I ignored them.

Beaky Nose kept trying to wriggle away, but I moved into his path of retreat and squatted down. He took one look at me and gave up.

I took his ID case and looked at it. The photo was bland and uninteresting. The name printed on the card was "Stephen Albert."

"Who sent you?" I asked him.

Instead of answering he leaned over and vomited. His eyes were glazed and his face had turned a bright red. Huge spasms racked him from hair to feet.

"Let's come back to that," I suggested, and went over to pick the pockets of the other agents. Baldy was Benjamin Carr, Scarecrow was John Woods Duke, and the Italian-looking guy was Mark Bucci. I didn't recognize any of the names. MindReader would get me every last detail about them, so I pocketed the IDs. I also took their guns and removed the keys from the ignitions of both cars. While I was at it, I checked the glove compartments and trunks of each vehicle and found nothing. The cars were as clean as if they'd just rolled off a Detroit assembly line. Not even a pack of gum or an owner's manual.

The only remarkable thing I found was a small rectangular piece of metal Agent Albert had in his pocket. It was about the size of a Zippo lighter, but thinner and with no moving parts that I could see. I would have dismissed it as nothing more than a piece of junk except for the fact that he carried it and had nothing else of a personal nature. So it wasn't a worry stone or a good-luck piece. It weighed next to nothing and was warm to the touch. I put it in my pocket.

Agent Albert was on his knees with his hands cupped around his balls, but his red face had turned gray-green. I squatted down in front of him.

"Who sent you?" I asked.

He tried to say something, but he couldn't make coherent sounds. His lips formed the words: *Fuck you.*

"You're not making this any easier on yourself, Albert."

He didn't respond to my use of his name. Not a twitch. His bug eyes stared at the puddle of vomit in which he knelt. People were coming out of buildings and stepping out of cars. A few began moving closer, but Ghost gave such an eloquent growl that they retreated to a minimum safe distance.

I leaned a little closer to Agent Albert. "Listen to me, asshole—I don't know what they told you when they sent you four morons out on this pickup, but they didn't give you enough information. You just stepped in shit and believe me when I tell you that a kick in the junk isn't the worst thing that could happen to you today. On the other hand, if you tell me who sent you and why, I can see your luck definitely improving."

All he did was give me a slow, stubborn shake of his head. I sighed. Twenty minutes ago I was in a warm bed with a beautiful woman. A beautiful naked woman. I'd intended on sleeping until noonish, then wake her up, romp with her some more, and afterward the two of us would go on a prowl for the thickest steaks in Baltimore. Instead, I was here. I felt like crap due to lack of sleep, residual booze in my system, a hangover that made my head feel like it was held together with duct tape and enough postconflict adrenaline to make my eyes twitch and my hands jump.

Plus there was that whole "the president has been kidnapped" thing that was setting fires in my head.

"Last chance," I said to Albert.

Another slow shake.

I sighed. "Your funeral, pal."

"Yo!" called someone from the crowd. "What's going on over there?"

I got to my feet and held up my ID. "Federal agent. This is a crime scene. Clear the street."

They milled but none of them left. Everyone seemed to be taking photos with their phones. In the distance I heard the banshee cry of sirens.

I made two quick calls. The first was to my brother, Sean, who was a detective here in Baltimore. I told him the details that mattered but nothing of what was really happening. Sean didn't really know what I did for a living—like most folks from my previous life, he thought I worked for the FBI—but he promised to pass along word that I was to be allowed to leave the scene. He said he'd call our dad, too. Dad's the mayor of Baltimore. Sometimes nepotism is the best grease for the gears.

Then I called Church and gave him the full story.

The sirens were really close.

"Theories?" asked Church.

"Not a goddamn one."

"Okay, get out of there as soon as you can. I'll handle things with Baltimore PD and we'll see about a transfer to bring those four to a facility where we can interview them. I'll also get Jerry Spencer out there to take samples and sweep their cars."

"Cars are clean. Doubt Jerry's going to get anything besides finger-prints."

"It's worth a try."

Jerry was a former DCPD who now headed up the DMS forensics unit. He was damn good at it, too, though he never seemed to enjoy it. World-class grouch. No visible social skills. One of the DMS guys privately described him as "Sherlock Holmes with hemorrhoids." Like that.

"Any news?" I asked, and he knew what I meant.

"No," said Church.

"Call me paranoid, boss, but I find it strange that these jokers took a hard run at me today."

"Because of this morning?"

"Maybe. Or maybe because the veep is now the commander-in-chief. Last time he was in the Oval Office he sicced the NSA on us. Could be doing the same with the FBI."

"You think that's likely?"

"Don't know. Timing's weird, though. And . . . the wattage is dialed up. These guys wanted to hurt me. They were drawing guns when I made my play."

"I'll make sure they land in our custody," said Church in a way that was not intended to suggest that these guys were going to spend the rest of the day getting blow jobs and eating bonbons.

"Cops are here," I told him as the first units screeched to a stop.

"Ghost—down and quiet," I said and he obeyed. With that command he'd even let me get cuffed—if it came to that—without doing anything that might get him shot.

I stepped clear of the cars and raised my hands; one was empty and the other held my NSA credentials.

The officers pointed guns at me. They yelled at me. They manhandled me. They took my gun. I had to reinforce my orders to Ghost because he doesn't like seeing people manhandle his pack leader.

"National Security," I said over and over again.

Ghost growled.

One of the cops drew his Taser and pointed it at him.

"Listen to me," I said in my most reasonable tone, "I am a federal officer involved in a matter of urgent national security. You can run my ID and do whatever you have to do, but if you Tase my dog I'm going to shove that gun so far up your ass you'll be shooting sparks out of your nose."

Maybe they weren't impressed by the trash talk, but nobody fired a Taser at Ghost. For his part, my dog held his ground, though he eyed them like they were items on a menu.

The cops tried to cuff me. I'm not stupid enough to try physical resistance, but I kept trying to stall them with credentials and the National Security angle. That worked only long enough for the juice to kick in. A call came down the line that made them suddenly back off and change their attitudes toward me. Maybe it was Sean, or my dad . . . or, more likely, Mr. Church. They handed me back my gun. The guy with the Taser holstered his piece and didn't meet my eyes.

The four agents I'd dropped were semiconscious. Officers were trying to question them, asking where they were hurt, who they were. The agents said nothing. Not a word.

A sergeant supervisor arrived on the scene and came hurrying over. When he saw my face he slowed to a stop, a confused half smile beginning to form on his face.

"Joe—?"

I grinned. "Hey, Tommy."

"The fuck's this all about?" he asked, closing in.

Tommy O'Malley was a good cop. We'd worked together at a couple of precincts—White Marsh and Essex. He took my identification wallet from one of the officers, looked at it, frowned, and handed it to me.

"I thought you were with the Feebs."

"I am, but . . . it's complicated."

He gave me a few seconds of the "cop" look. Frank and suspicious. "Uncomplicate it for me."

But, I shook my head. "Can't do it, man. And I hate like hell to do this to a friend, but I have to stonewall you. This really is a national security matter and I can't tell you anything more than that."

Tommy was shorter than me, and he had one of those thin, freckly Irish faces that are no good at hiding their emotions. I saw the sudden shift as our relationship changed from Tommy and Joe to street cop and fed. Or, as we used to say when I was on his team, street cop and fucking fed.

I could feel him take a mental step back from me, and even after we'd hurried through the necessary steps and I was back in my car, the weight of his disapproval was heavy on my shoulders.

It depressed me. I was no longer one of that brotherhood.

Chapter Twenty-four

Little Palm Island Resort
Little Torch Key, Florida
Sunday, October 20, 6:39 a.m.

"Where are you going?" asked Berenice.

Erasmus Tull looked up from the suitcase he was packing. Berenice stood in the bedroom doorway. She still wore the bikini bottoms but she'd pulled on a loose white cotton shirt. His shirt. It hung open and unbuttoned. Purple shadows painted her skin and darkened the undersides of her breasts.

"I have to go to Maryland on business."

She came in and leaned against the dresser. "I thought you were retired."

"I am," he said, stuffing his shaving kit into the corner of the bag. "But I take it in installments. Now I have to go back to work to pay for the next installment."

She stepped over and removed his shaving kit from the suitcase, unzipped it and held it out. The small .22 pistol was wrapped in blue silk. She whipped off the silk and held out the pistol flat in her pam. "And so what business is this?"

Tull gently took the pistol from her. "My own."

"Are you a criminal?" she asked, her green eyes searching his. Concern etched a single vertical line between her brows.

Outside the window a mockingbird taunted Tull in a hundred voices.

"No," he said. "The gun is protection."

She straightened and her features hardened. There was a small crescent scar on her cheek, a souvenir from a baby moray they'd encountered in the waters off Osprey Reef in the Coral Sea. When she was hurt or angry that scar darkened to the color of autumn wine. As it did now.

"Am I a fool that you lie to?" she demanded. "Am I some little beach bunny that you hump and dump?"

"Don't be vulgar."

"Why? Is it less polite than lying?"

He sighed and tossed the gun down onto his folded pants. "I thought we agreed not to talk about our pasts?"

"Easy for you," she said. "You already know mine. Donderbus Elektronica is hardly unknown and I may be last in the line of succession to take over the company. I am still an heiress, which means that you could Google everything you need to know about me."

Tull had to force his lips not to curl into a smile. When they'd first met, he had done exactly that. "I know, but you still agreed to the arrangement."

"Because I didn't think it mattered." She indicated the pistol with a curt uptic of her chin. "Until this."

"This doesn't involve you—or us," he insisted. "I've got a small matter to handle and then I'll be back."

"What is this 'matter'?"

"It's confidential," he said. "I can't discuss it with anyone, not even you. Considering what your family does, I'm sure you can appreciate the need for secrecy in some aspects of business." He reached to take her hand. "Look, I'll be back as soon as I can."

Berenice took a step back from him.

"So that's it? You just up and leave and to hell with me and us and everything we've—"

"Believe me," he said, "I'll be back."

"How many times have you said that? How many women have stood where I stand now? Involved with you, in love with you, fascinated by everything that you know and all the mysteries you never shared? And then—what? Abandoned? Is that what drives you? To seduce and abandon?"

Tull laughed. "Seduce? As I recall, Berenice, you seduced me. Or as near as. You came up to me at that party in Marseilles and dropped a killer line on me. What was it? 'I'm a lot more interesting than anyone you'll find here. Escape with me.' You had me on your hook from the beginning."

The stern expression on Berenice's face flickered momentarily. "I was only telling you the truth. We were more interesting than those inbred swine."

"No argument. The point is, you're not a victim of my irresistible seductive powers and I'm not the love 'em and leave 'em type."

"Oh? What type are you?"

"Mostly," he said, "I'm alone."

Berenice came and sat down on the bed. The action caused her shirt to flap open, revealing a perfect breast. The nipple was as dark as her scar and fully erect. Caused by anger, he knew, but that was a form of passion, too. He busied himself with folding his shirts so that he did not stare at her.

"How long will you be gone?" she asked.

"I—don't know. A few weeks at least. Maybe longer."

"What am I supposed to do while you're gone? Sit here and pine?"

"Cut it out, Berenice," he said softly. "You define your own life and always have. That's why they don't like having you at board meetings. It's why you picked me out of the crowd at that party. So, skip the guilt trip. You're playing the wrong card."

The mockingbird hopped onto the windowsill and regaled them with a schizophrenic diatribe.

"Will you have to use that gun?" she asked.

He picked up the blue silk and rewrapped the pistol.

"You're not answering me?" she said. "Is it because you don't want to lie? You'd rather say nothing?"

"What do you want from me?" said Tull. "I told you this is confidential . . . Can't we leave it at that?"

"Not if you want to be able to find me when this is over," said Berenice. He looked at her.

"That's what it comes down to, Tull," she said. "We're both adults, so if this is the end of what we had, then have enough respect for me to say so."

"I—"

She stood up and moved in close, pressing her body lightly against his. Tull was infinitely aware of her animal heat, of the familiar curves and planes of her body, of the insistence of nipples hard enough to be felt through the fabric of her shirt and his. She looped her arms around his neck and looked up into his eyes.

"I can bear any truth," she breathed, "but never lie to me." She reached for his belt, unbuckled it, popped the top button of his trousers, slid the zipper down.

"I . . ."

His trousers fell down. Her fingers, clever and cool, slipped inside his boxers, found his hardness, squeezed it, stroked it.

Tull closed his eyes and leaned his forehead against hers. He was breathing as hard as if he'd run up a flight of stairs. So was she, and for a moment they breathed the same breath back and forth.

"Berenice . . . ," he murmured.

"Please," she whispered.

And then his lips were on hers. On her lips, on her face, her throat, her breasts.

He reached out and swept the suitcase off the bed and then they crashed together onto the sheets. Their mouths breathed fire, their hands were everywhere. The bird stood on the window sill, silent now, wise enough not to mock this.

AN HOUR LATER, Berenice lay naked on the tangled sheets, the sweat still drying on her skin. Tull could see her through the open bathroom door, through the gap between the shower curtain and the wall.

When he'd left the bed to go into the bathroom, he'd taken the pistol. It lay on the closed lid of the toilet, wrapped in a towel.

Waiting.

While he and Berenice had made love, his thoughts kept drifting from the beautiful woman under him to the gun.

To *its* elegant lines. To its potential.

To the way in which it simplified things.

He wished she hadn't asked him about it.

He wished she hadn't asked him about where he was going. Or when he was coming back.

As the hot water rinsed away the soap and their commingled oils and the scent of her passion, Erasmus Tull tried to keep her in his thoughts. Only her.

But the gun was there. So close.

It never asked anything of him.

It never complicated things for him.

He closed his eyes and leaned into the spray.

And wondered what to do.

What was the right thing to do?

What was the human thing to do?

The shower pounded on his back, his head. The questions pounded inside his mind.

He ached for Berenice. To be with her. To be normal with her. To be able to be normal.

He ached for the gun and its simplicity.

In the past, when he was torn like he was now, the gun always won.

It always won.

Always.

Chapter Twenty-five

VanMeer Castle
Near Pittsburgh, Pennsylvania
Sunday, October 20, 6:59 a.m.

Mr. Bones left Howard with the staff doctor and went into his office to take a call. He listened to a very trusted and capable operative tell him very bad news.

Per his e-mail of earlier that morning, a team was sent to pick up Captain Joe Ledger of the DMS. They were supposed to hold him for a length of time, then release him. During the detention, agents were to collect his fingerprints for use in building an evidentiary case that Ledger was involved—or perhaps directing—the cyber-attacks. They would also drug him with one of the many compounds useful for eliciting a cooperative mental state. In such a state a subject could be asked to sign his name to any kind of document, or make simple calls, record messages, and even stand for photos. The memories and personality tics would still be in play, but the conscious control would be detached from the events. It was a lovely thing to see; something the Russians had developed a bit too late for it to be of value in the closing days of the Cold War.

The whole process would have taken Ledger out of play for an entire day, and additional drugs like some of the modern benzodiazepine variations would do that. The newest generation of midazolam was always fun for these sorts of things. Then Ledger would be returned to his car with a mild sedative, where he would have awakened to a world that had suddenly decided that he was a very bad man.

It was a simple operation. Ledger would never have been able to adequately explain his brief absence and the evidence would be ironclad. Mr. Bones had ordered variations on this at least a dozen times, never with a hitch.

Except that today there was a definite hitch. Captain Ledger had brutally beaten all four men sent to handle the pickup. Suddenly a very minor detail in a day that had much more important concerns was now a major issue.

"That is very disappointing," said Mr. Bones.

The caller was silent. Mr. Bones let him sweat for a while.

"I will have it cleaned up, sir," said the caller.

"Well that would be nice," said Mr. Bones icily and disconnected.

The good news was that Erasmus Tull was on his way to Maryland. Tull would never have fumbled so easy a play as this. In Mr. Bones's knowledge, Erasmus Tull had never fumbled anything. The worst that could be said of him was that once or twice he retreated from overwhelming odds, but that was simply good sense.

Mr. Bones activated Ghost Box and began reading updates and reports.

The air show was still on schedule. The prototype of Specter 101 had been safely delivered to VanMeer Castle, and the grandstands were already erected. Not that it really mattered, he mused. He really didn't care about the plane, nor did Howard, who privately referred to it as the "flying red herring." But for now, for today, all appearances must be maintained—and that was even more important if the thing in D.C. caused the air show to be postponed.

Christ, that really would give Howard another heart attack. It was a mercy that the minicrisis brought on by the news from Washington was only a "concern" rather than an "event."

Mr. Bones clicked on to the next item.

The tech teams had managed to launch several flocks of the new pigeon-size surveillance drones. How lovely. Ten flocks in Baltimore, ten in Brooklyn, and five each in nine other locations. The drones were one of Bones's own toys. Darling little machines. When Howard discovered him, Mr. Bones was the senior designer at AeroVironment, a nano aerial vehicles shop funded by DARPA's Defense Sciences Office. He'd been building unmanned aerial vehicles that looked like birds. The one that sold the project to the DoD was the hummingbird, which was beautifully painted and could flit and fly just like a bird—unless the observer was an expert on hummingbirds. The pigeon drones were more durable and their larger bodies allowed for the inclusion of technical packages for secondary objectives.

It amused Mr. Bones to imagine those flights of pigeons winging their way toward the Warehouse in Baltimore, the Hangar in Brooklyn, and the nine DMS field offices.

Another check mark on his to-do list.

Nice.

He scrolled through more items. More reports of UFOs. He dismissed any sightings in Washington State, Pennsylvania, Utah, Nevada, New Jersey, and New Mexico because the rubes were seeing experimental craft of one kind or another. With the air show pending, everybody in the industry was out test-flying their latest machines. That was fine. The reports from Upstate New York, Rhode Island, Iowa, Wyoming, and Central California were not as easy to dismiss. Frowning, Mr. Bones coded that for investigation and forwarded it to the field team supervisor with a request for twice-daily updates.

The minutes ticked by as he waited to hear from the doctor.

His phone rang and he saw the code word "Aqualung."

Erasmus Tull. Odd to get a callback so soon after initiating an assignment. It was too soon for Tull to even be at the airport yet. He picked up the phone, engaged the scrambler, and said, "Yes?"

"I need a cleanup."

"Already?"

Tull did not reply.

"Where?" asked Mr. Bones.

"The bungalow at Little Torch."

Mr. Bones took a moment to put that together. Tull was down there with the daughter of Matthijs de Vries, CEO of Donderbus Elektronica.

"Oh, dear," said Mr. Bones. "Has there been an accident?"

Tull said nothing.

The line went dead.

Chapter Twenty-six

The Warehouse, Department of Military Sciences field office

Baltimore, Maryland

Sunday, October 20, 6:44 a.m.

I rolled past security at the Warehouse, parked badly, killed the engine and hurried over to where the squat and muscular Sergeant Gus Dietrich— Mr. Church's personal aide and private bulldog—was waiting for me. Ghost was right at my heels.

Dietrich said, "You look like shit, Joe. Can't hold your booze like you used to? Too many Jell-O shots out of the navel of that Italian broad you brought to the party?"

"Fuck you," I said.

"There's that," he agreed.

I told him about the attack on the street.

"Well damn, son," he said. "You okay?"

"A bit rattled, highly suspicious, and mightily pissed off."

"Are you sure these clowns were feds?"

"I'm not sure of any-damn-thing, Gus. All I can tell you is that they weren't friends." I handed him four ID cases. "I doubt they're legit, but let me know if we get anything."

"Sure."

"Oh, and there's this." I dug the small piece of metal out of my pocket and handed it to him. "Took this off the lead agent. No idea what it is."

Gus weighed it in his palm. "Don't weigh nothing. And it's warm. Could be a tracker or something. I'll run some scans. But that can wait. Better haul ass—the big man's waiting for you."

We piled into a golf cart. Ghost tried for shotgun but I banished him to the back. Gus got behind the wheel and we whizzed off down the halls.

"I took the liberty of calling in your whole staff, Joe," Gus said. "Top Sims is already here, and he's got everything in hand."

Top was my number two. He was the smartest, toughest, and most organized noncom I've ever met—and that made him smarter, tougher, and more organized than just about any officer I'd ever heard of. Like Gus, Top was proof that nothing of any historical military importance has ever happened without the presence of good sergeants.

"Something came in right before you got here," Gus said. "A video file sent by an anonymous source. Wait till you see this, Joe, it'll blow your socks off."

"What's on it?"

He shook his head. "You better see for yourself."

The Warehouse is the third largest DMS field office. The biggest was the Hangar in Brooklyn and a small step down from that was Department Zero in L.A. The Warehouse was the office whose active range covered D.C., and it was all mine. I ran four field teams out of it—Alpha, Echo, Dogpack, and Spartan—and, including technical, maintenance, and general support, I had a total staff of about two hundred. Right now the whole building was at high alert and there was nobody loitering in the halls, no one anywhere except where they should be.

Gus dropped me outside my office. Church was already there, seated behind my desk with his laptop open. Church glanced at me and Ghost but didn't say a word. Didn't ask if we were okay. Didn't even offer to let me have my own chair. Apparently he forgot to bring his compassion to work today. Again.

Instead, he spun his laptop around and showed me an image. It was the president.

"This came in seven minutes ago," he said.

"They found him?"

"No," he said. "Watch."

He reached out to press a button. The static image of the president resolved into a video. The president sat in a straight-backed chair. He was not visibly restrained, but he sat unnaturally stiff and straight. His skin looked bad, blotchy, as if his blood pressure was firing on the wrong cylinders, and there was a weird glazed look in his eyes.

He spoke in a monotone, without inflection or pause. A tumble of words that had no life at all in them. It reminded me of the computer voice used by Stephen Hawking.

"Rector," he said, "I need you to do something. I need you to find the Majestic Black Book. You need to find the Majestic Black Book. You must find the Majestic Black Book."

Then the image abruptly changed. Instead of the president's face, the screen was filled with an image of an island somewhere in the middle of a blue ocean. There was a line of rocky ridges from some ancient volcano.

The president was back. "You need to find the Majestic Black Book."

Another image shift, this time showing a satellite image of the whole volcano. It was situated just off-center on an island. The island was small, the volcano was big. The image shifted again to show the same island from a much higher altitude, and that allowed us to see other landmasses.

"Where—?"

Before I could ask a question the image changed once more. Instead of static images, this was a series of video clips. First there was the storm surge as Hurricane Katrina smashed its way through the levees. Then a smash cut to the president repeating: "You need to find the Majestic Black Book." Then another cut to the tsunami that pounded Thailand the day after Christmas in 2004. Back to the president, same message. Then multiple images of a wall of ocean water sweeping across the coast of Japan. Back to the president. And then something even weirder—something scarier. The waters of the Atlantic rose up and slammed into the coastline of New York, sweeping over the Statue of Liberty, striking the docks, sending deadly waves through the streets, sweeping away cars and buses and all the people. The video clip ended and the satellite image of the volcano was back. That held for ten seconds and then we saw the president again.

"You need to find the Majestic Black Book," he said. "You don't have much time."

The screen dissolved into snow.

Chapter Twenty-seven

Office of the Attorney General of the United States, U.S. Department of Justice

Washington, D.C.

Sunday, October 20, 6:49 a.m.

Mark Eppenfeld looked up as his secretary entered the room. Eppenfeld's desk was covered with books and papers on constitutional law and the process of succession in times of national crisis. Although it was right and proper for Vice President William Collins to immediately step up so that there was no gap in the administration of the country, Eppenfeld was making notes on topics he knew would come up in the endless press conferences that would commence as soon as this story was released.

"What is it, Marie?" he asked.

"Sir . . . I have a Mr. Alden Funke on the phone. He's with the IRS office that liaises with Homeland. He said that he has a matter of great importance to discuss and his immediate superior is out of the country at the financial summit in Stockholm."

"Tell him to make an appointment, Marie," Eppenfeld said irritably. "I'm a little busy right now."

"Sir, he says that this involves that man, Mr. Church at the DMS."

Eppenfeld gave her a bleak stare, then nodded. "I'll take it."

He punched the blinking light on his phone. "What can I do for you, Mr. Frank?"

"Funke, sir. Alden Funke. I—I'm so sorry to interrupt you," stammered the caller in a thin, nervous voice, "however, I have some information that I believe is of grave national importance and—"

"So I understand. What is that information, Mr. Funke?"

"Well, sir, we were asked to review the financial records of employees of the Department of Military Sciences . . ."

"Asked by whom?"

"Um, the request came from the office of the vice president."

"When?"

"Several days ago, sir."

Eppenfeld leaned back in his chair and began chewing on the eraser of his retractable pencil. "Go on."

"I believe we have found something. A rather large something, to be quite frank, in the personal banking records for Captain Joseph Edwin Ledger."

Chapter Twenty-eight

The Warehouse, Department of Military Sciences Field Office
Baltimore, Maryland
Sunday, October 20, 6:55 a.m.

I looked at Church. "What the hell was that?"

"What does it look like?" he asked.

"If this was any other day . . . I'd say it was a joke."

"I seriously doubt we are being punked," he said. Church was a big man in his sixties who looked like someone who had spent his life doing the kind of stuff I do now. Age didn't have its claws in him yet, and he still looked like he could give anyone in the DMS a serious run for his money. Myself included. Dark hair shot with gray, a blocky build, and calculating eyes behind tinted glasses.

Right now, though, he looked more stressed than I'd ever seen him. A stranger couldn't tell—to anyone else Church looked like a man in complete control of every aspect of his life—but I could see the cracks at the edges of his calm.

"Who sent it to us?"

"Unknown. I've tried to backtrack it but MindReader keeps coming up with an error message."

"I thought MindReader could track any e-mail or Web site."

"So did I."

That hung in the air for a moment, weird and ugly.

"That footage of the wave hitting New York," I said. "That's from a movie. I recognize it but I can't grab the name."

"I thought so, too. A film about the end of the world. Bug will know. I sent this to him, so we can expect his call any minute."

Bug was the DMS computer supergeek who was also a pop culture nerd of legendary status.

"Who else has seen this?" I asked.

"I forwarded it to Aunt Sallie at the Hangar, of course, and to Linden Brierly. Otherwise, no one."

He sent the video from his laptop to the big HD screen on the wall and we watched it a couple of times. It didn't make any more sense the third time than it did the first time. It was equally freaky and equally frightening.

"The name the president used. Rector? That's you, right?"

Church nodded. He had a lot of names and as far as I've been able to determine, none of them are his real name. Most folks in government circles refer to him as "Deacon." I often wondered if his own daughter, Circe, knew her father's real name. I doubted it.

"It's a name I haven't used in a while," he said. "The president knows it from a matter that predates his presidency and may have chosen to use it as a code. However, if I am supposed to infer a specific meaning from it, then so far I am drawing a blank."

"You're going to have to show this to Bill Collins, you know."

Church nodded. "That's something Linden Brierly will have to manage. I am officially barred from this case."

"Barred? Why?"

"The acting president has some doubts about my loyalty."

"Shame I'm not drinking coffee," I said. "This is a classic moment for a spit-take."

He almost smiled. "Apparently President Collins variously believes me to be the villain who has been using MindReader to launch the cyberattacks or a fool who has mismanaged access to MindReader."

"Remind me again—I know assassination is against the law, but is there a rule against slapping some stupid off of an idiot playacting at president?"

"He is a difficult man to admire," conceded Church.

I stared at the screen. "What's this book the *actual* president kept mentioning?"

"The Majestic Black Book," Church said, putting the full name out there.

"Which tells me nothing. What is it? What's in it? Who wrote it? And why would you capture the president of the United frigging States to get a copy? I'm guessing it's not available on Amazon or Barnes and Noble."

You can't read Church's eyes. He wears tinted lenses for that very purpose. It's impossible to guess what he's thinking or where his thoughts are wandering. While he considered my question he used the tip of his index finger to trace a slow circle on the desktop.

"Until now I believed that it was an urban myth," he said slowly. "One of those elaborate conspiracy theories that have grown up around secret governments."

"Ah, secret governments," I said glumly. "I never get enough of secret governments."

"They do exist, Captain," said Church. "Any government as large as ours is compartmentalized. Divisions, departments, and groups splinter off, sometimes because they've been authorized to go deep and remain off the bureaucratic grid and sometimes to pursue other less official agendas. Congress knows about some of these and provides a degree of oversight, even if buried under layers of secrecy. Others manage to function within our government but without oversight. A case can be made that America would never have become a country had not a secret society of Freemasons taken charge."

"Yeah, yeah, I've read Dan Brown."

Church didn't smile. "Some of these groups believe—or claim to believe—that they are acting in the best interests of the nation. A case can be built to substantiate some of those claims, just as a case can be built that such manipulation generally has a profit-based agenda attached at some level."

"And this Black Book? How does this tie into that?"

"To be determined. What little I know of the Black Book comes secondhand from a more knowledgeable source."

I cocked an eyebrow. "You have a friend in the conspiracy theory industry?"

"Actually, I have several," he said, reaching for his cell phone again. This time, however, he surprised me. The image on the HD screen changed and suddenly there was Bug.

"Dudes!" he said brightly. "The Majestic Black Book? Are you freaking kidding me here? How cool is my job?"

His name was Jerome Taylor, but everyone called him "Bug." Even his mother. He's the only person, aside from Church, who has total access to the MindReader computer system. Bug was a former child-star computer genius who hacked his way into Homeland because he thought it would make a good senior project if he found Bin Laden. He'd been arrested and then Church hijacked him for the DMS. Even though Bug's early attempt at taking down the head of Al-Qaeda hadn't worked, years later when he had the full resources of MindReader at his disposal, he was largely responsible for putting Uncle Osama in the crosshairs of the heroes on SEAL Team Six. Bug currently ran the MindReader center at the Hangar in Brooklyn. The high-def screen made it look like he was right there in my office.

"Glad you're amused," said Church. "However, we do have a national crisis on our hands."

"Yeah, I know. The president, end of the world. Sucks. But . . . *the Black Book?* So cool." He beamed at us like it was Christmas morning. "Tell me we're really going after it."

"First things first," said Church. "Give me your assessment of the video."

Bug gave a dismissive shrug. "Meh. It's poor-quality alarmist trash. Crap like that wouldn't even get much play on YouTube."

"Pretend it's real," I said.

"Oh, I have no doubt it's real," Bug amended, "it's just that terrorists always make crappy videos. Kind of disappointing because anyone can buy the right software and do a decent job. It speaks to standards and—"

"Bug," said Church very quietly.

Bug blinked in a very buglike way. A cartoon bug. "Um . . . right. Sorry."

"The disaster clips?" I asked. "Are they—?"

"Most of them are real, sure. News footage. I can locate the sources, that won't be a problem. I'm doing a search now to find the island with the volcano. Oh, and that last clip they showed was from the movie *The Day After Tomorrow*. Made by the same guys who did *Independence Day* and *2012*. They got this thing about destroying landmarks."

"Do any of those movies deal with the Majestic Black Book?" asked Church.

"Nah." Bug screwed up his face as he thought about it. "Actually . . . I don't think I've ever heard of the book mentioned in a movie. Well, not in a theatrical movie. Not in fiction. You see it all the time in documentaries and on TV, though. Lot of nonfic books about it."

"Get me a list of those books and documentaries," said Church. "And the names of any experts associated with the Black Book."

"That's easy," snorted Bug. "But why not go straight to the source?"

"Source?" Church and I asked at the same time.

"Sure. Junie Flynn."

"Who's that?" I asked.

"She's the one who first broke the story about the existence of the Black Book," said Bug. "She's on all those documentaries."

Bug tapped keys and suddenly his image shifted so that he shared a split screen with a photo of a beautiful woman who looked like a 1960s flower child. Masses of long, wavy blond hair, sky-blue eyes, a smile so wholesome it could cure cancer, and a splash of sun freckles across her nose. The photo had been taken against a field of daisies, daffodils, and sunflowers.

"Wow," I said.

"I know," said Bug with enthusiasm. "She's hot, right? She's also one of the top experts on conspiracy theories—I mean she's up there with George Noory and Bill Birnes and guys like that. Written like twenty books and she's been on Nat Geo, the History Channel, Discovery, and all the others. Junie tracks all of the conspiracies. Her Web site has this great searchable database and there's tons of stuff about the Majestic Black Book. I'm telling you, man, she's like a hot version of Yoda."

"Then we need to talk to her," I said. "How fast can you get me her contact info?"

"Pretty fast, Joe, she's right here in Maryland. She lives in that old lighthouse in Elk Neck State Park."

"Turkey Point Lighthouse? Right at the head of the Chesapeake Bay?"

"That's the one."

"I thought the lighthouse was decommissioned," I said. "They turned it into a light station."

"No, they put it back into operation a year ago and she's the official keeper."

Church turned to me. "You can find this lighthouse easily?"

"You kidding?" I asked. "I know every inch of that place. I camped at Elk Neck with my family all my life. I took my nephew there half a dozen times."

"Good," he said. "Take a helo and go out there. If you think she's a viable information source—and if she's cooperative—then we'll set up a coded video conference call with her, Bug, Dr. Hu, and Dr. Sanchez. If she stonewalls you, arrest her and bring her back here."

" 'Arrest her'?" I asked, smiling.

"Feel free to use charm if that will work better, Captain. Whatever gets the job done. If this threat is real then we need to get ahead of it and we don't know what our timetable is."

Before I could even reply Church called Gus to prep my Black Hawk.

"Whoa, hold on," I said. "Before I go gallivanting off I'd like a few answers. I mean, what the hell is this book? What's the connection to all of those natural disasters? And why would someone go to such insane lengths as to capture the president of the United States in order to get it?"

"Are you serious?" Bug asked, appalled at my apparent stupidity. "There are people making *billions* off that book."

"According to rumor and speculation," murmured Church.

"Who's making that kind of money?" I asked. "And how?"

"Probably half the big shots with defense contracts," Bug said. "Anyone working on advanced stealth technology, space-based phasers, military space fleets, hypersonic technology vehicles, the High Frequency Active Auroral Research Program, cloaking devices, antigravity drives—"

"C'mon, Bug, we can't do most of that stuff yet."

"You don't know that, Joe," said Bug. "We're researching all of it. And, hey, that nifty microwave pulse pistol you brought in the other day? That's the sort of thing people like this would build."

"Wouldn't most of that fall under DARPA's umbrella?" I asked.

DARPA—the Defense Advanced Research Projects Agency—is a big group within the Department of Defense. They're the geeks responsible for a lot of major scientific breakthroughs from the Internet to combat exoskeletons.

"DARPA works with independent contractors, too," said Bug. "GE, Shelton Aeronautics, and like that. DARPA doesn't do all of its own research in-house, and it sure as heck doesn't do its own manufacturing. It only has a three-billion-dollar budget. And, there's a lot of extremely weird and highly profitable stuff being done in the private sector based on ideas either borrowed from DARPA or gotten from some other source—like the Black Book. And I'll bet that's where DARPA got most of its stuff, too. It's all there in the book, man, that's the bible for weird tech."

"You're talking like I should know what that book is and I don't, Bug. What the fuck is it?"

Bug took a breath. "Okay, Cliffs Notes version. On September 24, 1947, President Harry Truman convened a special group of scientists, military leaders, and government officials—a dozen of them—for the express purpose of studying wreckage recovered from a crash site in New Mexico. This group was called 'Majestic Twelve,' or MJ-12. However, according to Junie Flynn, MJ-12 was only the front for an even more secret group, a deeper level of shadow government called 'Majestic Three,' M3. A trio of people who had been given control of an enormous black budget to study the wreckage in case there was anything of military value. Bear in mind, these were the early days of the Cold War. The international arms race was already spinning out of control. Junie says that the members of M3 created a book that was a catalog of all parts recovered from the crash. The only complete catalog, they say, with exact specifications, which makes it particularly valuable."

"Whoa, slow down—what crash site in New Mexico? Are we talking Russian spy planes or—"

"Joe," said Bug, amazed, "haven't you been listening? This is the Majestic Project. The Black Book is a complete catalog of all the parts salvaged from the UFO that crashed in Roswell."

Chapter Twenty-nine

Camden Court Apartments, Camden and Lombard Streets
Baltimore, Maryland
Sunday, October 20, 7:04 a.m.

They looked like giant insects the way they swarmed out of the stairwells at both ends of the hall. Twelve men in black BDUs with Kevlar body and limb pads, helmet-cams, and full SWAT kit. The whole unit was split into four-man teams, with two men armed with MP5s, a point man carrying a ballistic shield and a Glock .40, and one team leader with a Remington 870 pump shotgun. Despite the speed of their approach they made almost no sound as they converged on the door to apartment. There were more men in the fire towers and in the lobby and out on the street. Two FBI helicopters were in the air.

The raid was being conducted entirely without assistance from local police. The suspect had ties to the police department as well as city government. His brother was a detective, and his father was the mayor.

The point man for the raid was Special Agent Sullivan, a twenty-year veteran with the FBI who had spent the last ten with Hostage Rescue. He was a tough, humorless man, very good at his job and totally unsympathetic to anyone who came into his operational crosshairs. When such a target was a crooked cop and suspected terrorist—well, Sullivan didn't figure he'd lose a lot of sleep if the bad guy was home and kicked up a fuss.

The teams clustered around the doorway, close but well back from any angle where a round fired from inside could hit them. The walls were brick but the apartment doors were only wood.

A burly agent hustled up with a breeching tool—a heavy weight with a blunt end and sturdy handles. He positioned himself in front of the lock and looked to Sullivan, who finger-counted down from three.

On zero the big man swung the weight and the wood around the lock turned to pickup sticks.

"Go—go—GO!" bellowed Sullivan and the men in the black body armor poured through the door into Joe Ledger's apartment.

Chapter Thirty

The Warehouse, Department of Military Sciences field office
Baltimore, Maryland
Sunday, October 20, 7:05 a.m.

I turned to Church, expecting to see him shaking his head in denial. Or smiling. Or telling Bug to stop shoveling the bullshit.

Instead he stood there, silent, the muscles at the corners of his jaw flexing.

After a long moment I said, "Oh, come on!"

"We need to remain open to any possibility," said Church.

Bug said, "Junie Flynn says that M3 keeps adding to the Black Book. Stuff from other crashes."

"Other crashes?" I demanded.

"Sure. There are UFOs all over the place. It's in the news, Joe, and lately there have been a ton of new sightings in the Southwest, all over Mexico, in Canada, Russia, Europe. UFO sightings are way up."

"Sightings or crashes?"

"Well, okay, sightings are up, but there have been bunch of crashes since the forties. The Black Book has data on all of them, and some stuff stolen from other governments, too. We're not the only ones doing this, but we're ahead of the pack because Roswell was the first crash in the modern era, and the first one where they were able to recover anything of value. The Black Book has specifications, schematics, analyses of materials, metallurgic reports, weights and measures. Everything. Like I said, the Majestic Black Book is the bible, Joe, the holy grail for reverse-engineering technology from alien spacecraft."

"No way," I said, shaking my head. "Maybe this book is packed with technological secrets but they're going to be from pretty ordinary sources. This is weird enough now without bringing aliens into it."

"Hey, man," complained Bug, his face flushing, "I wasn't the one who brought up the Black Book. The president himself just asked us to find it."

"He didn't say anything about little green men."

"It's implied, Joe, it's implied."

"Can we take a moment here," I said, "maybe take a breath, return to the real world? We're talking UFOs. We're involved in a conversation in which UFOs are an actual thing. I know we deal with some very weird shit here in the old D of MS, but do you really think we should waste our time running down a lead like this? You want me to drop everything and go talk to a conspiracy theory nut who lives in a lighthouse?"

"Tell me, Captain," he said quietly, "what other lead were you planning to follow?"

I opened my mouth to fire back a crushing reply, but there were no words on my tongue. Ghost gave a low, significant *whuff*.

To Bug, I said, "How many copies of the Black Book are there? Maybe we should send teams to every possible location and—"

But Bug was already shaking his head. "There's only one copy. *The* copy. It's supposed to be kept in this incredible safe with all sorts of booby traps and stuff."

"Uh-huh," I murmured skeptically. "And are there trolls and dragons guarding it?"

"I'm just repeating what Junie said. She also says that the Majestic charter does not allow the book to be photographed or copied in any way, and for anyone to see it the book has to be checked out by one of the three governors of M3."

A knock on the door saved me from saying something that would probably have hurt Bug's feelings. Gus Dietrich poked his head in. "Got some news about those four guys you tussled with, Joe."

"What kind of news?" I asked.

"Bad, very bad, and strange," he said, stepping into the room. "First the bad news—those names are bogus. Stephen Albert, Benjamin Carr, John Woods Duke, and Mark Bucci are names of dead American composers."

"Somebody has an interesting sense of humor," mused Church.

"Ha-fucking-ha," I groused. "What else?"

"That's the very bad news. They were taken to the ER at Harbor Hospital. At least that was the plan. A pair of ambulances showed up, EMTs loaded them, and they took off with a patrol car leading the way. The ambulances made a sudden left and by the time the cruiser saw them turning and circled the block to find them, the two ambulances were gone. Cops tried to radio the EMTs and got nothing. Helicopter flyovers failed to locate the vehicles. Police are searching for them, but there are a million warehouses, multicar residential garages, and boathouses in that section of town."

Bug looked at me from the big screen on the wall. "I can put somebody on that. Lot of ambulance services have GPS units, so we can probably track them. The ambulance company might also have a remote vehicle disabling system. Lot of them do because of all those warnings from Homeland about how easy it would be to use a vehicle like that as a car bomb."

"Gus," I said, "send everything you have to Bug and keep me posted."

He nodded and headed for the door.

"Wait," I said, "what's the 'strange' news?"

He turned with an enigmatic smile. "Oh yeah . . . that little metal doo-dad you found? I had the geek squad look it over. Get this . . . they can't identify the material. They're not even sure it is metal. But it might take a while for them to figure out what it is."

"Why?" asked Church.

"Because X-rays won't penetrate it and when they tried to run it through the MRI there was some kind of system failure. The geeks are trying to reboot the medical computers now."

"What happened?" I asked. "Did that metal thing cause the crash?"

"That's what they're trying to figure out now."

Church pursed his lips for a moment, then nodded. "Okay, Gus, keep us posted."

But Gus lingered for one moment more. "Oh, and Joe—your bird's smoking on the roof. You want Echo Team on deck?"

"No, this is just a pickup. We don't want to scare our expert more than we have to. Flight crew only. I'd rather have Top meet with the cop who lost the ambulances. Tell him to spread the team out and help with a search of the harbor area. I want those vehicles found."

"You got it." He left, closing the door firmly behind him.

To Church I said, "We need to add more numbers to today's weird-o-meter, 'cause that just pushed it past 'ten.' I got a bad vibe from those four jokers from the jump."

His answer was a stern grunt.

"Is that connected to the president's abduction?" asked Bug. "I mean, I'm with you on not liking the coincidence, Joe, but I really don't see how those two fit."

"Neither do I, Bug. All I have to go on here is gut, and my gut is telling me that there has to be a connection. Has to be."

"Then we need to find it," said Church. "I've called Dr. Sanchez and he's on his way in. I believe he has some interest in this field and—"

I was surprised. "He does?"

"Sure," said Bug, "he and I talk about it a lot."

"You do?"

"I've participated in some of those discussions," said Church. "It's by no means an uncommon topic around here."

"It isn't? Where the hell was I when all this was going on?"

Bug shrugged. "Out shooting things, probably."

When I looked at Church, he spread his hands. "You would probably be surprised at how the support staff manage their time while the field teams are going to or coming from the field."

I grunted.

"My point," said Church, "is that Dr. Sanchez will want to help and right now information gathering is going to be a primary concern. Knowing that the Black Book is our focus helps us make some decisions about which other elements of this may be related. I'll draw up a list of useful contacts for him to call."

"Okay, but if we get our hands on the Black Book—then what? How do we let the kidnappers know?"

"Presumably they will contact us. I don't want to be caught empty-handed when they reach out."

"No shit. Then I guess I'll go and see if Junie Flynn will help us."

I could think of twenty reasons why this was a bad idea and a waste of time.

But I was already out the door.

Four minutes later Ghost and I were in a big UH-60 Black Hawk, lifting off from the roof of the Warehouse. The DMS birds were as black as their names except for thin red lines around the doors and along the tail. The muscular General Electric engines raised the six tons of mass into the morning air and the pilot turned the nose toward the northeast. Elk Neck State Park was sixty miles away. In scant minutes we were screaming through the air at two hundred miles an hour, racing as if the tick of each fragile second was one digit less on some bomb that we couldn't see.

The president was missing. Taken from the White House in a scenario we all agreed was impossible. Actually impossible.

A mysterious video from a source even MindReader couldn't trace threatened terrible destruction if we didn't obtain a copy of a book that, fifteen minutes ago, even Mr. Church believed was a myth. A book I'd never heard of. A book that, had I first heard about it on one of those cable science shows, I would have dismissed with a laugh and channel-surfed over to an old *Baywatch* rerun.

A book that was supposed to hold secrets.

UFOs.

I mean . . . seriously? UFOs? Did I have to start believing in them now?

Or was this one of those things—like the Seven Kings—where it was misinformation layered over disinformation layered over insane conspiracy theory mumbo jumbo? The Kings had wanted us to believe that a goddess was punishing human iniquity by sending new versions of the old Egyptian Ten Plagues. When all the smoke cleared, that was just another bunch of terrorists playing on human fear and paranoia in order to make a buck.

Was that what we had here? Were we catching the outside edge of another massive con game?

I actually hoped so. The alternative was . . .

I looked at Ghost, who was crouched down on the helo's deck. He felt me watching him and stared up at me with big, brown, bottomless eyes.

"This is nuts," I said.

Ghost gave me another *whuff*, and left it entirely up to me how to interpret it.

Chapter Thirty-one

Over the Atlantic, due East of Hilton Head
Sunday, October 20, 7:19 a.m.

Erasmus Tull preferred to fly his own jet. It eliminated the need for any other staff besides his longtime partner, Aldo Castelletti. Much easier for keeping secrets.

The Mustang soared over the blue Atlantic, heading toward a private airstrip in Maryland, the engine muted to a soft growl by the cabin soundproofing. Tull glanced at Aldo, who was poring over a report on his iPad.

"Jeee-zuss, Tully," swore Aldo. "Did you read this shit?"

"I read it."

"Did you see that video Mr. Bones hijacked from the DMS?"

"Sure."

"Think that's really the president?"

"Yes."

"Christ on the cross, man."

Tull cut him a look. "What do you think?"

"What do I think? I think this is fucked up, man. Half of me wants to think this is a big steaming load of horse shit. The other half of me wants to run and hide. The main thing is that this doesn't make any sense." Aldo had heavy features, a thick mustache, a large crooked nose, and Tull thought that he looked like every Italian pizza shop owner he'd ever seen on a TV commercial. The coarse features and drooping eyelids were a terrific natural disguise that hid a keen and calculating mind. Unlike Tull and a few of the other top operators among the Closers, Aldo was not part of the family. He had a real mother and father. He had been born in a hospital, had sucked milk from a breast, had gone to preschool and all of that. Tull envied him.

Sometimes Tull got Aldo on a talking jag, just ruminating about growing up in Little Italy, being part of a huge family. About being real. When Tull was talking to people—like Berenice—he sometimes borrowed those memories. They were full of rich detail. Those kinds of stories put people at ease. They never looked at you as if you weren't like everyone else. That always felt better.

"Which part doesn't make sense?" asked Tull.

"The part about abducting the fucking president," said Aldo. "I mean, who in their right mind would abduct the president of the United States? Granted, that shows some heroic clanking steel balls—but what's the point? It's too much. It's like showing off, you know? Does it make any sense to you?"

Tull shrugged.

Aldo waited for more. "That's it? I ask you a serious question and you give me a shrug?"

"What's there to say?"

"For fuck's sake, Tully, we're flying right into the middle of this thing and you don't know what to say?"

"No, I don't. We don't have any solid intel on the abduction, so our role is a wetwork. Take out a few players, turn it over to the cleaners, and walk away. What is there to say, Aldo?"

"That's a piss-poor answer."

"Yes," agreed Tull, "it is."

"They want you to take the Deacon and his band of psychos off the board and you don't have a comment?"

Tull gave him another shrug. "I made some suggestions to Mr. Bones, so the surveillance is already in place. Pigeon drones, that sort of thing.

We have full teams on deck, satellite support, and by the time we have boots on the ground Joe Ledger will be a wanted man and we'll be the good guys bagging a terrorist. I think they've planned this out so well they probably don't need us."

"Then why the fuck did you take this gig? Why blow off retirement?"

They flew a lot of miles before Tull answered that question. "You know that I worked for the Deacon for a while."

"Sure. And then you split, but I never did hear why."

Tull thought about it, shrugged, and said, "This was before Deacon formed the DMS. He was doing some problem solving within the government, hunting terrorist sleeper cells, that sort of thing. I was topkick for a five-person team. Deacon received intel that a group of Lithuanians were bringing some old Soviet implosion-type devices into the country redesigned as suitcase nukes. Nothing too big, just enough pop to level a couple of city blocks and up the local cancer rate by three or four thousand percent. Stuff that would be used at places like Grand Central Station at rush hour, Madison Square Garden during a concert, or Times Square on New Year's Eve. It was junk from Kazakhstan, but it was something you wanted to take seriously. Only about halfway through the mission I get word from the Fixer—remember him? He was the acquisitions governor before Mr. Bones came on board."

"Yeah, sure. He woke up with his throat cut. Chinese got him, I think. Pretty nice guy."

"That's the guy. Anyway, the Fixer gets in touch and tells me that the Lithuanians were not bringing in suitcase nukes. What they had were two satchels filled with debris from that old crash at Tunguska in 1908. They'd swiped the stuff from a testing lab in Siberia and were hoping to sell it to some Chinese buyers who were going to meet them up by the Canadian border. Problem was, I had four guys running with me, all of them loyal to Deacon. The kind of guys you couldn't recruit into the Closers. Real GI Joes."

"Yeah? So what happened?"

Tull shrugged. "What could I do. If we nabbed the Lithuanians then we'd have to turn the satchels over to Deacon. Imagine what would happen if he got a good look at actual debris. M3 has invested millions just to stay off of his radar. It was why I was planted in his group. But . . . the clock was ticking. If I had more time maybe I could have finessed a way out and been able to keep my cover inside Deacon's organization."

"What happened, man? Don't leave me hanging."

"Oh . . . I killed everyone and took the satchels, what do you think happened?"

Aldo stared at him. "Four of Deacon's boys and the whole Lithuanian team?"

"There were only three Lithuanians."

"Jesus, Tully, you are one cold motherfucker."

Tull shrugged. "You have to do what you have to do."

They flew in silence for a while. Tull was aware that Aldo occasionally cut sly looks at him.

Without looking at his friend, Tull said, "Y'know . . . I was retired, Aldo. A couple of hours ago I was in paradise with a beautiful and intelligent woman, with nothing to do but work on my tan, make love, catch fierce little fish, and forget that I ever did this sort of thing."

"Sounds pretty great, man, but c'mon—you can't change who you are."

Tull sighed. "No, I guess not."

"You going back to her when this is over?"

Tull reached into his shirt pocket and removed a pack of gum, popped two pieces out of the blister pack and chewed them, savoring the sugary sweetness. His eyes roved over the wisps of clouds beyond the windshield.

"I didn't leave that door open," he said.

Aldo studied him for a while, lips pursed, his gaze as much inward as directed at Tull.

Without turning, Tull said, "Don't look at me like that."

"Like what?"

"Like I'm a monster."

"I'm not."

"Yes, you are. You're thinking that I'm a coldhearted freak."

"Hey, fuck, man, I'm not going to throw stones. I'm not welcome at church picnics, either."

Tull cut him a sly look. "Maybe not, but you can go to confession and square it with God. Get a fresh coat of whitewash on your soul."

Aldo shrugged. "Last time I checked that option was open to every-body. You should try it sometime."

That made Tull laugh. A dark and bitter laugh.

"What's so funny?" asked Aldo.

"You can't whitewash something that doesn't exist. I got a lot of nifty extras, Aldo, but I'm pretty sure a 'soul' was not part of the deal."

Chapter Thirty-two

Over Maryland airspace
Sunday, October 20, 7:25 a.m.

My cell rang seconds after the Black Hawk lifted off. I looked at the screen display and debated whether to let the call go to voice mail. Apparently of its own accord, my thumbnail hit the button.

"Joseph?" said a deliciously familiar voice.

DMS helicopters have pressurized cabins to allow for conference-quality silence. Violin's voice was soft and hearing it filled me with a memory of her that was rich and immediate and intense. Nestled between her thighs, our hungry mouths speaking each other's names through gasps and cries, the way her skin is always cool even at the height of passion, and how my heat seemed to flow into her and back into me as we soared over the brink.

"I'm sorry I had to leave you like that," I said.

"Work," she said, not pitching it as a question. She understood.

"Work," I agreed.

"Speaking of which," she said, "I saw a car outside as I was leaving. A black one. Crown Victoria, with federal plates. Friends of yours?" She described the men and gave me the plate number. It wasn't one of the two cars that had boxed me.

"No idea," I said, "but there's a little trouble going on. I'll call that in to my boss and they'll send someone out to take a look."

"Probably nothing, then," she said.

I heard sounds behind her. People. "Where are you?"

"The airport. I caught a cab after you took off."

"You're leaving?"

Violin laughed. "I told you that I had a job."

A job. A nice little euphemism for what she did for a living. When she went to work, someone died. No one I'd miss. No one the world would miss. Lately her work was focused on men who used to belong to the Red Order. And a few of the highly dangerous and incredibly creepy Red Knights. They kept trying to hide from Violin and her sisters in the group code-named Arklight. They tried, but Arklight is very good and very determined. Also, Mr. Church let them have some limited access to Mind Reader. It made Violin's job easier.

"When will you be back?" I asked.

She was a long time answering.

"Violin?"

"Let's not worry about when," she said. "I'll call you when I can, okay?"

I said that it was okay because it had to be okay. This was as close to an arrangement as we had. Probably as close to a real relationship as we would ever have. I tried hard to resent it, though. I tried hard not to let it feel like a convenience.

"Stay safe, Violin," I told her.

"You, too, Joseph."

She was not the kind of person to ever say *I love you*.

Maybe I wasn't, either. Not anymore.

The line went dead.

I sighed. Then I called in the info on the guys outside my apartment. Bug's assistant, Yoda, took the details and said he'd run it. Oh, and, yeah, Yoda was the kid's name. His parents were *Star Wars* freaks and, much as I love a little pop culture craziness now and then, those bozos ought to be horsewhipped. Kid's sister was Leia.

That done, I sat back against the cushions and stared at the walls on the inside of the helo and on the inside of my brain. Before I could sink too deeply into glum musings, my cell rang again. Rudy. The last time I saw him he was dressed in black socks and boxer shorts, covered in Silly String, and drunker than anyone I have ever even heard of. No, we didn't trick him into any naughty intrigue with hookers, but we staged a bunch of faked photos to make him think we did. Those photos were on my cell, but I hadn't yet found the right moment to send them to him.

"It lives!" I said into the phone.

Rudy gave me a deep, protracted groan that was equal parts shame, anguish, physical pain, and moral outrage. "Believe me when I say this, Cowboy, I will find a way to kill you."

"Hold on, I'm about to faint from sheer terror. No . . . no, that was just gas."

His next comment was in Spanish and it insinuated that my ancestors frequently and enthusiastically fornicated with livestock.

"Where are you?" I asked once his tirade wound down.

"On the toilet," he said grumpily.

"You're calling me from the toilet?"

"Over the last few hours I've become quite found of this toilet. We've shared so much. Now I seem to develop separation anxiety of a very unpleasant kind if I get too far away from it."

I laughed so loud Ghost woke from a doze and barked at me.

"You are not a very nice man," said Rudy.

"I don't call people while I'm taking a deuce, Rude."

He told me where to go and what to do when I got there. For a cultured man, he had a nasty gutter vocabulary.

"Circe home yet?" I asked.

"Not until Wednesday."

Rudy and Circe shared a very nice place in the Bolton Hill section of Baltimore. Right now, though, Circe was at the end of a book tour for her latest bestseller, *Saving Hope: The Seven Kings and the Face of Modern Terrorism*. When she'd heard about the bachelor party, Circe extended her trip by a few days. I think she wanted to clearly separate herself from the indefensible antics of men she otherwise respected as professional colleagues. Rightly so. We were very, very bad.

"Wednesday, huh? Well, maybe you'll be out of the bathroom by then."

Rudy gave another groan. "Last night was . . ."

"Fun? A romp with the guys? A last blast for the single man?"

"An inexcusable descent into the worst kind of excess. My liver may never recover."

"That's only because you're getting old. The old Rudy would have matched me Jell-O shot for Jell-O shot."

"Believe me, this Rudy is very old." He sighed. "Oh, with everything you inflicted on me, I never got to tell you about what happened when I met Mr. Church yesterday. You may not believe this, Joe, but it was the father-of-the-bride talk."

"You're shitting me."

"Sadly, no."

"What did he say?"

And he told me . . .

Twenty-four hours ago

"Come in, Dr. Sanchez," said Mr. Church. "Close the door behind you."

Rudy Sanchez entered the conference room, closed the door, and looked around. The room was empty except for the two of them. Most of the lights were out except for a single table lamp with a green globe whose glow barely illuminated the cut-glass carafe of water, two elegant glasses, and the plate of cookies. The only other object was Mr. Church's laptop, and as Rudy sat, Church consulted the screen, tapped a few keys, and closed the computer.

Church poured them each a glass of water and handed one to Rudy.

"I hear that Captain Ledger is throwing you a bachelor party," said Church without preamble.

"That is my understanding," said Rudy after only the slightest pause.

Church sipped his water and set his glass aside. Even in this gloom he wore tinted glasses.

There was no sound in the room. No clock ticked on the wall, no faucet dripped, no exterior sounds intruded. Rudy sat and waited.

After almost a full minute, Church selected a vanilla wafer, bit off a piece, munched it quietly, and set the rest of the cookie down atop his closed laptop.

"Doctor," said Church, "you know that Circe is my only living relative."

He made it a statement, but Rudy responded, "Yes, of course."

"You know that I keep the nature of our relationship confidential."

"Yes."

Silence.

Then, "There are many people who would give a lot to have a lever they could use against me. If they knew that Circe was my daughter, then they would have that lever."

"I—" Rudy began, but Church held up a finger. It was a small gesture, the index finger lifted an inch.

"In a different kind of world, Doctor, this would be the point where I, as the father, would have a frank and open discussion with the man who wanted to marry my daughter."

"I suppose," agreed Rudy. "Yes."

"A discussion filled with advice and cautions."

"Yes."

Church picked up the cookie, tapped some crumbs off it, and ate it slowly. He had a sip of water. He ate another cookie. He had some more water. Seconds passed with infinite slowness. Then minutes.

Mr. Church ate a third cookie. He did it slowly, taking small bites, chewing thoroughly, washing it down with sips of water. Five minutes passed.

Ten.

In all that time there was no sound in the room except for the faint crunching of the cookies. Rudy did not move. He did not reach for a cookie. He sat and watched Mr. Church, who sat and looked at him. Behind the barrier of tinted lenses, Mr. Church's eyes were almost invisible and totally unreadable.

After a dozen minutes had burned to cold ashes, Mr. Church stood up.

"I believe we understand each other," he said.

And quietly walked out of the room.

Leaving Rudy there. Confused, bathed in sweat. More than a little terrified.

"Dios mío," he breathed.

Now

I couldn't stop laughing.

"It's not funny," insisted Rudy, but he was laughing, too.

Then we both got calls at almost the same time.

"Mr. Church is calling me," said Rudy. "You don't suppose he was listening?"

"No, you paranoid freak. Something's up. He'll fill you in. But Bug's calling me. Catch you later, brother."

Before Rudy disconnected he asked, "Is everything okay, Joe?"

"Is it ever?"

Chapter Thirty-three

Over the Atlantic, due east of Hilton Head
Sunday, October 20, 7:26 a.m.

"Hey, Tully, we're getting something," said Aldo. "An update from Bones. He says that they managed to put a bunch of those pigeon drones on most of the DMS offices. He forwarded this clip from the Warehouse in Baltimore. One of the drones is on the ledge outside of the Deacon's office window."

He turned up the volume and replayed a series of audio clips. They were conversations between the Deacon and various individuals. The Ghost Box voice recognition software pinged the other parties as Captain Joe Ledger, Dr. Rudy Sanchez, Secret Service Director Linden Brierly, and computer expert Jerome Taylor. They listened to all the calls.

Most of it was intel they already had, but Aldo replayed one section over again. Jerome Taylor—the geek they called "Bug"—was telling Church and Ledger about a UFO expert living in a lighthouse.

Aldo's face went pale. He switched the audio files off and turned to Tull. "We are in some deep shit, son."

Tull grunted. "Why do you say that?"

"Didn't you listen? Ledger's going after Junie Flynn."

"Why is that a problem? She's a civilian."

Aldo gaped at him. "Are you serious? She's way too dangerous to—"

But Tull shook his head. "You're looking at this the wrong way, Aldo. You always look at these things like piecework. You need to step back and look at all of this as one project, not a bunch of items to be checked off a list. Junie Flynn is dangerous, no doubt, but she's only as dangerous as M3 wants her to be."

"Bullshit, Tull. They should have let me clip her when she first started talking about the Black Book."

"Why?"

"Why? *Why?* Dude, if it wasn't for her nobody outside of the Project would ever had even heard about the Black Book, that's why."

"And that is exactly why the governors gave a no-touch order."

"That doesn't make any kind of sense," groused Aldo.

"Sure it does, but not from close up. You have to step way back and look at it from a distance. M3 see things from a big-picture perspective."

Aldo eyed him suspiciously. "How do you know about this stuff? Since when are you that far into this that you know the inside track?"

Tull laughed. "I was born into it."

That shut Aldo up for a few seconds. Then he said, "So what do we do about this? This Ledger character's on his way to pick her up."

"Hey," said Tull, "we're quarterbacking this thing, remember? You and me. What do *you* think we should do?"

Aldo considered. "Big picture?"

"Yes."

"I'm leaning toward a scorched earth approach, man. I don't want to engage these cats hand-to-hand. Not that I'm turning into a pussy in my old age, but I've read the reports. I don't need that kind of grief."

Tull reached over and patted Aldo's thigh. "You see, now you're getting the idea. That, my friend, is a big-picture way of handling things."

"You agree?"

"Absolutely."

Chapter Thirty-four

The Oval Office, the White House
Sunday, October 20, 7:29 a.m.

Acting president William Collins closed his eyes and smiled as he listened to the detailed information being shared with him by the attorney general. There was an almost orgasmic flush sweeping through his body in hot waves. Each word, each detail, each amount, brought him closer to an actual physical response, he could feel it in his loins.

When Mark Eppenfeld, the attorney general was finished speaking, Collins had to clear his throat and take a sip of water before he trusted his voice to speak.

"And all of this is verified?" he asked.

"Yes, sir," said the AG. "Once I got the tip I had it verified by three separate sources."

"What are the chances that this is a frame job?" asked Collins. "Could these funds have been placed in Ledger's account?"

"If the money just appeared there, sir, I would say yes, but I have print-outs of Ledger's banking records going back fourteen months. There is a clear pattern of deposits. As you know deposits of ten thousand dollars or more are reported by banks, so what we're seeing are multiple deposits in smaller amounts of three to six thousand, but there are a lot of them, and they're spread out over a number of accounts. Plus there are purchases of IRAs, bonds, and other products that establish that Ledger has been try-ing to hide some of the money, or keep it off the IRS radar. We got his tax returns for last year and more than ninety percent of this money was never reported. And, sir, that doesn't even take into account money paid into his brother's bank account, and the rather large sums that appear to have been sent to numbered accounts. We're going to have to get subpoe-nas for that, though the Cayman Island banks will stonewall us."

"How much, Mark? Give me a ballpark figure."

Eppenfeld sighed heavily. "It's bad, Mr. President. Adding in the bank accounts, guesses on the offshore deposits, the certificates, and bonds, we're talking just shy of four million. But that might be the tip of the ice-berg. We have Treasury and FBI at Ledger's apartment now and they've found paper records of cash purchases."

"What kind of purchases?" asked Collins, feeling that throb deep in his groin.

"Real estate. Five properties, paid for in cash."

"Jesus. And this is all legit? None of this is planted? I need to know that we're not being handed a live hand grenade here, Mark."

"I don't think so. We've run down two of the Realtors so far and they've identified Ledger from photos. No . . . he's dirty."

Collins gripped the phone so hard the plastic case creaked. "Why would he be this clumsy about it?"

"He's not being clumsy," said the AG. "We didn't know about this until Funke at the IRS picked out some anomalies in banking records be-ing matched against government employee tax returns. Otherwise, Led-ger might have flown under the radar for at least a few more months, and who knows what he would have cooked up by then to hide this. If he was even still in the country. With his knowledge and resources he could go off the radar at the drop of a hat. He still might if we don't move on him quickly."

Collins swiveled his chair around to stare out the window. The White House lawn never looked so clean and bright and beautiful before.

"And Deacon?"

"Well," said Eppenfeld heavily, "that's a different kettle of fish. By executive order all of his records and personal information are sealed."

"How do we unseal them?"

The attorney general was slow to answer. "That's problematic, sir. Mr. Church has a great many friends in Congress and if we push too hard or too fast and it turns out that he is not involved in Ledger's criminal activities, then we lose those people."

"You're afraid of Church?"

"I . . . respect who and what he is."

"Who and what he appears to be, you mean."

"No, sir," said Eppenfeld. "I respect Mr. Church and even now, with all this about Ledger coming to light, I find it extremely difficult to believe that he is involved in any criminal misconduct."

That took some of the joy out of the moment. "Ledger is the Deacon's pet shooter. How can Ledger be crooked and Deacon arrow-straight?"

"I can't act on supposition, Mr. President. We do not have anything on Deacon. Nothing. And, I believe it is in our best interests to approach him about this as soon as possible."

"No," said Collins firmly. "No damn way."

"May I ask why not, Mr. President?"

"MindReader is why not."

"Sir?"

"That goddamn computer system is at the root of all this. Ledger is clearly being paid—and paid well—to use MindReader to carry out the cyber-attacks on the defense contractors."

"I . . . don't know that we can draw that conclusion, sir. We know that Ledger has been receiving large sums of undeclared money. We have no evidence as yet about its source or the reasons for which he was paid."

"Don't be an idiot, Mark. Why else would Ledger be taking that kind of money?"

There was a pregnant silence and when the attorney general spoke again there was frost in his voice. "With all respect, Mr. President, I—"

"Oh, Christ, Mark, I apologize. Forget I said that. This situation has me on edge."

"Yes, Mr. President, I understand." The frost was not totally thawed.

"Can we get a warrant to confiscate MindReader?"

"No, sir. That is the private property of Mr. Church, and as I said—"

"Can we get a warrant for a thorough search of the Warehouse?"

The AG thought about that. "I can issue a warrant for search and seizure of anything in Ledger's office."

"What if there is a MindReader unit in his office?"

"Then, yes, we can take that, his laptop, and anything else that is either Ledger's property or that is included in the inventory of his office."

"Do it."

"What about Mr. Church?"

"If he interferes in any way I expect you to arrest him for obstruction of justice. Unlike you, Mark, I don't believe that the Deacon is lily-white. I think he's dirty and he runs a dirty shop, and I'm damn well going to see him taken down."

Chapter Thirty-five

The Warehouse
Baltimore, Maryland
Sunday, October 20, 8:06 a.m.

The screen display on the ringing phone said "Jerry Spencer." Mr. Church punched a button to put the call on speaker.

"Go," he said.

"I'm at the car stop scene," said Spencer, the former Washington police detective who now headed the DMS forensics unit. "I went over the two vehicles used to box Joe. They've been wiped pretty clean."

"So we have nothing?"

"Did I say that?" asked Spencer with asperity. He was a gruff and unsociable man most of the time, and this morning was even more irritable for having a hangover. He'd been at Dr. Sanchez's bachelor party, too. "I said it was wiped pretty clean, but nobody wipes down every single inch."

Church waited for the details, choosing not to provoke Spencer by prodding him.

"I pulled two prints off the underside of the gas-cap release, flash-scanned them and ran 'em through MindReader. Got an instant hit. Prints belong to a Thomas Erb. Former Marine Force Recon. Did a two-year knock for giving a Taliban drug convoy a free pass. Got out twenty-two months ago and has been working for Blue Diamond Security ever since."

"Blue Diamond," mused Church. "Now isn't that interesting."

"I matched his prison ID to the phony credentials Joe got and it matches one of the guys."

"That's excellent work—"

"I'm not done. You want all of this or should I just go fuck myself?"

"Of course," said Church carefully, "please share whatever you have."

"MindReader pulled his tax returns for me, and he draws his paycheck from a local Blue Diamond office here in Baltimore. Payroll for that shop says there are twenty-four active operatives. Bug hacked their database for me and pulled up the IDs of the others. We pinged the others Joe danced with."

There was a long silence.

Then Spencer said, "You going to say anything or do I just stand here with my dick in my hand."

"Excellent work, Detective. I'll roll Echo Team on the Blue Diamond office."

"Sure, fine, whatever."

Spencer disconnected the call. Church punched the in-house line for Gus Dietrich.

Interlude Two

People's Liberation Army Navy Secure Base
Changxing Island
Yangtze River Delta, China
Twenty-nine hours ago

The craft was there, right in front of him. Sleek, dark, massive, and absolutely immobile.

Admiral Xiè bent down, his knees creaking under his ponderous weight, as he attempted to peer under the craft.

"So!" he breathed in wonder and delight. There was an unobstructed view all the way to the far side of the bay. The only limit to visibility was a very faint distortion, like a heat shimmer. Otherwise, nothing. No wheels, no support framework, no landing struts. Merely a faintness of disturbed air. Xiè held out a hand to his aide, who helped him up.

To his left, six officers in crisp uniforms stood to attention. Caps perfectly squared, pressed trouser seams as straight as sword blades, eyes staring into the middle distance with equal discipline and affected obliviousness to everything around them. Xiè would expect the same expressions if fire imps appeared or if orangutans appeared out of nowhere and began copulating on the floor. These men were the very cream of the People's Army. None of them wore a name tag, unit patch, medals, or other identifying insignia except a single number stitched onto the front of their hats and the sleeves of their left arms. They were known only by these numbers. Even Xiè did not know their names offhand. He would have to access classified documents and open sealed files.

And it did not matter. These men were never going to rise further within the People's Liberation Army Navy than they were now, and they were never going to find comfortable seats in any history books. They had signed away those rights, and all others, in exchange for the honor of being part of this project. And, Xiè mused, for some financial considerations for families they would never again see.

Xiè turned to the six officers and they immediately saluted. He returned their salute and walked over to them with his aides in tow. Even when he tried to make direct eye contact with them, the men stared into nothing.

Very good, he thought. *Like machines*.

For Xiè, the measure of military discipline was how well an individual or group of soldiers acted like parts in a greater machine. Well oiled, perfectly designed, carefully maintained. To think of these men as men would be to invite empathy and compassion, and that was a short path to weakness and self-doubt. These were parts to be added or replaced as needed. That these particular parts were of the highest standard merely meant that the machine could run at a new level of productivity. And how lovely a thing was that?

After a few long moments of study, Xiè turned to his chief aide. "Now," he said.

The aide barked a terse order and the six men turned smartly and began trotting in unison along a metal catwalk, heading for the nose of the craft. If "nose" could even apply to so improbable a design. The front of the craft was whichever direction it was pointed. The cockpit, as such, was in the center—six sunken chairs arranged in a ring, facing out toward a larger circle of curved screens that allowed a three-hundred-and-sixty-degree exterior view. Additional screens above and below them combined to create a nearly perfect spherical view, and the cockpit was positioned on gimbals to allow it to turn in any direction. The design philosophy was lovely, elegant, and limited only by the fact that pilots— even top fighter pilots like these six—were never truly adapted to spherical thinking. Ten years in zero-gravity flight simulators, however, had pushed them far out onto the edge. Perhaps the next generation of pilots, the ones raised in a world where this craft was part of everyday reality, would be better suited. That jump in perception and mental processing would come. Everything comes in time.

As the pilots reached the end of the catwalk, a panel slid open on the side of the craft and a short boarding ramp extended. The pilots entered the ship, the plank retracted, and the door slid shut.

Admiral Xiè moved to the handrail and leaned on it, eyes narrowed to study the craft. So much was riding on this. The seven previous craft, though successful in one way or another, had also been spectacular failures. Whole laboratories had been destroyed, there had been test-firing side effects of catastrophic proportion, the loss of valuable staff, and the waste of so much money. After the first debacle in Tangshan, Hebei, back in 1976, the whole project was nearly scrapped. Back then the creation of the Dragon Engine was deemed a fanciful waste of time and resources. Only the scope of the disaster itself was the thing that saved the project from termination. That one prototype engine had exploded, causing the single largest earthquake of the twentieth century.

That was power.

It demonstrated a potential that was unlike anything previously guessed. If it could be harnessed, there would be none of the suicidal clumsiness of nuclear power, none of the slow process to enrich plutonium. No radiation, no contaminated waste to be hidden somewhere. The Dragon Engine, for all of its terrible destructive force, left no chemical or energetic signature behind. This was the true face of clean energy, and it eliminated the threat of mutually assured destruction, leaving in its place only the destruction of the enemies of the People's Republic.

It meant that for the first time since the dawn of the age of superpowers, a global war could be fought and won, with a guarantee of life on a living planet afterward.

That kind of power could not be ignored, and so the program continued. So did the disasters. The Kunlun earthquake of 2001, Ruichang earthquake of 2005, and the Sichuan quake of 2008. All failures of prototype Dragon Engines.

Of course, the very fact of that kind of power made everyone in Xiè's division curious to the point of paranoia. How close were the Americans or the Russians or the British? Was the Haiti earthquake of 2010 a natural disaster, or the spectacular failure of someone else's own prototype engine? One of Xiè's spies even worked up a credible paper to suggest that the eruption of Mount St. Helens in 1980 was an early attempt to fire an engine. Xiè believed that report. It fit the estimates of where the Americans were at that time. And it explained why their progress had been stalled for so long after that.

His aide stepped forward to be noticed. When Xiè nodded to him, the aide said, "The pilots report that they are ready, Admiral Xiè."

"Tell them that they may proceed."

The aide hesitated. "Admiral Xiè, perhaps you would be more comfortable in the telemetry room?"

That room was in a reinforced bunker on the other side of the island. A quick trip by underground air car. Xiè shook his head.

"We will all witness it from here," he said.

The aide nodded and stepped back. He, too, was trained not to let his emotions show on his face. Xiè was faintly amused.

The craft remained perfectly still. Although there were lights all around it, there was no glow from its metal skin. The entire ship was coated in nonflective polymers. On a dark night, with the running lights off, the ship would be invisible at a hundred yards. Against a night sky, it would vanish entirely except where it passed across the moon or a star cluster. There were plans in research phase now for the new generation of cloaking technology that had been developed by the Americans. Thousands of tiny cameras on the upper surface of a craft fed real-time images to LED panels on the bottom so that a ground observer would see what he expected to see when he looked up at the sky. The American Locust bomber program was being used to test the latest generation of that technology, and Xiè's team would have those results and all related science within a few weeks.

That was part of a barter whose specifics had taken many years to work out. The American government was not involved, of course. Xiè dealt with Howard Shelton for such matters. That man—that reptile of a person—was sometimes willing to throw scraps to Xiè and thought that his *generosity* gave him a clear window into the status of the Dragon Engine project. The view Xiè provided, however, was very much a window display. Shelton had no idea what the true status of this project was. Or so Xiè told himself, hoping that his intelligence was accurate.

As Xiè waited, his eyes flicking over the craft, he tried to discern the exact moment when its main drive systems went online. There was supposed to be absolutely no exterior signature. No heat bloom, no shudder as the engine went from its station-keeping mode to full operation. If there was so much as a tremble, Xiè was going to have someone shot.

After three long minutes, Xiè turned around to glare at one of the scientists.

"Am I to stand here all day?"

"Admiral Xiè," said the scientist, a sweaty little stick-bug of a man, "if you please."

He gestured to the ship. Xiè sighed heavily and turned around.

To see nothing.

The ship was gone.

That fast, that silently. Gone.

Xiè's mouth hung open.

When he could speak, when he could command himself enough to form a thought and put it into words, he stammered, "W—where is it?"

The scientist indicated a large status board mounted high on the wall to the left of the bay. Everyone turned toward it. It showed a satellite image of the Shanghai area, with Chongming at the top and the midstream islands, Changxing Island and Hengsha Island, lower down. There were two red lights glowing on the board. One indicated the laboratory here on Changxing. The other identified the craft. As they watched, the second light moved away from Changxing at incredible speed. It flew high, paralleling the G40 Hushan Expressway toward the mainland. Within seconds it was moving toward the heart of Shanghai. And this, Xiè knew, would be the ultimate test. It was a cloudy night and the sky would be a featureless and uniform black. Even so, Shanghai was the most populous city on Earth, with twenty-three million people, and so many of them with cell phones and cameras. If there was one picture, one clip of video, then the great secret would be out.

The craft kept going.

And going.

As he watched, Xiè thought of who he wished he could tell about this. No, not tell . . . Xiè thought about whose nose he would like to rub in this. It was easy to conjure an image of the man's sneering face and superior smile. Shelton, who loved to brag about how far along the M3 Project was . . . and offer false sympathy for the many setbacks in the Dragon Engine's development. Xiè would have given much to see Shelton's face at the precise moment when he discovered the truth.

Well, he mused, *now the worm has turned. And in turning, revealed itself to be a dragon.*

Xiè was not a man much given to profanity, but there were moments for everything. As he held the image of Shelton in his mind he murmured, *"Cào nǐ zǔzōng shíbā dài."*

Fuck your ancestors to the eighteenth generation.

Admiral Xiè closed his eyes and took a nice, long, deep breath of perfect contentment.

Chapter Thirty-six

The Warehouse
Baltimore, Maryland
Sunday, October 20, 8:38 a.m.

"So," said Top to the five members of Echo Team, "that's what we got so far. Questions?"

They were in a mission briefing room and Top had brought them up to speed on the president, the Black Book, the video, and everything else that had happened.

"UFOs?" said Lydia Ruiz, the only woman on the team. "Holy shit."

Bunny had a pair of Oakleys pushed up on his head, a mouthful of pink bubble gum, and an expression of profound indifference on his face. "We are not alone. Got it. What's the big?"

The others looked at him.

"Um, dude," said Sam Imura, the team's new sniper, "aliens and all? That's kind of big, wouldn't you say?"

Bunny shrugged. "After all this shit we've seen you guys are actually surprised that this was going to happen at some point? Wait till you cats have rolled with the captain a couple of times, Sam. Aliens don't even seem that bad. I mean, on my first gig with Echo we did zombies."

"Read about that," said Sam. "Zombies. Jee-sus. I wish I could tell my little brother, Tom. He's a total *Night of the Living Dead* freak."

"I did genetic supersoldiers when I was on Hotrod Team in Detroit," said Ivan Yankovitch, a lantern-jawed piece of granite who had transferred to Echo right after the Red Order mess in Iran. "A Russian kill team that had twenty percent more muscle and bone mass. The smallest of them could bench six-fifty. That was some serious mad scientist shit."

"Well that's my whole damn point," complained Bunny. "I mean, after all that stuff, if they told us the op was taking down radioactive cockroach ballerinas I'd just lock and load, but I wouldn't get my panties in a bunch. I am officially not surprised by anything."

There was a ripple of laughter, but it all sounded a bit forced. Top said nothing, letting them absorb it and deal with it in their own way.

"But," continued Bunny, "we have an even longer list of stuff that wasn't anything at all. 'Member that thing in May, when Al-Qaeda said that Bin Laden's ghost was advising them? Fricking stooge dressed up as Bin Laden. And remember how everyone panicked when we got a report that there was a *seif al din* outbreak in Times Square on New Year's Eve? Turned out to be a flash mob dressed as zombies doing the *Thriller* dance. More than half the stuff that comes onto our radar is bullshit. We get all worked up, teams get scrambled, and half the time we find out that our supervillain du jour is some toothless hillbilly cooking meth in a cave."

"My little Bunny's got a point, Top," said Lydia. "Do we even know if this is real? I mean, how do we know if the shit is about to hit the fan or if somebody just farted in a draft?"

"We *don't* know," Top said, "but, to paraphrase Mr. Church, do you really think we have the luxury to wait and watch?"

Sam shook his head. "No, First Sergeant, we do not."

Ivan cleared his throat. "What's the status? Are we at DEFCON One?"

"We're in an elevated alert state," said Top. "The official status for the military is REDCON-2 as part of an unannounced training exercise. The DMS status is FPCON Charlie."

There were five levels on the Force Protection Condition scale. FP-CON Charlie was the fourth level, one used in situations when intelligence reports that there is terrorist activity imminent. Similarly the military had its Readiness Conditions. REDCON-2 had all personnel on alert and ready to fight, but they had not yet kicked the tires and lit the fires on the fighter jets.

Top added, "All of this was initiated when the president went missing because it was presumed that terrorists had somehow infiltrated and therefore compromised White House security. The joint chiefs advised the acting president to maintain that alert for now, at least until we have some confirmation that there is no immediate threat."

"What kind of confirmation they lookin' for?" asked Pete Dobbs, a shooter recruited from an ATF team working the drug wars in the Appalachians. "ET hanging ten on a monster wave rolling up Pennsylvania Avenue?"

No one laughed.

The phone rang and Top took the call, listened, said, "Yes, sir."

As he hung up he grinned at Echo Team.

"Turns out the thugs who pissed off the cap'n this morning work for Blue Diamond Security." He saw sour and hateful expressions blossom on their faces. Like their chief competitor, Blackwater, Blue Diamond was a global security company, which is a polite way of saying that they provided top-of-the-line mercenaries to power players in American politics and big business. They were the go-to company for everything from protecting U.S. oilmen in Iraq to serving as "advisors" for commercially inconvenient political uprisings in third world countries.

"Mr. Church would like us to go have a few words with them."

All five of them grinned liked wolves.

Chapter Thirty-seven

Over Maryland airspace
Sunday, October 20, 8:43 a.m.

"Hey, Bug," I said into the phone. "We anywhere yet?"

He told me what Jerry Spencer had found out about the Blue Diamond connection. "Top's heading over there with Echo Team."

"Great, they get to have fun while I heroically sit on my ass in a helicopter." I sighed. "Look, what can you tell me about this Junie Flynn character? Why's she so obsessed with UFOs and that stuff? She see a flying saucer once?"

"Not that she's ever claimed. In fact I bet she'd give a lot to see one. She's very harsh with people who claim to have seen craft but who Junie thinks are faking it."

"Why would someone fake a claim like that?" I asked.

"Why do people claim to have seen Bigfoot, Joe?"

"There's that." I scratched Ghost between the ears. "Is the Black Book her only message or is she a general interest conspiracy nut?"

"She's not a nut, Joe. Junie's one of the most lucid speakers I've ever heard. But . . . to answer your question, the Black Book and Majestic Three are pretty big with her, but she also talks a lot about the need for disclosure. She keeps throwing challenges out to the U.S. government to 'fess up and admit that there are aliens and that we've recovered crash vehicles."

"Good luck with that."

"She's been leading up to something. She's been talking about something she's going to reveal to the world this week. I think it was on last night's podcast. I have it taped."

"Dude, don't you think we should already be on that?"

"Sure, but you wouldn't believe how many things the big man has me on right now, just related to the president. Besides, her podcast is like three hours long, so I have to find the time to go through it."

"Find the time."

"Yeah, yeah. Oh, and other areas she hits a lot—alien-human hybrids."

"Really? What's that all about?"

Bug laughed. "Jeez, you really are clueless."

"I have that on my business cards. C'mon, Bug, hit me."

"Okay, Junie says that the reason we haven't figured out how to make maximum use out of the alien tech is that it requires a biological interface. Now I know you know about that because we sat through that lecture."

"That was DARPA, not *Plan 9 from Outer Space*."

"Junie says that DARPA is only one group working on a way to develop technology that will allow a human being to bond with an aircraft on a biomechanical level. Maybe on a psychic level, too. That way a craft will move with the speed of human thought and without the lag time between thought and physical action on, say, a joystick or any other instrument."

"So how does that involve alien-human hybrids?"

"She said that bodies were recovered from some of the crashes, and that we've been trying to do gene therapy with alien DNA so that an alien craft would recognize the pilot and respond according to how the ship was designed. Junie said that the hybridization program began in the seventies and viable hybrids were born or grown or whatever in the mid-eighties. The hybrids were supposedly raised in labs and trained in special camps, but some of them were seeded into the human population so scientists could study how well they blend in."

"I'm really sure I saw this movie."

"Just telling you what she says on her podcasts."

"Sure, but, since you believe in this stuff, Bug, what do you think about all this?"

"If I tell you are you going to make a snarky comment?"

"Snarky? Me? You wound me, Bug. Wound me, I say."

"Joe—I'm being serious here. This is something that matters to me."

And there it was. I really liked Bug. He was a true innocent and definitely one of the good guys. He was also way too easy a target for a barbarian like me, who tended to throw stones at everyone.

"My word, Bug," I said. "Serious business."

That seemed to mollify him. "Well, yeah . . . I think there are aliens and I think they've visited us. Consider the math, Joe. There are somewhere between one hundred and four hundred billion stars in the Milky Way. That's a lot of wasted real estate if there's nothing out there."

"Lot of empty space in Antarctica, too. Not a lot of life."

"Tell that to the penguins. Besides, there's all sorts of bacteria and viruses frozen there, and some of it is viable when thawed."

"You're beginning to sound like Dr. Hu."

"Bite me in an ugly place," said Bug. He and I both hated William Hu, the DMS science director. "Look, Joe, there are some things to consider. In 1976, the Mars landers detected chemical signatures indicative of life. The following year, the radio telescope at Ohio State University detected a very weird thirty-seven-second-long signal pulse of radiation from somewhere near the constellation Sagittarius. The signal was within the band of radio frequencies where transmissions are internationally banned on Earth, and natural sources of radiation from space generally cover a wider range of frequencies. Now, understand, the nearest star in that direction is over two hundred million light-years away, so this was either a massive astronomical event that was not visible to any other telescope, or an intelligence with a very powerful transmitter created it."

"Oh," I said.

"And there's those Martian fossils they discovered in meteorite ALH80041, which was from where? Oh, wait, was that Antarctica? Oh no!"

"Wasn't that disproved?"

"Challenged," corrected Bug, "not disproved. Also, back in 2001 some brainiacs did a serious upgrade on the Drake Equation, and—"

"The what?"

"Did you skip *every* science class?"

"I was very hormonal and all the hot girls were in art class."

Bug snorted. "Uh-huh. Well, back in the early sixties this astronomer Frank Drake came up with an equation to try and estimate the number of planets in our galaxy that could reasonably host intelligent life and also be potentially capable of communicating with us. His estimate was that there had to be at least ten thousand earthlike planets."

"Okay . . . wow."

"It gets better. In 2001, scientists applied new data and theories about planets that could be in the 'habitable zone' around stars, where water is liquid and photosynthesis possible. They now believe that there are *hundreds of thousands* of worlds that could support life as we know it. And that's just life as 'we' know it. What about life that exists outside of that range? After all, penguins can live in Antarctica. There's a bacteria that thrives in the hot springs at Yellowstone—an environment where the waters are near the boiling point and acidic enough to dissolve nails. There's another bacteria that lives at the bottom of an almost two-mile-deep South African gold mine in one hundred and forty degrees Fahrenheit. It fixes its own nitrogen, and eats sulfate. There are microbes thriving off the acid runoff from the gold, silver, and copper mines on Iron Mountain in California, and other microbes that live in the stratosphere miles above the Sahara. And there are some insanely complex ecosystems in utter darkness and under intense pressure way at the bottom of the ocean. I'm not talking fish, I'm talking about tube worms living in volcanic undersea vents, thriving in sulfur-rich waters. Down there you got the worms, all sorts of microbes, barnacles, mussels, and shrimp, in an environment that, prior to its discovery in the late seventies, scientists swore could not support life. Now, step back for a moment and let's look at the red color of Europa, one of Jupiter's moons. One of the leading theories is that the color comes from frozen bits of bacteria. Joe . . . you can't be a rational person and tell me that there's no chance at all that we're alone in the galaxy."

I said nothing, digesting the implications.

"Besides," continued Bug, "over the past decade a slew of reputable scientists have begun making a case for the likely existence of extraterrestrial life. Guys like Stephen Hawking and Lachezar Filipov, director of the Space Research Institute of the Bulgarian Academy of Sciences."

"Wait, Hawking actually said he believes in aliens?"

"Oh, yeah . . . and he's gone as far as strongly urging against any attempts to engage them. He was on one of those Discovery Channel documentaries, and he referred to aliens as 'nomads looking to conquer and colonize.' That's some heavy shit from a guy who everybody considers to be one of the top brains on the planet. You want to call him a fruitcake, or ask him if he wears aluminum-foil hats?"

"Stop kicking me in the shins here, Bug. You're making your point."

"Let me toss this in your lap, then. There was a theory advanced a couple of years ago by Arizona State University physicist Paul Davies, who said that he believed that some microbes on our planet may be derived from alien civilizations. Right after that, Chandra Wickramasinghe, a professor at Cardiff University, claimed there was new research showing that human life started somewhere other than the planet Earth. You see, a lot of this new interest in the possibility of alien life is growing out of the new technologies that are enabling a more thorough search for other habitable zones in the galaxy. You watch, Joe, as this movement keeps gaining momentum from the top minds, then we're going to see skepticism about UFOs shrivel up and die."

"Maybe," I said grudgingly, "but you're talking about guys who are taking a careful approach. Are any of them saying that the aliens are actually here now? Are any of them talking about technologies looted from crashed vehicles? Or even saying that they believe that we've already been visited?"

"Some," said Bug, "but you're right—they're careful. They have to be, because they're with universities and stuff like that, and one whiff of anything questionable and they lose their grants or their chair. This is why Junie Flynn is building such a strong case for full governmental disclosure. She wants our government to do it and if we do then others will follow suit."

"Not a chance," I said with a laugh.

"You don't think they should?"

"If it's true? Maybe. But, I don't think they ever will. C'mon, Bug, if flying saucers crashed and we actually did recover the wreckage we would never—*ever*—admit to it. We'd study that stuff in secret in hopes of building advanced craft, new weapons systems, and anything else that would put us out in front in the arms race."

There was a significant silence.

"Bug . . . ," I said slowly, "tell me you didn't just trick me into making your point for you?"

"How's that shoe taste, Joe?"

I laughed again. "Okay, okay, you sneaky bastard, I can see the shape of it. I can build a good case for us creating secret R and D divisions to study this stuff, if it exists. That's a logic exercise based on an understanding of how paranoid all governments are and how the military mind-set works."

"Uh-huh," he said.

"Doesn't mean that there is actually something to disclose. Your Junie Flynn could be yelling in a windstorm."

"Or maybe she's onto something."

"If she is, no matter how loud she yells it's not going to make the government disclose. And maybe they shouldn't. Imagine public reaction to the existence of aliens. You know what that would do to organized religion?"

"Prove that the universe is a bigger and more wonderful place than people give it credit for?"

His innocence was a wonderful thing. I think we need a lot more people who not only see the glass as half full, but half full and a waiter is coming with a pitcher. Most of the rest of society is so cynical and jaded that they think the glass is always half empty and filled with bacteria.

"Where does the Black Book fit into the disclosure equation?" I asked. "Why does Junie Flynn rant about that? What set Junie on this path? What made her an evangelist for this particular cause?"

"I really don't know," said Bug, sounding surprised. "She came onto the scene with a bang and she never talks about herself. She always keeps it about the message, about the need for disclosure, about how we need to believe the truth, and how the Black Book will set us free."

"Set us free? How?"

"I don't know that, either," Bug admitted. "All I know is that she's been building up to something lately. Whatever it is, it's supposed to be big. She says that soon the governments of the world won't be able to keep us in blinders and they won't be able to hide the truth anymore. Or words to that effect. Maybe it was on her podcast last night. I'll go through it."

"Okay, let me know what you find out. And, Bug? About this UFO stuff?"

"Yeah?"

"I *do* want to believe," I said. "I just don't yet."

" 'Yet' is a pretty significant word, Joe."

He disconnected.

Chapter Thirty-eight

Blue Diamond Security Regional Office #5
East Pratt Street
Port of Baltimore, Maryland
Sunday, October 20, 8:44 a.m.

When Black Bess rolled off the AM General assembly line in South Bend, Indiana, it was a Humvee intended for use by the United States Army. This particular vehicle was purchased as part of a fleet by Mr. Church and turned over to Mike Harnick, the head of vehicle maintenance. Now she had extended shock-absorbing crash-plate bumpers, a reinforced frame, and her already considerable fifty-nine hundred pounds was amped up to sixty-eight, most of which was the result of a retractable cannon platform for launching TOW missiles or a M134 Minigun. The sides were heavily armored and the advanced ALON window glass could take sustained fire from a fifty-millimeter heavy machine gun.

Black Bess was neither a very fast nor highly maneuverable vehicle, but it was as close to a tank as Harnick could make it without putting an Abrams on the street. Black Bess also had faux spinner hubcaps, a vanity plate that read GAMER, and lots of decorative chrome. It looked like a big, expensive toy for a slacker who'd made some money.

Sam Imura was behind the wheel. Top Sims sat beside him. Ivan and Peter were in the backseat. Bunny and Lydia were already on the far side of the Blue Diamond compound.

"Call it, Top," said Sam.

The regional office of Blue Diamond Security was a short block away, a squat one-story box tucked behind a security gate with a barrier bar. Behind it, massive tower cranes lifted containers from cargo ships and stacked them into multicolored mountain ranges.

A thermal scan of the building showed where everyone was. Most of them were clustered in neat rows in what was probably a mess hall. A few others were scattered around the building. No one in the receptionist office on a Sunday morning, and no one in the rear loading bay. Eighteen men in all.

Top tapped his earbud for the team channel. "Okay, kids, we're going in softball. Nobody dies but don't take any shit. Combat call signs from here out. Hellboy, you're on street sweep."

"Copy that," said Ivan. He slipped out of the car and ducked down behind a parked Honda.

"Prankster, as soon as we're inside make some noise."

Pete Dobbs said, "Rock and roll."

"Okay, Ronin, let's bust down some doors!"

Sam Imura—Ronin—kicked down on the gas and Black Bess rolled forward, slowly at first, but as her mass got into motion the ponderous vehicle picked up speed. By the time it hit the drop-bar barrier at the front gate Bess was cruising at sixty. The barrier disintegrated into splinters. Two guards threw themselves out of the way, landing hard, rolling awkwardly, rising to their feet in shock but still reaching for their guns. Ivan dropped them both with beanbag rounds from his combat shotgun. Each round was a small cloth pouch filled with number-nine birdshot. They went down hard.

"Green Giant," growled Top, "knock loud and knock hard."

There was a five count of silence and then a huge *whump* shook the whole building as Bunny's blaster-plaster blew the back door off its hinges and hurled it twenty feet into the loading bay.

Black Bess was racing at her top speed of seventy-five miles an hour when she slammed into the front of the building. The double doors exploded inward across the empty reception office, smashing the desk flat against the far wall and then punching all the way through into the main room beyond. This room was a large empty training hall, with a walled pistol range, taped-off combat circles, free weights, and racks of practice weapons. Sam jammed on the brakes and spun Bess around so that she slewed across the gym in a big turn that destroyed equipment, vending machines and the outer wall of the shooting range. Then he threw it into park and he, Top, and Pete piled out.

Pete pulled flash-bangs from his harness as Top yanked open the door to the next room—a crowded mess hall. The flash-bangs arced over the tops of the long mess tables. Men tried to dive out of their chairs, to turn and run, to crawl through each other.

In all those things, they failed.

The flash-bangs exploded with massive booms, filling the mess hall with blinding white light.

Men screamed and fell, pawing at eyes, pressing hands to ears, temporarily blinded, deafened, and shocked.

One man clung to the frame of the doorway, dazed but still on his feet as he clawed for his holstered pistol. Top drew his sidearm, an X26-A multishot Taser, which had a three-shot magazine with detachable battery packs. Top shot the man in the chest and immediately the battery sent fifty thousand volts into him. Top then released the battery pack to allow his gun to automatically chamber the second round. The dropped battery was still connected to the target by silver wires and would continue to send a maintenance charge through the flachettes until the twenty-second battery ran dry. As the man fell, Top saw that the back door of the mess hall was open and Bunny and Lydia were already rushing in to join the fun.

Bunny grabbed one man by the sleeve and hair and whipped him around in a half circle, giving the swing a vicious upward tilt so the man left the ground and crashed into two of his colleagues. Then Bunny grabbed one of the big mess tables and with a growl like an angry bear upended it atop men who were trying their best to get out of his way.

But Lydia was there. She was lightning fast, firing beanbag rounds as fast as she could pump, but when that ran dry she didn't bother reloading or switching to the Taser. She waded in with wickedly precious kicks to calves and knees and groins, and used crosscutting palm strikes to wrench necks and smash noses.

"Warbride," Top called to her, "on your six."

She whirled to face a big man with a steak knife in his fist, but Top sat him down with the Taser, and took out a second man who was swinging his pistol up. Those were the last two charges of his Taser, so Top dropped it and drew a short black rod holstered at his hip. With a flick of his wrist it snapped down to the length of a baton. It was made of durable sponge rubber over a tight spring. The rubber kept it from being lethal, but it was not a toy. Bones broke and men screamed.

One of the Blue Diamond men managed to get off a single shot, but suddenly he pitched back and out of the corner of his eye he caught Sam Imura leaning in through the window, a smoking shotgun in his hand.

Counting the two men at the gate, there were eighteen Blue Diamond guards to Top's six-person team.

Eighteen wasn't enough. The flash-bangs had changed those odds, and the brutal efficiency of Echo Team had skewed the math in their favor. When the last man fell—Ivan head-butted the man; Ivan wore a helmet, the other man did not—the room dropped into sudden silence.

"Cuff 'em," snapped Top, and everybody pulled out fistfuls of plastic flexcuffs.

Some of the men were conscious and very vocal, threatening legal action, threatening worse. One, a shovel-jawed bruiser with a gray buzz cut and a livid bruise in the shape of Lydia's fist over one puffed eye, seemed to be in charge.

Top directed Bunny to bring the man into what was left of the other room. The man wasn't yet trussed up, so Bunny hauled the man to his feet, screwed a pistol into his ear and said, "This one's loaded with hollowpoints, dickhead."

When they were in the adjoining room, Top kicked a chair toward the prisoner and Bunny shoved the man down into it.

"What's your name?" asked Top.

"Fuck you."

"Well, Mr. Fuck-you, would you like to tell me why four of your people thought it was a good idea to pull a car stop on a federal agent this morning?"

The man's eyes narrowed. "I don't know who the fuck you think you are, Tupac, but I'm going to hang your balls from my rearview mirror."

"Is that a genuine fact?" asked Top, raising his eyebrows as if interested.

"Bunny . . . why don't you go in the other room. Mr. Fuck-you and I are going to sort out a few talking points. I believe he wants in his heart of hearts to tell me who ordered a hit on Captain Ledger."

Bunny looked from Top to the seated man, then he smiled and left.

Top was smiling, too.

Chapter Thirty-nine

VanMeer Castle
Near Pittsburgh, Pennsylvania
Sunday, October 20, 8:47 a.m.

Mr. Bones knocked quietly and came into Howard's bedroom. The old man was awake, sitting propped up, a Ghost Box on his lap and open file folders scattered around everywhere.

"So much for resting," said Mr. Bones, arching an eyebrow.

"I'll rest next week."

"It's Sunday, it is next week." Mr. Bones dragged over a heavy hand-carved wooden chair, flopped into it, crossed his ankles, and laid his heels on the edge of the bed.

Howard waved a hand. "You know what I mean. The doctor said it was stress and exhaustion. Big surprise. Said all I needed was some rest . . . so I'm resting."

"How are you feeling? No bullshit."

The old man took off his reading glasses and tossed them onto the bed. He rubbed his eyes and sighed. After a moment he said, "I know this is what I wanted," he said. "I know this is what I've worked my life for . . . but sometimes getting what you want is such a goddamn pain in the ass." He cut a look at his friend. "No, don't say it: It's like a man complaining because he has to count every penny in a heap of treasure he found. This isn't something that's going to take me off the path. I'm not going to come to my senses and devote the rest of my life to charity and good works. I'm a monster, Bones, and I like being a monster."

"But it's still a pain in the ass to count all that treasure," said Mr. Bones softly.

"It is. Am I weak for saying that?"

"You're human. And I'll bet every hero and every conqueror in history had these moments. Alexander the Great probably needed to hang out in his tent, get drunk, fart, read some trash scrolls."

Howard nodded. "They should show that in the history books. Downtime of the rich and powerful."

"We can fund a reality show," said Bones, *Kicking Back with Kings.*"

They laughed about it. Quietly, respecting the needs of the moment. And then they sat in companionable silence for a time, listening to the drifting music from the speakers mounted high in the corners of the room. A playlist of old blues. All covers of Willie Dixon tunes.

"We could bag it," said Mr. Bones, and when Shelton looked at him in surprise, he continued, "We could. All of it. We could let the air show be just an air show. We'll have everyone here to fly their planes and we'll be affable hosts. We could let Yuina continue to do what she already thinks she's doing. We could stop the cyber-attacks and let Ledger and the DMS dig their way out from under without any further interference from us, we could call off the Closers and tell Tull to go back to trying to be a person."

"What about the Chinese? I can't help feeling that they're closer than we think."

Mr. Bones shrugged. "We initiate the tapeworm and turn their project to junk, and let the rest of the world go back to the arms race they think they've been running since the Cold War ended. We could do all of that, Howard."

They both nodded, thinking about it. It wasn't the first time they'd had some version of this conversation. It wasn't the tenth time.

Howard said, "What's wrong, Bonesy? Nervous there at the wobbly end of the high dive?"

"Of course. No matter how many times we run the math, there's still a chance this could all go flooey."

" 'Flooey'?"

"Flooey," agreed Mr. Bones. "There might be something we haven't thought of, some X-factor that makes it all go wrong."

"There isn't."

"That's what we believe, Howard, but we can't know everything. No one has ever done what we're about to do."

"That's what makes being the first so much fun."

"What if the joint chiefs and the DoD suits won't be bullied? What if we lay it all out and give them our terms and they call our bluff?"

"We're not bluffing," said Howard.

"What if they force our hand?"

Howard Shelton lay back and stared at the ceiling for a few moments. "I said I wanted to get out of the fast lane for a few minutes, collect my wits, get my second wind. I never said that I wanted to lose the race." He closed his eyes and smiled. "No fucking way."

Chapter Forty

Over Maryland airspace
Sunday, October 20, 8:53 a.m.

My cell rang again. Church.

"Dr. Hu has watched the video," he said, "and he'd like to share some thoughts."

I thought that I probably didn't want to hear anything else. The day was already sliding downhill, but I flipped open my tactical laptop and the screen showed Mr. Church with a Chinese-American man in his mid-thirties. William Hu was an awkward, ungainly man with an incredible brain filled with deep knowledge in a lot of areas of science. A genuine supergenius, which is why Church hired him. Church doesn't employ many second-stringers.

When I first joined the DMS, Hu and I had failed to bond on an epic level. He regards me as a mouth-breathing semiliterate Neanderthal and I think he's a heartless prick who would improve the world by stepping in front of a bullet train. Neither of us pull any muscles trying to play nice.

"Okay, Doc," I said, "what's your take?"

Hu wore an X-Men T-shirt—vintage Dave Cockrum—and thick glasses with bright red frames. He removed them and polished the lenses thoughtfully on his shirt. "The president looks doped," he began. "Not drunk, nothing like that. He's too rigid for sodium amytal or scopolamine. Maybe amphetamines of some kind, considering the way he kept running his sentences into one another. Could also be one of the compounds that Ukrainian guy, Keltov, was playing with a few years ago. Whatever it was, the president appears to be acting according to chemical coercion."

"Could be more than that," I said. "Some of his nervousness could be from the fact that he was abducted, and his captors could have threatened him."

Hu gave a derisive snort. "No way. You can't bully someone like him."

"You can threaten anyone," I said. "Especially if the threats aren't directed at him. He's a husband, a father."

Hu shook his head. "I don't buy it."

"Says the man who lacks the compassion to reach for a fire extinguisher if his own family was on fire," I said.

Hu ignored that. "I'm drawing a blank on the Majestic Black Book, whatever that is."

Church did not yet elucidate. Nor did I.

"The rest of it's pretty clear, though," said Hu.

"Clear?" I asked, and he gave me a pitying look.

"Obvious to anyone with half a brain, sure. They showed a series of natural disasters and each time they cut to the president telling us that we have to find this book. Simple enough, find the book or bad things w happen." He smiled at me. "You didn't get that?"

"Yes, I got that," I lied. "But you said it yourself, they were 'n disasters. How can you threaten someone with that? Last I heard Nature wasn't taking contract hits."

Hu rolled his eyes, just like a thirteen-year-old girl havin an iPhone app to her Luddite maiden aunt. "That's why t the volcano."

Church gave a small nod; apparently he was right th

"What about the volcano?" I asked.

"Well," said Hu smugly, "the short-bus versio this book or they'll arrange a disaster for us. We could simulate a natural disaster. Hence the Speaking of which, I don't recognize—"

"*The Day After Tomorrow*," I supplied.

"Oh. Right." Hu looked annoyed tha that Bug had told me. "And before y cause we haven't had a tsunami hit home a point, make it personal."

Though it galled me to adm

message and I could see it now. "At the risk of getting a demerit from Professor Snootypants," I said, "is it really possible to engineer a tsunami?"

"Sure," said Hu. "An artificially induced earthquake could do it. Drop a nuke in a volcano, or detonate some underground device on a fault line. Maybe hit the exterior wall with nonnuclear cruise missiles. Couple of bunker busters at the right spot might do it. But, artificially induced or not, that volcano could definitely do it. No question about it."

"Why that particular volcano? Is it active?"

"It doesn't need to be," said Church.

Hu nodded. "Absolutely. That volcano, even cold, is a disaster waiting to happen."

"How do you know? Did Bug find it for you?"

"No, I recognize it," said Hu smugly. "It's Isla de La Palma in the _ Islands, and the volcano is Cumbre Vieja."

_e of the volcano with his forefinger. "See that ridge? ___" he said, leaning on the word "known" as if ___nce was in on this, "that a failure of the ___se a mega-tsunami."

___ut if you wanted to ___n of explosive ___ We're talking ___n a massive ___ean. Local ___ hundred ___ conver-

___-bent ___"

___ bite me." ___ward from

"Shit," said Hu. "You'd lose the whole African coast in the first hour. Southern England a couple of hours later. And then in five, six hours it would hit the eastern seaboard of North America. Mind you, by then it would have diminished to, say, thirty to sixty meters, but that's more than enough to wipe out Boston, New York, maybe as far inland as Philadelphia . . . all the way down to Miami. Call it fifty million people wishing that evolution hadn't taken away their gills."

I gaped at him. "Are you fucking kidding me here?"

"No," said Church. "He isn't."

"How do people not know about this?" I demanded, appalled.

"*People* do," said Hu. "How do *you* not know about this? Don't you ever watch Nat Geo?" He cocked his head to one side then snapped his fingers. "Actually, now that I think about it, this wouldn't actually be the first mega-tsunami to hit America. There was one in Alaska. Lituya Bay, I think, back in 1958. Five-hundred-meter high wave stripped trees and soil from the opposite headland and swamped the entire bay."

"How many people were killed?" I asked, aghast.

"Only two. It was nothing. Boring. Wrong location and time of year for anything interesting."

" 'Interesting'?" I echoed.

Hu shrugged again, unabashed by his delight in the subject. "If our bad guys can knock down Cumbre Vieja then things would get really interesting really fast."

He looked delighted at the prospect. I wondered how long I would have to punch him before I felt better. "So . . . who would do this?" I asked.

Hu shook his head. "I have no idea."

We stared at the image on the screen. Seconds burned themselves to cinders around us as the strange implausibility of this warred with the terrible implications. Hu replayed the video and we watched the president with his glazed eyes and dead voice repeat his warnings over and over again.

There was a question that had to be asked. No one wanted to put it out there, so I did.

"Is this really going to happen if we don't find that book?" I asked. "Guys . . . do we believe this?"

Church and Hu looked at the screen, at each other, then at me.

"What choice do we have?" said Hu.

"Oh," said Church, "it gets worse."

"'Worse'?" I said. "I don't want to hear it. I'm half a bad decision away from jumping out of the helicopter right now."

Hu grinned at the prospect.

"A few minutes ago Linden Brierly sent me a series of photographs taken in the Rose Garden," Church said. "The pictures are of something that Secret Service agents discovered on the lawn minutes after the president went missing. There are some additional details," he said, "but right now I want you to look at the pictures and tell me what you think it is."

Hu and I exchanged a look. It was clear he didn't like this kind of lead-in any more than I did.

Church sent the picture to our screens. There were twelve photos, all from different angles and heights. After cycling through them, Church took the clearest one and expanded it to fill the screen.

"Brierly's people took exact measurements," said Church. "It is a little over three meters across."

I was no whiz when it came to conspiracy theories or UFOs, let's all agree on that, but even I've seen this sort of thing before. Clearly, so had Hu. I saw the expression on his face. This image twisted him into an entirely new mental state and all sorts of expressions warred on his features. Denial, anger, shock. Fear.

He said, "No fucking way."

I was having a hard time with this myself. "Okay, I'm throwing a flag down on this play. Are you trying to tell me that there's a goddamn crop circle on the White House lawn?"

"Apparently so," said Church.

So, I said, "Okay, then tell me how in the hell it got there?"

"No one knows," said Church, and he filled us in on how the circle was discovered.

Hu kept shaking his head in denial, but at the same time he leaned close and peered at the pattern. "Wait a damn minute . . . you said that this was a little over ten feet. Did they do an *exact* measurement?"

An enigmatic little smile curled the edges of Church's mouth. "As a matter of fact," he said softly, "I anticipated that question, Doctor. After seeing the image I requested that they take a new set of measurements. I asked them to be as precise as possible. It is ten feet and three point six eight inches across. Or, to put it another way, it is three point one four one five nine meters across."

"Wait," I said. "Why do I know that number? It sounds familiar."

"It should," said Hu, "if you ever stayed awake in math class. It's the value of pi."

Church nodded to the image. "Doctor . . . what does the pattern itself tell you?"

"It's *pi*," he said, his voice dull. "It's all pi."

"Be a bit more specific."

"This is bullshit."

"Doctor, I would appreciate a little focus here," said Church mildly. "Please give us an analysis of the image."

"Okay, okay, damn it," snarled Hu. He began jabbing his fingers at different parts of the pattern. "This is basic math. Those radial lines corresponded to a grid dividing the circle into ten equal slices. The grooves in the circle spiral outward with orderly steps at various points. Each step occurs at particular angles, and the circle itself is divided into ten equal segments of thirty-six degrees each. If you start at the center, you can see that the first section is three segments wide; then there's a step and underneath this step is a small circle. That's the decimal point. The next section is one segment wide and then there's another step. The next section is four segments wide, and so on until the final number encoded is three point one four one five nine two six five four. *Pi*." He paused, then added, "Fuck me."

"And how long after the president vanished did this appear?" I asked.

"Minutes," said Church.

"Made by little floating lights," I said. Just saying it. Putting that on the wall for us all to look at.

"Fuck me," repeated Hu.

Chapter Forty-one

Private airfield
Near Baltimore, Maryland
Sunday, October 20, 9:34 a.m.

Tull brought the Mustang down out of a clear sky and landed on an empty runway in a deserted airfield. Except for Aldo seated beside him, the world could have been completely empty of people. There were no cars at the airport, no other planes taking off or landing. Only the Mustang. Tull taxied it toward the lee of the tiny airport's main hangar.

Tull debated letting this all go. He could pull a gun on Aldo, force his friend off the plane, and then take off again. He had enough fuel to get to West Virginia or Pennsylvania, find a place to refuel and then vanish off the grid. Tull had enough identities prepared, accounts in a dozen names, safe houses and bolt-holes. Even some friends in low places who could help him get so far off the radar that even M3 couldn't find him.

Would that do it? he wondered. If he cut all ties with the Project, with Majestic Three and the Closers and all of it, would that be enough to allow him to change who he was? Would it allow him to finally be human in every sense of the word? Most of him already was, maybe the rest was buried somewhere, like junk DNA waiting for the right trigger to activate it. If M3 was totally out of his life, would that give him a life?

And . . . what would that feel like?

Most of him yearned to find out, ached to know.

A smaller part of him cringed back from that thought. What if becoming fully human meant that his conscience would try to catch up on all of the sins he'd committed? He wondered if taking Aldo's cue and confessing to a priest would really save him from the agony of feeling something about what he'd done.

What if he got away and then every time he closed his eyes he relived that last moment with Berenice? Even now, when he thought about the surprise and doubt and sudden horrible understanding in her eyes as she stared past the barrel of his pistol and into his eyes, there was some flicker of something deep in his mind. Was that a nascent conscience fearing to be born?

"Yo," said Aldo, and Tull realized that it wasn't the first time his friend had spoken. He blinked his eyes like a reptile and then he was back in the present moment.

"What?"

"Earth calling Erasmus Tull. Where the hell'd you go?"

Tull sighed. "Getting my head in the game is all."

Aldo gave him a curious look, but said nothing.

As they unbuckled and gathered up their gear, it occurred to Tull that if he did try to run from M3, the governors would almost certainly send Aldo after him. It saddened him. Not that his friend would accept the hit, but the thought of killing Aldo. Tull had no other friends.

They opened the door, folded down the stairs and deplaned. Tull was pleased to see a car waiting for them when they descended from the Mustang. It was three-year-old black GMC Yukon. Clean but not gleaming, with visible wear on the bumpers and some scuffing on the sidewalls. Bumper stickers on the back from half a dozen family resorts where fishing was an attraction. Strip across the back window that said their kid went to Morgan State University. Trailer hitch. The kind of vehicle no one would look twice at.

Tull nodded his approval.

The key was in a magnetic box under the rear fender. They stowed their gear on the rear seat and went to the back. The spare was a fake and it opened on a hinge to reveal a flat steel safe. Aldo punched in the code and opened it to uncover the first layer of goodies. Two Sig Sauer pistols and multiple preloaded magazines, two microwave pulse pistols with one extra battery each, various small electronic gadgets, a spare battery pack for the Ghost Box, and leather wallets with ID, cash, and credit cards in six different names each. They lifted out the top layer and poked at the devices snugged into carefully molded foam-cushion slots.

Aldo whistled. "Holy rat shit fuck. They weren't joking about the clean sweep."

"Be prepared," said Tull. "A million Boy Scouts can't all be wrong."

They replaced the top layer and studied the weapons. Tull had his personal .22 pistol strapped to his ankle, but he selected a 9mm Sig Sauer, dropped the empty mag that had been put in place for transport, worked the slide to make sure there was no bullet in the chamber. He removed a full magazine of hollowpoints, slapped it into place, set the safety, and snugged the gun in a shoulder holster. Aldo did the same.

They stuffed several gadgets into their pockets, closed the false tire into its compartment, and shut the rear door.

After they climbed into the cab, Aldo said, "What's wrong?"

"Nothing, why?"

"You're making a face."

"No I'm not."

"Yes, you are."

"What kind of face?"

"I don't know. A face. Like something's grabbing your balls. You sweating the fact that we have to take a run at your old boss?"

"No, it has nothing to do with that." Tull gave him a short, bitter laugh and clapped Aldo on the shoulder. "I just think that it would be better for everyone if I'd stayed retired."

"Yeah," said Aldo, eyeing him dubiously, "well life's a kick in the nuts sometimes."

"Yes it is."

"You really out after this?" asked Aldo. "For good, I mean. No more farewell tours."

"Definitely. What about you?"

Aldo looked up into the dark blue sky. "You're gonna laugh, but I always wanted to open a barber shop. Not a hair salon, nothing faggy like that. I mean a real barbershop. Old school, Brooklyn style. Two, three chairs. Red and white pole outside. Maybe me and my two cousins cutting hair and talking shit all day with the wiseguys."

Tull stared at him. "Really? You want to retire and cut hair?"

"Better than cutting throats for a living."

It was said as a joke, meant as a joke, but neither of them laughed, and the truth behind Aldo's words darkened the day.

"If I had a time machine," said Aldo, "maybe I'd go back and do that instead."

"And miss out on serving your country?" Tull asked in a voice heavy with irony.

"Serving my country." Aldo shook his head. "Man . . . I don't even think I know what that means."

They smiled at each other. One of those moments where what they were saying aloud was substantially different than the conversation they were actually having.

Then Aldo stiffened. "Shit—look."

A bright blue jeep had just rounded the corner of a hangar a hundred yards away, between them and the exit. Even at that distance they could see the white shield on the hood.

"Security patrol." Aldo looked at his watch. "Somebody screwed up. These jokers aren't supposed to be here for another half hour."

"And yet . . . ," said Tull with mild exasperation. He jerked the door handle and got out, waving to Aldo is stay where he was. "I got this."

Tull waved at the security patrol. He shoved his hands into his back pocket and began strolling slowly toward the approaching jeep, smiling a broad amiable smile.

The blue jeep rolled to a stop sideways to Tull and about eight feet away. Two uniformed guards stepped out. Aldo rolled down his window to try and hear the conversation. He needn't have bothered. All he heard was the first guard say, "Is there a prob—?"

Tull stepped forward and from four feet shot them each twice in the head.

It was so fast that Aldo never saw Tull reach for his piece. The two guards lay slumped in their seats and the breeze blew the gun smoke away.

Tull looked from them to the gun in his hand. He sighed, turned and climbed in behind the wheel.

"Okay, brother," said Tull, "let's go save the world."

He put the car in gear and spun the wheel. In seconds the airport was empty and as still as death.

Chapter Forty-two

Over Maryland airspace
Sunday, October 20, 9:55 a.m.

I stared out the window of the helo as we hurtled toward Elk Neck State Park. I don't like Dr. Hu, but I respect his knowledge. Seeing how badly this stuff rattled him made me depressed and more than a little scared.

As if this was all possible.

As if it was real.

Once the call ended the image on my laptop defaulted to Junie Flynn's pretty face.

"I hope you have some answers, sister," I said.

Chapter Forty-three

Dugway Proving Ground

Eighty-five miles southwest of Salt Lake City, Utah

Sunday, October 20, 9:56 a.m.

Colonel Betty Snider touched the lucky coin in her pocket. The face on the coin was nearly worn away from the frequent rubbing of her thumb, a habit Snider fell into when things got dicey. Lately things were more often dicey than not.

There were twelve congressmen seated on bleachers erected under a canvas awning to protect them from getting their congressional brains scrambled in the unforgiving Utah sun's glare. The rest of the bleachers were crammed with officers of every wattage, from captains on the rise to generals who wanted to catch a last dose of reflected glory before they mothballed their uniforms. And there was a moody little contingent of snooty-looking men in off-the-rack dark suits who perched like a row of pelicans. Defense department bean counters.

In an ideal world, Colonel Snider would have had three or four more months to run her shakedowns before a party like this, but Senate appropriations committees got to call these shots. Not officers like Snider who had risen to her rank quickly twenty years ago but had since managed only a lateral slide

Even if today's test was successful, it wouldn't step her up to a star. She'd retire a full-bird colonel and that was that, thanks for your service.

She cut a look at the gathered faces and stifled a sigh.

Fucking bureaucrats, she thought. Best thing for the whole country would be to have the jet crash into the stands.

Maybe that would get her that star.

Down on the field the jet was beginning to taxi past the stands. The Locust FB-119 was on the very cutting edge of stealth aircraft. It was the first generation of jets to use a radical new design philosophy that did not use faceted surfaces like the earlier stealth craft. Instead, the Locust could disguise its infrared emissions to make it harder to detect by heat-seeking surface-to-air or air-to-air missiles. It also had fast-adapting cameras and display panel so that the skin immediately changed its underbelly colors to match the skies through which it flew, with a lag time of point zero nine three seconds. The design would put all existing stealth craft to shame, and very likely steal the thunder from tomorrow's air show at the Shelton estate.

This test flight should have happened eighteen months ago, but the original testing facility out at Area 51 in Nevada had been totally destroyed along with all six prototypes, a victim of the Seven Kings terrorist campaign. The setback was tragic in a lot of ways, but the silver lining was that it allowed the design team to make some important tweaks and add a few new features.

A young lieutenant came hustling over and snapped off a salute. "We're ready, Colonel. The spotter planes report all clear and the wind is down to two knots."

"Very well," she said. Snider held out a hand for a walkie-talkie and accepted it from the lieutenant. "Captain Soames, we're green to go. Make us proud."

"Roger that," was Soames reply.

Colonel Snider turned and gave a short address to the audience that was part hype and part sales pitch. They'd all heard it before, but they listened with varying degrees of interest, especially now that the engines on the Locust were spitting flame.

"I can assure you, ladies and gentlemen," concluded Snider, "that you will see something you have never seen before."

The flagman on the runway gave the signal and the Locust began rolling forward.

The jet did not look particularly aerodynamic. It was roughly triangular, with only a slight bump to indicate the cockpit. The surfaces were painted flat black and the engine roar was muted by a series of internal baffles—part of a hushed engine design that reduced burner noise by 67 percent. That alone, Snider knew, should have made the bean counters reach for their checkbooks—or would have if any of those pencil necks had ever worn a uniform.

The engine gave its soft, deceptive growl and the Locus began rolling faster down the runway. Again, this was deceptive. Because the tarmac was painted flat black and so was the plane, it was hard to judge its ground speed.

Then bang!

The jet's nose lifted and as if shot by a cannon, the massive fighter-bomber bounded up and away from the ground, accelerating smoothly. Snider knew that by the time it leveled off at ten thousand feet it would already be at Mach 1.

"Go, baby, go . . . ," Snider said under her breath.

There was a sonic boom as the jet broke the sound barrier. Then the pilot put the pedal down and Locust seemed to fade into a blur that was too fast for the eye to follow.

Snider heard the first gasps from the crowd and wondered how much of her budget it equaled. Probably 10 percent. But that was okay, because the rubes hadn't seen anything yet.

The Locust rose high and did a wide, fast circle around a big chunk of the eight hundred thousand acres that comprised Dugway. The broad, flat expanse of the proving grounds was bordered on three sides by mountains that created a lovely backdrop for the test flight.

Snider lifted the walkie-talkie. "Captain Soames, give me a low, fast pass. Take their hats off, son."

"Roger that."

The Locust came out of its turn at the far edge of the Great Salt Lake Desert, turned its blunt nose toward the bleachers that could not have been more than flyspecks to the pilot, and turned up the heat. The jet dropped low, scorching above the deck at one hundred feet, but punching through the still air at three times the speed of sound. It was far from the bird's top speed, but this close to the stands it would be supernaturally fast to the spectators. Gasps turned to cries as the Locust ripped past at what appeared to be an impossible speed.

"Okay, Captain," said Snider, "go high and go away."

The jet rose and rolled and made an improbably tight turn. That was another of Shelton's design breakthroughs—a combination of inertial dampeners and internal gears that allowed sections of the ship's mass to pivot on gimbals in a way that sloughed off the stress. Snider had a masters in physics and it was voodoo to her, but damn if it didn't work. In a high-speed pursuit, the Locust would be able to shake the tail and then whip around behind with the kind of dogfighting agility not seen since the days of the old P-51s in World War II. Agility was not considered possible for craft as big or as fast as the Locust.

Snider turned once more to the audience.

"Now, ladies and gentlemen," she said, "we just scrambled four Lockheed Martin F-35 Lightning IIs to pursue the Locust. For those not familiar with the F-35s, they are single-engine, fifth-generation multirole fighters designed to perform ground attack, reconnaissance, and air-defense missions with stealth capability. In short, these birds are capable of stopping anything with wings and they'll do it with style and an awesome grace."

She paused, watching confusion and doubt play over the faces of the bean counters and politicians.

"We've asked the F-35 pilots to pursue the Locust and get a missile lock. Naturally no missiles will actually be fired. Everyone is carrying dummy warheads today anyway. Now . . . statistical probability gives the Locust a six percent survival rate in a four-to-one confrontation with the Raptors. Lieutenant McMasters will be happy to take your money if anyone wants to bet on the outcome."

There were a few smiles. Not many.

Fine, you humorless fucks, thought Snider, *maybe I should take a bet on how many of you shit your pants in the next five minutes.*

She raised the walkie-talkie, switched the feed to the main speakers so everyone could hear, and said, "Ground to Lightning One. Go get 'em, boys."

Suddenly a flight of dark gray jets came screaming over the mountain ridge like a swarm of monstrous wasps. Snider was taking a bit of a risk using four combat-ready craft that had a flyaway cost of nearly two hundred million each. But she needed a lot of money to put the Locust into mass production. The Air Force had sixty-eight of the F-35s, with contracts pending for ten more. Snider wanted to piss on that contract and see Shelton Aeronautics get the big money for the next ten years' worth of stealth fighters. If the F-35s were generation five, Snider personally regarded the Locust as an evolutionary leap forward. Generation ten at least.

The four F-35s tore across the sky, then split into two pairs, with one group flying a direct intercept with the Locust—which was coming out of its long circle—and the other group rising to come above and around for a drop-and-kill.

The Locust flew straight toward the first group and Snider heard the murmurs begin in the stands. Maybe they thought that the Locust pilots were so busy trying to figure out how to fly their new plane or maybe they thought the pilots didn't realize the exercise began, but Snider overheard several derisive comments. The gist was that the audience thought this was going to be a very short exercise and one that was, in its way, every bit as much of a disaster as what happened at Area 51.

The four F-35s closed in like the snapping jaws of a crocodile. So fast, so hard, so certain.

"Lightning One to Ground," began the team leader, "I have a missile lock on—"

And the Locust vanished.

It was there one moment and then it was simply gone.

Everyone in the stands gasped. They all froze for a moment and then jumped to their feet. The F-35 pilots all began jabbering at once.

"Lightning One, do you have the target on your scope?"

"Lightning Three, who has eyes on—?"

And on like that. The four F-35s split apart, turning and rising to check the four quadrants of the sky. One of them circled low to drop almost to the deck, looking for the Locust on the desert floor.

It was not there.

Then a voice shouted out in alarm. "Lightning Three, who has a missile lock on me? Who has a damn missile lock on me?"

There was a burst of squelch and then another voice said, "Locust One to Lightning Three. You're dead, baby."

Far above, there was a shimmer and suddenly the Locust was there. It seemed to melt out of the sky, shedding the dark blue like a chameleon stepping off a leaf. The Locust shot past the F-35 and did a neat little roll. *A "fuck you" roll*, thought Snider.

Lightning Two and Four abruptly angled down, driving toward the Locust with a renewed pincer attack.

The audience yelled and pointed.

At nothing.

The Locust vanished again.

The F-35s burst through empty air and parted, rising up and away to try and find their target.

Then Lightning Four's voice broke from the speakers. "Showing a missile lock. Goddamn it . . ."

The Locust blipped into view again, right on Lightning Four's tail, six hundred yards back, lined up for an easy kill shot.

"Sweet dreams," laughed the Locust pilot. Then he was gone again.

The crowd was yelling now. No, Snider realized, cheering.

Two F-35s in under two minutes. It was so beautiful it was horrifying. Even the bean counters were grinning like kids at a World Series game.

The two "destroyed" F-35s flew out of the test area, and Snider could swear she saw their wings droop with frustration and disappointment. These pilots were combat pros who had seen action in Iraq, Syria, and elsewhere. They were the kind of pilots who killed what they hunted and always came home without a dent in the fender. Now they would have to put this on their résumé. The only consolation was that these were the kinds of pilots who might be in the first full class of Locust pilots. They would want that. They would burn for that.

The remaining F-35s were watchdogging each other, changing formation, doubling back, making random turns to shake pursuit. This part of it would sell the maneuverability of the F-35 to even a hardened skeptic.

But then Lightning Two announced that there was a missile lock on him. It sounded like the words were being pulled out of his mouth with rusty pliers. The laughter of the Locust pilot did not soothe his feelings one little bit, and the Locust appeared again, momentarily switching off its chameleonic disguise. One moment it was invisible against the far mountains, the next moment it was there doing its cocky little victory roll, and then it was gone again.

"Son of a bitch," said a voice and Snider saw that it was the senator who was the chairman of the arms appropriation committee. "Son of a goddamn bitch."

Snider picked up the walkie-talkie. "Locust One, come out of the closet and go head to head."

"Roger that, Ground."

The Locust appeared again and in a part of the sky where it should not have been, clear evidence of its ability to turn and accelerate. The pilot of the last of the F-35s, Lightning One, growled something that sounded like, "You're mine, asshole." Everyone laughed.

The two jets were three miles apart and high above the desert, flying toward each other at incredible speeds. This would be over in seconds.

The crowd was cheering, stamping their feet, waving hands and shaking fists. The Locust screamed toward its prey.

And suddenly the sky was filled with fire.

The blast was silent for a moment and then the shock wave of an incredible *BANG* punched its way down out of the sky and slammed into Snider and all the spectators. They staggered, some fell. Snider stumbled backward and would have gone down had not the young lieutenant leaped forward to steady her. Then the two of them froze, staring upward at the fireball. Flaming pieces of metal fell slowly down toward the desert. There was one piece that did not look like debris. It looked like a person. A man. Burning as he fell.

The Locust was gone.

The F-35 peeled off and angled away from the burning cloud.

Snider snatched up the walkie-talkie and screamed into it. "Ground to Lightning One—what the fuck have you done? Who gave you permission to go weapons hot? My God!"

The pilot responded at once and his voice was clearly shaken. "Lightning One to Ground, that is a negative engagement. Weapons are off-line, repeat, weapons are off-line."

"Then what the hell just—?"

"Ground, report hostile at eleven o'clock."

"Identify, identify!"

"Hostile is . . . holy God . . ."

But now Snider could see the hostile. Everyone in the stands could see it. The craft was larger than the fighters. Sleeker. Triangular.

There were no visible wings.

No visible markings. No windows. No rocket pods.

No one spoke. They stared. They pointed. They covered their gaping mouths.

For a long, terrible moment the hostile just sat there in the sky. Unmoving, gleaming like a drop of molten silver.

"Ground, permission to engage," called Lightning One, "permission to engage."

"Engage with what?" murmured Snider. The F-35s had flown with dummy missiles and unloaded guns. All to prevent any chance of a mistake.

The F-35 to flew as tight a circle as its design would allow, turning to meet this craft, determined, at least, to do a close flyby. Maybe catch some identifying marks. Maybe to . . .

To what? thought Snider.

Then the hostile moved. Not merely away from the jet that screamed toward it. The bogey rose straight up.

Straight.

Up.

Five miles above the sand, it changed direction without slowing and shot away toward the west. It moved so fast that the eye could not follow it.

All of this in front of eighty-one witnesses and twenty-six high-definition video cameras.

The last of the burning wreckage of the Locust crashed to the salty sand, sending up a dust plume that looked like a mushroom cloud.

"Colonel," said the lieutenant in a child's frightened voice, "what was that?"

Snider didn't answer. She didn't need to. Everyone there at Dugway, in the stands, in the control booth, and even the pilot up in the F-35 knew what it was.

No one wanted to say it, though.

Because this was the U.S. military, and the U.S. military does not believe in flying saucers.

Chapter Forty-four

VanMeer Castle
Near Pittsburgh, Pennsylvania
Sunday, October 20, 10:04 a.m.

Mr. Bones and Howard Shelton sat side by side on the couch in one of the small salons in VanMeer Castle. One wall was dominated by a massive plasma screen on which was the feed from a discreet high-quality camera clipped to the lapel of the senator from the great state of Arizona. A man whose entire political career had been financed by Shelton money. A man who understood without reservation on which side his bread was buttered.

Right now they could hear that same man panting like a nervous dog on a stormy night, the gasps interspersed with small protestations and prayers.

Not that Bones or Howard were really paying attention to those cries. They were making almost identical sounds as they watched the flaming wreckage of the Locust bomber drop in improbably slow motion toward the unforgiving desert below.

Even that, even the wreckage did not dominate their minds.

All they could really see was the craft.

Or the empty sky where the craft had been.

The impossible, impossible craft.

Mr. Bones turned very slowly to Howard Shelton. He tried to say something, but words utterly failed him.

Interlude Three

Gurgaon, suburb of Delhi, India

Nine years ago

The five of them met in a lovely little house on a quiet street. Green trees cast soft shadows during the hottest part of the day, and there were always songbirds hiding among the leaves. Children played on the lawns. They were well behaved, well dressed, and their games were innocent. Small feet kicking footballs, a make-up-the-rules-as-you-go version of cricket, adventures with ornate dolls.

Erasmus Tull saw all of this through the sheer curtains. Behind him, Tull heard the *chink* of ice on glass as his employer built another drink. His second since they'd arrived. Tull did not like that his employer drank while they were on a meet, though he had to admit, however reluctantly, that it had never seemed to interfere with the man's ability to negotiate.

"Anything?" asked Howard Shelton.

Tull was about to say no when a white Land Rover turned the corner and drove slowly up the street.

"They're here," he said.

Behind him Howard knocked back the second Scotch, sighed and said, "Let the games begin."

The driver parked the Land Rover outside and four men got out. The driver remained with the car—Tull evaluated him and discounted him as a significant threat. Two of the others were different. They were small but very fit young Nepalese men with clean-shaven faces and the erect postures and expressionless faces of former Gurkhas. Considering the buyer—a slippery man named Sheng—these two were probably from the Gurkha contingent based in Singapore. Tull's appreciation for the buyer went up a notch. Gurkhas had a centuries-old reputation as fierce and efficient warriors who were also intensely loyal and disciplined. Although they would willingly die to protect anyone in their charge, they would also very likely pile up a hill of bodies on the way down.

The Gurkhas flanked a waddling fat man. Sheng. Half Chinese and half German, though his looks clearly favored his Asian side. His personality, however, favored that of head lice. This was the third time Howard had met with the man to barter goods for goods. The last two times Sheng had been accompanied by a pair of former Yakuza from some Japanese slum, but the grapevine said that last March one of Sheng's buyers in Cambodia turned out to be with Interpol. Some creative mayhem ensued. Sheng escaped with his life, and everyone else managed to die. Now Sheng had an upgrade in personal protection.

At the soft knock, the governor sank into a chair and Tull answered the door.

One of the Gurkhas stood between Tull and Sheng, dark eyes suspicious and alert. He struggled with the English translation of the code phrase.

"We are looking for the home of Mr. Patel."

Tull pulled the door wider. "Mr. Patel is on a call. Would you like to come in and wait?"

The Gurkha gave a single sharp nod and entered as Tull faded back, keeping his back casually to the wall. The Nepalese glanced around the room, then turned and said something very quick and rapid to Sheng in bad Cantonese.

Sheng beamed a great smile as he waddled into the room. "My friends," he said in passable English. "So good to see you again."

Howard did not stand to shake hands. No one offered to shake hands, not even Sheng. Nor did he bow. The smile was all the cordiality that this encounter was likely to have, and that was false.

"Feel free to make yourself a drink," said the governor, waving a hand toward the wet bar. There was a bottle of Scotch, a bottle of gin, and a bottle of tonic standing next to a tray of cheap glasses and an open plastic bag of ice cubes. Everything was disposable. Howard wore latex gloves. Tull did not, but aside from the doorknob he hadn't touched anything in the house, and he'd deliberately smeared his fingerprints on the knob. If, for some reason, he didn't have the time to properly wipe the door, then the residual prints would be useless.

The six Styrofoam containers lined up on the coffee table would not take a fingerprint; and Tull had been careful not to touch the tape that sealed each container.

Sheng looked at them with interest. His Gurkha guards stood on either side of him, but well back, hands clasped lightly in front of their lower abdomens, feet wide apart. Tull noted that they kept their bodies tilted slightly forward so that their weight was balanced on the balls of their feet. The posture looked moderately casual, but these men were ready to spring into action. Tull approved of it.

"I see you have brought some presents," said Sheng.

"As agreed," said Howard.

"And . . . how many were you able to obtain?" asked Sheng, eyebrows arched, mouth smiling.

"There are three in each container," said Howard. "Eighteen in all. And if we like what you've brought us, we'll give you the key and location of a cold storage unit where you can find the other eighty."

"So many! How wonderful. And the, um, provenance . . . ?"

"They were donated."

"By?"

"Local laborers who signed release forms and who were paid. Twenty-five hundred per."

"That is a good price," said Sheng. And Tull knew that he was doing the math. Eighteen kidneys from healthy donors at a per-unit cost of $2,500 meant an investment of a quarter million. Sold locally, the kidneys would bring in at least double that, probably triple. In certain places—Europe, for example—they would fetch as much as five times that amount. A broker as clever as Sheng would opt for the better market, which made a million and a quarter easy money for someone like him.

It would all be pure profit, Tull knew, because he knew for certain that Sheng did not pay a dime for the item he planned to trade for the organs. Sheng would barter with the devil himself, and probably come out at least even on the deal.

Sheng went over to the first of the Styrofoam containers, slit the tape with a thumbnail, opened it, waved aside the dry-ice vapors and studied the contents. Then he nodded to himself and closed the container.

"Where is this cold storage unit?" he asked, his voice very casual. Like someone asking the time of day.

Howard smiled. "Somewhere in India. We give you the location and the key once we see what you've brought us."

Sheng's smile momentarily flickered, and suddenly Tull understood the play, and why Sheng had brought the two Gurkhas with him. Sheng had no intention of making a swap. Or, at least he hoped he didn't have to. Which brought up the ugly question of whether Sheng had brought the thing he promised.

"Do we have a deal?" asked the governor, leaning back in his chair and crossing his legs.

Sheng licked his lips. "Of course, of course."

Howard nodded, his smile as false as Sheng's. "Then let's see it. This is already taking too long. I've shown you mine, now you show me yours."

For one fragile moment Tull thought Sheng was going to go for it. The man's eyes flicked from the row of containers, to the door, then to the nearest of his guards. But, ultimately he gave a heavy sigh, as if having agreed to sell his virgin daughter into slavery, and barked out a command to the Gurkha closest to the door. The man nodded and opened his jacket.

That fast Tull had a gun in his hand and the barrel screwed into Sheng's left temple.

"No," he said.

The Gurkhas froze in postures of near-attack, their hands caught in motion toward their concealed weapons.

"No," Tull said again. Very quietly.

Sheng hissed something at the Gurkha by the door. Tull didn't know the language but whatever Sheng said it sounded vile. The Gurkha winced a little and colored.

In English, Sheng said, "Slowly and with care."

The Gurkha nodded, bowed slightly to Tull, and used two fingers to very gingerly pull back the flap of his jacket. There, tucked into the waistband of his trousers back near his hip bone, was a small parcel wrapped in green silk. He raised his eyebrows inquiringly at Tull.

"Like the man said . . . slowly and with care."

The Gurkha used two fingers of his other hand to remove the parcel. It was about the size of a paperback book, though narrower and a little longer. The green silk was bound with red cord.

"Put it on the chair," said Tull, indicating an empty easy chair with an uptic of his chin. "Good. Now step back and stand by the door. Hands in plain sight."

The man did as instructed and backed away.

Sheng said, "You are denting my head."

He tried to make a joke of it, but his voice trembled too much.

"Sir?" said Tull, and Howard uncrossed his leg, leaned over and picked up the parcel. He weighed it in his hand.

"Feels light as balsa wood."

"Better make sure it's what we're paying for."

"It is," insisted Sheng. "It is exactly what I promised to bring. I am not cheating you. No one here is cheating you. Please, let us all be calm about this."

"Sure," said Tull, though he didn't move the gun away.

Howard unwrapped the parcel, peeling back the layers of silk with great care and delicacy. Inside was a second wrapper, this one of tissue paper, and Howard peeled that back as well, revealing a piece of metal that was nine inches long and four inches wide. The metal was a dull gray, flat, and unremarkable. The governor picked it up and turned it over in his hands, studying it from every angle and holding it up to the light to look for scratches or pits.

"It's perfect," he said, and his voice was now filled with wonder and passion. "God, Tull, it's fucking flawless. Not a scratch on it."

"It's real?" asked Tull. "Not a phony?"

Howard removed a small device from his pocket, activated it with his thumbnail, and ran it along the side of the device. A tiny digital meter showed a series of colored lights that fluctuated for several seconds before turning all green.

"Oh, it's real. Holy shit, Sheng." He looked up and grinned at the broker. "Holy mother of shit. You weren't lying. You delivered the goddamn goods."

Sheng's eyes kept darting nervously sideways toward the gun. "As promised," he said, "Sheng delivers. Now . . . if you please . . ."

The governor began rewrapping the bar. "You got any more of this stuff? Tell me you can get me some more."

"Alas, no," said Sheng. "That is the only specimen to have come into my possession."

"You're sure?"

"Quite sure."

"You can't swing some deals and get me something else? This is only one component, there are others that—"

"I am quite familiar with these items, sir," said Sheng. "And if you had approached me last spring we might have been able to do considerably more business. But those other items have moved on, and although the demand is very high, the market is quite threadbare."

"Who bought the other pieces?" demanded Howard.

"Oh," said Sheng, contriving to look pained, "as a businessman of some reputation I could not possibly tell you that."

"My man still has a gun to your head. Doesn't that put you in a mood to share?"

"I . . ."

Howard suddenly laughed. "Sorry, I'm just fucking with you. We know you sold one piece to North Korea and two to China."

Sheng's face went pale.

"It's all cool," said Howard. "It's all about business."

"Of course," said Sheng. "Business is—"

Erasmus Tull shot him through the head.

The Gurkhas were shocked for one fraction of a second and then they moved. Tull shot the one by the door in the face. The second one managed to whip out his kukri knife and Tull had to danced backward to keep from losing his gun arm. As it was the deadly blade struck the pistol barrel with such force that the weapon was torn from Tull's hand. It hit the carpet with a heavy *thud* as the Gurkha lunged at Tull.

Tull was unarmed against a Gurkha—one of the fiercest warrior classes in history. The man was a master of that blade and he came at Tull with blinding speed and terrible precision.

Erasmus Tull took the knife away from him and cut the Gurkha's throat. He stepped aside to avoid the spray of blood.

The whole thing had taken less than four seconds.

Howard stood up and smoothed his trousers. He looked down at the three dead men and wrinkled his nose at the mingled smells of cordite and fresh copper. Gunpowder and blood.

"Messy," he observed.

Tull shrugged. Howard carefully rewrapped the component. His eyes held an almost erotic glaze

"We made a good start," said Tull as he began wiping every surface they may have touched. "We're nearly halfway there."

"Halfway is a long way from actually being there," grumbled Howard. "The frigging Chinese are going to beat us to the finish line if we don't put some topspin on this."

"You think they'll actually recover from the setback in 'seventy-six?" asked Tull. "They lost eight components in one day. Eight."

"Sure, but now they have four and we only have five." Howard hefted his precious bundle. "Halfway is nowhere at all. C'mon, let's get the fuck out of here."

Part Four
The Closers

A good plan violently executed now is better than a perfect plan executed next week.

—GEORGE S. PATTON

There are not enough Indians in the world to defeat the Seventh Cavalry.

—GEORGE ARMSTRONG CUSTER

Chapter Forty-five

Turkey Point Lighthouse, Elk Neck State Park

Cecil County, Maryland

Sunday, October 20, 10:07 a.m.

The Black Hawk came in along the curve of a sheer bluff that rose above the headland of Chesapeake Bay. Elk Neck State Park was sprawled across twenty-one hundred acres of dense forests, hills, marshland, and sandy beaches. I'd hiked every one of the trails, roasted marshmallows and hotdogs over campfires, sung bad songs very loudly with other boys, done my first wilderness training and orienteering, and experienced some of my happiest moments here. I look back at the last summer we'd camped here as the last clean breath before my life became polluted by the urban trauma that scarred me and transformed me into the killer I've become. That summer was before Helen and I had been attacked by a group of teenage boys. Before they'd stomped me half to death and then assaulted her. It was the last time I was unmarred by life. The last time I was innocent.

Here in this forest.

I could feel my mouth wanting to smile at those memories, but that's always tough for me, because I have to view them through the lens of what happened so soon after.

And yet . . .

We'd played here. Helen and me, when her family came camping with mine. My brother and me, the two of us hunting for Apaches and dinosaurs and savage tribesmen on those forgotten trails. Maybe one day, maybe when the war let me stop long enough to catch my breath, I'd come back here and find one of those old trails and walk it. With Ghost beside me and ghosts around me. Would I be able to hear the echo of old laughter here? Does the world ever grant a killer that much mercy?

It was a bad day to ask those kinds of questions.

The shadow of the Black Hawk flickered across a flat green lawn and flitted up the white tower of the Turkey Point Lighthouse. From a distance the lighthouse looked blunt and squat, but it was deceptive. A hundred feet high and as white as a gull's breast.

I was surprised to see that there was a house adjoining the tower. Our scoutmaster had told us that the lightkeeper's house had been torn down in 1972, years before I was born. But now there was a two-story Victorian cottage that had an improbable number of porches and cupolas and little towers sticking out in all directions. In contrast to the stark simplicity of the lighthouse, the cottage was on the charming side of untidy. Japanese black pines stood guard beside an inviting walkway, and an herb garden was embowered by beach plum, bayberry, and hydrangeas.

The pilot, Hector, set us down on the far side of the two-acre lawn.

"You want backup, Cap?" he asked. We'd left Baltimore with a crew of three: Hector at the stick; a former field agent with an artificial leg called Slick riding shotgun; and a red-haired woman nicknamed—creatively— Red along as crew chief. They were support staff, but they were also combat vets; each partially disabled but still tough as nails.

"Stay on station," I told Hector. "I don't know if this is a hello-goodbye waste of time or if we're going to need to get this Flynn woman back to the shop. Cut the rotors but stay ready."

"You got it."

Red rolled back the door and once I hopped out she handed me a ruggedized laptop bag. A MindReader substation. She gave Ghost a wink as we got out. She said, "Don't go chasing no 'possums."

Ghost gave her a snooty look and followed me through the fading rotor wash. The turbines whined down to a whisper and then fell silent as I approached the garden path.

The day was cool and clean. There wasn't a cloud in the sky and despite the time of year the air was alive with the last of the season's hummingbirds. They whipped and whizzed around us, dancing with swallowtail butterflies, and Ghost jumped and barked like a puppy. The scent of roses was infused by the rich salty air, and as the breeze shifted I could smell rosemary and sweet grass. As I approached the cottage I marveled at the variety of flowers, some of which were way out of season. Pansies, impatiens, and dianthus thrived alongside tulips, crocuses, and a dozen kinds of roses. And there was a row of hollyhocks with their paper-thin blooms fluttering in shades of pale pink, lemon yellow, and deep magenta, some of them towering nearly ten feet high.

I stopped and looked around, and despite everything—my errand, the video, the crisis—I smiled.

Then the door opened and Junie Flynn stepped into my life.

I know how that sounds. Absurd, dramatic, corny. But there are moments in life—precious and rare—when no matter what else is hanging fire or clawing at your attention, you have to simply pause and focus all your attention. You do so because something of great importance is happening and you are suddenly aware of it. Maybe not in a conscious away, but deep down, on the level where your instincts trump your thoughts. The voice of your essential self whispers to you: *Behold*. And you stop because you must. You know that to fumble the moment through inattention or to pollute it through triviality is to lose something of great value. Even if you cannot then—or ever—ascribe precise parameters to that value. You are acutely aware, though, that if you blunder through the moment without giving it its proper due you are one very dull fellow. This, you are sure, is an event in life so rare and significant that it can only be described as having a flavor of importance.

That is what I felt when the lighthouse door opened and Junie Flynn stepped from soft interior shadows into the golden sunlight of early afternoon. She wore a loose peasant skirt with a complex Mexican print, a white long-sleeved sweater unbuttoned over a coral t-shirt with a deep V, and no shoes. Her wavy blond hair was tied back in a loose ponytail. She wore no makeup, but there were silver rings on most of her fingers, a jangly ankle bracelet on her left leg, and at least a dozen bracelets on each wrist—layers of silver, white gold, red gold, and copper. An emerald pendant hung from a gold chain around her neck, half lost in the shadows between her sun-freckled breasts.

She walked up to me, smiling and asked, "Are you here to kill me?"

Chapter Forty-six

VanMeer Castle
Near Pittsburgh, Pennsylvania
Sunday, October 20, 10:11 a.m.

The golf cart's top speed was twelve miles an hour, and Mr. Bones tried to will it to go faster. The labyrinthine underground structure of basements, subbasements, laboratories, warehouses, firing chambers, and other rooms was more than triple that of the massive castle above. They had to endure two freight elevators and more than a mile of tunnels in order to get to Howard's design lab. It was a ponderous distance at the best of times, and now it was excruciating.

"Why don't you move the fucking lab closer to the elevators?" Bones growled.

"Why don't you stop whining and steer? Nearly clipped my elbow back there."

The sniping war continued all the way to the big security door. Then they piled out and went through the steps necessary to open the airlock door. It required two palm prints simultaneously applied. There was a secondary entry method for those times when Mr. Bones was not at the estate, but that had a number of extra steps and many safeguards in case Howard was being made to access the lab under duress.

The airlock hissed open, belching refrigerated air at them. Despite the nervous hostility during the trip, they weren't mad at each other. They were terrified. The disaster at Dugway was dreadful.

Beyond the airlock was a large laboratory with state-of-the-art computer systems lining three of the walls. The fourth wall was completely covered by a line of heavy gray drapes.

Once inside they hurried to the central Ghost Box station, which was a massive affair with over twenty networked screens built in a semicircle around a console with two wheeled leather chairs. Mr. Bones held the chair for Howard and paused to feel the old man's pulse and press a palm against his forehead. Howard was flushed, but the blood pressure medicine seemed to be keeping him stable. His pulse was elevated, but not dangerously so.

Howard waved him away with mock irritation.

They logged onto Ghost Box and immediately called Yuina Hoshino. A hologram of her appeared above them, almost life-size but just her head and shoulders. She wore her glasses and peered owlishly at them.

"Howard? What is it? I'm in the middle of—"

"I tried to call you, damn it."

"I turned my phone off," she said. "We're working on the slave circuit and—"

"To hell with the slave circuit. Never turn your goddamn phone off," snarled Howard. His voice carried such savage emotion that Yuina straightened and removed her glasses. "Look at this."

Howard replayed the last few seconds of footage from Dugway.

Her face was a total blank. No expression, no emotion.

"Again," she said. "Play it again."

They played it twice more and then a third time in slow motion. Mr. Bones opened some video-editing software, froze the best image and blew it up, but as good as the senator's lapel cam had been it was still not sophisticated enough. As the picture expanded it began to blur and then to fragment into blocks as the computer isolated individual pixels and assigned them colors. Annoyed, Mr. Bones reduced the magnification until they had the largest clear picture.

"They're back," said Howard. "Holy mother of God, Yuina, they're back and—"

"Don't jump to conclusions," said Yuina slowly. She put her glasses back on and bent over her keyboard for a few seconds. Then a second image appeared in an inset box. The craft in this picture was a triangle of unreflective black metal with one bright light near each of its three points and a larger light in the exact center. The sides were dark, alternating black and smoke gray. The top and bottom of the machine were slightly larger than the center section, creating an eavelike overhang all the way around. In the second picture, the craft stood on three metal legs made from steel struts. The vehicle was apparently in a cave with rough walls but on the closest wall there appeared to be some kind of rough structure. When Yuina increased the size of the inset box it became more evident that the structure on the wall was the reconstructed skeleton of a dinosaur.

The craft in the inset and the craft at Dugway were a perfect match.

"Wait, wait," said Shelton. "What are you saying here?"

"Isn't it obvious?" answered Yuina. "The ship in the cave is the one found at the Dadiwan dig in the excavation site in Zhangshaodian Village, in Tianshui City. The one they found in 2013."

"Bullshit . . . that ship was trashed," Howard fired back. "Tull got in there. He took photos of everything."

Yuani gave him a pitying look. "Haven't you ever put used parts from one car into another? Or am I the only tomboy in this group?"

"Son a bitch," breathed Mr. Bones. "The fucking Chinese did repair it."

"Are you sure they're the same?" demanded Howard. "Look, the lights aren't exactly—"

"If there are differences it's because the Chinese rebuilt or remodeled the craft," said Yuina.

"This craft just shot down the Locust bomber they're testing out at Dugway," said Howard. "That's an act of war, Yuina. You actually think the Chinese are looking to declare open war on the U.S.?"

Her face was impassive. "I'm not so sure I'd call this war, Howard."

"Then what?"

"A war is two-sided. The DoD has been hoping to use the Locust to put us way ahead in the international arms race. Much like we're hoping to do with Specter 101. But if that vehicle is Chinese, then they've just told us in no uncertain terms that the arms race is over." She leaned toward the screen, dark eyes intense. "And they just won."

Chapter Forty-seven

Turkey Point Lighthouse, Elk Neck State Park
Cecil County, Maryland
Sunday, October 20, 10:12 a.m.

Junie Flynn's words seemed to hang burning in the air.

"Kill you?" There may have been a crooked smile on my mouth, but I wasn't sure. "That's a pretty strange way of answering your door."

Ghost whined faintly.

Junie Flynn shielded her eyes with her hand and squinted up at me.

"You landed on my lawn in an unmarked black helicopter. What else would I think?"

My crooked smile twitched. "Actually, I can make a pretty good list of reasons why someone would land on a lighthouse lawn. That list includes free rides for lucky kids and extremely aggressive Jehovah's Witnesses. Killing people, however, would be moderately low on the list."

"Only 'moderately low'?" she asked, smiling.

"I could be Santa Claus gone high-tech."

"It's October."

"The Great Pumpkin, then?"

"In a black helicopter."

"It's not entirely black. Look, we have snazzy red sports trim. It's just an ordinary everyday heli—"

" 'Ordinary'? Why would an ordinary helicopter have—and this is just a guess off the top of my head—a pair of GAU-19/A Gatling guns, seventy millimeter Hydra rockets, probably a round dozen AGM-114 Hellfire laser-guided missiles, and thirty millimeter M230 gun pods?"

"Geese are a hazard to air traffic," I said. "We're being proactive."

Junie Flynn laughed.

I laughed with her. Ghost wagged his tail.

Not sure in what proportions our laughter was constructed of false and honest humor. In the background, the Black Hawk crouched on her lawn like a giant insect from a Godzilla flick. She glanced down at Ghost, who, despite extensive and costly training, was wagging his tail like a puppy. She held out her hand to him.

"Don't," I warned quickly. "He's a trained combat dog."

My trained combat dog licked her fingers and then flopped on the ground to show his belly, tongue lolling and tail thumping. Junie squatted down and began rubbing his tummy while Ghost's eyes rolled up and one leg started kicking.

"Who's a good little combat dog? Who's a good little combat dog?" cooed Junie Flynn in a singsong voice.

"Um . . . he's not usually like that with people."

"Dogs understand me."

Ghost was apparently understanding that her clever fingers on his fur was the equivalent of a crack pipe.

"Why did you think I was here to kill you?" I asked.

Junie stood up and shrugged.

"That's it?" I said. "Shouldn't there be a whole 'nother part to this conversation?"

"You haven't read a single one of my books, have you?"

I said, "Um . . ."

"If you had, you'd know that I am not a cheerleader for any part of the government that employs bullies and thugs. And you'd know that I've had my share of bullying and thuggish behavior."

"I'm not here to bully you, and I am seldom thuggish to total strangers."

"Just close friends, then?"

"Cute, but no. Look, Ms. Flynn, I'll admit that I haven't read your books, watched your videos, or listened to your podcast. In fact, until this morning I'd never even heard of you."

"Oh?" Her blues eyes flashed with challenge. "Do you know *anything* about me?"

"Just basic stuff. You were an orphan who was adopted at age five by Jericho and Amanda Flynn. Your foster dad was a physicist, your mom was a developmental psychologist. They were killed in a car accident when you were in your senior year of college. They had no other children, no family except for you, so you inherited. You finished college, but you switched your major from art history to political science. After college you went to grad school at the University of Pennsylvania, but dropped out a year later after you were injured in a car bombing while on vacation in Egypt. After you returned to the States, you began to write articles about conspiracy theories, UFOs, alien abductions, shadow governments, and the Majestic Black Book. You've published twenty-three books, four of which were *New York Times* bestsellers and two of which were *USA Today* bestsellers. You are on the UFO and conspiracy theory lecture circuit, which means that you travel at least half the year. You are the go-to expert for several topics related to UFOs, though the real basis of your celebrity is the Black Book. You wrote the first books on it—which, I admit, I haven't read—and you've filed over one hundred requests via the Freedom of Information Act in an attempt to have the contents of the book released." I paused. "Did I leave anything out?"

Her face remained bland through my recitation, with only a momentary tightening of her mouth when I mentioned the death of her parents and her own injuries in Egypt. "You didn't mention my arrest record."

"Eleven arrests in seven years, all related to organized protests to humanitarian issues. You've been on talk shows with Martin Sheen, Don Cheadle, and George Clooney following various arrests."

"What does that tell you?"

"That you're a social activist and I probably agree with some of your politics."

"Says the man with the gun, the helicopter, and the combat dog."

"Being a patriot isn't the same thing as being a radical. Right or left."

She digested that. "You left out that I'm a freak. That shows up in a lot of field reports. I've seen some of them, so I know."

" 'Freak'? I wouldn't use that word."

"What word would you use?"

"Gifted?" I suggested. "Maybe uniquely gifted. In middle school you demonstrated qualities consistent with eidetic memory—photographic memory—but later that diagnosis was modified to include hyperthymesia, which I believe is what they call a superior autobiographic memory. In short, you don't forget anything."

"Can't forget," she corrected. "And . . . it's not very much fun."

"I'll bet. There are whole years of my life I'd like to forget."

"Me, too."

We looked at each other for a moment, letting all of that sink in.

"What do they call you?" she asked, shifting topics abruptly enough to strip the gears.

I offered my hand. "Captain Joseph Ledger."

She didn't immediately take my hand. "Captain of . . . ?"

"You won't have heard the name of the organization I'm actually with. We don't have badges."

"Let me guess. It's one of those 'we're so secret that if you told me the name you'd have to kill me' things?"

I laughed. "That's almost exactly what I said to my boss the first time I met him."

"He didn't kill you."

"Not so far. Guy's twitchy, though, so we'll see what my retirement plan looks like."

"A gold watch and two in the back of the head?"

I liked this Junie Flynn. She was a civilian and I could have stood there and sold her some kind of bullshit, but with some people deception is like lying in church.

"The name isn't really important," I said. "You wouldn't have heard of it and to tell you I'd probably have to make you sign a mountain of non-disclosure papers. Do you really want to do that?"

"No."

"Then let's leave it at this: I'm not with the IRS, so that means I'm not pure evil. I am definitely not here to kill you. And I consider myself to be one of the good guys."

"The American flag and mom's apple pie?" she asked skeptically.

"My mom's dead. She died of cancer. And . . . I don't really know why I told you that."

"People talk to me," she said.

"I guess they do." I offered my hand again. "The name's Joe."

Junie considered that, her smile wavering only a little. Then she took my proffered hand.

"Junie," she said. Her hand was slender but strong, with long fingers and interesting calluses. Yard work, maybe. No shooter's calluses, though.

She looked into my eyes and something happened. There was a very sudden and very weird bit of chemistry between us that created a connection I didn't really understand. In one split second it felt as if a door opened in my mind and Junie Flynn stepped through. Just like that she seemed to know who and what I was. I'd known other people who had a similar gift. Some of them were screeners who worked for the CIA and FBI. They didn't need a polygraph machine because for whatever reason they were wired differently than the rest of us. Maybe they could smell subtle changes in body chemistry, maybe they could feel the vibrations of other human hearts. I didn't know how it worked, but they were human lie detectors. And then there were some who had an even deeper level, a second and separate gift. They could look into your eyes and see who you were, your real self, down deep behind the artifice and affectation. Junie was that kind of person. I didn't know it until we touched hands and looked into each other's eyes. It was all so immediate, so fast. And it was like having an X-ray focused on my soul.

There are so many things about me that I don't show people. I am not, by any clinical definition, entirely sane. I am functionally warped as a result of the brutal attack on my girlfriend and me when we were fourteen. We both lost ourselves that day. Neither of us ever really came back. After I healed from the physical trauma I found every way possible to make myself tough. Martial arts, boxing, weights, endless reading about psychology, warfare, the physics and physiology of the destruction of the human body. As the corny saying goes, I became a weapon. My mind, though, was not something that could be sweated back to fitness in the gym any more than it was something the docs could stitch back together. My personality had become splintered and over the years a number of unique personality fragments emerged, some quite self-destructive. Others were shockingly violent. Through endless hours working with Rudy Sanchez—a doctor who became my best friend—I learned to exert control over them. I edited out most of the bad ones, but three aspects still remain. One is the Modern Man—the Civilized Man—and he's the one who still carries the last cracked pieces of my idealism and innocence. In recent years he has taken a serious beating.

Then there's the Cop, and he's the closest thing I have to a central personality. The Cop is frequently in charge. He drives the bus most of the time and that's a good thing because he's smart, calm, passive, sensitive, and intuitive. He'd rather solve a problem than pull a trigger.

But the third part of me is the Warrior. Or, as he prefers to be called, the Killer. That part of me was born on that terrible day. With each stomping foot, with each punch and bash and crack he fought his way into the world. He is the skull-cracker, the neck-breaker, the eye-gouger. He is not evil, but he is not nice. The Warrior paints himself with camouflage greasepaint and crouches in the tall grass waiting for the bad guys to come by, and then he hunts them with a cruel and savage delight.

Helen became lost in that carnival funhouse of the damaged mind, where all images of her destruction and violation were reflected in twisted

and deformed mirrors. And in that darkness she became so utterly
without hope that she needed to find a permanent way out.

Which she did.

I found her—too late. The Warrior in me rose up and screamed so
loud that it broke the fragile shell of mercy that hung around his neck.
There is no mercy left in him now.

As Junie Flynn looked into my eyes I tried not to let her see any of this,
but I knew that she did. Somehow, impossibly, she did.

All in one tiny moment.

I saw it register in her eyes. They widened a bit, and her face went
death pale. I expected her to yank her hand back. To at least turn away in
disgust. Instead she reached up with her other hand and touched my
cheek. Despite the fact that we were strangers it was an oddly personal
gesture, intimate and familiar, as if she and I shared some history beyond
a few seconds of banter and verbal sparring.

"I'm sorry," she said.

I closed my eyes.

Her fingertips lingered for a moment and the connection was gone.
When I opened my eyes, she had indeed stepped back. But it was not a
retreat from me. Instead she'd stepped back into a neutral space, which
was the only way we could both move forward from this moment.

"So why are you here, Joe?" she asked in a tone that held no trace of
what had just happened.

It took me a second to find my footing, and my voice. "I . . . need your
help to find a copy of the Majestic Black Book."

Her eyes flicked to the parked helicopter and back. "I don't have it."

"I know."

"Then—"

"I need to get a copy of it. Any copy. Today."

Her eyes were thoughtful, her mouth formed into a half smile, and I
waited her out.

She said, "Then I'd better make some tea."

With that Junie Flynn turned and went back inside, leaving the door
open for me to follow. I glanced down at Ghost. He gave me a "hey,
you're the super secret agent guy; I'm just a dog" look.

We followed her inside.

Chapter Forty-eight

Turkey Point Lighthouse, Elk Neck State Park
Cecil County, Maryland
Sunday, October 20, 10:14 a.m.

The inside of the cottage was a wonderful mess. It was clean but a long way from neat, and the way in which the living room was arranged seemed to suggest that there were at least two distinct sides to Junie Flynn. One half of the room was given over to big squashy armchairs, comfortably lumpy couches, brightly colored throw rugs, endless decorative pillows, tables piled high with art and craft magazines, a half-finished macramé bedspread, and hardwood stacked haphazardly by a massive stone fireplace still cluttered with cold ashes. Christmas lights framed the windows and ran along the edges of the walls even though this was still October. Or perhaps they were last year's lights never taken down. The floors were polished wood covered by overlapping rugs with Navajo and Turkish weaves. A guitar stood against the hearth and various handmade instruments—a buffalo horn, a tube zither, reed pipes, tongue drums, and several brightly colored BaTonga Budima Drums. In one small glass-fronted cabinet were dozens of packs of tarot cards, some new and some very old. The decks were interspersed with crystals and semiprecious stones. Deep purple amethyst, yellow citrine, dark blue lapis lazuli that was flecked with red, golden tiger eye, watermelon tourmaline, and sky-blue turquoise. These were quality pieces and even though they were indoors they seemed to radiate light that was as rich as the bright sunshine outside.

If that was all that I saw of this woman's home I would not have been surprised. It was in keeping with her garden, her manner of dress, and her apparent lifestyle. A dull and unimaginative person might dismiss her as one of those soft, fringe people, a latter-day hippie, a child of the New Age.

The other half of the room showed a different aspect of Junie Flynn; a separation so dramatic that it suggested a true dichotomy, or perhaps a mind in schism. Still too early to tell. There was a functional desk on which was a high-end ruggedized laptop, laser printer, scanner, podcasting equipment that included a good camera on a tripod and a quality microphone. There were six steel file cabinets in a neat row, and a side table on which was a wire sorting rack filled with neatly arranged papers. The chair tucked into the desk was a leather business model similar to the kind I had in my own office. Everything was neat and precise and functional.

Standing between the two halves of the room, almost as a deliberate bridge between them or a doorway from one to the other, was a tall bookshelf crammed with books on every subject: physics, astronomy, linguistics, symbology, politics, genetics, molecular biology, engineering, religion, and medicine. The walls directly adjacent to the bookcase were covered, floor to ceiling, with framed pictures of Egyptian cartouches, a semaphore signaler, an obviously blind woman touching the face of a child, Maori body art, strange animals carved as geoglyphs into the hardpan of a Peruvian desert, and even crop circles.

There were two things that made me go "hmmmm." Standing neatly side by side near the front door was a bulging suitcase; and leaning against the wall just inside the doorway was a good old-fashioned Louisville slugger.

I nodded to the suitcase. "Planning on going somewhere?"

"I was going to drive up to Philly, my friend just had a baby." She was a pretty good liar, but not a great one.

"Glad I caught you," I said. "And the baseball bat?"

She shrugged. "I live alone."

"You didn't bring it with you when you went outside to meet me. A guy you thought was here to kill you."

"I didn't really think you were here for that," she said with a laugh.

"Oh? What tipped you off? My boyish good looks? Crinkly blue-eyed smile?"

She plucked at the sleeve of my Orioles shirt. "The kind of killers the government sends dress better."

"Hey, I'll have you know this is a genuine 1983 World Series away-game shirt."

"Okay."

"Tippy Martinez wore this shirt when he got the save against the Phillies in game four!"

"Tippy who?"

"My dad gave me this shirt when I turned eighteen."

"Your face is turning red."

"Baseball," I said, the way most people say "religion."

"Baseball seems like a lot of time with men standing around spitting tobacco and scratching their crotches. I like football. Things happen in football."

Before I could construct a properly devastating reply, Junie waved me toward the couch. "Sit."

"I'd like to set up a video conference call," I said, hefting the case I'd brought. "Okay with you?"

"Sure. You can set up on the coffee table. Just push the magazines and stuff onto the floor." She vanished into the kitchen.

I set the case down but instead of opening it I stepped to the far side of the living room and pulled out my cell to call Church. When he answered I said, "Where do we stand?"

"Nothing new," he said. "Have you made contact with the Flynn woman?"

"With her now. She's a bit paranoid, thought I was here to kill her."

"That's interesting," said Church. "Try not to do that."

"Very funny. I'll patch you in as soon as I've prepped her."

I disconnected, sat down and opened the MindReader substation. It had a powerful satellite uplink, a 128-bit cyclic encryption system, and a battery good for forty-eight hours.

Junie came in carrying a tray of cups and fixings, which she set down on the edge of the coffee table. I covertly watched her eyes take in the sophisticated machine. Her appraisal was cool and I saw the tiniest lift of one appreciative eyebrow.

"My tax dollars at work?"

"Nope," I said. "This system is privately owned and its use is loaned at no charge to Uncle Sam under very restricted circumstances."

Junie poured tea from a Japanese pot decorated with cherry blossoms, selected a fat slice of lemon and squeezed the juice through the steam. I accepted the cup, sniffed, took an experimental sip. The tea was far richer than I expected, and it swirled with several flavors that I could almost but not quite identify.

"Delicious," I said, setting the cup aside.

"What's your dog's name?"

"Ghost."

"Ah," she said, nodding. "That figures."

"Pardon?"

"He can see spirits. This place is haunted."

"Okay," I said, mostly because how else do you reply to a comment like that? It didn't help that Ghost sat beside the couch staring at the empty air across the room. He turned his head slowly as if watching someone idly strolling from the window to the front door. I wanted to tell him to knock it the hell off. "I thought this house was brand new. The old one burned down, right?"

"This house is a hundred and sixteen years old. It was dismantled and brought here from Cape May, New Jersey."

"That sounds expensive. Why bother?"

She looked puzzled. "Why not?"

"Good point."

"So, why are you looking for the Majestic Black Book?"

"That's—"

"Classified?" Her smile was very charming and a few degrees below freezing. "Have a safe flight back, Joe. I can put your tea in a travel mug."

"Hey, it's not a joke. This is an actual matter of grave national importance. No bullshit."

She snorted.

"You don't believe me?" I asked.

"You're with the government," she said, as if that said it all.

"Wow, cynical."

"I tried naive faith in all people but that became a drag."

"You're paranoid, too."

"I prefer the term 'realist,'" she said. "Surely you're not going to tell me that the government has never spied on its citizens, denied them their rights, violated their constitutional and civil rights . . . et cetera. You're not going to go there, are you, Joe?"

"I wouldn't dare."

Ghost was watching this exchange like a spectator at a Wimbledon match.

"Maybe I'm going about this the wrong way," I conceded. "How's this—I'd like to hire you as a paid consultant."

"A consultant on the Black Book."

"Sure," I said. "On the book and where I can find a copy."

"Paid?"

"Yes."

"How much?"

I shrugged. "What's your standard fee?"

"You couldn't afford it," Junie said with a sour laugh.

"I have pretty deep pockets."

"You still couldn't afford it."

I sipped my tea. "Try me. What's your price?"

"The truth," said Junie Flynn.

"Ah . . . now that is expensive."

"And nonnegotiable."

"Even though this is a matter of—"

"Grave national importance," she finished. "Yes, you said that. But how can I believe there's any crisis at all unless you tell me the truth?"

I sat back and crossed my legs. "How would you know that I am telling the truth?"

"I'd know."

"I'm a very good liar," I said. "It's a professional requirement. You know, working for the Man, and all."

"I'd know," she insisted. She didn't lay into it, she wasn't selling it. She was telling me.

"What? Can you read minds?"

"Not in the way you're thinking. It's more empathy than telepathy. I don't know what people are thinking, but I can tell if they're being honest or not."

"That's a useful skill."

"Yes," she said. "Though often disappointing and disheartening."

"I'll bet."

We sipped our tea.

"Even if I can meet your price," I said, "it doesn't mean that I can tell you everything."

"I wouldn't expect you to," said Junie, "but I don't want to be lied to."

"Guess I can promise that much. If there's something I can't say, I won't." I set my cup down. "So . . . what is it you want to know?"

She blew out her cheeks. "Lots of things. Everything. I guess the first thing, though, is why there's such a rush to get the Black Book? Why right now? It's been around for years."

A dozen lies and two dozen variations on the truth occurred to me, but what I said was, "Someone has cooked up a pretty damn good way to extort the United States. A lot of people could die and the country would never recover. Never. Because of certain circumstances related to this matter, we believe that this is a credible threat."

"How does the Black Book play into that?"

"Apparently, that's the price to keep America safe. We obtain the book for them and they don't make good on their threat."

"I thought America didn't negotiate with terrorists."

"That's really more of a guideline than a rule," I confessed. "It's all a matter of what kind of leverage they have. Threatening to blow up a school bus or release anthrax into a Grand Central Station is one thing. Bad as those events would be, the disaster would be, to a degree, containable."

"What about all those lives?"

"We're at war, Junie," I said, and it hurt my mouth to say those words. "And for all practical purposes the nature of war has changed. It isn't a matter of who can put the biggest army in the field. The Taliban taught us that, just as they taught the Russians before us. War is about threat, leverage, bribery, duplicity, subterfuge, and political gain."

"Wow," she said softly, "you're really not lying to me."

"No."

"It takes a lot to tell the truth."

"I get my strength through purity."

"Just like Lancelot." She cocked her head to one side. "Didn't he steal the girl and betray his best friend, though?"

"Best not to look too closely at heroes," I suggested. "They often have feet of clay."

"Very sad, but also very true." She pursed her lips. "What kind of threat are we talking about? And using what leverage? A terrorist bomb? Anthrax?"

There was no way I was allowed to answer that question. I could get fired. I could get locked up. But . . . sometimes, with some people, you simply have to take a chance.

"They've threatened to cause a mega-tsunami in the Canary Islands that would totally destroy the coastlines of Africa, Great Britain, and the eastern United States."

"Cumbre Vieja," she said automatically.

I leaned forward and very quietly asked, "Now, how the hell do you know that?"

Interlude Four

Hotel Riu Palace Aruba
J. E. Irausquin Boulevard 79
Palm Beach, Aruba
Six years ago

Erasmus Tull knocked on the door of room 67, waited for ten seconds. Knocked again.

When there was no answer, he leaned close to the door, listening for sounds from inside the room. There was a faint mutter of voices on a television turned low. Nothing else.

Tull knocked one more time.

Nothing.

The hallway was empty. Most of the tourists were baking by the pool or crammed into faux pirate ships on the way out to prime snorkeling spots. Late morning was the deadest time in a resort hotel, especially on floors reserved for time-share swaps. The cleaning staff only came here by appointment and the mass exodus that required extensive cleaning wouldn't happen until Friday afternoon.

Nevertheless Tull waited for a full minute to make sure the hall would remain empty before he dug a small device from his pocket. It was about the size of an old Zippo lighter but had no visible moving parts. At a glance—and even on close inspection—it looked like a piece of metal. Aluminum or magnesium. Something pale and light.

Tull moved close to the electronic door lock, using his body to shield it from view as he pressed the blunt edge of the metal right below the keycard slot. There was no sound at all from the device he held, but the light on the card reader shifted from red to green and there was a faint *click*.

Easy as pie, he thought as he gently body-blocked the door open, careful not to touch the handle or wood with his hands. The door swung inward and Tull stepped quickly and cautiously into the room.

"Mr. London?" he called.

The man he was there to meet, Thomas London, was a broker of some note on the international technologies scene. London was in his late sixties and had navigated the treacherous waters of the black market ocean since his boyhood apprenticeship with father, brothers, and uncles. If something with wires, gears, circuits, or hard drives was needed and there were no conventional means of obtaining said item, the London Brothers could get it for you. Quickly, cleanly, discreetly, and at a good price.

Tull's employers, the three governors of M3, had authorized Tull to reach out to the Londons in order to obtain an exceedingly rare and extremely valuable piece of debris. Thomas and Tull met four separate times to haggle over price for the item, the purchase being complicated by the presence of other bidders who were—as London put it—very aggressive and passionate.

Competition creates a seller's market, and the price skyrocketed from its initial $1.2 million to its current $4.5 million.

Even at that amount, Tull thought it was a bargain. After all, this was not a top-quality facsimile—which abounded on the market—or one of the damaged items that circulate and circulate, waiting for the unwary enthusiast to snap them up. No, this piece was very nearly perfect. A few minor dents and some scorching. Operationally sound, though, and that was all that mattered.

Or, rather, as far as M3 and Tull knew at the time, that was all that mattered.

They would later learn hard lessons about the dangers of using D-type components with any surface damage.

Tull stepped aside to let the door swing closed behind him.

He immediately dropped the metal device into a pocket and darted his hand under his jacket to pull his gun.

Thomas London lay sprawled on the floor. Most of him. Some of him was on the bed, and some was spilled out onto the balcony. The walls and carpet and drapes were painted with blood. Tull stared at the carnage, his mouth suddenly going paste-dry. London was not merely dead—he had been destroyed. Torn apart.

Blood dripped from the lampshade and a pool of it spread out beneath each ragged piece.

Realization shot through Tull's shocked brain in a microsecond.

Blood dripped. It still pooled. In a dismembered corpse. That could only happen if the slaughter had taken place seconds ago.

Tull threw himself to one side, turning in midair, bringing his gun up toward the corner as the closet door swung open. He did not see the killer; all he saw was the snout of a weird-looking pistol.

Both guns fired at the same time.

Tull felt a blast of superheated air scorch past him as if some monstrous fire demon had exhaled at him. The lamp on the bedside table exploded into a thousand fragments and the tabletop split down the middle.

But there was no second shot from that strange gun.

The gunman sagged slowly down to his knees, canting forward in slow motion as he toppled bonelessly out of the closet, the gun clattering from his hand. A red hole glistened in center of the man's chest and a bloody bubble expanded from the hole and then popped as the man fell forward onto his face.

Tull lay on the carpet, gun held in both hands, staring at the dead man.

"Jesus Christ," he gasped, and abruptly drank in a huge lungful of air.

He scrambled to his feet, aware that his shoulder and thigh were smeared with blood. Not his own, but still hot.

He hurried over to check that there no other surprises. The bathroom was clear. So was the balcony. He was alone in the room with two dead men.

Thomas London was barely recognizable. There were enough parts to add up to a human being, but the damage was so severe that the police would need to use DNA or dental records.

The other man was another matter. Tull rolled him over. The killer was Asian; though Tull didn't think he looked Chinese. Possibly Korean. Slim, wearing the uniform of a hotel maintenance man, but when Tull checked his pockets he found a wallet belonging to another man, a local, who did indeed work at the hotel. That man was also dead somewhere, Tull thought. The only thing in the killer's clothes that did not appear to belong to the genuine maintenance man was a thick bundle jammed down into the left front trouser pocket. It was the size of a large bar of chocolate.

Tull hastily opened it and when he saw what it was, he let out a huge lungful of air.

"Thank God," he murmured.

The stabilizer.

One of the rarest D-type components of the Device, the one most often damaged during a crash or misfire.

Howard Shelton would be so happy.

Though admittedly less so for the loss of an important contact like Thomas London.

Tull rewrapped the component and slipped it into an inner pocket of his jacket. Then he bent and retrieved the odd-looking pistol. It was far lighter than he expected, and badly designed. Square and clunky. Instead of a barrel opening there were four prongs at the business end. Tull glanced down at London and over at the destroyed lamp, and he remembered the blast of heat.

He took a cell phone from his pocket and hit a speed dial.

When it was answered, Tull said, "This is a secure line."

"Very well," said Howard. "How did it go?"

Tull told him.

"That's unfortunate," said Howard. "And the component?"

"Secured."

"Thank God." The governor put so much emphasis on the last word that it came out like a prayer from a devout supplicant. Tull thought that was as accurate a picture of this man as any he'd had. To Howard, the Device was God, and the arduous process of obtaining D-type components were quests to obtain relics. What did that make him, he wondered—Percival?

"We're getting so close," breathed Howard. "We're going to do this and we're going to change the world."

"Save it, you mean," corrected Tull.

"Of course. Save it. That's what I meant."

Chapter Forty-nine

VanMeer Castle
Near Pittsburgh, Pennsylvania
Sunday, October 20, 10:15 a.m.

Howard Shelton paced back and forth while Mr. Bones watched. The big plasma screen was blank now. Yuina Hoshino had gone back to work, leaving them with her observations and their shared fears.

"She can't be right," said Howard for maybe the tenth time.

Mr. Bones did not comment. They'd already wrangled through this. If Yuina was right, then sixty years of the Majestic Project was an exercise in futility, and M3's belief that they were well ahead of the competition was so much vain fluff.

That was a problem, though not at all in the way Yuina thought it was. To her the Project was everything. Her entire adult life had been building toward this.

"How come she didn't look more upset?" asked Mr. Bones. "She seemed to take it pretty well."

"Don't kid yourself," countered Howard. "I know her and I could see it in her eyes. Two seconds after she got off the phone with us I guarantee you she was curled into a fetal position, screaming her lungs out. If this is all what it looks like, then we have to be really careful with her." He paused and made a mouth while he considered that. Then he snatched up a phone and made a call to one of his people at her lab, advising them to keep a close eye on Dr. Hoshino. "And I mean close. She just got a pretty hard knock and we have to make sure she doesn't do something unfortunate."

He ended the call and flung himself into his chair.

"What does this do to us?" asked Mr. Bones. "After that . . . they're definitely never going to let the air show go on."

Howard chewed a crumb of skin off of his thumb.

"I want like hell to believe it's those fucking Chinese," he muttered. "I have half a mind to call that prick Admiral Xiè and shove this in his face."

"He'll deny it," said Mr. Bones. "He's a backstabbing shit and he'll deny it was them."

"Son of a bitch takes our money and then does this."

"If it's him," said Bones. "If it's the Chinese."

"It has to be."

"This and the president?"

"Has to be," insisted Howard.

They sat in silence, thinking about it. Howard could almost hear his plans crashing to ruin around him.

"If it is," said Howard slowly, "then they have to know where we stand with the Project. I can build a case for that, Bonesy, I can make sense of that. If they had a spy inside our Project, then they'd know what we have planned for the air show."

"*Had* planned," Bones corrected sourly.

"Had planned, whatever. If they know that, then this was an attempt to trump us. To make the statement that we'd better not get any fancy ideas because they're already up and running and ready to kick us in the nuts."

"Okay . . . so what?"

Howard got up and walked over to the wall of curtains. He touched a button and the curtains parted and slid away to reveal huge glass windows beyond which was an enormous limestone cavern. Far below, standing on three steel struts, connected to computer systems by a hundred pendulous cables, was a massive triangular craft. Dozens of technicians swarmed like ants around the thing. Dangling above the center of the machine was an engine made from gleaming metal, supported by chains, swaying slightly. Dozens of similar engines, each in various stages of completion, stood on metal trestle tables that lined one wall. Howard leaned on the windowsill and put his forehead against the cold glass. After a moment, Mr. Bones got up and came to stand next to him.

"You know, Bonesy," said Howard Shelton very softly, "we might be going about this the wrong way. I think we are trying to win a battle instead of going straight for it and winning the whole damn war."

Chapter Fifty

Turkey Point Lighthouse, Elk Neck State Park
Cecil County, Maryland
Sunday, October 20, 10:17 a.m.

"How do I know about Cumbre Vieja?" she asked, puzzled. "With you coming to me, I thought that meant someone in the government watched my shows, listened to my podcasts, or maybe read my books."

"Others in our group have. I haven't. Tell me something that's going to lower my blood pressure and my sudden urge to reach for a pair of handcuffs."

"Joe—it's in all my stuff. I did an entire podcast about this stuff."

"About what stuff? Stop talking around it."

"I'm not," she snapped, but then paused to take a calming breath. "Okay, so you came here to interview me but you haven't done your homework. Typical government."

"Can we save the target shooting for later?"

"Sure. I did an entire book about the dangers of WMDs based on retro-engineered technologies."

"Retroengineered from flying saucers."

"Alien craft," she corrected. "Most of them aren't round. Only the small scout craft."

"Really?"

"Most of the ships have been triangular. T-craft, they're called. And there are some fully automated craft that are round—they look like glowing balls. It's probably the basis for the myth of the will-o'-the-wisp."

"Not swamp gas?"

"Swamp gas doesn't change direction at right angles, accelerate and decelerate over specific locations, and—"

"Okay, got it. We're off topic already."

She nodded. "That might happen because everything you want to know has context and you clearly don't know the context."

"True, so you can be my study buddy, but let's try to stay as close to a straight line as possible. We were talking about alien WMDs."

"No, we were talking about weapons of mass destruction made by humans based on alien technology. That's not at all the same thing. I'm talking about weapons that have been openly discussed in the media and scientific journals but which never seemed to go past the stages of basic research or early experimentation. Particle-beam weapons, cold-light phasers, satellite-killer superlasers, things like that."

"The government is researching all kinds of stuff—" I began, but she cut me off.

"Of course they are, and some of it is the natural outgrowth of our own very human desire to kill each other."

"I wouldn't put it that way . . ."

"No? Remind me again which nations were formed without conquest and bloodshed?"

"Touché," I said weakly.

"There are a lot of universities, private labs, and corporations doing advanced work funded by government dollars. Who has first dibs on any useful developments? The Department of Defense."

"I know this, Junie, but nothing so far suggests that a race of evil alien space monkeys is behind it."

"Joe," she said with eroding patience, "please try to let this sink in—this is not aliens. This is us using their technology."

"How? By discovering how to use their—what do I call them? Ray guns? Space bombs? I'm not trying to be a smartass here, Junie, but I don't know the vocabulary for this conversation. Help me out. Pretend I arrived on the short helicopter."

She laughed. "Okay, and I'm sorry if I get a little, um, passionate about this."

"No, I get that. We're cool."

Junie nodded, collected herself for a moment, then launched in. "Let me begin by saying that I am a believer in aliens, alien visitation, and alien technology. I am not, however, the kind of person who believes everything. There are a lot of things attached to the world of 'UFOlogy' that I don't believe in. Some of it are things that just don't hit me, but I can't prove or disprove—I'm just not sold on it yet. And, yes, the 'yet' was intentional."

"I want to believe," I said, quoting *X-Files*.

"Some of this stuff I don't believe because I know it to be a lie."

"Who's putting those lies out there?"

"A lot of them are from people who want to belong to any group that will have them and they use false stories to latch on to the UFO community. It's a very accepting community, even when it comes to outlandish stories. After all, no one has yet been able to provide the world with absolutely irrefutable proof of alien life and visitation. At least . . . no one has been able to survive an attempt to do so."

"Yeah, we're going to have to come back to that point," I said.

She nodded, and continued. "I've been exposed to this world since I was little, I grew up with it. But my parents—well, adoptive parents—were both scientists. Especially my father. He was skeptical of everything that couldn't be measured. He engendered within me a similar skepticism. I don't take things at face value. Sure, I'll discuss them on my podcasts and in my books, but I really don't believe everything. However, just as science is unwilling to accept what can't be measured, it cannot by its own structure discount anything that cannot yet be measured."

"Meaning?"

"We know that there are billions upon billions of stars in this galaxy. We know for a fact that there are worlds orbiting many of those suns. We cannot state with any degree of scientific certainty that those worlds can or cannot support some form of life. We cannot state with any degree of scientific certainty that advanced life has not developed on any of those worlds. Or that these potential life forms have or have not developed technology allowing them to travel through the vast distances of space. Along the same lines, we cannot prove or disprove time travel or interdimensional travel. As our own science moves forward, we gradually—and reluctantly—reevaluate the limits of what we are able to believe because we can now prove it and what we are willing to believe because it now fits within the revised guidelines for possibility. In recent decades, with the marked decrease of the prejudice against quantum physics, we're seeing proof that our universe is much larger and more complex than we ever thought."

I nodded. "So far I'm absolutely sold on the statistical possibility of life in the galaxy. Drake's theory, right? Which was recently updated."

"Wow, look at you for knowing that."

I spread my hands. "What can I say?" What I didn't say was that Bug told me this a couple of hours ago.

"So, science can't take a serious stand against the possible existence of alien life or discount the possibility that we've been visited by aliens. That's point one. Point two is that there have been sightings and purported visitations throughout recorded history, and in virtually all world cultures. With me so far?"

"Yup."

"Point three, there are instances of radical leaps forward in human development, particularly in certain fields of science that are not yet explainable."

"The building of the pyramids," I ventured.

"Are you trying to be the teacher's pet?"

I said nothing. Was that a flirtatious twinkle in her eye when she said that?

"Point four. It is reasonable to postulate that nothing lasts forever, or to put it another way, everything breaks down. From plant life ending its life cycle to suns burning out. Manufactured items that are heavily used tend to ultimately break down because of that hard use. Point five is that vehicles built to cross the gulfs of space qualify as items being heavily used. We can expect that the demands of such travel might wear them out."

"You're building a case for crashes," I said.

"Exactly. If you look at the great exploration fleets of human history, you see that a percentage of all long-range fleets fail. That's true from the Phoenicians to Columbus to the NASA shuttle program. Friction, vibration, material fatigue, temperature changes, intended and unintended impacts, and other phenomena will degrade the internal and external integrity of any craft."

"Still with you," I said. "But if these craft crashed on earth and we've salvaged the wreckage, why don't we have a fleet of saucers . . . er, triangle ship thingies?"

"Ah, that's the right question and you get your first gold star."

I tried not to preen.

Junie said, "Let's look at it from the perspective of the target culture. If a wrecked Phoenician ship washed up on the shores of the Hudson River a couple of thousand years ago, how long would it take the Iroquois Indians to repair it and sail it?"

"Ah," I said. "But we're more educated than the Indians."

"We're more technologically advanced. The Iroquois were very smart—for their time and their place in their own history. Don't forget that the United States Constitution was based in part on the Iroquois system of government. However, they lived in a resource-rich environment that did not require the development of certain technologies."

"They didn't even have the wheel."

"They didn't need the wheel," she amended. "Now, spin that around, crash a World War II German Messerschmitt in Galileo's backyard. Or Newton's. These were clearly very smart men. Could they have repaired and flown that plane? What about a Los Angeles—class nuclear sub found damaged and drifting off the coast of Japan in, say, 1938. Or even Russia in 1944. They even had a fledging nuclear program by then. Could they have repaired it? Refloated it? Driven it?"

I sighed. "We can't fix the crashed UFOs because we're not smart enough."

"Oooh, and he loses his hard-won gold star."

"Wait—how?" I demanded.

"It isn't about being smart, Joe. Look how smart Ben Franklin was. And Da Vinci. Yet they would be flummoxed by any fifth-grader's entry in a school science fair."

"Not if it was explained to them," I said. "They could grasp the concept."

"If someone was there to explain the concept. And if they spoke the same language and used the idiomatic references particular to that era and location. What if that fifth-grader was from one of the regions of China where only five hundred people speak their dialect? The cultural differences would significantly decrease the likelihood of a meaningful exchange. Now step back and expand that communication gap. A theoretical physicist, born and raised in an affluent family in New England working at the Large Hadron Collider to a member from a Amazonian tribe whose people have never before held a conversation with an outsider. That tribesman may be the leader of his people, a shaman whose understanding of healing might be the result of ten thousand years of word-of-mouth training, and it might involve plants and compounds found nowhere else on earth. Tell me, Joe, where is the basis for understanding? How long before that tribesman can calibrate that collider?"

"You think the gap is that wide?"

She laughed. "I think the gap is about a million miles wider, and this is not a two-way conversation. The aliens are not guiding us through this step by step."

"Surely we're starting from a more viable point than a guy whose culture hasn't invented any machines. If a Roman chariot-maker found a bicycle wheel he might eventually make a breakthrough in his understanding of materials, design, and other areas. That's basic human reasoning. What if he found an antigrav hoverboard, like the ones in *Back to the Future*? There's no design corollary in his experience, none in any culture he would have exposure to even though Rome was the center of the civilized world. The item would sit there, maybe for centuries or even thousands of years before someone figured out how it works.

"Is that what's happening now?"

"To a degree" she said. "We've recovered so much from the crashed vehicles, and some of it we've been able to figure out. Basic things like chairs, control panels, stabilizers. Mostly stuff that's pure mechanics. However the deep science has been a lot more elusive because it doesn't fit any of the design philosophies we understand. Even when we reassemble some of the parts, we can only guess what the result is or does."

She bent forward and rested her elbows on her knees.

"Joe . . . tell me the truth," she said. "Is all of this just nonsense to you, or do you believe?"

"I don't know," I said. "I started the day with a hangover and a belief that we were alone in the universe. Since then a lot of very bad things have happened and most of them seem to be tied to a book I never heard of that's supposed to be filled with information about alien spacecraft. Maybe I'm inching my way toward believing, but right now I think I'm too scared and too confused to know what to believe."

Her eyes searched mine. "You're telling the truth."

"Yes," I said, "I am."

We sat there, looking into each other's eyes for almost a minute. The room grew quiet around us. Ghost looked from me to her to me, as if he was watching a Ping-Pong match, or following a conversation, but we weren't saying anything.

Before I could open a new doorway into the conversation, my cell rang again. Church.

I excused myself and stepped outside to stand among the flowers while I took the call.

"Tell me this isn't more bad news," I said.

Church said, "How often do I call you because I enjoy small talk?"

I sighed. "Okay . . . hit me."

"We received another video. Like the first it came from an untraceable source. And, like the first one, it shows the president," he said.

"What's the message this time?"

"Are you alone?"

"Yes."

"Then I'll send the video. In the meantime, what is the sit-rep there?"

"Miss Flynn is being cooperative. We can do the conference call as soon as you're ready."

"Watch the video first."

Church disconnected but my screen display told me I'd received a video. I plugged in an earphone so I could watch it silently.

It opened on a tight shot of the president's face, then pulled back to show him sitting on a nondescript chair against a blank wall. There was a small table placed between them on which was a small black box. The president said, "You must find the Majestic Black Book."

The image abruptly changed and the screen was filled with an image that was frighteningly familiar. A circle divided into concentric rings and sections. The diagram of pi. It was the same image that had been stamped onto the White House lawn, but it was not a picture of the lawn. This was a precisely drawn image, possibly a computer graphic.

"You must find the Majestic Black Book."

Blank faces, toneless voices. Then the president half turned and pressed a button on the top of the black box. Red numbers appeared on the face of the box. The display read 4320:00. Then the numbers changed.

4319:59

4319:58

A countdown. Seventy-two hours. Four thousand and twenty minutes, ticking away with silent, inevitable precision.

Simple.

Eloquent.

Terrifying.

"Holy shit," I said. Around me there were beautiful wildflowers and a sky bright with clean sunshine. The Chesapeake was blue perfection and the air was as clean as any I'd ever breathed.

But there was nothing right about any of it.

4319:51

Then a series of numbers ran across the bottom of the screen. I recognized the pattern. A radio frequency restricted for military use. The one we use for the most severe catastrophic events.

It was a very clear message. Get the book, broadcast the fact on that frequency . . . and keep a billion people from dying.

Clear. Simple.

Good Christ.

I hurried back inside.

Chapter Fifty-one

The Taiwan Strait, South China Sea
Sunday, October 20, 10:22 a.m. eastern standard time

The Seventh American Fleet was spread out across the dark waters of the Taiwan Strait. Thirty-eight of its sixty ships were moving into position, carrying with them more than half of the fleet's sixty thousand men and three hundred and fifty aircraft. Even without the rest of the fleet, this was a show of sea power that could conquer most nations on Earth. Some of the ships possessed the potential for more destructive power than all the bombs used in World War II, and that did not include the missiles with nuclear warheads.

Miles away, China sprawled, vast and powerful, secure in its personal power. Or, so it wanted the world to believe. Most of the civilian world believed that the Chinese military machine was only a half step behind America's, but that was a by-product of China's disinformation and misinformation campaigns. Whereas they could put a far larger army on the ground than anything America could hope to match, every military strategist in the world knew that such a ground battle would never be fought. Not directly. Not without intermediaries like the Koreans, the Vietnamese . . .

The real fight, if it ever came to it, would be with sea and air power.

The Seventh Fleet did not have an equal in China.

Not yet.

China had two aircraft carriers to America's eleven. Twenty-one destroyers to America's fifty. A defense budget of sixty billion compared with the U.S. commitment of over five hundred billion. The only area where they were nearly on a par was in the number of submarines. China claimed sixty-eight and America admitted to seventy-five.

This is what the generals and the admirals knew. This is what the chairman of the Joint Chiefs of Staff knew every bit as well as the chief of PLA General Staff.

Knowing this, seeing the demonstration of potentially overwhelming force riding the waves within fist strike of mainland China, it would be stupidity or madness or naïveté to put fighters in the air.

Philosophers have long suggested that all men are fools. Not all the time, but often enough. Else why would wars ever start?

The Shenyang J-15 is a carrier-based jet fighter aircraft based on the Russian-designed Sukhoi Su-33. Twenty of them crouched on the deck of the ROCS *Hu Yaobang,* the second of Chinese domestically built aircraft carriers. The jets were all primed, the pilots on deck, the flight and deck crews ready.

No one is certain—or will admit—who gave approval for Pilot Deng to climb into the cockpit of his J-15, belt in, fire up the engines, and launch his craft. No one on the deck crew tried to stop the action. It was as if they were all complicit, although in interviews following the incident, each man claimed to have received orders. They could not, however, remember who gave those orders, and there was no entry in any log that authorized the launch.

And yet Deng's J-15 leaped into the air and drove toward the Seventh Fleet.

Within minutes a swarm of Boeing F/A-18E/F Super Hornets had been scrambled and they screamed out to meet the J-15.

Although these two jet types had never before been pitted against one another in real combat, analysts theorized that the J-15 had superior aerodynamic capabilities to all other known fighter aircraft with the possible exception of the F-22. It had 10 percent greater thrust to weight ration and a 25 percent lower wing loading than the Super Hornets. In a one-to-one contest, it should have been a turkey shoot for the Chinese fighter.

But there was only one of them in the air, and five of the Hornets.

The J-15 picked the fight, everyone was clear on that. It flew straight at the Hornets, playing a crazy game of chicken, thrusters punching it to Mach 1 for no sane reason. The Hornets spread apart to let the fighter pass, but then they rolled and turned and followed because the Chinese pilot was still moving forward toward the fleet. Toward the lead carrier.

The game of chicken became a chase.

Politicians will argue for years over who fired the first shot. It is not even clear what Pilot Deng's intentions were. To buzz the tower on the carrier? To make a statement? To provoke a first shot?

Or to attack the carrier with missiles and a death run.

All calls went unanswered. Calls to the plane, calls to the Chinese carrier.

The gap between the J-15 and the fleet was decreasing at incredible speed. There was a stopping point, a line of sanity, where everything could have been dialed down. But that point came and went with a scream of jet engines. And then there was a second stopping point when the pursuit craft locked on to their targets and went weapons hot.

Even then, the J-15 could have peeled up and away and everyone would be able to breathe.

But that stopping point melted away.

"This is Bloodhound Five," said the lead Hornet pilot. "I have a sweet lock on the joker."

There was only a moment of hesitation from the carrier. "Bloodhound Five, you are cleared to fire."

"Bloodhound Five, fox three."

A simple code for the firing of an AIM-120D AMRAAM missile.

The missile burst from under the Hornet's wing and drove above the choppy sea toward its target.

It was exactly halfway there when the missile exploded.

The Hornet pilot said, "What—"

"We have a missile malfunction," said the pilot. "Bloodhound Five, fox three."

The second AMRAAM blew up so close to the Hornet that the shock buffeted the jet into a dangerous tilt. It took every ounce of the pilot's skill to keep from stalling.

"Missile system failure," he bellowed. "Disengaging."

Ahead of him, the J-15 was still closing on the carrier with the rest of the Bloodhound team in close support. The Hornets had to cut wide and change angle to keep the ships out of the line of any misfire.

Bloodhound Two and Three fired missiles.

The missiles exploded almost immediately.

Shock waves swatted the jets away and they wobbled like wounded birds, trying to regain a measure of control.

Suddenly the J-15's angle of approach made a radical change. The pilot peeled up and away and as soon as he had a clear line of escape he hit the afterburners and scorched his way out of there. In seconds he was a dot on the horizon, heading away from the fleet.

"What the hell was that all about?"

The radar man from the carrier cut in. "Bloodhound Squadron be advised, there is a second bogey coming low and fast out of the—"

But the pilot of Bloodhound Five saw it before the radar man could finish his sentence. It moved in an arrow-straight line, coming back along the path the J-15 had taken, but moving many times faster.

Many times.

"Holy moly look at that mother *move*."

The T-craft closed the distance from the horizon to the fleet in seconds.

"He's clocking Mach fifteen," cried Bloodhound Three.

But he was wrong.

The T-craft cut through the center of the fleet at Mach 20, shooting between a destroyer and a cruiser, pulling behind it an air mass that rocked both ships. It bore down on the carrier too fast for any practical reaction. There was only time to cut in the collision sirens as the gray mass of it hurtled toward a certain impact.

And then it turned.

At Mach 20, it turned.

In its own length it went from a lateral glide path to a straight vertical rise. A ninety-degree turn. It rose one thousand feet into the air and turned again.

Another ninety-degree turn. As precise as if written onto the moment with a ruler.

As thousands of men watched—through binoculars, goggles, portholes, the windscreens of jets, and with naked eyes—the T-craft became a blurred dot and then vanished.

Over mainland China.

Bloodhound Five opened his mouth to make a report, but any words he might have said died on his tongue, replaced by a single word.

"God . . ."

Chapter Fifty-two

Turkey Point Lighthouse, Elk Neck State Park
Cecil County, Maryland
Sunday, October 20, 10:24 a.m.

"What's wrong?" Junie asked as I came back into the house. "God, you look like you just saw a ghost."

"That would be a comforting break, actually."

I sat down and poured myself some hot tea, stared into the cup, and didn't drink any of it. Ghost, roused by what he thought was the mention of his name, whined to be petted. I ran my fingers through his fur and stared into the middle of the air, hoping that answers would appear out of nowhere.

They didn't. What a surprise.

"Joe?" murmured Junie, concern in her voice.

I rubbed my eyes. "Things have gotten worse."

"Can you tell me?"

"I think we'd better leave that to my boss. I'm going to video conference him in now, along with a couple of other people from my team."

"Okay," she said dubiously. She fluffed her hair, which did not make any appreciable change—it was just as wild and lovely—and smoothed her skirt.

I hit some keys on the MindReader keypad and suddenly we had a very weird little party. The large computer screen was broken into several smaller windows, each filled with a high-res 3-D image. Mr. Church, Bug, Dr. Hu, and Rudy Sanchez—who I was gratified to see was at the Warehouse and no longer on his toilet at home.

"Wow," said Junie Flynn. "I feel like I'm on a game show."

The big guy took the lead. "Ms. Flynn . . . my name is Mr. Church. Before I make introductions, I need to know if you are willing to cooperate with us in this matter."

"I am," she said, "but only as long as I feel that I'm doing the right thing. I'll tell you straight up front that I don't trust most government agencies and I have good reasons for that. If I think you're manipulating me or trying to pull a fast one, then we're done. You can arrest me or whatever."

Mr. Church gave her a small, faint smile. "That is acceptable."

But Junie wasn't finished. "I negotiated a consultant's fee with Joe. He's agreed to pay me what I asked."

Church nodded but did not ask what that price was. I saw Rudy's eyebrow lift a little; he must have caught some nuance to her tone. I gave him a tiny nod. Hu seemed to have recovered from his earlier shock and now contrived to look bored. Bug was clearly in love.

"You gave us your conditions, Ms. Flynn," said Church, "now here are mine. I expect that the content of this conversation is to be kept confidential. It is not to be talked about, written about, or otherwise shared except with my permission. Agreed?"

"Agreed."

"The names of any organizations I choose to share with you, and the identities of the people involved in this matter fall under that agreement of secrecy."

"Agreed," said Junie. "Do you need me to sign anything?"

Church shook his head. "I've found that a signature on an agreement of secrecy is no guarantee of anything other than a basic ability to write one's name. Either your word is good or it's not. From what I have heard about you, I believe you to be a person of integrity."

That put a smile on Junie's face. Mine, too. Church was actually being mildly charming. The scoundrel.

"Are you going to tell me who you people are?' asked Junie.

"You won't have heard of us," said Church. "I am the director of the Department of Military Sciences, the DMS. We are a small agency that operates under executive order. We are answerable to no other agency within the government. We are not answerable to Congress. Does that disturb you?"

"Yes."

"It disturbs me, too," said Church. "There should be no need for an agency like ours to exist. However the world is not a calm or safe place, and there are many people who would like to see it burn. Just as there are people who would like to see everyone in chains—real chains or those created by political, religious, ideological, informational, or theological manipulation. I am not one of those people. I employ people who share my view of fairness, freedom, and justice. Does this sound corny to you?"

"Actually," she said, "it doesn't."

Church gave her a small nod and another small smile, and I had a totally irrational flash of jealousy. I felt as if all three of my inner personalities suddenly looked askance at me.

"Very well," continued Church, "let me introduce the others who are working on this problem." His introductions were brief and moderately nondescript. "Bug, head of computer division. Dr. William Hu, chief of science and research. Dr. Rudy Sanchez, a psychiatrist who consults on matters related to trauma."

There was a very brief flurry of greetings. Hu as dismissive, Bug was obsequious, and Rudy was charming. No one was paving new ground.

"For the most part these men are participating as observers," explained Church. "Captain Ledger and I will ask most of the questions, but having the others here trims down the time we'd waste sharing your remarks with them."

Junie took a breath, gave me a brave smile, and nodded to the wall of faces.

Then Church hit her with the problem. He told her about the abduction. He showed her the videos—the original one and the second video I'd just watched. I studied Junie's body as the information and images slammed into her. She straightened and stiffened and all the humor drained out of her face, leaving her drawn and deathly pale.

"Oh my God," she breathed.

"Indeed," said Church. "Now you know what we know, and you can see why Captain Ledger arrived unannounced and in such an unorthodox manner. He probably did not mention that he was also attacked this morning by four men who claimed to be government agents and who subsequently vanished without a trace. Someone else knows what's going on and they've already made a move to obstruct our investigation. We have no clue who they are or what their motives might be."

Junie glanced at me. "You didn't tell me you were in a fight."

"It wasn't much of a fight," I said.

From her expression I could tell that she didn't believe me.

"You're not hurt?"

"Didn't even get my hair mussed."

"If we can stay on point," interrupted Church. In his own little screen, Hu was making a gagging sound. Rudy looked amused.

"Yes," said Junie. "This is all . . . just so much so soon."

"I wish we could offer time for you to get up to speed," said Church, "but we don't have that luxury. We need to know about the Majestic Black Book."

"How much do you already know?"

"Some," he admitted, "but why not give us your take on it."

She nodded, thought about it, then dug in. "Joe admitted that he doesn't know a lot about UFOs and the related conspiracies. What about the rest of you?"

"I know a lot," said Bug, beaming.

"So do I," said Hu sourly, "but I think this is all a waste of time."

"I don't know a tremendous amount," said Rudy, "but I believe we've been visited. However, I never heard of the Black Book before today. Neither, I believe, has Dr. Hu or Joe. So, please don't assume any useful knowledge on our part."

Church said nothing and when it was clear he was not going to comment, Junie said, "Then let me start with some things everyone needs to know." She took a breath. "It started with a group called Majestic 12—or MJ-12. That was a group of scientists, government officials, military officers formed by a secret executive order from President Harry S. Truman. The initial agenda for MJ-12 was to investigate the recovery of the UFO that crashed north of Roswell, New Mexico. The government denies that MJ-12 ever existed, however UFOlogists uncovered a collection of documents in 1984 that state that the group was formed based on a recommendation by Dr. Vannevar Bush and Secretary of Defense James Forrestal. In 1985, another document mentioning MJ-12, dating to 1954, was found in a search at the National Archives. The FBI naturally attacked these documents as fabrications and continues to deny their authenticity."

"But you don't accept that denial?" asked Rudy.

"Hardly. Since the eighties, thousands of pages of other government documents mentioning MJ-12 have leaked out. The preponderance of evidence shows that there is an ongoing government cover-up of the existence of UFOs and the recovery of technologies from crash sites. According to these papers, the members of MJ-12 were Rear Admiral Roscoe H. Hillenkoetter, who was the first director of the CIA; Dr. Vannevar Bush, who chaired the wartime Office of Scientific Research and Development, which was the predecessor of the National Defense Research Committee. Dr. Bush also set up and chaired the postwar Joint Research and Development Board (JRDB) and then the Research and Development Board (RDB) and was president of Carnegie Institute in Washington, D.C. Then there was James Forrestal, the secretary of the Navy and the first secretary of Defense. When he died, he was replaced on MJ-12 by General Walter Bedell Smith, who was the second director of the CIA."

"Wow," I said.

She began ticking the others off on her fingers. "Next you have General Nathan Twining, who headed Air Materiel Command at Wright-Patterson AFB, and who was later the Air Force chief of staff from 1953 to 1957, and then the chairman of Joint Chiefs of Staff from 'fifty-seven to 'sixty-one. General Hoyt Vandenberg, who directed the Central Intelligence Group in 'forty-six and 'forty-seven and was Air Force chief of staff from 'forty-eight through 1953. General Robert M. Montague, a noted guided-missile expert and commander of the nuclear Armed Forces Special Weapons Center, Sandia Base. Dr. Jerome Hunsaker, an aeronautical engineer from MIT. Rear Admiral Sidney Souers, first director of Central Intelligence Group and first executive secretary of National Security Council. Gordon Gray: secretary of the Army and a top intelligence and national security expert as well as a CIA psychological strategy board. He was also the National Security advisor from 1958 through 'sixty-one. Harvard astronomer Dr. Donald Menzel, who was also a cryptologist during World War II and a security consultant to CIA and NSA. Dr. Detlev Bronk, a medical physicist and aviation physiologist who went on to chair the National Academy of Sciences, National Research Council, and become president of Johns Hopkins and Rockefeller universities. And last, but not least, Dr. Lloyd Berkner, a physicist, radio expert, and the executive secretary of Bush's JRDB."

"Again I say . . . wow."

Dr. Hu looked like he'd rather be arranging his sock drawer than listening to any of this. He kept rolling his eyes like a thirteen-year-old girl.

Junie shook her head. "The point is that they were only the top level of administration. Advisors more than players. They never got their hands dirty beyond writing policy for the government on how it would handle UFOs and alien technology. These are the people who created the levels of misinformation and disinformation. They created Project Blue Book and commissioned the Condon Report, both of which were never intended for anything else except to present to the public a fabricated message that UFOs don't exist. These men paved the way for generations of credible witnesses to be discredited, humiliated, maybe even killed. They are the ones who created the image of the aluminum-foil-hat-wearing delusionists who claim to have seen little green men. And yet all along they knew the truth. The MJ-12 documents include diagrams and records of tests on UFOs, memos on measures to prevent leakage of information, and descriptions of the president's statements about UFO-related issues."

"And they keep that truth from everyone?" suggested Rudy.

"Not from everyone," said Junie. "There are hundreds, perhaps thousands of people who work for some aspect of the part of the defense industry that exists to exploit these alien technologies. Some people believe that a lot of the R and D is done by private companies in order to keep it outside of government oversight and to smooth the way for plausible deniability."

"Absolutely," agreed Bug. "I started a pattern search for people and businesses who fit this kind of profile. I've . . . um . . . been trolling your Web site for keywords to use as search arguments."

"Fine by me," said Junie.

I said, "And M3? Where does that come in?"

"They are the ones doing the actual work," she said. "MJ-12 is the bureaucracy, but the Majestic Three are the true research and development people. They're called 'governors,' and each one handles a specific area. Acquisitions, Research, and Development. The head of Acquisitions is generally the only nonscientist of the group, though occasionally the governor in charge of Development is more of an industrialist than an actual scientist. He or she hires scientists to develop the products that come out of the Research."

"How do you know this?"

Junie paused and drummed her fingers on her knee for a long time before answering. "I . . . had a source."

"A source?" asked Church. "What kind of source?"

"Someone who was on the inside," she said evasively.

" 'Was'?" asked Hu, jumping on that.

"Was," confirmed Junie, but she didn't immediately explain. "My source was involved in the active R and D on recovered artifacts. That research required that he consult generations of notes that had been entered into the Black Book. Interesting to note that no one ever called it the Black Book, of course, and it was absolutely forbidden to mention words like 'alien' or 'UFO' at any of the labs or testing facilities. It all had to seem very normal, like they were reverse-engineering a captured MIG or some piece of Chinese spy technology."

"Which it probably was," muttered Hu, but everyone ignored him.

"All the research and development fell under one umbrella, though," continued Junie. "They called it 'the Project.' "

Church asked, "Your source was on the inside of this Project?"

"Very deep inside," she said. "He was a senior researcher and designer. He led one of the most important teams, though like most of the senior scientists he consulted on several projects because so many research lines overlapped. They had a lot of these experimental lines going at once. Radical engine design, artificial intelligence, human-computer interfaces, organic computer memory, biological hybridization, even some work on psychic enhancement."

" 'Psychic'?" echoed Hu, smiling. "Please."

"Doctor," said Church quietly. The smile vanished from Hu's face.

"Yes, psychic," said Junie with a bit of frost. "They wanted to develop pilots who were completely integrated with their craft, and who could think their commands instead of using control panels or joysticks. That was a big part of the Project. It was way more practical than the eye-head controlled operations we use now. It would have been the most important military development since the invention of the airplane. Maybe more so.

It would be an incredible leap forward. A quantum jump forward in terms of the arms race."

"How so?" I asked.

"The human mind is so much faster than a computer," said Junie. "Not in data recall, of course, but in reaction time, decision-making, intuition, and creative reactions to critical encounters."

"How much information did your source share with you?" asked Church.

"Yeah," said Bug, "it sounds like a lot."

Junie glanced at me and then down at her hands, which were folded nervously in her lap. "It was a lot."

"Did he write any of it down?" asked Bug.

"He had notebooks," she said, nodding almost absently. "Over a period of fourteen years he managed to copy every single entry in the Majestic Black Book."

We all came to point like a pack of birddogs.

"Ms. Flynn," said Church very quietly, "where are those notes?"

She raised her head and met his eyes. "Destroyed," she said. "They're all gone. My source was in a car accident and the notes were incinerated."

The silence was crushing. I felt like I'd been hoisted up into the sunlight and then dropped right back down into the slime.

Rudy said something under his breath. Bug looked away; Hu gave a triumphant smile as if this was the kind of news he wanted. The man was deranged.

But Church continued to study Junie.

"What exactly happened to your source?" he asked. "How was it that all his research notes were with him when he had his accident? That seems strange to me."

Junie nodded. "They found out that he was duplicating the Black Book. When he realized that they knew, he gathered together everything he had, notebooks, printouts, drawings, flash drives, all of it and took off. This was in Virginia, in a lab in Arlington. My . . . source . . . tried to make it all the way to D.C."

"What did he hope to accomplish there?" I asked.

"Exposure," she said. "There was an important bill being debated in the Senate. It was all over the news. That jobs bill a couple of years ago.

My source wanted to get to the Capitol building and . . . I don't know . . . crash the Senate."

"The security would have stopped him."

"He was terrified, he didn't know where else to go. He thought that if he yelled out the right names right there, with all those congressmen and all that press, then maybe he could force his way into the public eye. He thought that creating a media sensation would keep him safe long enough to get the truth out there."

"Guy sounds like a fucking idiot," said Hu.

Junie gave him a withering look. "He was naive. About that kind of thing . . . he was very naive. That's how they hooked him in the first place. They played on his idealism. They sold him on a story that he was working on a project that would help save America and maybe even prevent future wars. Considering what he was working on, that seemed reasonable. It still could be, or would be in there was a genuine public welfare in the minds of those bastards in M3."

"How so?" asked Rudy. "What were they working on?"

"In simplest terms they were trying to re-create the engine of the crashed UFO. That engine is enormously powerful, capable of flying all those light-years across space. My source was told that if this power could be tapped and controlled, then it could be the basis for an entirely new kind of clean, renewable energy."

"Oh, wow," said Hu, "a cliché."

"Doc," I said, "if you make one more crack I'm going to beat the living shit out of you. Tell me if I'm joking."

"That's enough," barked Church, though I don't know if he was directing that at Hu, me, or both of the yapping dogs.

In the ensuing silence, Church focused all his considerable personality on Junie.

"Ms. Flynn," he said, "we know that your source never made it to Congress. What happened to him?"

"They got him," she said.

"Who got him?" asked Church. "Specifically who?"

"The Closers."

"And they are?"

"Most people call them the Men in Black."

Chapter Fifty-three

The Harbor District
Baltimore, Maryland
Sunday, October 20, 10:25 a.m.

The black Yukon drove at a sedate speed past the long double chain-link fence that bordered the street side of Cobbler Records Storage. At the corner, they made a turn and drove away, tucked into traffic, hiding in plain sight.

"Okay," said Aldo, "so that's where it is. We could have seen it on the Ghost Box. There are pigeon drones all over the place."

Tull shrugged. "It's always better to put eyes on something. Hard to tell about architecture and building materials from a video feed, and the building plans are no longer on public record."

"Church pulled them?"

"He made them disappear," said Tull.

"Driving past the place is a piss-poor substitute for a blueprint."

"Not always," said Tull. "And not in this case."

Chapter Fifty-four

Turkey Point Lighthouse, Elk Neck State Park
Cecil County, Maryland
Sunday, October 20, 10:28 a.m.

Dr. Hu said, "So you're telling us that Will Smith and Tommy Lee Jones abducted the president of the United States."

Junie gave him an arctic glare. The fact that she was taking a quick dislike to Hu made me like her even more.

"Yes, Doctor," she said icily, "we've all seen the movies, ha-ha, but in the real world the Closers are anything but wise-cracking heroes protecting us from the scum of the universe."

"Then who do you think they are?" asked Church.

"They claim to be government agents."

And suddenly I thought about the four goons I met today. Four men in black suits claiming to be government agents. Church's eyes flicked toward mine for a millisecond. He was right there with me.

"They show up after significant UFO sightings or crashes," said Junie. "That's been happening since Roswell. They harass and even sometimes threaten witnesses."

"What kinds of threats?" asked Rudy.

"It varies," she said, crossing her arms under her breasts. "Sometimes they threaten to arrest people on the grounds of national security. Sometimes they hint that 'accidents' might happen if the witness doesn't stop talking. Sometimes their threats are very direct."

Rudy frowned. "Threatening physical harm?"

"Threatening to kill witnesses. Or the families of witnesses."

"Has anyone actually been harmed?" Rudy asked.

"There are several cases in there about people who have been brutally beaten. Some people have gone missing. And there have been a number of unexplained or unexpected deaths of witnesses. Car accidents, heart attacks, cancer, viruses, street muggings . . . all sorts of things."

"Bug?" murmured Church.

"Already on it. Compiling a list now."

"Have the Closers ever taken a run at you?" I asked.

She shook her head. "I've never actually witnessed anything. Wish I could say otherwise. God, I'd give anything to know . . . to really and truly know."

"I thought you were a believer."

"The Pope believes in Jesus," she said, "but I bet he'd like to actually meet him."

Everyone smiled at that. Even Hu.

"True," I admitted.

"Who do you think the Closers are, Ms. Flynn?" asked Church. "And what do you think they're trying to accomplish?"

"I have theories, but that's all they are. They claim to be from the Air Force, the CIA, or the FBI. Andrew Meyers, who used to be a major voice in UFO research, believed that these men are really members of the Air Force Special Activities Center, based in Fort Belvoir, Virginia, and working under operational authority of Air Force Intelligence Command centered at Kelly Air Force Base in Texas."

"Bug," said Church.

"On it," Bug replied.

"This guy, Meyers," asked Rudy, "you said he used to be a major voice. Did he die?"

"No. He retired from UFO research. No one seems to know why."

Before anyone could say anything, Bug said, "On it."

"You said that this was Meyers's theory. What's yours?"

She said, "I think the Closers work for Majestic Three."

"Which could connect what happened this morning in Baltimore to this case," said Church.

Junie turned suddenly toward me. "The men who attacked you were Closers? How come you didn't say that?"

"I didn't know who they were," I protested. "I still don't. As much as it pains me to say it, Junie, there are a lot of people who would like to see me dead."

Barely under his breath, Hu said, "And some of them work with you."

"Ms. Flynn," interrupted Rudy. "What exactly happened to your 'source'?"

"He was in a car accident on the George Washington Parkway. His car was run off the road into an oncoming truck. He and his wife were both burned to death in the wreck."

"Whoa," I said, "there's a pretty significant median between opposing lanes."

"Not down by the foot of the Mount Vernon Trail, off the ramp from the Curtis Memorial Parkway," said Junie, and it took me a moment to recall that part of the highway.

I nodded. "Okay, but that's a dangerous road, though, accidents happen all the time."

Junie gave another shrug.

"So," said Rudy slowly, "it's your belief that your source systematically made a copy of the Black Book, and when M3 found out about it they sent these Closers to arrange a fatal traffic accident."

"Yes."

Bug asked, "Do you have any idea who might have a copy of the Black Book? I mean . . . Do you know the names of the current members of M3?"

"Or any previous members?" I added.

Junie laughed. "I've spent the last ten years of my life trying to figure that out. I have a list of about a hundred possibles. A lot of those names are going to be on the list of industrialists profiting from radical technologies your Mr. Bug is compiling."

"She called me Mr. Bug," said Bug, apparently to himself.

"Do any names stand out for you?" asked Church, and I knew that this was the key question. Church asked it casually because we didn't yet know how far we could trust Junie Flynn, or how deep her true knowledge ran. If she was, after all this, just a conspiracy theory nut, then any guess she made could be worthless. Or, if she was as well informed as she claimed, then she might have what we needed. Either way we didn't want to spook her. This all had to be done right the first time.

Junie thought about it and then gave Church a careful nod. "There are seven living people that are on my 'most likely' list. They are Ernest Foster Gould of Gould Cybersystems; Charles Osgood Harrington III, Harrington Aeronautics, Harrington-Cheney Petrochemicals, Harrington and Mercer Fuel Oil Company; Rebecca Milhaus, president of Brantley-Milhaus-Cooper Aviation and wife of H. Carlton Milhaus, CEO of Milhaus and Berk Publishing; Howard Shelton, owner and CEO of Shelton Aeronautics; Reese Sunderland of Sunderland Biological and Sunderland Integrated Systems; Joan Bell-Pullman of MicroTek International; and David Robinette of Robinette Development Associates."

My breath caught in my throat and I cut a sharp look at Church. All of those names were well known to us. Laboratories, computer systems, and factories of every single one of them had been targeted by the cyberattacks. Church gave me a tiny shake of his head. For now he didn't want that information shared with Junie Flynn.

I think she caught something though, because her eyes darted from me to Church; however, Church asked her, "Is it your belief that one or more of these people are members of M3?"

Junie shook her head. "No, I think that all the current members of M3 are probably on that list, and maybe one or two former members."

"Please explain."

"It's circular logic," she said. "In almost any industry, most companies develop products in a kind of dead heat. Company A might bring out a new widget that seems to be ahead of the market, but looking back you can see that it's a natural step in the progression of research and development. Companies B and C tear that product apart to find what their own R and D missed, but they're so close behind already that they can get a competing product out in the same calendar year. Look at the cell phone business and you see what I mean. The Samsung-Apple court case is a prime example."

Church nodded.

"But every once in a while someone comes along with a product that is a radical jump," continued Junie. "It's so innovative that it's freaky, and even if you take it apart and look at the science you can't backtrack it to any kind of developmental process. It appears to be the result of an intuitive design leap."

"Right," I said. "So?"

"So, sometimes it's only that. Someone has a dream about a new kind of widget and it's nothing more than a true flash of intuition. However, the seven people on this list have done this time and again. They're not doing it in ways that clearly build off each other's research. The products are in totally different areas, as if they have agreed not to compete with one another. That's not normal, and those design jumps definitely aren't. An intuitive leap is really rare. It might make a fortune for a company, that's happened plenty of times, but it's usually going to be in a single area. Even if that kicks off a new avenue of design philosophy, it's still a single line. The people on this list seem to be able to come up with patents for radical jumps in a lot of different areas of technology. Military and private sector stuff. Big jumps, where there's no backtrack at all. Nothing."

"Unless," I said, feeding her the prompt she wanted.

"Unless he's drawing on another source," she confirmed.

"Like the Majestic Black Book?" said Church.

"Right. It's more than just a catalog of parts. The Black Book has measurements, weights, schematics, information on material composition, stuff like that. It also has a complete list of the ACL."

"Isn't that a ligament in the knee?" I asked.

"Alien Code Language," explained Bug. "Don't you ever watch Nat Geo?"

"I watch the *Dog Whisperer*," I added. Beside me, Ghost whuffed at the mention of that show. Cesar Millan was a god to him.

Junie smiled at me. "There are symbols on most of the T-craft and on all the parts recovered from crashes. They look like the pictograms you see on Egyptian tombs. A language based on images rather than letters or words."

"All of that's in the Black Book?" asked Rudy.

"Yes. That and a catalog of all the parts. Not just from Roswell, but from every crash. There have been a number of them. Kecksburg, Tunguska, Rendlesham, other places. Some estimates say that there have been as many as sixty crashes, some of them centuries ago, maybe longer than that."

Bug said, "I heard there was a black market for stuff from crashes."

Hu made a face of complete contempt.

"There is," said Junie. "My source said that occasionally the governor of Acquisitions would bring in a brand-new piece, something obtained from unnamed sources. My source believed that M3 was purchasing or bartering these D-type components."

"If this crap really existed," said Hu belligerently, "why the hell would anyone ever part with any of it? That doesn't make sense."

"Two hammers," said Junie.

"What?"

"If you have two hammers and no saw, wouldn't you consider trading with someone else who had a saw?"

Hu glared at her, but he didn't attack the logic. It was too sound. He sulked instead.

There was a brief pause as we all considered this.

Church said, "Could you put these seven names in order of most likely, by your estimation?"

"No. I keep rearranging that list, but I really don't have it locked down other than I think they're all involved in some way. Some of them are old enough to have been governors who have since stepped down."

"David Robinette is pretty young," said Hu. "I've seen him at trade shows. He's not even thirty-five. And he's no scientist."

"He's one of my votes of the current governor of Acquisitions." She shrugged. "He's a wildcard, but his family has long-standing ties to Defense Department contracts, and he goes missing for long periods of time. No one knows where."

"You think he's on buying trips?" I asked.

She nodded.

"One more thing," said Church, and he hit the key to bring up the picture taken by the helicopter early this morning. "What can you tell me about this image?"

Junie didn't even blink. "It's a crop circle—though it looks like it's on a lawn somewhere."

"Do you recognize the pattern?"

"Of course. It's the pi crop circle, like the one that appeared in a field in Wroughton, Wiltshire, England, in June 2008. But this isn't that one. Where was this taken?"

"This appeared on the White House lawn at approximately the same time the president disappeared."

Junie stared at him. She was surprised, but not totally shocked.

"There seem to be a lot of theories as to what crop circles are," said Church, "including strong evidence that many of them are faked."

"Sure. Doug Bower and Dave Chorley have made a bunch of the ones in England. There are companies that pay to have them made with their logos as advertising gimmicks. There have been over ten thousand of them since the early seventies. All over the world, too, and probably eighty or ninety percent of them are faked."

"Not all?" asked Rudy.

"You tell me," she challenged. "Did a couple of pranksters put that one on the White House lawn?"

No one answered that.

"What are they?" Rudy asked.

"No one knows for sure, but when you see something like this one, I think that the point is pretty clear."

"Tell us," encouraged Church.

"Communication," said Junie. "Pi is a universal constant. Pi is math, and math is immutable. It will be the same here as it will be across the galaxy. Ten plus ten equals twenty no matter where you are. Same goes for, say, geometry? A circle is always a circle and its circumference is always calculated the same way no matter where you are. The same holds true for any other geometric figure like triangles, squares, or rectangles." Her eyes shifted to Hu. "Isn't that right, Doctor?"

Hu grunted something unintelligible.

Church nodded and gave Junie a pleasant smile. "Thank you. Bug, do you have enough to begin a comprehensive pattern search on the names Ms. Flynn provided?"

"More than enough."

"I've run those kinds of searches," said Junie. "Hundreds of them, with all kinds of software, but I hit too many walls, and there are simply so many variables."

Bug laughed. So did I.

She looked from him to me. "What?"

"We have a pretty spiffy computer," I said.

"I've used university networked supercomputers and—"

"And we have a pretty spiffy computer," I repeated.

She stared at me, her eyes imploring me to explain but she didn't ask. She understood that I couldn't. After a few moments she nodded, then turned to Church.

"Mr. Church," she said, "this—all of this—is really about stopping a disaster? About saving the country?"

"Our country, England, and a good part of Africa."

"And you believe that if you get the Black Book you'll really be able to do that?"

"It's our hope and belief, yes."

She sat there, chewing on her lip, fingers twisting nervously in her lap, clearing agonizing over a very difficult decision.

"Maybe . . . ," she began hesitantly, "Maybe there's an easier way . . ."

Mr. Church opened his mouth to ask what she meant.

Suddenly the MindReader screen went blank and then dissolved into the static of white noise.

"Ah, crap," I said, reaching for the controls.

"What's wrong?" asked Junie.

"Looks like we lost the satellite connection. Damn it." I tapped my earbud. "Bug, I need a new—"

There was static in my ear, too.

"Joe?" asked Junie, a note of doubt creeping into her voice.

I pulled my cell.

The display told me that there was no service.

Junie looked down at the screen and then up at me. "Joe, what's going on?" Doubt was turning into the first faint traces of alarm.

Before I could say anything there was a knock on the door.

"Must be my guys," I said, rising and crossing the living room to reach for the knob. "Radio must be out on the Black Hawk, too."

But as I turned the knob I heard Ghost begin to growl. I told him to be quiet as I pulled the door open.

Two men stood there.

Big men. Strangers.

Both of them were dressed in black.

Both of them were pointing guns.

Chapter Fifty-five

The Warehouse
Baltimore, Maryland
Sunday, October 20, 10:37 a.m.

Mr. Church sat in Joe Ledger's leather chair and stared at the blank square of screen that moments before had held the image of Joe Ledger and Junie Flynn. Now all it showed was static.

"Bug?" he snapped.

"Working on it."

"Work faster."

Rudy Sanchez sat on the other side of Joe Ledger's desk, fists balled in his lap.

Dr. Hu smiled down from the wall-mounted plasma screen. "Ledger probably spilled his coffee on the keyboard," he suggested.

"Stop being a child," said Rudy, and it shut Hu up as surely as a slap across the face.

In the lower corner of the big screen was the digital clock that Church had started after receiving the second video.

4316:12

4316:11

4316:10

"Bug," he said again.

"This is weird, boss. We got a total communications dead zone that extends in a perfect circle around the lighthouse."

Hu looked suddenly interested. "A jammer?"

"A mother of a jammer. It's even killing the satellite uplink."

Rudy frowned. "I thought Joe once told me that a jammer couldn't do that."

"It can't," said Hu. "C'mon, Bug, you're reading it wrong."

Bug flashed information onto the screens from half a dozen sources, including a Defense Department satellite and two general communications satellites. "Yeah? Then you show me how to read it right."

Hu stared at the data. So did Church and Rudy.

Church snatched up his cell phone and hit a speed dial. "Gus. I want Echo Team wheels up for Turkey Point Lighthouse right now. Make it happen. Captain Ledger is in trouble."

4315:55

4315:54

Chapter Fifty-six

Turkey Point Lighthouse, Elk Neck State Park
Cecil County, Maryland
Sunday, October 20, 10:38 a.m.

"Oh God," cried Junie.

"Get inside," said the taller of the two men.

There was a black SUV parked on the lawn halfway between Junie's front door and the helicopter. A third man stood by the car. There was no movement at all from the chopper, and that did not make me feel good. Hector and the others should have signaled me. They should be out in the field and up in the faces of these three goons.

They weren't. The chopper sat there as silent and cold as a dead bug.

Junie touched my shoulder from behind and whispered, "Joe . . ."

Behind me, Ghost continue to utter a low growl of obvious intent.

One of the two men in the doorway shifted his pistol from my heart to Ghost's head. The other one looked me in the eye. The gun he held was not an automatic. It was square and clunky, with four curved contacts at the business end. A microwave pulse pistol, an MPP. It was a scary-looking piece of hardware and it was pointed at my dog.

"You call the play," said the man.

I half turned. "Ghost, ease down."

Ghost stopped growling and sat. The man turned the MPP away from Ghost and pointed it at me, and the man who'd spoken gave me a nod, pleased that I'd made the sensible choice.

We'd see about that. "Ease down," in the private and coded language I'd created when I trained Ghost, did not mean what these guys apparently thought it meant. Misunderstandings can be very useful.

"Get inside," the man said again. He was the leader of this team. Unlike the clown act that had attacked me on the street in Baltimore, these guys were younger, tougher looking, and dressed in black battle-dress uniforms. No insignia of any kind. No rank. Everything was black, and their trousers were neatly bloused into black boots. They wore gun belts with extra magazines. They had white wires curling behind their ears and small wire mikes hovering at the corners of their mouths. The leader was a light-skinned black man, the guy behind him was white. They both wore identical mirrored sunglasses, right out of every cheap 1970s highway cop flick you ever saw. Neither of them was smiling. Mr. Black raised his barrel from my heart to my head, the four metal contacts were aimed right between my eyes.

Despite the exotic guns, the rational part of my mind wanted me to believe that these were a couple of working stiffs from the FBI or NSA and that we'd get this all sorted out as soon as we swapped IDs, and then we'd all laugh about it over tea.

The rational part of my mind was sometimes a fucking idiot.

The rest of me knew who and what these guys were, even if I hesitated using the word.

Closers.

Jesus.

I backed up with my arms wide to shield Junie but also guide her backward. Ghost rose and backed up, too, as the Closers herded us inside.

When we were all inside, Mr. Black looked past me. "Are you Miss June Cassandra Flynn?"

"I—" she began, but I cut in.

"Hey, let's dial this down, fellows. I'm a federal agent. Please identify yourself and your reason for being here." I pitched it in my best officer's voice. Flat and authoritative.

Mr. Black and Mr. White turned their mirrored glasses toward me for a microsecond.

"Shut up," said Mr. White.

"Look, chief, I think there's been a big misunderstanding here," I said, still keeping it in neutral. "If this is a jurisdictional thing, then we can get it straightened out. Who cut your orders for this pickup?"

"Raise your hands and do not interfere," said Mr. Black.

"I can show you my identification," I said. "NSA. We're on the same—"

Mr. Black lashed out with the barrel of his pistol and slammed me across the face. A line of heat exploded along my cheek and the force spun me around and dropped me to one knee. Ghost barked and started to go for the man, but even with my eggs scrambled I knew that they'd kill my dog and then me. Which would leave Junie alone and probably the target of the next Shot. I lunged sideways and hooked my arm around Ghost's throat.

"No!" I yelled, shouting it to anyone and everyone.

"Don't shoot!" shrieked Junie. She darted forward, as if she wanted to put herself between the guns and us. Mr. White stepped toward her and jammed the hard metal points of his gun against her breastbone.

"Get the fuck back," he said in a deadly voice.

Junie gasped and stepped back, bumping into me where I knelt. Ghost strained against my arm.

"No," I begged in a fierce whisper. "Don't."

There was no shot. Not yet.

"Control that dog," said Mr. White. "Do it now."

"Ghost," I pleaded. "Ease down, ease down."

He trembled in my arms, but despite his primal need to defend the pack leader, he eased down. Just as he was taught. There was blood on his shoulder and I touched my face. My fingers came away slick and red. I didn't think my cheek was broken, though. Small mercies. The gun may look plastic, but it hit like steel. I dearly wanted to take it away from him and shove it up his ass.

After a moment I climbed to my feet. Mr. Black's gun followed me, always pointing at my heart. There was a small, cruel smile on his mouth. "Stand there and shut the fuck up. When we want you to speak we'll ask you a question. If you open your mouth before then, I'll put you down."

I raised my hands, palm out, head high, and unthreatening. Whoever these guys were, they played in a whole different league from the clowns who braced me on the street in Baltimore. They had been Triple-A ball and these guys were major league all the way.

"What do you want?" demanded Junie.

Instead of answering, Mr. Black said, "Check her."

I thought he was ordering a pat down, but Mr. White reached into a pocket and produced a cell phone, thumbed a few buttons and pulled up a photograph of a pretty, blond, smiling woman. He held it up to compare it with the pretty, blond, unsmiling woman standing with me.

"It's her."

"Good," said Mr. Black. They turned toward us. Toward Junie.

That's when I knew what was going to happen next.

I couldn't see their eyes, but I can read body language. They teach us about that in Ranger school, in the cops, in the DMS, and in martial arts. No matter how cold a person is, no matter how detached they believe themselves to be, it is impossible to kill without some psychological and physiological reaction. Even machete-wielding Hutus, mob button men, and mercs who will spray a whole village with automatic weapons fire feel something. That reaction might manifest as a curl of a lip in real or pretended loathing for the victim. It might be a mad light in the eye as the inner voice whispers that to kill is to prove a sort of godhood. It might be a flinch at trigger pull as the mind tries to erect screens around the action in order to compartmentalize it from the more ordinary parts of life. Some have to scream or yell or laugh louder than the sound of another piece of their own soul cracking off as if ricochet bullets pinged and pocked it. Some go totally cold, their conscious submerging into a dark place so deep inside their fractured minds that there is no name for where it goes.

There are a hundred different reactions.

But everybody reacts.

There is always a sign that the mind has ordered the body to break that most ancient of taboos—the ending of a human life.

Practiced killers try to hide their own involuntary reactions.

Warriors look for that small sign, that inevitable tell, because it is both a warning and a doorway.

I saw Mr. Black's mouth tighten. Ever so slightly, and as it happened the muscles in his arm steadied in anticipation of the force of the gunshot and the recoil of the weapon.

I moved first. My hands were already high, hands open and loose. With every scrap of speed I could muster I whipped my open left palm across the barrel of his gun, knocking it away. It is not a move you try if there are any other options. And you don't wait to see if it worked or how he's going to react. All you can do is commit. Totally and with as much savage aggression as you can manage.

I can manage quite a lot.

My right hand darted out, fingers straight and stiff and stabbed Mr. Black in the eyes.

Before he felt it, before he could scream, I went for Mr. White, but Ghost, who had been waiting for this kind of move, was already in motion. He is big but he is very fast. And he is every bit as savage, every bit as vicious, and maybe after all he's been through, every bit as crazy as me. He came in low and went straight up, jaws wide to take the wrist of the gun hand.

There were two shots. Mr. Black and Mr. White each managed to get off a shot in the same split second. One shot each is all we allowed them.

No bullets. The guns made that weird, hollow *tok* sound, and suddenly there was a flash of intense heat that burned past my face. The wall behind me exploded in a cloud of superheated plaster and charred wood. The other missed the top of Junie's head by a hand's breadth and hit the Mind-Reader substation. The computer blew up—a big, gaudy explosion that took the sofa and half the wall with it. All the pictures on the wall crashed to the floor.

My brain recorded all this, but I was in motion. It was all happening fast now.

Ghost took Mr. White's wrist. There was a red moment of crunching and worrying and growling and screaming. He took the wrist and the hand with it.

I pivoted to Mr. Black. He had one hand clapped over his eyes and the other tried to bring the gun around. I grabbed the gun and gun hand and wrenched it all in a vicious circle. The trigger guard is curved metal, it's sharp. At the right speed and with enough leverage it can become a blade. As I took the gun I saw the finger fall.

Junie screamed and kept on screaming. At the blood or at the ugliness or in terror.

Everyone was screaming. Mr. Black, Mr. White.

Me.

I buried the pistol under the soft palate of Mr. Black's chin and pulled the trigger. If it was a regular pistol it would have blown the top of his head off.

This wasn't an ordinary pistol.

There was that hollow *tok* sound and then Mr. Black's head exploded.

Yeah.

Exploded.

All over me, the wall, the ceiling. A huge blurp of superhot blood and brain matter.

I am pretty damn sure I screamed. You want to blame me? You make someone's head explode and see how calm you stay.

As the corpse fell away from me, I turned and saw that Mr. White, despite the loss of his hand and the agony he must feel, was trying to hammer at Ghost's head with his remaining hand. Ghost evaded the blow and clamped his fangs around the man's thigh. Mr. White's screams rose to the ultrasonic, but then I shot him in the face.

Same effect.

A *tok*.

And his head exploded.

I didn't scream that time. Junie was screaming loud enough for both of us. I gagged. Everything I'd eaten since the late nineties wanted to come up.

But there were shouts from outside.

Not one man's voice.

Two of them. More.

I shoved Junie down and ran to the open door. Two of the Closers were running toward the house with their M-16s ready to fire. I took the MPP in both hands and fired two shots. They both flew apart.

But there were still shouts.

No, a single voice. Not in front.

There was the sound of breaking glass, and Junie screamed, "Joe! The kitchen door—"

A man shouted at Junie.

Ghost was already in motion. He was a red-streaked white blur, a torpedo in dog shape who blasted through the living room, into a short hallway and out of sight. The man's yells changed. Became screams. Became wet.

Stopped.

I crouched, listening.

Nothing. No sound.

"Ghost!" I called. "Hunt!"

I heard his nails skitter on kitchen floor tiles and then he was gone.

"Oh my God," cried Junie, her eyes filled with the horrors that lay around her. There was blood everywhere. On her skirt and coat, too. On her legs. All over me. "Joe! Oh my God . . . what did you . . ."

"Get down behind the couch," I ordered.

Her mouth snapped shut and without a further word she scuttled behind the couch and dropped down out of sight.

I looked down at the gun I held. Mr. Black's gun felt wrong in so many ways. It felt intensely freakish in my hand, so I tossed it down and drew my Beretta. I tapped my earbud for the team channel. "Hector! Hector! Give me a sit-rep. Red! Slick! Do you copy?"

There was no answer. The communications were still down.

"Joe," cried Junie, peering out from behind the couch, "are you hurt?"

"No. Stay down."

She disappeared again.

I edged outside, fanning the Beretta across the lawn. The only movement was the swaying of tall flowers. With the pistol leading the way, I ran toward the helicopter. It sat there, eerily still in the sunlight.

There was no doubt of what I'd find.

Of what I did find.

Hector, Red, and Slick.

What was left of them was sprawled behind the Black Hawk. That gun—that weird gun—had blown them apart. Three good people were now fried meat and drying blood. Not even recognizable as the people they'd been. Red lines of blood snaked through the grass. Exactly the same color as the red trim on the helo.

Eight dead. My three friends, and five of the Closers.

What the hell was happening?

As I ran back toward the house, Ghost came running around the corner of the building, stopped and stared at me, waiting for orders. "Watch. Call, call," I ordered and he faded back, ducking into the shadows of the house. If anyone else showed up, Ghost would warn us with a couple of loud barks, and then he would go back to hunting.

My face hurt like hell from where Mr. Black had pistol-whipped me, and blood dripped onto my shirt. All the drinking I'd done last night, the violence twice today and the accompanying adrenaline dump, and the sheer exertion of terror was all taking its toll. Kicking my ass. I didn't know how much I had left to spend on this game. It felt like I was down to my last couple of chips and I didn't like the cards I was being dealt.

Exhausted, frightened, and sick at heart, I turned and ran back inside house.

Chapter Fifty-seven

Over Maryland airspace
Sunday, October 20, 10:43 a.m.

First Sergeant Bradley Sims looked up from the flat tabletop tactical computer screen that showed a topographical map of Elk Neck State Park. The rest of Echo Team was clustered around in a semicircle, checking their gear, thumbing fresh rounds into spare magazines, laughing and joking. Swapping the kind of trash talk that was meaningless in itself but useful as a way of coaxing courage into the heart and adrenaline into the veins.

Five of them. Four men and a woman.

All combat vets, all first-team shooters. None of them virgins when it came to a firefight, even if they had not all taken fire together in the same battle. Bunny, the hulking kid to his right, had been with Top and Captain Ledger from the jump, the three of them signing onto the DMS on the same day—and that day had been a nonstop series of battles. In the two years since, the lineup of Echo Team had changed so many times.

Lydia, the woman sitting beside Bunny, had been on the firing line for half that time, which made her the third in team seniority. The other three—Pete Dobbs from Kentucky, Sam Imura from California, and Ivan Yankovitch from the Motor City—were all new to Echo.

So many others had fallen. Every night of his life, before he went to sleep and in lieu of prayers, Top Sims murmured the names of every other member of the team who had stepped up to the line and then gone down in the heat of a fight. Some were still alive but because of injuries received on the job were no longer field certified. Big Bob Faraday, who had taken a chestful of bullets during the Jakoby affair, now ran mission support out of a substation in Virginia. DeeDee Whitman, who'd taken a facial laceration and permanent eye damage while aboard the *Sea of Hope,* was a talent scout for the DMS—cruising the top guns in JSOC for Echo and other teams. Gunnery Sergeant Brick Anderson, formerly of the Denver office, now ran the special weapons shop two blocks from the Warehouse.

And the others, the ones who had fallen and not been able to get back up. Top remembered every name, every rank, every MOS. He remembered why and where they'd fallen.

As the Black Hawk tore through the skies toward Turkey Point, he glanced at the five faces around him. So often in military PR they call all soldiers heroes, and to a degree there was a heroic sacrifice made when enlisting. But these five were actual heroes. Each of them had been in DMS actions—either with Echo or other teams—and had put their lives on the line to protect the country, and in some cases the whole goddamn world.

Top chewed on a wooden kitchen match, dancing the stick from one corner of his mouth to the other. He was at least ten years older than the oldest of them, and almost twenty years older than the youngest. He was older than Captain Ledger. There was no other active field agent in the whole DMS agent that had hit forty yet, and Top was a few years past that milestone. He could feel it, too. He wasn't sure how many more of these missions he had left in his bones. What was the expression? It ain't the years, it's the mileage?

Bunny tapped his arm and offered him a bottle of vitamin-enriched water. The big young man leaned close.

"You okay, Top?"

"Thinking 'bout the cap'n," said Top, pitching his voice low enough so that only Bunny heard him. "Wondering what he's got himself into now."

"You think he's in trouble?"

"Day ends in a 'y' doesn't it?"

Bunny sighed. "Did Dietrich tell you anything? Everyone's on alert and now the captain goes off the grid. I only saw Mr. Church for a second this morning but he looked like he was ready to cut throats. We know what kind of shit is hitting the fan?"

Top shook his head. "Don't know. Don't want to find out."

"Yeah."

"Tell you what, Farmboy . . ."

"Yeah?"

"If someone's finally put their mark on the cap . . . I am going to tear their world apart."

"Hooah," agreed Bunny.

That threat, Top knew, was not empty trash talk.

The Black Hawk flew north with all the speed and ferocity of a dragon.

Interlude Five

Dadiwan Excavation Site, Zhangshaodian Village
Northeast of Qinan County in Tianshui City
People's Republic of China
Two years ago

"Doctor, you must come quick! The diggers have found something!"

Dr. Wen Zhengming looked up from the small fossil he was cleaning and peered at a young graduate assistant who had burst into his office. The assistant's face was flushed, his eyes wide, brow beaded with sweat.

"Is it more of the hadrosaur?" asked Dr. Wen hopefully. Three weeks ago they had found a thigh bone and part of a vertebra from a hadrosaurid that might be as big—or even bigger—than the great one found in the 1980s. Dr. Wen had been part of the team that had unearthed the earlier one, and so far it was the largest of its species unearthed anywhere. Back then he was a junior member of the team; if they made a significant discovery here, he would be the one to receive the accolades. That would mean greater support from the government and possibly a speaking tour of the United States.

The young man snatched his cap off his head and fidgeted with it. Whatever this was it had deeply affected him.

"Doctor," he said in an almost strangled voice, "you had best come and see for yourself."

Dr. Wen frowned and set down the brush with which he had been cleaning the fossil. "You're not one of mine, are you?"

"I am with Professor Yao's team," said the young man.

"Ah," said Wen. "Then I will come at once."

Despite his name, Professor Yao was an American from the University of Pennsylvania, and he was not part of Wen's team of paleontologists. Yao was an anthropologist and the senior member of a very important international team made up of experts in a number of fields ranging from ethnobotany to archaeologists. His team had come here to China primarily to study the excavation of a nearly pristine village of the Dadiwan, a Neolithic culture that once lived in Gansu and western Shaanxi. The original Dadiwan-type-site was excavated between 1975 and 1984. Although the Dadiwans lived between 5800 and 5500 B.C., their village stood on grounds that were rich in dinosaur bones dating back one hundred and seventy million years. Scientific teams came from all over the world to study everything from the world's largest fossilized dinosaur footprint—which measured one and a half meters across—to Neolithic pottery kilns. The region was so rich in varied history that Professor Zhao Xijin, the chief paleontologist at the Institute of Vertebrate Paleontology and Paleoanthropology famously labeled it "the garbage dump of time."

Three days ago Professor Yao made a very interesting and intensely curious discovery. While excavating the ruins of a Dadiwan roundhouse, Yao had removed an oddly placed floor stone and discovered that it partially covered the entrance to a tunnel. Neither Yao nor Dr. Wen quite understood what that tunnel had been used for or why it had been carved out of the calcium-rich sediment. After getting approval from Professor Zhao in Beijing, Yao's team had begun to painstakingly excavate the tunnel, photographing, weighing, and cataloging every piece of rock they removed. As of last night, Yao reported that the tunnel angled downward at twenty-eight degrees but so far was only filled with rocks of no remarkable nature.

However, from the look on the face of this young man, it appeared that Yao had found something other than chunks of rock.

"Have they reached the end of the tunnel?" he asked.

The young man licked his lips and repeated what he had already said, "You had better come and see for yourself, Doctor."

Dr. Wen sighed and stood up, his knees and lower back popping audibly. He pulled on a sweater, fitted a knit cap over his bald head, and followed the assistant out into the teeth of a raw northerly wind.

A large tent had been erected over the site of the roundhouse and from the way it glowed Wen could tell that every light was on. But as they approached he hesitated. Instead of the usual graduate student standing guard outside, the tent opening was guarded by two more of Yao's assistants. A Norwegian boy who towered over everyone else in the camp, and a diminutive Senegalese woman. Wen could not remember either of their names; both were unpronounceable anyway.

The dark-skinned woman stepped forward to meet them, and she looked even more stressed than did the young assistant who fetched him. So did the Norwegian boy. Despite the cold, they were all sweating.

"Where is Professor Yao?" asked Wen, his pulse quickening as the first tickles of alarm shivered through him.

"Inside, Doctor," said the Norwegian. "He is down in the pit."

The Norwegian stayed outside to guard the tent while the girl led the way. Wen was beginning to have a bad feeling about this. Had Yao's diggers found something they weren't supposed to? It wouldn't be the first time, and such events were always calamitous. Just a few years ago another team of diggers had gotten into very bad trouble in Jilin when they unearthed a cache of bioweapons that had supposedly been destroyed thirty years ago following an international arms agreement. Changes within the government and the overall culture of secrecy had resulted in the cache being first mislabeled in the government computers and then lost altogether. The scientists who had found it were harshly rebuked and several of them vanished entirely.

Dr. Wen hoped that Yao was not next in line to disappear.

Or, himself.

The inside of the tent was large but cluttered, with rows of wood and metal shelves along one side, each of them crammed with tagged artifacts and plastic trays of materials to be analyzed and cataloged. At the far end, scaffolding had been erected over the entrance to the tunnel and a row of dented wheelbarrows groaned under the weight of rocks taken from this new find. Directly beside the tunnel mouth was a mound of dirt and chunky clay. A pair of shovels stood up from the side of the mound.

The mouth of the tunnel yawned round and black at Wen's feet.

Professor Yao came hurrying over, and he was every bit as flushed and sweaty as the others. "Doctor Wen! Thank god," he gasped. "Please, you must come see this."

"What is it?" asked Wen. "What, have you found my hadrosaur?"

Yao gave him an enigmatic smile. "We found some bones," the professor said evasively. "And something else. Something quite . . . extraordinary. Please, Doctor, come see for yourself."

Yao led the doctor into the hole. A line of small yellow lightbulbs strung on a wire threw a pale glow along the slope. Wen grunted at how long the tunnel was. There were chalk marks to indicate distance and through the gloom Wen could see that the tunnel extended many meters into the earth.

"This is much longer than we thought," he said. "How did you excavate this much of it so quickly?"

"This arm of the tunnel is ninety-two feet," said Yao. "The obstruction did not extend all the way. As of last night we had cleared nineteen meters of the tunnel, and today we got through another five. Then the next two meters of the tunnel were filled with dirt packed on either side by red clay. There was nothing remarkable about the clay—no markings of any kind, so we photographed it and then broke through." He nodded to the rest of the tunnel. "Beyond the dirt was empty tunnel. And then this . . ."

They emerged from the tunnel into a chamber whose floor was flat and smooth. Perfectly flat, perfectly smooth. Natural caves are never smooth and the Dadiwan were incapable of this kind of symmetrical stonework.

Wen was suddenly alarmed. This was exactly what he had feared.

"Professor," he said carefully, "you realize that what you have found here is very likely a base, or a weapons storehouse. We are both going to be in a lot of trouble and—"

Yao was shaking his head. "You don't understand, Doctor. Your government did not build this chamber. Nor did the Dadiwan."

"How can you be so certain?"

Yao fished inside his trouser pockets and produced a heavy Maglite. He dialed the powerful beam up to its highest setting and then aimed it carefully at the closest wall.

Dr. Wen nearly screamed.

His heart leaped in his chest and he felt a spasm of pain shoot through him as he stared at the wall.

The wall was as flat as the floor, the ancient stone smooth as glass. But Wen saw none of that. Instead his eyes goggled open at what was in the wall. Extruding from the stone, like a display at a museum or a piece of decorative art, were the bones of a hadrosaur.

A complete skeleton. Articulated, assembled, perfect.

And impossible.

The bones were fused into the wall so precisely that the dinosaur seemed to rear up above them.

"I—" Wen began, but Yao turned slowly and shone his light along the wall. Beyond the hadrosaur was another skeleton, one that Wen recognized at once—the great predator *Zhuchengtyrannus magnus,* a cousin of the *Tyrannosaurus rex* first discovered in the city of Zhucheng. Four meters tall and ferocious.

But beyond that . . . more skeletons.

So many more.

Each of them carefully reconstructed and fixed by some unknown means into the wall. This was not the result of lava capture or a mud slide—no, even through his deep shock Wen could clearly see that these skeletons had been placed here.

Preserved.

And it was absolutely impossible.

He snatched the flashlight out of Yao's hand and used it and his own smaller light to sweep along the walls as he walked down the line of them. Then he was running.

Stopping. Gasping. Crying out.

Weeping.

There was a massive armored *Huayangosaurus.* A titanic *Mamenchisaurus.*

A complete *Shunosaurus,* and an *Omeisaurus* with its improbably long neck and absurdly small body. And a perfect *Tsintaosaurus* that was at least a meter taller than any specimen Wen had ever seen.

There were many others. Too many to count.

Hundreds of them.

Species Wen had never seen before. Species he was positive were unknown to the fossil record. He stood there, trembling, tears running down his face.

Yao came hurrying up to him and gently took the Maglite from his hand.

"How . . . ?" Wen asked. He gripped the professor's arm with desperate force. "Who did this? How could they? I don't understand. You must explain this to me . . ."

"Doctor," Yao said in a haunted, hollow voice, "this is still not what I brought you here to see."

It took Wen several seconds to process that statement. "W-what?"

"We don't have much time. The news about this find is already out. One of the diggers working on my team is a spy. I didn't know it at first, but I know it now. I caught him making a cell phone call to one of your government offices. Officials are probably already on their way."

Wen's heart nearly stopped in his chest.

"But I wanted you to see this before they arrive," said Yao. "You deserve to see this."

Yao raised the flashlight again. Not toward the wall this time, but into the center of the chamber. Dr. Wen's eyes followed the beam.

"No," he said.

Yao said nothing. He walked over and switched on the strings of lightbulbs that he and his assistants—his terrified assistants—had erected here in the darkness.

"No," said Wen once more.

Yao nodded.

They stood looking at the thing that sat in the middle of the chamber.

A thing that was far more impossible than the perfectly round walls and museum of dinosaurs.

"No," said Wen one more time. "Dear God . . . no."

Dr. Wen Zhengming lay dying.

All the heat was leaving his body, spreading out around him in a dark pool.

"I don't . . . understand . . . ," he said, but his voice was a whisper, only the ghost of a sound, growing fainter even to his own ears.

He turned his head. It was so hard to do, requiring so much of what little strength he had left. But he had to do it. Not to look at the group of men who stood a few yards away. Not even to stare reproachfully at the government officer who had shot him.

No, Wen needed to see it again.

The thing that Professor Yao had brought him down here to see.

The impossible thing.

By turning his head, Wen saw the other shapes that lay sprawled on the ground. The young woman from Senegal. The Norwegian boy. The young assistant. Others. The whole international team. And all his own people. Sprawled in heaps. Dying or dead. Sacrificed on the altar of political and military gain.

Wen distantly wondered how the government would explain these deaths to the rest of the world. A plane crash over the ocean, perhaps. Something where the bodies could never be recovered.

His own death? That would be easier. He was old. He had a well-documented heart condition. Would they spin the story so that his heart attack was brought on by grief and shock over the deaths of so many of his colleagues?

He coughed wetly.

I have blood in my lungs, he thought. Would that make it easier to die? Would it make it hurt more or last longer?

He had never thought that he could be afraid of death. As an archaeologist, he worked among old bones every day, and each fragment was proof that nothing and no one lived forever. If they left him here, left him to turn to bones down here in this cave . . . Wen could bear that. Perhaps his ghost would spend a thousand years studying the gigantic skeletons that lined the walls. There were worse hells and no better heavens that he could imagine.

The group of men began walking and Wen watched them pace off the thing in the center of the cavern. The one who had shot him—Colonel Li—still held his pistol, though now the barrel pointed to the stone floor as he followed behind the group of scientists sent by the Fourth Bureau of the Ministry of State Security. Wen had been compelled to report what Yao had found. There was no way to avoid it.

Yao had begged Wen to be allowed to communicate the information to his own people back in the United States, but Wen had refused. They had to follow proper protocols.

Proper.

Now those protocols were playing out. Yao lay ten feet away with half his face shot away. Their colleagues were all dead. Each "properly" handled by the uniformed thugs who accompanied the science team here from the capital.

Wen tried to hear what these men—these killers—were saying, but he could only hear fragments. His ears rang constantly and everything was getting so dim, so far away, as if the entire cavern was receding from him.

". . . there is no other opening . . . ," said one of the scientists.

". . . since that is clearly impossible, we should search for an entrance cave . . ."

". . . ground-penetrating radar . . ."

The voices faded and then came back as if the men were casually pacing the room while engaged in an idle conversation. *So strange*, thought Wen.

". . . such a shame that it is so badly damaged . . ."

". . . there are several components in perfect shape, Admiral Xiè . . ."

". . . and a line on more. My sources inside the Majestic program assure me they can smuggle . . ."

". . . with what we already have, Admiral Xiè, perhaps it will be enough to rebuild the Dragon Engine . . ."

The voices faded again. They were only fragments anyway. Some of them made sense, most were meaningless. Or, they were becoming meaningless as Wen became detached from the moment. Perhaps detached from himself.

A tear burned at the corner of his eye. As stunning as this discovery was, it was not his discovery. It did not matter to him as much as it mattered to the others. To Yao. To the government. To these men from the

Fourth Bureau or the uniformed killers who traveled with them. They were all focused on the silvery wreckage in the center of the cavern. They barely even looked at the walls. At all the wonders there in the walls.

All those dinosaurs.

All that perfection. Not a bone out of place. Not a bone missing.

Hundreds of them. At least half of them unknown in the fossil record.

Would these government thugs even stop to consider them?

Or would they blast them apart in order to remove the wreckage from this chamber?

Wen closed his eyes for a moment, tasting the grief of that potential loss.

When he opened his eyes again he was much colder. The men were nowhere in sight. He had no idea how much time had passed. The chamber was silent. The others from Yao's team and his own lay in utter stillness. How Wen—the oldest and frailest of them all—lingered while the others had died was a mystery. Wen doubted that he was in any way "luckier" than the dead. They were already beyond pain and fear, and he was not.

Wen lay with his face pointing toward the twisted metal.

"No," he said in his ghost of a voice.

This is not what he wanted to see with his last moments of sight.

He wanted to see his precious dinosaurs.

One last time.

Wen summoned the last of his strength, took a final ragged breath, and tried to turn over. It was a simple act, if he could move far enough then gravity would do the rest, and he would see the bones in the walls.

He tried.

With everything he had left, he tried.

But his body would not move. He was too weak. There was simply not enough left in him to turn even the frail scarecrow of a body that he owned. Not even his head would move now.

Red poppies blossomed in his eyes and the breath burst from Wen in a final gasp of defeat.

He lay there and all that he could see was the impossible machine.

It was the last thing he saw as the darkness of the cavern swallowed him whole.

Chapter Fifty-eight

The Warehouse
Sunday, October 20, 10:45 a.m.

"Talk to me, Bug," said Church in a voice that was getting harsher by the minute.

"I can't break through the jammer, boss. Joe's going to have to get to a landline or a computer with a cable. Whoever these bastards are, they're killing the air."

"Is Joe all right?" asked Rudy, but before Church could reply his phone rang.

Church frowned at the name on the screen display. He hit a button to mute Bug and held up a finger for Rudy to remain silent as he answered the call. "Yes, General," he said. He listened for a moment. "Yes, you can send me a coded video. I'm in a secure location."

Church hit a few keys on his laptop and watched a video file, but he did not turn the laptop so Rudy could see it. Church plugged earbuds into the speaker jack and listened in silence as he watched.

Rudy crossed his legs and sat back as he studied Church's face. After two years he was still trying to catalog the man's reactions. They were very subtle and generally too well hidden to read at all. Once in a while, though, that iron control slipped.

He watched it slip now, and he wondered which of the day's crises was unfastening the bolts on that legendary calm.

"General . . . ," said Church after the video was done, "tell me everything you know about this."

The conversation was mostly one-sided, with the general doing most of the talking. As Church had not put it on speaker there was little more than a few soft encouraging grunts to go on. That, and a gradual change in Church's body language. The man slowly straightened as if his body was being pulled into a posture of terrible tension. The hand holding the phone was white-knuckle tight. The other hand lay on the desk and Mr. Church slowly opened it, pressing the palm and splayed fingers flat and pressing them against the polished wood.

"General," said Church, "there is a high probability that this incident relates to what's happening in Washington right now, and to other matters currently unfolding. You will need to speak with General Croft for further information. He will inform you of today's . . . developments. Speak to no one else about this. Detain everyone who was there and confiscate all cell phones. No, I don't care who they are. This matter supersedes all other concerns. Lock it down, General. Do it now."

Church closed the phone and set it down on the desk. He removed his tinted glasses and rubbed his eyes.

"I'm almost afraid to ask what that was about," said Rudy.

Before he answered, Church removed a pocket handkerchief and cleaned his glasses. He kept his eyes down, focused on the phone as he did so, and Rudy knew that Church was unwilling to let anyone see his eyes without the barrier of the tinted lenses.

He put the glasses on, took a long breath and breathed it out through his nostrils.

"That was Major General Armand Schmidt," said Church. "He's in charge of the stealth aircraft program out at Dugway along with his aide, Colonel Betty Snider."

Rudy nodded. "I believe I met him at a State Department dinner. I took him to be a highly competent officer."

"He is, and he's not prone to hysteria. However, today they were doing a mock combat test of the Locust FB-119, advanced-design stealth fighter-bomber."

He turned his laptop around, pulled the earbuds from the jack and replayed the video. When it was over, Rudy found that he could not speak. He tried, but he simply could not articulate his reaction to what he'd just seen.

"What do you think, Doctor?"

Rudy found his tongue. "Is this . . . is this . . . I mean, this can't be real . . . Can it?"

Church did not bother to answer.

Of course it was real.

Rudy felt as if the floor was dropping away from under him. His hands were ice cold and his mouth was dry.

"What is happening?" he asked.

Church looked at him and said, plainly and frankly, "I don't know."

Chapter Fifty-nine

The Hangar

Floyd Bennett Field, Brooklyn, New York

Sunday, October 20, 10:46 a.m.

While Bug labored to solve the problem with the jammer, Dr. William Hu shifted his focus back to the project he'd been working on for the last few days.

The microwave pulse pistol.

The lab was filled was smoke, and he engaged the blowers while his assistants cleared away the debris and erected a fresh stack of bricks. Currently the microwave pulse pistol was clamped to a cart and placed twenty feet from the target. At five, ten, and fifteen feet the destructive power of the MPP was appalling.

And delicious.

This was fun, this was his idea of science. Not that UFO bullshit Joe Ledger and that daffy broad in Maryland were trying to get him to believe. You could measure this, you could prove this. Who cared if someone stomped out a crop circle on the White House lawn? Those things could be faked.

But this—the guns—this was real science.

Hu grinned as he paced off twenty-five feet, then locked the cart's wheels. The assistants patted the target—a wall of red bricks, cinder blocks, and a couple of big river rocks brought in from outside the Hangar.

His assistant, Melanie, clipped leads to various places on the gun and watched the meter of a small device she held.

"This is crazy, Doctor," she said. "The meter still reads 94.189 percent after nine test fires in five minutes."

"I know," said Hu, "I love it."

They grinned at each other like a couple of kids.

Hu turned and pulled his protective goggles into place. "Clear the firing line!"

Everyone moved behind thick Lucite shields.

"Firing," he yelled and pulled the trigger.

Tok!

The wall of debris exploded.

"Outstanding," cried Hu. "Absolutely outstanding. Melanie, is there any power drain?"

Melanie ran the meter again and shook her head. "Ninety-three point seven seven six percent."

They tried five more distances, and only when they neared forty feet did the destructive force of the MPP begin to diminish. By sixty feet it had little effect.

They kept testing the gun. Against blocks of ice and sheets of metal, firing through glass, firing at sides of beef to determine the effect on tissue. The gun had been delivered to Hu late on Thursday and now it was Sunday. It had been fired a total of 607 times. On arrival at Hu's lab the gun had a charge of 99.00034 percent. After all those firings, after all that destruction, it had a charge of 90.0957 percent.

Hu removed the clamps and picked up the pistol.

It was ugly in design, but beautiful to his eyes.

And those numbers. The range, the effect, the incredible amount of power held in reserve.

"Who made this thing?" asked Melanie. It was probably the hundredth time she or someone at the Hangar had asked that question. "Who could have made it?"

Hu shook his head. Over the last couple of days he had spoken discretely to several who were on the cutting edge of microwave technology and they told him that they were decades away from a man-portable microwave gun like this pistol. The current estimate was that to fire a gun like this you'd need a battery the size of a Jeep Cherokee. And yet when they'd dismantled the gun, all they found in the battery compartment was a piece of drab metal approximately the size of an old metal cigarette lighter. The metal had no discernible features, and the gun fired no matter which end of the battery was inserted first. Ledger had found a second battery in the pocket of one of the men who'd ambushed him this morning.

Then Melanie stuck a pin in Hu's enthusiasm. She got a call, listened, frowned, hung up, and said, "That was Mitchell in metallurgy. He finished his analysis of the scrapings he did on the other battery."

"And?"

"And he's never seen anything like it. He looked at it under the electron microscope and it appears to be an alloy composed of two metals. It's approximately twenty percent iridium, but the other metal is unknown."

"Meaning that he hasn't identified it yet?"

"No," she said, "meaning that it is a metal currently unknown to science."

Chapter Sixty

Turkey Point Lighthouse, Elk Neck State Park
Cecil County, Maryland
Sunday, October 20, 10:47 a.m.

"Junie," I yelled, "do you have a landline?"

"No, only my cell," she said, rising shakily up from behind the couch. "Wait—there's one in the lighthouse. Emergency use only, it goes direct to the Coast Guard."

Even before she finished saying it she was running toward the kitchen. I followed and tried to get ahead of her to body-block her view of whatever Ghost left of the Closers, but I was a step too late. She did not scream. Instead it was an intake of breath so deep and sharp that it was like a reverse scream, all of the terror driving back into her. Ghost acts like a puppy a lot of the time and he can be as playful as a house pet, but not when he's working. He is by breeding and training a combat dog. A fighter and killer true to all of the lupine genes that fire in him every time the moment turns ugly. What he left was a man, but you had to look closely to tell. We didn't look all that close.

I gave Junie a gentle push and she turned away, shaking her head in denial and disbelief. She looked up at me with her troubled blue eyes.

"Is this what you do?" she asked in a voice that was filled with pain.

I turned away, not willing—or perhaps able—to let her read that particular truth. It was a coin I did not want to spend, and it was a fee that would hurt her to accept.

Or so I thought.

Her fingers touched my cheek and she gently, firmly turned my head so that I faced her again. I looked into her eyes and searched for revulsion, for the judgment that was my due for being who and what I was. Inside my head the Killer tried to stare her down, but even he could not.

Maybe I'm not sure who looked back at her. Cop, Killer, Civilized Man. Or someone else.

Pain flickered across Junie Flynn's face. It darted like lightning through her eyes.

"I'm so sorry," she said.

Then it was she who turned away. Not because she was unable to hold that contact, but because she had seen what there was to see. She passed me and reached for the handle of a door set between two pantries, turned it, and went through it.

I took a ragged breath and followed.

Beyond the door was the huge, round base of the lighthouse and there was a wooden stairway winding its way around and up toward the light. The moment kept wanting to whisper symbolic meanings to me. I told it to shut the fuck up.

Junie was already running up the stairs, and I followed.

The stairs vanished through the floor of a wooden platform. Junie disappeared through that. As I came up through the floor, I saw that we were right at the top of the tower, with heavy windows in metal frames on all sides. The view was magnificent, with the October lushness of Elk Neck State Park behind us, the bluffs below, and the lovely bay spread out in front. In any other moment it would have been a breathtaking view. I was feeling less touristy than I might otherwise, however. Junie crossed to a serviceable-looking desk on which were various logbooks, charts, timetables, and a big, old-fashioned white phone.

She picked up the handset and listened. Her eyes lit and she smiled. "There's a dial tone!"

Junie began punching numbers. I bent close and listened through five excruciating rings before a male voice answered, "Coast Guard, this is Petty Officer First Class Johnson Byrnes. Please identify and state the nature of your emergency."

I snatched the phone from her hand. "Petty Officer Byrnes, this is Captain Joseph Ledger with the National Security Agency. I am calling from the Turkey Point Lighthouse in Elk Neck State Park, Maryland. We are under attack by multiple hostiles. This is a terrorist attack. This is a matter of national security. Put your commanding officer on the phone right now."

Byrnes began to react as if my call were a joke, but his training overrode his natural skepticism. He said, "Sir, please hold the line."

A moment later an older, gruffer voice came on the line, "This is Command Master Chief Petty Officer Robles. Please identify yourself."

"Command Master Chief, this is Captain Joseph Ledger, currently attached to the National Security Agency and working under an executive order." I gave him our location. "We are under attack by hostile forces of unknown type or number. We have three KIA and multiple hostiles down. All radio, sat-phone, and cell-phone communication are being jammed. I need you to send all available assistance. I need you to contact my superiors at the following number." I gave them a special number that would ring on Church's cell. "I have one female civilian with me and a white shepherd combat dog. We are in the lighthouse and if possible we will remain here until assistance arrives. We are armed."

I waited for him to say something.

He didn't.

He couldn't. The line was dead.

I set the phone down.

Junie asked. "What's wrong?"

"They cut the phones, too."

She looked around as if expecting to see Closers leaping out of the shadows.

"Do you think he understood what you were saying?" she asked breathlessly. "Do you think they understood?"

I wanted to lie to her, to tell her that Robles heard and understood it all. But, she was Junie Flynn and you can't lie to Junie Flynn.

"God . . . ," she whispered.

I took her by the shoulders and turned her around to face me. "Junie . . . can you think of any reason why these Closers would want to kill you?"

"W-what?"

"Downstairs . . . they weren't after me. They had your picture, they were hunting for you. Why?"

She hesitated, clearly unwilling to tell me. Her pale face flushed red. Was it tension? Embarrassment? Shame?

"Joe," she said tentatively, "I . . . may have done something really stupid."

"Why? What did you do?"

"I think I may have gotten us killed."

Chapter Sixty-one

The Warehouse

Baltimore, Maryland

Sunday, October 20, 10:48 a.m.

Rudy Sanchez perched on the edge of the visitor chair, feeling immensely useless as Mr. Church and the rest of the DMS threw its resources against the current problem—including the loss of communication with Joe Ledger. Rudy's stomach was turning slowly to a soup of hot acid.

Across the desk from him, Church was making a series of phone calls. To the acting president, to Linden Brierly, to Aunt Sallie, to two members of the Joint Chiefs, to four separate DMS station chiefs, to the Coast Guard and the Maryland State Police. At least half of his efforts were bent toward getting help out to Joe Ledger, but so far there was nothing Rudy could do to help. His advice was not even sought.

In a moment of dismal depression he mused that, as a trauma specialist, he might only be able to help Joe after this whole thing was over. Or, worse yet, to help those who cared about Joe if this situation continued to spin downward. He wished Circe was here. She was one of the world's top analysts in matters of terrorism and, no matter whatever else this was, this matter was terrifying. Privately Rudy admitted that he simply would not mind having his hand held by the woman he loved.

Then the screen on the wall flashed and Bug reappeared. "Boss," he said to Church, "we got a problem. Actually—maybe two problems."

"Of course we do," Rudy said to himself.

Church took a breath. "Tell me."

"This is about our expert. It's about Junie Flynn. I've been doing deep background on her, and you know she was adopted, right?"

"Yes."

"No, she wasn't."

Church said nothing.

"I ran her adoption records and they're passable fakes. They used that old trick of lifting a Social Security number from a real orphan who died a few days after being born. Junie was never in an orphanage. The paperwork was entered into the system by someone who's pretty good at this stuff. Good enough that it took MindReader to figure it out."

"Then who is she?" asked Rudy.

"Good question," said Bug. "Here's more. She was homeschooled until she went to college."

"So . . . ?"

"I went into the system to pull any records I could find on her. Medical, vaccination, anything."

"And?" asked Church.

"There's nothing."

"I don't understand," said Rudy. "Have her records been removed?"

"No," said Bug, "if they'd been expunged it would leave a trace in the system and MindReader's programmed to look for that sort of thing. You can't hide from MindReader . . ."

"But . . ."

"Unless you're not in the system at all, and Junie Flynn is definitely not in the system. She's never been in a hospital, at least not under that name or the name on the phony birth certificate. She's never been to a dentist, she's never been vaccinated, she's never been to an ER. Never been to a shrink, as far as I can tell."

"How thoroughly have you looked?" asked Church.

"I got a couple of guys on this and they're going all the way down the rabbit hole, but Alice isn't there."

Church pursed his lips and said nothing.

Rudy asked, "But what does that mean? Is she . . . a spy? A mole, or something like that? Is she operating under a false identity?"

"We don't know," said Bug. "It's not Witness Protection or anything like that, and I don't make her for a deep-cover mole."

"Doubtful," agreed Church.

"As far as the system goes," continued Bug, "prior to entering college she didn't exist. Most of what we have is really recent stuff, what she put on her Web site and the content of her podcasts."

"Put people on those podcasts," said Church. "I want summaries of everything she's said."

Bug made a strange face. "Way ahead of you. I have a whole bunch of my guys on that. I started them on the podcasts as soon as Joe headed out to Turkey Point. Most of the stuff is general conspiracy theory material, and a lot of speculation on the Black Book, M3, all of that. But then Joe suggested we listen to last night's podcast. If the thing with the president wasn't already taking up so much manpower we'd have gotten to this sooner. But man-oh-man-oh-man."

"What is it?" asked Rudy, gripping the arms of his chair.

"Last night Junie Flynn announced that she has obtained a complete copy of the Majestic Black Book and that tonight she plans on sending it to every newspaper and university in the world. And to every nonprofit organization, every grassroots organization . . ."

Rudy gasped. "She . . . she lied to us."

Church sat back in his chair. "So it seems."

"I'm embarrassed to say that," Rudy said, "except for the obvious deception about her source, I believed that she was being straight with us. I caught none of the eye shifts, body language changes, or facial tics typical of someone who is lying. And considering the pressure of the situation, at least some of those elements should have been there."

"What do you infer from that?" asked Church.

"That she is either a very practiced liar, or she is—for some reason— unaware that she is lying."

"No other options occur to you, Doctor?"

"Not immediately."

Rudy saw a twitch on Church's mouth that might have been a smile. "Let me know if you have any additional insights to share."

"If I may," said Rudy, "Bug—could you go through those podcasts more carefully? If she's made this bold a move then there may be some precipitating event. She may have hinted at it in some way that will give us a clue as to what she has planned."

" 'Planned'?" asked Bug. "I told you, she's going to release the Black Book."

"There has to be more to it than that. She's openly challenging M3. Surely she knew that they would respond. If they killed her parents, then she would have to be aware of the threat to herself. Until now she's only talked about the Black Book. Now she not only claims to have it, but has threatened to release it in a way that will force M3 to move against her, to stop her."

"I agree," said Church.

"We need to figure out what game she's playing."

Chapter Sixty-two

Turkey Point Lighthouse, Elk Neck State Park
Cecil County, Maryland
Sunday, October 20, 10:52 a.m.

I stared at her.

"What do you mean you got us killed? Junie . . . what did you do?"

She hugged her arms to her body, but a shiver swept through her, raising goose flesh on her skin. "Joe . . . when we were on with your boss, Mr. Church, and those other men . . . I was scared. I . . ." She shook her head like she was trying to shake off angry bees. "It's so big! The president, the crop circle . . . this is the kind of stuff I podcast about and write about, but now it's here, it's right here, and I guess I kind of freaked. I flaked out on you. And the thing is . . . I still don't know how much I can trust you."

"Jesus Christ, Junie, I just saved your life from a hit team."

"I know . . ."

"What more do you want?"

She stood several feet away from me, near the top of the stairs, tension rippling through her as if she was trying to decide whether to tell me or to make a break for it down those stairs. I tried to get inside her head and see it from her perspective, but maybe she'd lived in the world of conspiracy theories and paranoia too long. Maybe a lack of trust was the only thing she could rely on. And really, who was I to her? Sure, we shared a couple of freaky moments of subliminal communication, but who's to say that wasn't brain chemistry misfiring because of all the trauma? Hey, it's not like I'm not crazy already, so I could have been reading a lot more into my first encounter with Junie than was ever there; and I didn't have Rudy riding shotgun on my sanity right now.

"Joe . . . I'll make a deal with you," she said at last.

"Can't wait to hear this, but sure, go ahead, let's see what's behind door number one."

"I'm serious."

"So am I. I'm like this when I'm serious."

That probably wasn't as comforting or amusing as intended. She filed it away.

"Here's the deal . . . you get us out of here, you get us somewhere totally safe, and I will put the Majestic Black Book into your hands."

I stared at her.

"What?"

"That's the deal."

"You have the book?" I growled. "After all this . . . you have the damn book?"

"Yes." There was some hesitation in her voice, but she repeated her answer. "Yes. What's it going to be, Joe? Do we have a deal?"

I towered over her, glowered at her. I wanted to yell at her, shake her.

What I did, though, was smile.

"Either you are one cool bitch," I said, "or you're every bit as crazy as I am."

Her smile was of a lower wattage. "Do we have a deal?"

I stuck out my hand. "We have a deal."

We shook on it.

Outside, Ghost suddenly started barking.

Then we heard the helicopters.

"The Coast Guard! Thank God," she said as we raced to the windows.

There were two of them, coming in low and fast a hundred yards above the blue water. Coast Guard helicopters are red and white, easy to spot against the sky or sea.

These helos were as black as the bottomless well of despair that had opened in my heart.

There was a puff of smoke, small and pale in the distance. It was a slender thing and I knew it for what it was. I've seen so many of them, up close and mounted. I've seen what they can do. A hundred pounds of metal and wire and chemicals; sixty-four inches long. Sleek and silver in the sunlight, moving at Mach 1.3. Nine hundred and fifty miles per hour. Like an arrow shot by a god of war, the Hellfire missile flew toward us.

"Run!" I screamed as I hooked my arm around her and hurled her toward the stairs.

Above and around us the world seemed to disintegrate into a burning fireball of pure destructive force.

Hellfire without a doubt.

Chapter Sixty-three

The Warehouse
Baltimore, Maryland
Sunday, October 20, 10:55 a.m.

"Give me something to do," Rudy pleaded. "If I simply sit here and do nothing while all this is happening I'll go insane."

"As it happens, Doctor," said Church, "there is something you can do."

He handed Rudy a sheet of paper on which was a list of names accompanied by notations about each person's credentials and contact information. Several of the names were highlighted in yellow.

"These are some experts who might be able to provide some useful information relative to this case."

"I recognize some of these people. George Noory? He has a conspiracy theory radio show. And Bill Birnes, he publishes *UFO Magazine*. They're both on TV a lot in all those UFO specials."

"Yes. The others are experts as well. Some areas of expertise overlap. You can speak frankly to any of the people whose names are highlighted."

"Why them?"

Church gave him the smallest of enigmatic smiles. "They are friends of mine in the industry."

Chapter Sixty-four

Turkey Point Lighthouse, Elk Neck State Park
Cecil County, Maryland
Sunday, October 20, 10:57 a.m.

We ran and hell followed after.

The whole lighthouse shuddered like a man does when he's taken a bullet but hasn't yet realized he's dead. The walls cracked, crooked lines ran from top to bottom. The wooden stairs groaned as the bolts tore themselves free from the juddering structure.

"Run!" I screamed.

But she was running as fast as she could. As fast as it was possible to run down a set of stairs that was rippling like a serpent, twisting itself into an Escher-esque impossibility. The top of the lighthouse was a fireball. Flaming debris rained down on us. There was a great cry of tortured metal and I looked up to see the massive reflector come plunging through the burning deck to drop like a fiery comet to the concrete floor below. I dove for Junie and nearly crushed her against the wall as tons of metal and wood and flame smashed past us, the jagged steel beams of the reflector's support reaching out to pluck at the handrail.

"God!" Junie shrieked.

The stairs were starting to collapse. I grabbed Junie's hand and pulled her as I ran down. Shocked and terrified as she was, she ran with me. Civilian she might be, but she was not falling apart. Chunks of building stone tried to crush us. The stairs wanted to die beneath us. Heat bloomed up from the growing mound of debris that now filled the center of the lighthouse.

There was a huge crack and I felt the whole last section of stairs cant outward, reeling like a suicidal drunk toward the fire.

"Junie—jump!"

Her hand locked tight around mine and then we were in the air with nothing under us but hot air and a hard landing.

Ten feet doesn't sound like a lot of distance to fall.

It is.

As we hit, I dropped into a crouch, taking as much of the impact as I could in my calves and thighs. I pulled Junie against my chest and twisted so that we hit the ground on my side and rolled over and over like a log, sloughing off the foot pounds of force. But I rolled a half turn too far. Into the edges of the burning rubble. Flames leaped onto my shirt and jeans.

With a howl of pain I thrust Junie away from me and I tried to roll fast enough to smother the flames. Then a shadow passed in front of me and Junie was there, on her feet already, tearing off her coat, swatting at me with it, killing the fires that wanted to consume me.

I scrambled to my feet, my clothes smoking but no longer burning.

"Thanks," I said breathlessly, and she managed, despite everything, to give me a crooked grin on a soot-smudged and fear-flushed face.

One hell of a woman.

There was another cracking sound and we looked up in horror to see a massive fissure snapping its way down the wall.

"It's all coming down," she cried.

"We have to get out of here," I snapped. "Right damn now."

Junie tossed her smoking coat away as we headed for the back door to the house. The door was still ajar and I shouldered through it, drawing my gun, pointing the barrel everywhere I looked. There was no one in the kitchen except the dead man Ghost had killed, sprawled in a lake of blood.

I heard Junie make a soft sound, a grunt that was an inarticulate and visceral reaction to the presence of violent death.

"Don't look at it," I said, but it was too feeble and too late.

Junie edged around the blood as if it were a hole into which she could topple and fall. I jumped over the corpse and ran to the window. She crowded in beside me. Perhaps it was an accident or maybe she had that much presence of mind, but she pressed against my left hand rather than my gun hand.

Outside, the helicopters were still hovering above us, admiring the destruction they'd wrought. One was stationed high, missiles aimed for another blast. The other was lower, angled sideways with the bay door open and the ugly snout of a minigun pointed straight at the house.

But we were inside, in shadows, and they couldn't see us.

"What are they doing?" asked Junie.

"Watching to see if anyone comes running outside."

"What can we do?"

Without getting too close to the window glass, I angled my head to look up and down the yard. I spotted Ghost. He was alive, crouched under a pine tree forty feet from the house. He looked terrified.

Lot of that going around.

"Are we dead?" gasped Junie.

It was so strangely worded a question that I turned to her. Usually people ask *Are we trapped?* or *Can we get out?*

Are we dead?

That was a different kind of question and it opened within my mind a window of speculation about her. It also provoked a response from my inner committee. The Cop barked a sharp denial. Cold and certain. The Warrior rose up and thumped his chest to prove that he was the toughest ape in the tree. But the Modern Man, the quietest and least often heard from of my inner selves, spoke in the clearest voice.

"No, Junie," he said, using my mouth, my voice, "we're going to live."

It was a clumsy line, awkwardly phrased, a bit of bad melodrama. And yet I knew that I meant it, and I knew that those words conveyed more than their surface meaning. I looked into Junie Flynn's blue eyes and saw understanding and trust and—something else. It looked like sadness, but she gripped my wrist and gave me a firm nod.

"Then let's get the hell out of here."

We backed away from the window and ran through the house to the front door. The dead men lay where I'd left them. Inside and out.

"Listen to me," I said. "Right now they don't know if we're alive or dead. They're going to shoot at anything that moves."

"What do we do?"

"We give them something to shoot at." I pointed to a stand of sassafras trees thirty yards to the right of the open door. "I'm going to draw their fire. You run for those trees like your ass is on fire."

She frowned. "What about you?"

"I'll be right behind you. Their focus is going to be the kitchen. As soon as you hear them open up, you move." I touched her cheek. "No matter what happens, stay low and get lost in the woods. You know this forest, you live here. Find people. Find help."

I fished a card out of my pocket. All it had on it was a phone number.

"As soon as you can, call this number. They'll connect you with my boss, the man you spoke to earlier."

She glanced at the card and handed it back.

"No, you'll—"

Junie recited the number back perfectly and tapped her head. "Like an elephant, Joe, I never forget."

I grinned at her. "Good brain you have there."

"At times."

As I made to move away, Junie suddenly grabbed my shirt and pulled me close for a very brief and totally unexpected kiss.

"For luck," she said as she pushed me away.

I goggled at her. "Wow," I said.

"Go!" she ordered.

I went.

The chopper with the minigun was slowly descending, clearly preparing to land on the lawn beside the flower garden. The kitchen was filling with smoke and I realized that pretty soon the entire place was going to be a bonfire. Junie was going to lose everything she owned. That gave me a flash of panic and I spun and ran back to the living room.

"Junie—the fire's spreading."

"No!"

"Your computer, the records about the Black Book. We need to get that stuff—we need to take that with us."

She shook her head. "No, it's okay. I have it all stored on my Web site in blind pages, and I've attached a lot of it to e-mails I sent myself. There's some stored in cloud servers, too. The rest of it . . ." She went to touch her head, but her hand faltered. She took a breath and tapped her skull. "I've got the rest of it here. I don't forget things."

Smoke was coming up from between the floorboards now. Some of the debris must have punched through into the cellar and now the fire was burning up. We were out of time.

"We need that information," I warned Junie.

"Then we have to get out of here. Get me to a good computer with a secure Wi-Fi and I'll get you everything you need."

I nodded and ran through the smoke into the kitchen. The chopper was ten feet above the grass.

Scary in one way, perfect in another.

With my Beretta in a two-handed grip, I leaned my thighs against the sink, aimed out the window and squeezed the trigger. The first shot hit the black metal beside the open door. The second shot hit the Closer who was crouched over the minigun. Not sure where I hit him, but it was solid enough to punch him back into the shadows of the helo. I paused to wait for the next man to swing into position to return fire. He did, leaping forward to grab the minigun, swinging the barrel around toward the house.

I took him in the face.

It was a long shot and I was aiming center mass, but it clipped him right above his snarling mouth. Lucky shot for me, damned unlucky for him.

Then the pilot turned the bird to bring his 30mm gunpods to bear.

"Kiss my ass," I yelled, then spun and ran like a son of a bitch for the living room even as the first bullets began tearing the rear of the house into splinters, broken glass and flying debris.

Junie was right there and I did not even pause. I shoved her toward the door and I was pleased to see that she took the force of my push and used it to settle into a nice, fast, efficient sprint. For a tall woman she ran well.

The machine gun fire was continuous, the sound enormous; with that din we never heard the sounds of the other helo firing its rockets.

We were a dozen feet from the sassafras trees when the house exploded.

A huge, rolling, tumbling ball of superheated gases chased us across the lawn, caught us, plucked us off the grass, and hurled us screaming into the forest.

Chapter Sixty-five

Hadley and Meyers Real Estate
Baltimore, Maryland
Sunday, October 20, 10:59 a.m.

Tull pulled to the curb outside of a real estate office that had a small parking lot. The windows were dark and the lot was empty. The lot was partly sheltered from the street by the exterior wall of a Dunkin' Donuts, so Tull pulled into the Dunkin' lot and killed the engine. Tull and Aldo got out, opened the back, stripped the cover off the false tire and removed several items from the safe. They packed everything into a pair of nylon gym bags, closed the car, and walked around to the back of the real estate office.

The place had an expensive security system. Aldo smirked at it. They were inside less than two minutes later.

The middle room had no windows, which allowed them to turn on lights without drawing attention. They cleared everything off a big work-table, and Aldo began emptying the bags while Tull set up the Ghost Box. Once it was booted, the system hacked the Wi-Fi, bypassing all security as easily as knife through wet tissue.

"Okay," said Tull, "I'm recalling the pigeon drones. Open the window in the back room."

"We're going to be deaf for a while. Can we risk that?"

Tull shrugged. "Not going to matter much if we move fast."

Chapter Sixty-six

The Warehouse
Baltimore, Maryland
Sunday, October 20, 11:04 a.m.

Rudy Sanchez sat in his office at the Warehouse. The door was locked and the anti-intrusion devices activated, however he felt as if covert eyes were peering at him. He scolded himself for allowing the pervasive air of paranoia to set its hooks in him. Rudy prided himself on his detachment, but today he found that increasingly difficult to manage.

The list of names and contact numbers Mr. Church had given him was placed neatly in the center of his desk blotter. Rudy fitted a Bluetooth onto his ear and punched in the first of the numbers. The call was picked up after a few rings.

"Hello?"

"Is this George Noory?" asked Rudy.

"Sure. Who's calling?"

Church had given Rudy a certain phrase to use when reaching out to the names he'd indicated were "friends in the industry."

"A mutual friend told me to tell you that 'Eden still burns.'"

There was a profound silence at the other end. George Noory was the popular host of the overnight radio show *Coast to Coast AM*, which was broadcast to well over five hundred radio stations as well as streamed over the Internet to more than ten million people a night. Rudy was a long-time listener and enjoyed the often lively discussions of everything from Bigfoot to flying saucers. More than once he caught elements related to DMS cases and he found it fascinating how public perception often spun stories into wild new forms. Looking back on those shows—and now knowing that Noory was a friend of Church's—Rudy appreciated the subtle way in which the host dialed down needless panic and kept the discussions in the realm of intelligent speculation.

Noory said, "You're a friend of the Deacon?"

"I am," said Rudy. "Dr. Rudy Sanchez, I am——"

"The house psychiatrist at the DMS," cut in Noory.

"You've heard of me?"

Instead of answering, Noory said, "What can I do for you?"

"The DMS is currently involved in a case that includes elements that are somewhat outside of our usual comfort zone."

"With the things you fellows deal with I'm surprised anything's outside of your comfort zone."

"Unfortunately the Fates seem to take each new day as a challenge when it comes to the DMS."

Noory laughed. "What are they throwing at you today?"

"We . . . have been tasked with obtaining the Majestic Black Book."

"Wow," said Noory.

"You've heard of it, I gather."

"Of course. How can I help?"

"We need to put together a list of persons most likely to possess a copy."

"Well, first understand that there aren't 'copies' of the Black Book. There's the original and that's it."

"Okay."

"Are you familiar with MJ-12 and M3, or do we need to start at square one?"

"No, I've actually read a couple of Junie Flynn's books."

"Good. Are you talking to her, too?"

"We're working on that but there have been some complications. Mr. Church said that you were also an expert on the book."

"Kind of him, but I wouldn't go that far. I've had Junie on the show a dozen times, but she's the one who knows everything."

"Miss Flynn was able to provide us with a list of possible current or former members of M3. If I share those names with you, might you be able to help us cull the list to the most likely? As Mr. Church is so fond of saying, time is not our friend."

"I can't make any promises, Doctor, but I can take a pretty solid swing at it. Is that the only thing Deacon wants from me?"

"Actually, I have a second request. This case involves groups of men Miss Flynn refers to as 'Closers.' "

"Men in Black, sure."

"I need everything you can tell me about them as well."

Noory whistled. "Tall order. I hope you have a comfortable seat, Doctor, this might take a while."

Chapter Sixty-seven

Elk Neck State Park
Cecil County, Maryland
Sunday, October 20, 11:06 a.m.

We slammed into the trees.

A month later and those trees would have been bare sticks and the crooked fingers of the countless branches would have plucked the skin from our bodies. But summer had lingered well into October and the trees were still thick with leaves. If those leaves were not as butter-soft now as they would have been in July, then at least there were a lot of them. Junie and I were curled into balls, arms wrapped around our heads, knees pulled to our chests like kids cannon-balling into a pool.

The blast punched us through the branches and gravity pulled us down to the thick grass. She hit first and then me, landing in a bad heels-first attempt at grace but powered by too much momentum. We tried to turn the landing into a clumsy run, but that was for shit. I lost sight of her as my body pitched forward and suddenly I was a big clunky wheel rolling over and over down a slope and I'm pretty sure I hit every goddamned moss-covered stone and fallen branch. Pain erupted all along my hide like a string of firecrackers. At the bottom of the slope I found a fragment of balance and ran halfway up the next hill to slough off the force. Everything hurt. My muscles hurt, my joints hurt, my teeth hurt, even my hair hurt. The world did a drunken Irish jig around me and my guts wanted to throw up everything I'd eaten since last March.

Instead, I whirled and looked for Junie. She was sprawled in a thick rhododendron. Her wild blond hair covered her face and one hand was flung out onto the grass. It was covered with dirt and ashes and blood.

She wasn't moving.

"Junie!" I cried and then I was racing down the slope toward her, dropping to my knees, sliding the last yard, reaching for her.

Her fingers closed around my wrist.

"Joe . . ." Her voice was a faint echo of pain.

I tore leaves and branches out of the way. "Are you hurt?"

"I . . . don't think so."

There was a sound behind me and I whirled, one hand scrabbling for my pistol.

Which wasn't there. I'd lost it in the trees.

Something moved quickly through the brush and then I saw a flash of white.

Junie looked past me. "Ghost!" she cried, and the fuzz monster came pelting down the slope. He was as much of a mess as we were. Sooty, singed, bleeding from a dozen shallow cuts, but for all that he was full of excitement to see me.

And he rushed right past me and began licking Junie's face.

With dogs, it's always an ego boost knowing that you're the center of their universe.

"Hey," I said, and Ghost gave me a quick token lick and half a wag.

He does more than that when he smells the neighbor dog's ass.

Nice.

There was another sound from up the hill. Men shouting, and I realized with a start that the helicopters were no longer overhead. They must have touched down to deploy their crews of killers.

The Closers.

I pulled Junie down behind some wild shrubs.

"Persistent sons of bitches," I said, then I gave her a shrewd look. "No offense, but this seems like a lot of firepower to kill one woman."

She shook her head. "I don't understand it. I don't know how to fight, they could have sent one man with a gun."

"Why do they want to kill you at all?"

She didn't answer.

"Junie . . . really, now's not the time to be coy."

"They're coming!" she said urgently. Indeed they were, a line of men hurrying down into the woods.

We edged away and as soon as we could, we bent low and ran for our lives.

Chapter Sixty-eight

Elk Neck State Park
Cecil County, Maryland
Sunday, October 20, 11:12 a.m.

Ghost tore ahead of us, plunging through the brush, picking out a rough path for us, and we followed. Junie next, me behind her, watching her back. Studying this enigma of a woman.

Despite the shock and trauma of the last fifteen minutes, she ran well, moving with a flowing grace, her stamina impressive. I'm bigger, heavier, and I've had more wound-repair surgeries than most people have had hot dinners. On a short sprint I'm a pale Usain Bolt, but after about fifty yards my knee starts sending me hate mail. After half a mile at full speed I can feel each separate inch of scar tissue, each area of knitted bone, each screw and pin.

Junie Flynn ran like a deer. Ghost was right beside her.

"No," I said in a grouchy wheeze, "I'm good, don't stop for me."

They didn't hear me and weren't meant to.

The land angled downward and wound through the woods. I looked over my shoulder and could no longer even see the column of smoke from the ruined lighthouse. The manicured lawn and beds of wildflowers were gone, replaced by a primal forest filled with deadfalls, gullies, hairy vines, twisted roots, and unexpected marshes. Once I heard a gunshot— the harsh boom of a shotgun—but it was ahead of us, far deeper into the woods. I almost stopped, but Junie flung two quick words over her shoulder.

"Deer hunters!"

Swell.

The lingering temperature kept fooling me about what time of year it was. It was fall, and fall meant hunting season was underway. Beginning in September, deer hunters begin walking these woods, armed with bows, shotguns, and even muzzle-loaders. And there are waterfowl blinds on the bay and along the Elk River. It would be so hilarious to have escaped helicopter-fired missiles and actual Men in Black with freaky weapons only to take a load of buckshot in the teeth. I'd die embarrassed.

As Junie jumped over a fallen log something fell from the loose pocket of her sweater. She felt it fall and turned, but I bent and picked it up.

It was one of the freaky-looking pistols. There was a single smudge of blood on the handle. Junie looked at it and then at me. She shrugged.

"I picked it up from the man in the kitchen."

"Do you even know what it is?"

She nodded. "Microwave pulse pistol."

"You say that like it's something everyone knows about. I play with guns all the time and I've never heard of anything like this."

Junie held her hand out for it, but I held on to it for a moment. "I need a gun."

"You need to answer a bunch of questions before I put a weapon in your hand."

We heard muffled shouts far behind us.

"Move!" I snapped, shoving the pistol into my waistband. Junie gave me a furious look, but she didn't press the issue. Not then, anyway.

We cut across a well-worn hiking path that I knew as the Lighthouse Trail. Junie wanted to go that way, but I pulled her back into the brush.

"We'd make better time," she insisted.

"And they'll know that. This is where they'll look for us." I flipped open my rapid-response folding knife, went ten yards deeper into the brush, cut a leafy branch, and used it to wipe out our tracks on the road. Then I tossed some stones and loose gravel across the spot I'd cleared, and picked up some leaves and let them fall haphazardly over the stones. The old trick of brushing out your trail is useful for fooling the inept, but a trained tracker will see the distinctive erasure marks. The key is to then disguise the marks of the branch. Best way to do that is with casual debris. If I had time I'd have found some deer poop and dropped it there, too. The older and dryer, the better. But in a poopless scenario, stones and dry leaves would do it. You work with what you have.

We started running again and I took the branch with me, finally discarding it a quarter mile away.

"Junie," I said, "we are going to have that talk."

She looked at me, then turned away and pretended to concentrate on picking a path through the woods. If we were back in the world and if what happened this morning in D.C. hadn't happened, then maybe I'd cut her some slack. She didn't strike me as an agent of evil or a closet super-villain, but she was clearly hiding something. A little time alone in a hold-ing cell or an interview room might give her a chance to sort through her options and make the right decision.

But we didn't have that kind of time. We had no damn time at all. With the jammers on I couldn't even check the countdown from the video, but I could feel the seconds burning, burning . . .

After ten more minutes I touched her shoulder to stop her, then sent Ghost out to scout. He's trained to do that several ways. For this I wanted him to stay out there as long as he saw nothing. If there was anyone within five hundred yards of us, he would come back at a fast, silent run.

"Okay," I said, "we're good. Let's talk."

She kept moving.

I took a big step forward and wheeled around in front her, forcing her to a stumbling halt.

Junie exhaled a ball of tension and nearly collapsed. She put her face in her hands and sat that way on the weedy edge of a shallow ravine, feet propped on a rock, body hunched.

I let her have about two minutes of that.

"Junie," I said, "we're going to have to have a conversation, you know that, right?"

She said nothing.

"I'm not screwing around here. This is more than just your life."

That did it. She raised her head and gave me a long, flat, uncompromis-ing stare. "You think I don't know that, Joe?"

"Frankly, sweetheart, I don't know what you know. You're hiding something from me and my patience for that kind of bullshit is wearing pretty thin."

She whipped an arm out and stabbed a finger in the direction we'd come. "Those men are trying to do more than kill me," she snapped. "They're trying to kill the truth."

"Oh, very nice. Can we use that as the tagline if someone makes a movie of your life?"

Junie glared at me. "I'm not being overly dramatic. The Closers want to shut me up because of something I said on my podcast last night."

"Which was?"

She closed her eyes for a moment, then raised her face and looked up at the sky. "Last night I announced that I had a complete copy of the Majestic Black Book and that I was going to share it with the entire world."

I stared at her for a long five seconds. "Well kiss my ass. Why in the world would you want to do something like that?"

She stared at me. "Do you even grasp what these people are trying to do?"

"According to you and my friend Bug, they're reverse-engineering UFO parts and making a shitload of money. What else do I need to know?"

"How can you be so naive?"

"I'm not naive," I said. "I lack information, and I feel like I'm being dicked around here. Instead of the dramatics, why not come straight out and tell me what's going on?"

"Joe . . ." She winced as if saying anything were physically painful for her. "During the conference back there . . . I didn't exactly tell you the truth."

"Really? Well gosh, Junie, I'd have never figured that out." I sighed. "If you're thinking that now's a good time to unburden your soul, then I'm all for it, 'cause we're ass-deep in it right now. I honestly don't think I've ever been this confused in my entire life, and believe me that is saying a hell of a lot."

She took a steadying breath. "Okay, I told you that I had a source who told me about the Black Book."

"Right, and the Closers cooked him in a rigged car crash. What about him?"

"He was more than a casual contact, Joe." Her eyes were bright with pain. "He was my father."

And I said, "Yeah, no kidding."

"Wait . . . you . . . know?" she gasped.

"I know."

"When did you figure it out?"

I grinned. "Right around the time everyone else did. My boss, Bug, Rudy, even that jackass Dr. Hu. I think Ghost knows, too. It's not like you built a mind-boggling web of deception around that part of it."

"Oh," she said, and I couldn't tell if she was relieved or deflated.

"But . . . ," I said, "I'm sorry, Junie. For your dad, and your mom."

She sighed and nodded. "Thanks."

"Right now, though," I said, "I need you to tell me how he got involved with M3, what he knew, why they decided to kill him, and why on earth you painted a bull's-eye on yourself by broadcasting that you're going to share their secrets with the world." I paused and gave her my most charming smile. "Really . . . start anywhere."

Chapter Sixty-nine

Hadley and Meyers Real Estate
Baltimore, Maryland
Sunday, October 20, 11:27 a.m.

"How's this actually work?" asked Aldo.

"I thought you took the tour . . . Didn't Dr. Hoshino go over it all?"

"Yeah, she went over a lot of bullshit science. The woman is a supergeek. Doesn't know how to talk to real folks. She couldn't explain the concept of chewing gum to a kid without making it sound like *Star Wars*."

"It's simple," said Tull. On the table were ten tiny components laid out on a long piece of red velvet, each piece separated by a block of rubber. "These are miniatures of the D-type components used in the Device. The stabilizer, the red generator, the green generator, the clock, the interface, the mother board, the master circuit, the slave circuit, the iridium heart, and the central switch. When President Truman authorized Majestic Twelve and Majestic Three, the initial goal was to rebuild the alien craft from Roswell. That was an immediate failure because the ship was too badly damaged. So, M3 began researching other crashes around the world, and when it began clear early on that there have been many crashes, Truman directed M3 to obtain as many D-type components as possible in order to cobble together one complete craft. All devices have these ten. The miniatures were made to run simulations, but they're actually too dangerous for that. We blew up a couple of labs before we figured that out."

Tull took two of the components. "Take any two of the—like this slave circuit and this green generator and put them in close proximity and look what happens."

He set the two pieces down within five inches of each other. Immediately they began trembling and suddenly they flew together. At first they merely collided, but as Aldo watched the components continued to tremble and turn until they finally reached the point where a tab on the green generator slid into a slot on the slave circuit. There was a flash of white light and when Aldo blinked his eyes clear the pieces lay immobile but completely connected. Tull handed it to him.

"They look like they're welded together. I can't even find a seam. Jeez-us."

"It's called charismatic magnetism. The pieces know they're supposed to be together and given the chance they'll always connect. Rubber blocks work pretty well, but for today we're going to coat one piece in ionized gel. The charge in the gel will be fed by the motors in the pigeon drones. Once in place, we shut off the motors and the gel gradually loses its charge, eventually allowing the last component to be pulled into place."

"That's some scary shit," said Aldo.

"You should see your face," laughed Tull. "It's not magic, man, it's just science."

Aldo grunted. "What was that flash? Nearly blinded me."

"Ah, well . . . that's the reason they stopped building the little ones, and it's the reason they've had so much trouble with the big ones. When the components connect they emit a strong burst of energy. No one quite knows why. Almost every previous attempt to construct a complete Device—or a synthetic Truman Engine—has resulted in such a massive energy discharge that it's been like dropping a nuke."

"Yeah, I heard some bullshit rumors about that. Did we cause Mount St. Helens to blow?"

"Sure, they had a geothermal research lab that was part of a clean power project. The governors of M3 at the time thought that the big turbines and batteries they'd built to store all that geothermal energy would be enough to contain the discharge."

"That didn't work out so great, huh?"

"Not the first big mistake, not the last."

"You're telling me that every single one of these engines is a potential disaster waiting to happen."

"Right," said Tull.

"So . . . ," Aldo said slowly, "why the fuck are we trying to build ten of them right here?"

Tull grinned. "When you were a kid, didn't you ever tie a firecracker to a cat's tail?"

"No, when I was a kid I was sane."

"Well, the man who taught me about the Device used to blow up cats." He paused and picked up another component. "I even tried it. So much fun."

Chapter Seventy

Over Maryland airspace
Sunday, October 20, 11:31 a.m.

There was a soft tone in Top's ear and he tapped his earbud.

"Go for Sergeant Rock," he said, using his combat call sign.

"It's Bug. I just intercepted a call from the Coast Guard. They got an emergency call from someone claiming to be Captain Ledger. Sounds legit."

"Tell me."

Bug replayed the message.

"Who's rolling on this?" demanded Top.

"Coast Guard has a boat inbound and a helo in the air. The helo reports smoke rising from the direction of the Turkey Point Lighthouse. They're eighteen minutes out. The Deacon wants to know your ETA."

"Instruments say we're about to hit the outer edge of the jam zone," said Top.

The pilot tapped Top's shoulder and pointed toward the northeast. A column of gray smoke curled up above the trees at the edge of the bay. Bunny leaned between Top and the pilot.

"Jesus, is that the lighthouse?"

"Wait," said Bug, "what did he—"

And they crossed into the jam zone. The pilot tried everything he could to reestablish contact.

"Sorry, Top," he said, "but nobody's talking to nobody in here."

Top felt his stomach turn from cold slush to hard ice. He pulled out the plastic-covered map and tapped a spot half a kilometer from the lighthouse. "Put us down right here, then go to this spot. Drop us, then haul ass outside the jam zone and call for serious backup. Next time I look up all I want to see is gunships. Copy?"

"Hooah," said the pilot. "What about Captain Ledger?"

He tapped a second point three klicks inland. "Sweep by this LZ every half hour. We'll find the captain and come to you."

Then Top turned in his seat and yelled in his leather-throated sergeant's voice.

"Echo Team—saddle up! Time to bring the pain."

Chapter Seventy-one

The Warehouse
Baltimore, Maryland
Sunday, October 20, 11:32 a.m.

Rudy's next call was to Bill Birnes, publisher of *UFO Magazine* and, like Rudy's fiancée Circe, a *New York Times* bestselling author. Although Rudy had seen Birnes several times on UFO specials and shows, it took Rudy a moment to realize that this was the same William J. Birnes who had written several landmark books on a completely different subject—serial killers. One of those books, *The Riverman*, coauthored by detective Dr. Robert Keppel, described how serial killer Ted Bundy helped police track Green River Killer Gary Ridgway. Rudy had read that book twice while working as a police psychologist prior to his being hired by Church for the DMS.

He used his laptop to run through Birnes' other publishing credits and noted that he'd coauthored books with George Noory as well. That was good. The conversation with Noory had yielded a great deal of information. About M3, about the Black Book, and about the Closers—those fearsome Men in Black. Everything, along with Rudy's notes and observations, had already been passed along to Mr. Church, Aunt Sallie, and Bug, and so the great investigative machine that was the DMS was already turning.

Rudy dialed the number and got Birnes on the line.

"How's the Deacon doing these days?" asked Birnes after the introductions. "Still tilting at windmills?"

"Every day."

"I'd expected nothing less. Tell me what you need and I'll tell you if I can help."

"I don't know what Mr. Church knows," confessed Rudy, "and he's not available right now. I am attempting to gather as much information as possible to assist one of our field agents. One area in particular seems to make no sense to me."

"Which is?"

"Funding. If a group like M3 exists, and they have been working for half a century to reverse-engineer technology from crashed alien craft, surely that would have to be an enormously expensive undertaking."

"Very."

"So—where is that money coming from? I know the popular belief is that it's all buried beneath levels of secrecy as part of Depart of Defense funding, but—"

"Some of it is, sure," said Birnes, "but not the bulk of it. And, you have to understand that we're not really talking about work being undertaken by hidden divisions within our own government. That would be a logistical nightmare. It's hard to hide something that big—and that interesting—inside a red-tape bureaucracy. No, a lot of this kind of R and D was transferred out of the government and into the hands of private contractors."

"Defense contractors?"

"Mostly."

"But that would still necessitate a lot of monies going to those companies as government fees."

"Sure, but not for what we're talking about. We're talking about companies that have massive projects under way that are totally legitimate. We contract out everything of military importance to whoever can design and build it according to the right timetables and price tags. Alien tech notwithstanding, we still need jet fighters and satellites and submarines, and that sort of thing. However, private corporations, even defense contractors, have other sources of funding, and this is where this all starts to get dirty."

"And that's probably the part I need to hear."

"I'll give you the short course in illegal black budget cash flow," said Birnes. "Each year the Department of Defense lists several coded entries that have nondescript names, like 'special evaluation research program,' that don't clearly relate to anything that sounds like any known new weapons system currently in development. These entries are simply covers for black budget items, and this provides a hefty slush pile for all sorts of things including covert operations, intelligence activities, and classified weapons research to be conducted without congressional oversight on the grounds that such oversight would compromise the secrecy essential for black ops. And to a degree that's true. However, some watchdog groups have tracked some accounting anomalies in the DoD budget that suggest that as much as a trillion U.S. dollars is annually being siphoned by the CIA into the DoD for secret distribution to unknown projects."

Rudy whistled.

"It gets better," said Birnes, warming to his topic. "Congress is always looking for a way to chop the DoD budget and to put a tighter leash on black operations of all kinds, especially anything connected to the CIA. At the same time, there are things the DoD and other groups want to work on that they know for a fact would never get official sanction or funding and, if it was discovered that they were being secretly funded, they would get the ax and some heads would roll. So, that's part of why we've seen the movement of critical and you could say 'radical' R and D away from the DoD and into private labs. Now, those labs still need to be funded and this kind of research is enormously expensive. We're talking amounts bigger than the national debts of some of our allies."

"Why so much?"

"Because a lot of these research projects chew up money and then hit a developmental dead end. Which means there are no items to sell to Uncle Sam and no items that can be repurposed and sold to the global nonmilitary technologies markets."

"So where does this funding come from?"

"Drugs."

"Drugs?"

"Sure," said Birnes. "Look, to understand it you have to realize that this has been going on for a long time and that the money doesn't go to fund a single project or even a related group of projects. A lot of it goes to funding any kind of operation that is so secret it needs to stay totally off congressional or public radar. That means there are a lot of dirty deals being made. During Vietnam—even before Mr. and Mrs. America knew we had an interest over there, the CIA was taking control of the flow of drugs as a way of funding our developing involvement. That includes everything from bribe money to providing weapons for locals who we'd turned into allies, to all sorts of things. That process didn't start there and it sure as hell didn't end there. CIA and other agencies have been managing the world narcotics market for decades because that is an inexhaustible and unregulated source of income."

"You're killing me with this," said Rudy.

Birnes laughed. "You asked. But I'm not taking wild shots at America. This isn't national policy, this is backdoor stuff and when the right people in Congress find out about it they shut it down."

"It doesn't sound like it goes away, though."

"Of course not," said Birnes. "Too much is at stake."

"National security?" Rudy said, pitching it as a sour joke.

"Actually, yes, to a degree. Some of it does serve the common good. But no government has ever been entirely honest, and there are all kinds of groups, big and small, that have their own agendas, and they know that they can't go to Congress to get funding. The fact that drug money can be used to fund these projects is too tempting to ignore. Even for those persons who abhor the damage drugs do, they often look at the risk-reward ratio. Many of them are absolutely convinced we're involved in a very serious arms race, and if we lose that race we'll lose more than economic superiority."

"Meaning?"

"Meaning that whoever cracks the alien technology in a practical way that allows mass production of a new generation of weapons of war will end the arms race right there and then."

"How? By shaking the biggest stick?"

"No," said Birnes, "through conquest. We could easily see a new age of empire that would reshape every map on Earth."

"With alien technology?"

"With alien technology," said Birnes.

Chapter Seventy-two

Elk Neck State Park
Cecil County, Maryland
Sunday, October 20, 11:34 a.m.

We heard sounds and moved to a new hiding spot. The sounds were probably deer sneaking away from hunters, but we weren't taking chances. I found a ravine that angled down into a little natural tunnel worn by rain runoff. It was ten feet long, with easy egress from either end. We could see and hear anyone coming, but in the dense shadows we were invisible.

So, we hunkered down to wait. I knew that help had to be on its way. Maybe the Coast Guard, definitely my guys from the DMS. All we had to do was not be seen and not get our brains scrambled by those freaky microwave pistols.

As the minutes dragged by, I used the time to gather as much intel as I could. They say that knowledge is power, and that's true enough, but knowledge is often a shield as well.

"Okay," I said, "now tell me how your father got access to the Black Book."

Junie tucked her legs under her and smoothed her skirt. In the shadows she was a specter, her pale skin painted a misty blue, her eyes dark and bottomless.

"My father was a brilliant physicist and engineer," she said. "He'd filed half a dozen patents during his first eighteen months at MIT. He won prizes in so many different areas of science. The Rolls-Royce Science Prize, the UNESCO Science Prize, the Bunsen Prize, the Sten von Friesen's prize, he even spent two years as part of a team in Austria and won the Erich Schmid Prize. He was so smart that he was unhappy with it. He hated it. He was depressed a lot of the time because everything he tried was too easy. There are people like that, you know, genius freaks who almost fit in with the rest of the world, but can't really. Maybe there was some Asperger's there. Maybe some autism, but it was never diagnosed. If he'd come along a half generation later they might have caught it." She shook her head. "The thing is, genius of that level gets noticed. He partnered with another young scientist for one of the DARPA challenges. The participants were given three pieces of a machine but no other information. No idea what kind of machine the parts belonged to or even if they belonged to the same machine. The challenge was to develop a way for those parts to work in harmony. Most of the entrants were part of the robotics crowd, and Dad was always into task-oriented robotics. Well, no surprise, but he won the challenge and was awarded a huge research grant and DARPA hired him for their robotics lab."

"So he worked for the military?"

She frowned. "Not exactly. His paychecks came from DARPA, but he never worked in their lab in Arlington. Instead he was brought into a separate lab nearby. The thing is, none of the DARPA people he'd met at the challenge were there except one of the judges, and that person was Howard Shelton of Shelton Aeronautics. He's a major defense contractor. His family's always done contract work for the government. Jets now, planes of every kind going back to World War I, and before that they made cannons and special guns."

"Shelton . . . he's on your list of possible M3 members."

"He's pretty high on my list, I suppose. He was the one who recruited Dad for the special DARPA group. I'm not sure if that means he's in M3 or is one of the people profiting from their research. A lot of people are, there's a trickle down among the superwealthy industrialists, especially those tied to the Department of Defense."

"What happened once your dad was in that group?"

"I don't know everything," she said. "I was little and even though he started telling me things later on, he never told me everything. He didn't have time. From what I've pieced together, they kept Dad on some non-critical projects at first. Stuff that was challenging and interesting, but nothing that was tied to anything from the crashed vehicles. That came later, after they knew they could trust him."

"Could they trust him?"

"For years, sure. He was very loyal to them at first. For most of the time, really," she said. "Because Dad was very patriotic. He had his idealistic side, but he was always a bit more of a hawk than a dove. Dad's grandfather died in World War II, at the Battle of the Bulge. His father was career military and had been wounded twice in Vietnam. Dad never served, but he had a lot of respect for those who did and he wanted to help create the kinds of technologies that would keep American soldiers safe.

He worked on tactical armor and antiarmor programs, infrared sensing for space-based surveillance, high-energy laser technology for space-based missile defense, antisubmarine warfare, advanced aircraft, and defense applications of advanced computing, and he did some of the earliest work on predators and other drones. He created some of the parts for the MARCbot, the Multifunction Agile Remote Control Robot, used to disable IEDs. Stuff like that."

"Good man," I said. "I know people who didn't die because those robots cleared IEDs off the road."

"He was a good man," she agreed. "A very good man. He wanted to do good things. They kept moving him from one project to another, and for a while he was frustrated by that because he never got to follow anything to completion. But then he realized that they were bringing him into projects that had stalled because the developers had hit a dead end or a limit in known science. Dad was the X factor that would take these projects in new directions or help them jump right over a design block. That was his gift. He was a developmental intuitive."

I could see the shape of it. A scientist like that would be a shot of adrenaline to any project. DARPA, like most other R and D groups, has more failed projects than successful ones. That's the nature of speculative science. Sometimes you don't know until you try, and you can blow through a lot of cash and a lot of research time on projects that sound good until they hit an immovable snag. A man who can come in and think through or over or around the problem would be worth his weight in gold. Actually, considering the price tag on some of these things, he'd be worth a hell of a lot more than that.

Junie explained how her father was coaxed inch by inch away from DARPA and into the more covert world of M3. They played on his patriotism—and perhaps his naïveté—so that he believed he was part of a think tank that was the last bastion between a safe America and the collapse of democracy in the face of enemies both foreign and domestic. It was a very good sales pitch, and it bought her father's total loyalty.

"Finally," she said, "they brought him a piece of equipment that he could not identify. They said that it was a component to a large device, but that's all they'd tell him about it. They called it a 'D-type component.' They said it was another test, like the DARPA challenge. They wanted him to figure out what it was and what it did. They let him work on the problem part of every day for months. Then he figured out what it did. It was a switch. That was all, just a switch, but clearly no one had ever figured that out before because it didn't look like a switch. It didn't resemble something whose design intention was to function as a switch. When Dad figured out what it was, everyone got very excited. They threw a party for Dad, they gave him a huge raise and better benefits. He became like a rock star at the lab."

"This D-type component," I said, "what was it?"

She cocked her head. "It's what you think it was."

"From an alien ship?"

She nodded. "The next day, when Dad came into work, the head of the lab brought him into his office and made him sign a whole stack of papers. Nondisclosure agreements and other documents, including one that essentially said that he waived his constitutional rights while working on what they called 'the Project.'"

"Yeah, I've seen crap like that," I said. "Some of the DoD bases require that for people working on the stealth aircraft program. Not a fan of that. Mind you, I'm okay with punishing someone for revealing secrets, but I've never been a fan of anything that actually strips away your legal rights. That's a slippery slope."

"Dad signed it, though. At the time he was happy to do it. And . . . once all the papers were sealed, that's when they showed him the Majestic Black Book."

"Ah," I said. "We get to the point before I die of old age."

She punched me lightly on the arm. "If I don't tell this in order then some parts of it won't make sense."

I held my hands up in a gesture of surrender.

"The Black Book has a list of all of the parts recovered from crashes. The most important part of that inventory is the list and exact descriptions of the ten D-type components that make up the Device. That's with a capital 'D.' Those ten D-type components are the stabilizer, the red generator, the green generator, the clock, the interface, the mother board, the master circuit, the slave circuit, the iridium heart, and the central switch. When President Truman authorized Majestic Twelve and Majestic Three, the initial goal was to rebuild the alien craft from Roswell. That was an immediate failure because the ship was too badly damaged. So, M3 began researching other crashes around the world, and when it began clear early on that there have been many crashes, Truman directed M3 to obtain as many D-type components as possible in order to cobble together one complete craft."

"If there were so many crashes, that should have been easy."

"No, Joe," said Junie, "it's very complicated and for a couple of very good reasons. First, the Device is the engine of the craft, and most of the crashes were the result of some kind of engine failure. We don't know why, but in a number of cases the engines blew up. The ten D-type components that form the Device are held together with what my father called 'charismatic magnetism.'"

"What the hell's that?"

"It's part of the science my father was studying. When certain D-type components are brought into close proximity, they would begin to pull on each other in way that simulated magnetism. Align the parts in approximately the right way and that pull allows them to self-assemble."

"Um . . . okay."

"However, when a Device fails or a crash occurs, the components reverse their polarity and fly apart. If the crashing ship hits sand, foliage, or soft dirt, the flying pieces might be recovered intact. But if they hit something harder, then most or all the components could be damaged."

"I think I see part of the problem. M3 has been trying to build a flying saucer with potentially faulty parts."

"That, and they don't have all the D-type components. Ever since Roswell, M3 has been able to recover six complete and undamaged components from various crashes, but they never had the other four—the stabilizer, the interface, the slave circuit, and the green generator. Other countries have been working on this, too. There are groups like M3 in Great Britain, Israel, Germany, Brazil, North Korea, China, and Russia. Most of these projects are far behind M3's Project. Brazil only has one part, a green generator. Israel and North Korea each have three parts, the Brits have five. Same with China and Russia. At least, that was the last count my source heard, and that was a couple of years ago."

I knew that I had to have a long talk with Church. How the hell could something this big be going on without the DMS being aware of it? Either Church and MindReader were a lot less efficient than I believed, or there was something hinky going on. Neither option made me want to sing Disney songs.

"In 1952, when it became clear that they might not be able to assemble a Device made from original D-type components, President Truman allotted a huge amount of money for M3 to begin a research program to synthesize the missing parts. The intention was to combine these parts with the genuine D-type components to create a complete and working Device. M3 refers to this hybrid machine as a Truman Engine."

"How close are they to pulling this off?"

"I don't know. Close, I think. One of the last things my dad told me was that there have been some recent breakthroughs, but that was a few years ago, before he was killed."

"But they must have had some success. I know for a fact that we have some radical engine designs in the works for the next generation of fighters and—"

"You're thinking about it the wrong way, Joe. You're thinking that this is about building a fast jet or stealthier jet, but the Device is more than just an engine. A lot more. From experiments they've tried where things have gone disastrously wrong, they know that there is an almost unlimited potential for power in those D-type components. You think they don't know that fossil fuel is going to run out? Coal and natural gas aren't the long-term answer. Nuclear has a million problems. And the technology for solar and wind power is not really as close as politicians make it. We're hurtling toward a power crisis unlike anything we've ever faced. Unless we want to see ourselves plunged into a new and very literal Dark Age, we have to find a new and inexhaustible source of clean power. And, Joe— this is about power. The first nation to control that kind of power will become the greatest superpower the world has ever seen." She touched her fingers to my chest. "Because unlimited energy like this can also be used for weapons. And nobody—no nation or group of nations—will be able to defend themselves against that kind of power. Whoever can solve the riddle of the Device will be able to conquer the whole world—and nothing and no one can stop them."

Chapter Seventy-three

The Warehouse
Baltimore, Maryland
Sunday, October 20, 11:44 a.m.

Rudy Sanchez made a total of twenty calls to Mr. Church's friends, and another thirty calls to people recommended to him by the first tier of contacts.

He spoke with experts on alien craft. "You're more likely to see something big and triangular than the classic saucer," Peter Robbins, author of a landmark book on the UFO crash at Rendlesham in the UK told him. "As far as who or what they are . . . I have no idea beyond a general belief that they are not from here. They are from somewhere very far away. That in itself is cause for grave concern."

Experts on alien abduction. "I was abducted last year in Phoenix," said Jeff Straus, a friend of a friend of a friend of Church's and the national technical director for the Mutual UFO Network. "They did the whole thing on me. Blood and urine samples, DNA, all sorts of meters and scopes. And an anal probe. I don't know why aliens have this thing about anal probes. What's up my ass that could help them understand the human race? That's just uncalled for."

Experts on alien-human hybrids. "The thing about alien craft," said Bud Sorkin, a physicist from Caltech, "is that the pilot is part of the engine. There is a definite biomechanical interface and without the pilot to control all of the engine functions the engine runs wild and blows up. That's why both the aliens and our own people are interested in creating hybrids. Not only will they be able to interface with the ships, but by doing so they'll be able to form some measure of meaningful communication between aliens and humans."

"Has there actually been any progress in terms of creating an alien-human hybrid?"

Sorkin chuckled. "Dr. Sanchez . . . they're all around us. You've probably met one. I know I have. The thing is . . . not all of the hybrids know that they're hybrids."

Another expert on that subject was Abigail DuFraine, a clinical psychologist who Rudy had met at conferences. A brilliant, if eccentric woman, who had twice been short-listed for a Nobel Prize. Her book *Of Two Worlds: The Question of Alien-Human Hybrids* was a bestseller and had been the basis of a History Channel special.

"While writing my second book," she said, "the one on alien abductions, I began to encounter a large number of people who claim to have had DNA, eggs, or sperm taken from them. And once, in 2005, I was introduced to a young man of about twenty-four who claimed to be a product of a government sponsored program tasked with creating hybrids. I was only able to interview the young man, sadly. I would very much have liked to do a full medical workup on him, particularly a DNA sequence. However, during our interview, he demonstrated a remarkable number of unusual qualities. In a leap to judgment you might think was indicative of savantism. He demonstrated prodigious capacities and abilities far in excess of those considered normal. He had an eidetic recall of any number sequence he had encountered, and when tested was able to calculate mathematical problems to six decimal points. However, with savants there is usually a prodigious memory of a special type that is very deep, but exceedingly narrow. Not so with him. He could recall every zip code, sports statistic, text and page numbers of every book he'd read, and so on. Understand, Dr. Sanchez, that it is exceedingly rare for a prodigious savant to have so many areas of interest and memory. From our conversation I counted twenty-six areas, and I don't think I scratched the surface."

"What happened to the young man?" asked Rudy.

DuFraine gave him a sad sigh. "I arranged to have him visit my office so I could do a more thorough interview. I said that I wanted to take some blood samples as well. However, on the way to that appointment he was killed in a traffic accident. What a sad loss to science."

Rudy murmured agreement, but he made a notation to have Gus Dietrich pull the records on that accident.

He asked DuFraine a follow-up question, "Did this young man claim that these abilities came about as a result of his being a hybrid?"

"Yes, but that's an odd thing. He said that these were not qualities he—and others like him—got from the aliens. He said that exposure to alien DNA unlocked these qualities in ordinary human DNA."

Rudy's next call was to a theoretical physicist, Dr. Kim Sung, who was a leading proponent of the theory that aliens were not from other worlds but from other times in our own future, or were visitors from neighboring dimensions. He leaned heavily on the interdimensional theory, which was the subject of the book he was currently writing.

"Why is that more likely than them being aliens?" asked Rudy.

Sung laughed. "We know that there are many dimensions. Superstring theory, M-theory, and Bosonic string theory respectively posit that physical space has either ten, eleven, or twenty-four spatial dimensions. However, we can only perceive three spatial dimensions and, so far, we haven't come up with any experimental or observational evidence to confirm the existence of these extra dimensions. One very hip theory is that space acts as if it were curled up in the extra dimensions on a subatomic scale, possibly at the quark-string level of scale or below. You following any of this or did I lose you around one of the turns?"

"I understood two or three of the smaller words."

Sung laughed again. He had a broad Southern California accent and a deep-chested laugh. "Okay, we think that there are a lot of dimensions and they're all pretty much right here. We just can't perceive them. Then again, without the right equipment we couldn't detect radio waves or see ultraviolet light. It takes the right meter. Anyway, it's conceivable that we could pass from our current dimension to another or maybe many others. Now, let's jump to pop culture. An abiding theory is that there are an infinite number of universes, each separated from the other by a veil as thin as tissue paper. All it takes is the right kind of device or energy to open a pathway. Whereas that might take a lot of energy, think of how much more energy—not to mention time—that it would take to traverse trillions of miles of interstellar space. Light-years. That's years of travel at the speed of light, which we can't even approach, let alone maintain. Weighed against that, opening a doorway to the dimension next door sounds like a piece of cake."

And Rudy spoke to many experts on shadow governments, political theorists, conspiracy theorists, and general UFO experts.

He asked every single expert if they had ever heard of Majestic Three and/or the Majestic Black Book.

Every one of them had.

Then Rudy asked them a crucial question.

"If you had to pick the top five people most likely to be a current or former member of M3, what would those names be?"

Almost everyone had an opinion on that.

It became clear to Rudy that the entire UFO community had given this a lot of thought, and although there was a strong likelihood that some names were being repeated because it was common knowledge that they were famously suspected of involvement, a few names began rising to the top.

Chapter Seventy-four

Hadley and Meyers Real Estate
Baltimore, Maryland
Sunday, October 20, 11:45 a.m.

Aldo always stuck his tongue out of the corner of his mouth when he was doing delicate work. It was something Tull found oddly endearing. He'd seen kids do that on TV, and sometimes when he looked into windows in the dark of night. That's how Tull learned a lot about families. Watching them through windows. He'd done it for as long as he could remember. Once he saw an old man doing the tongue thing while he rewired a toaster.

"Last one," said Aldo, his tongue back in his mouth, small beads of nervous sweat on his forehead. He set the modified pigeon drone very carefully on the desk and pushed his wheeled chair away.

"You're sure they can take the weight?" asked Tull.

Aldo shrugged. "I stripped out everything but the motor and the GPS. As long as we don't want them to fly high or for long, they should be okay. We got to be careful not to let 'em fly into a telephone pole or something. The central switch is only held by a little bit of that ionized gel stuff. Hit it too hard and . . . well, that would suck very, very large moose dick."

"Noted," said Tull.

They each took one pigeon and carried it to the rear window, then went back for the others. There were ten of them in all and they made slow, careful trips, staying well clear of each other or obstructions. With each trip, Tull noticed that Aldo was sweating more heavily. He found that strange. He'd seen Aldo in firefights looking cool as a cucumber. Why should this make him more frightened? People were funny.

When the pigeons were all in the back room, Tull fetched the Ghost Box and set it on a stack of boxed SOLD signs. He squatted down and as Aldo read the serial number stamped on the first drone's leg, Tull typed it into the computer. Then Aldo leaned out the window with the pigeon cradled gently in his cupped palms, then he gave it a little toss, like a Disney princess setting a songbird free. Tull kept that observation to himself.

One by one Aldo released the pigeons and Tull watched them appear on the tracking screen.

"And that's all of them," said Aldo with obvious relief. He squatted next to Tull and they watched the white dots on the screen flying at rooftop height through the streets of Baltimore.

Chapter Seventy-five

Elk Neck State Park
Cecil County, Maryland
Sunday, October 20, 11:46 a.m.

"You know, Junie, 1947 was a long damn time ago. What's taking this project so long? If there are supergeniuses like your father involved, what's taking so long?"

"Think about what they're trying to do," she said. "The science is so completely different than ours, the whole design philosophy follows a way of thinking that simply does not harmonize with human thought. Even their methods of communicating are so . . . well, so alien that it doesn't in any way mesh with ours. Think of it in terms of the way we study languages in animals like dolphins and whales. We can record their language and we think we can understand some of the gist of it, but that's not the same as being able to actually communicate with them. Not in any meaningful way. The differences are too great, there's no commonality. We don't have a *Star Trek* universal translator, and I don't think the aliens do, either. I think . . . I think that's one of the problems. I think that's one of the reasons there hasn't been any true or meaningful communication between them and us. We don't have a shared language."

"What about the crop circle? The pi thing. I thought math is the universal language."

"It is and it isn't," said Junie. "Sure, we can both look at a simple equation—two plus two equals four—and that will be a universal constant, but what does it tell you about them? Or us? How does math explain Van Gogh or Lady Gaga or hot chocolate? How does it explain how the love you have for your country is different but equally as important as the love you have for your family or a puppy? How does math give insight into why you like one TV show over another? Or why you think baseball is a good way to spend a Saturday afternoon when I'd rather shop on Saturday and watch football on Sunday. Math is a common ground, but it isn't a language."

"Let's go back a bit," I said. "You said that at first your dad was dedicated to the Project. What changed? Why'd he lose faith in the space race?"

She gave me a sharp look.

"This isn't a space race," she said. "It never was. Even the space race of the 1960s was never about simply going to the moon. God, do people still really think that? This is an arms race, Joe. That's what it was then and that's what it is now. It's about having the most powerful weapons, because weapons equal power on the global scale. Before World War II, before Hiroshima and Nagasaki, do you think we were viewed as a superpower? No, we were one of many powerful nations. Those bombs changed the game. Everyone knows that. Now we're in an age where the technology race is getting too close to call. China is becoming the world's leading economy and it's almost reached the point where it is the most powerful nation. Do you think our government—your government—will sit by and let that happen if there's any way to give us back our edge?"

Her eyes were fierce even in the darkness.

"Truman foresaw this time," she continued, her words whispered but her tone intense. "Maybe he was really smart or maybe really paranoid, or both, but he knew that there would come a point in time when America would need another dramatic edge. Something on the scale of nuclear weapons, but something that would give an edge once other countries acquired nukes and caught up to us. Welcome to now."

"That doesn't answer why your father left, Junie," I said. "And it doesn't explain how you know so much about your dad's classified work."

"The deeper he got the more he understood about the nature of the Project. It became clear that M3 was operating totally without congressional oversight. They were so deep into the black budget, and covered by so many levels of subterfuge that none of the last six presidents even knew the Project existed. The whole thing was being run as if M3 and the Project were actually separate from America. It made Dad wonder where the funding for something this big was coming from. How could you hide tens of billions from congressional accountants year after year? Dad decided to find out, so over a period of a few years he ingratiated himself more and more with the governors of M3 while at the same time using that increased access to take covert looks into their computers. It was painstaking work, but he figured it out. Dad always figured things out. He found out where the money was coming from."

I thought I knew, but I let her tell it.

"Drugs," she said triumphantly. "It was all drug money. The same way the CIA has been getting most of its funding since the fifties. Air America, the Iran-Contra thing, today in Afghanistan. Our own government agencies have been deeply involved in drug trafficking on a massive scale. This isn't even a secret anymore. Our so-called War on Terror is funded by drug money and most of the time we're in bed with the very people we claim we're taking down."

"I know," I said. "The DMS has had some dealings with a few of those groups, and we've put some of them out of business. I wish I could say that we made more than a casual dent, but . . ."

"Do you know where your funding comes from?" she demanded.

"No," I said. "But I'll say this—even though I don't believe for a millisecond that Mr. Church is paying our light bill with drug money—if I found out he was, I'd put a bullet in him."

She pushed me over so that my face was in the light. Junie studied my eyes for a long time, then she nodded to herself.

"Okay," she said.

"Okay," I said. "Now, about the funding . . . Did your dad find this out for sure or was this guesswork?"

"He had proof. That was part of what he wanted to bring to Congress. Real proof."

"And that's why they killed him," I said.

"Yes."

"Shit."

"But . . . ," she said.

"What?"

"I hacked my dad's computer."

"You did what? Why?"

"Because I thought he was a bad man," she said glumly. "I thought he was a government flunky working on something very bad. In a way I was right, but I misunderstood my father. He was a lot more complex a person than that, and less politically astute. When I saw him start getting more and more depressed I figured it was guilt for the bad things he was doing for the government. I hacked his computer so I could confront him with the proof." She stopped and shook her head. "I read everything I could find. Hundreds of pages of materials, and records, and evidence."

"Jesus."

"Then I confronted Dad, but not with accusations. I begged him to go to the world media with the story. Not just one newspaper or station, but all of them. A blast of truth. But he said that doing something like that could damage the government and even then he didn't believe that the entire government was corrupt. He was determined to make Congress react and then act."

"He took all his notes with him? His computer records, the copies of the Black Book pages, all of it?"

"No," she said. "He took one complete set. The rest was on his computer at home and on several portable hard drives he kept in a wall safe."

"Thank god! We can—"

"The house was burgled the night he was killed," she said. "They took everything. They tore the safe out of the wall, tore his desk to pieces, and even took my mom's laptop and mine. They ripped open all the walls, tore up floorboards, pulled down the ceilings. The police said that it was the most thorough search they'd ever seen. When I tried to explain why this was done, they gave me very tolerant smiles. I saw them laughing about it outside. I was a grief-stricken conspiracy theory goofball. They said that the house was probably targeted after my parents' names were announced on the news. They said it happens all the time."

"It does."

She punched me again.

"But hold on, hold on," I said. "If all of your father's records were destroyed, then how were you planning on revealing all the secrets of the Black Book? Did you somehow make a copy?"

"You forgot," she said.

"I what?"

"You forgot. That always amazes me," she said. "I see it all the time, hear about it, read about it, but it still amazes me."

"What does?" I asked, totally lost.

"That someone can actually forget something. I never could."

And it hit me with a very nice one-two punch. I said, "Jesus, I even said it when I was showing off and reading out your bio. Eidetic memory—photographic memory, and that thing where you can remember every day of your life."

"Every day, every hour, every minute," she said. "Hyperthymesia."

"And you saw your father's notes."

"Yes."

"All of them?"

"Yes."

"You remember all of it . . ."

"Every single word. Every formula. Every measurement and description." She smiled. It was a strange, intense, almost otherworldly smile that put goose bumps all along my arms and down my spine. "Joe . . . for all intents and purposes I *am* the Black Book."

Chapter Seventy-six

Hadley and Meyers Real Estate
Baltimore, Maryland
Sunday, October 20, 11:59 a.m.

Aldo and Tull watched the ten white dots move across the tracking screen. One by one the dots stopped moving. Telemetric feeds provided exact locations via a satellite uplink.

"Perfect," said Aldo. "Every single one of them. Nice!"

"Very nice," agreed Tull.

Chapter Seventy-seven

Elk Neck State Park
Cecil County, Maryland
Sunday, October 20, 12:01 p.m.

There were a million questions I wanted to ask Junie, but suddenly Ghost came racing down into the tunnel, gave me a sharp whuff, then turned around and stared back along the path he'd come. We froze and listened, and after five long seconds we heard it. Men's voices. Terse and harsh.

"God," whispered Junie, "they found us!"

I shook my head. "No, if they did they'd either be yelling or making no sound at all. I think they're following that trail." I nodded to the one we'd been paralleling. "Maybe there's another team coming up from the far side and it's our bad luck we're in the middle."

"What do we do?"

I held a finger to my lips and she nodded and fell silent. I left Ghost with her as I climbed out of the tunnel and up onto higher ground, ready to ambush them if they found our hidey-hole.

Five minutes passed and the voices faded.

Then we heard new voices coming from a different direction.

We waited them out, too.

Minutes crawled by.

The voices finally went away.

After they were gone, I drifted back down to Junie.

"Are they going to find us?" she asked. She leaned very close to whisper in my ear, and despite the blood and ash on our clothes I was very deeply aware of the sweet faintness of her perfume and the heat from her soft cheek.

You're a frickin' idiot, growled the Cop inside my head. *Keep your head in the game*.

I cut a sideways look at Junie's beautiful face, and I told my inner Cop to go piss up a rope.

"No," I said. "I'm going to go find them."

Her hand darted out and closed around my wrist. "You can't! They'll kill you."

"I need to go take a look," I said. "We need to know if we can wait here or if we're in the center of a net."

Junie touched my arm. "You'll be careful, won't you?"

Her question caught me as I was rising, and for a moment I settled back down into a crouch. "Yes," I said. "I'll be very careful."

That coaxed a smile from her. Small, but damn if it didn't light up the day.

But I lingered a moment longer. "Junie . . . when we get out of this, when we get back to the world . . . you understand that my people are going to need to know everything you know about the book. You get that, right?"

She nodded.

"This isn't about you getting revenge for what they did to your parents. And it's not about sharing alien technology with the whole world. All personal considerations are back burner."

"But—"

I took her by the shoulders and shifted around so that we were face to face. "Junie, this is about saving a big chunk of the world. The southern coast of Africa, all of England, Scotland, and Ireland, a sizable chunk of Western Europe, and the entire eastern seaboard of the United States. Do the math, honey, because that racks up to about a billion people who are going to drown under the worst tsunami in recorded history if we don't stop it."

"How can we stop it?" she demanded. "What if whoever took the president wants the Black Book destroyed? Will you shoot me? Or will you let Mr. Church do it? He seems cold enough."

"You tell me what I should do," I growled. "You saw the videos, you know the score. What should I do?"

"I think we should try and get the actual damn Black Book. There's only one copy. Maybe that's what they want you to get. They don't even know about me."

"Who are 'they,' Junie? Who do you think took the president?"

She took a moment before she said, "Them."

"Say it."

"The aliens, okay. I think the aliens took the president and they want the Black Book."

"How does that make sense? If they can abduct the president, how come they don't just take the Black Book?"

"Maybe they don't know where it is."

"How can they not? They're aliens."

"Does that automatically make them psychic? Who knows what the problem is? Maybe it's taken them a long time to figure out how to communicate with us. Maybe there aren't that many of them. Maybe they simply don't know who has the Black Book."

"Then why go to these lengths to get it?"

"I don't know. Something pushed them," she said with heat. "They've been silent all this time, but something changed. But they clearly don't know everything. I mean . . . their ships crashed. A lot of them. That has to say something about them as fallible beings. Maybe they only just learned about the Black Book and realized what kind of threat it poses. I don't know, Joe. I'm just guessing, too. All I know is that there are at least two copies of the Black Book. M3 has one and I'm the other. You have to decide which one you want to give to the aliens."

I sat back on my heels. "Your aliens are playing some serious hardball. They're willing to kill a billion people to get that book."

"No," she said. "We don't know what they're doing. The fact that you can make a comment like that shows how much you don't know about them."

"Junie, I don't know anything about them. Even if I am starting to edge toward accepting that this is real, I don't know one single thing about whoever built the crafts that M3 is studying. What are they like? Did they come here to conquer us? Are they studying us to determine our weaknesses? Is this some kind of alien seedpod invasion?"

"What they look like isn't important, Joe. You're like everyone else, you keep trying to ascribe human emotions to them. You think that if a race is powerful then they could only get that way through military force."

"You saw the video . . ."

"Okay, we both saw the video. Do you understand what it means? I mean, really understand it? How do we know it doesn't have multiple meanings? How do we know that it's even a threat? It could be a warning."

"Pretty harsh for a warning."

"That's because you think like a soldier and you think they think that way, too. They haven't attacked us after all these years, what makes you believe that they're even capable of violence? Maybe they're warning us of what could happen if somebody else builds a working Device. China, Russia . . . They could be trying to help us. No, we just can't assume they're violent. Not everyone is."

I shook my head. "Show me a culture that isn't violent. Even the Swiss used to be warriors. Ditto the Tibetans. There were armed soldiers in the service of the Dalai Lama. Soldiers and armed police guard the Pope. History and every holy book you can find is filled with stories of war and conquest. It's a side effect of being a predator species. We may aspire to civilized and harmonious behavior, Junie, but it's not natural to us."

"I'm not saying it's not natural to them either."

"Then what are you saying?"

"I'm saying that they are alien, so we shouldn't make assumptions. We have to stop trying to understand them based on what we know of ourselves. That's polluted thinking."

"Okay, okay," I said, and rubbed my eyes. "I should have stayed in bed today. I was nursing a well-earned hangover and . . ."

My words trailed away as my mind conjured a picture of Violin. I glanced away from Junie, not wanting her to read anything in my eyes.

"Time's flying away from us," I said. "No more talk. Get down and hide. I'll leave Ghost with you. If there's something he can't handle he'll make some noise and I'll come running."

"Where are you going?"

"It's hunting season, right?" I asked, and left it there. "Now come on, hide."

She did as directed, vanishing completely in the dense undergrowth. All Ghost had to do was lay down and he became invisible in the tall grass. I moved off, veering away from our back trail and then heading upwind of the sounds.

I tried my earbud again, but got only dead air. Bug and Church had to know I was off the grid by now, even if the Coast Guard call didn't go anywhere; but what was the best-case scenario for a rescue? Half an hour? An hour?

That was not encouraging. I didn't know how many of the Closers were out in these woods. They had helicopters, too. Maybe thermal imaging.

290 | Jonathan Maberry

I regretted not grabbing one of the long guns, but when the lighthouse blew up my mind was more focused on not burning to death than on arming for a prolonged war. Now I wondered if I should have circled around and made a smarter choice. I had my Beretta and a couple of full magazines, and I had my rapid-release folding knife, a lifetime's study of jujutsu, and a lot of years camping in these woods. How did that stack up against the Closers? We'd have to see.

Best-case scenario was that the Coast Guard took our call seriously and a fleet of choppers and half a dozen Zodiacs crammed with sailors were about to bring down six kinds of hell on these Closers. Sure, I told myself, and the charge would led by the Easter Bunny and Santa Claus.

Inside my head a debate was raging. The Modern Man aspect of my personality was yelling at me to *Run, run, run*.

The Cop wanted answers and he was losing patience. When he did that he tended to act more like the Warrior. And that part of me, the Killer, wanted to turn this reconnaissance run into a hunt. He was telling me that if you run then you're prey. That's weak, that's vulnerable, and it would probably get Junie killed as well as me.

Hunt the hunters, whispered that merciless voice.

I slowed from a light run to a crouching walk and then to stillness. Shallowing my breathing. Listening to the woods.

At least one of the helicopters was up there, but it was far away. North and west of where I crouched. Searching down near the main part of the campground, blocking the most natural exit from the park.

When you hunt like this you learn to tune things out. It's not that you don't hear them, but once a sound is cataloged you allow it to fade into the background so that other sounds can present themselves for identification. The same goes with movement. The forest is a living thing, it's always moving, it's always making sound, even in the very depths of winter. Here, in this freakish holdover of a summer that did not want to relinquish its grasp on these Maryland woods, there were a thousand sounds. Birds and animals moving through the leaves, the creak of trees in the breeze, the exhalation of the forest as its breath passed between and through the millions of intertwined branches.

There were no more voices.

I waited, letting the Closers hunt Junie so I could hunt them.

The Closers.

Over the last hour that name had already been burned into my private lexicon. I thought of them as "Closers," but on another level I had a different word for them.

Prey.

I heard a man's voice, speaking low and quiet. Just two words.

"This way."

Inside my head, the Warrior grinned.

Yes, he whispered, *come this way.*

Chapter Seventy-eight

VanMeer Castle
Near Pittsburgh, Pennsylvania
Sunday, October 20, 12:04 p.m.

Yuina Hoshino called a few minutes after noon.

Howard and Mr. Bones sat down at the Ghost Box console to take the call and immediately they could tell that the nervous little scientist had been crying. Her eyes were red and puffy and there was some white paste at the corners of her mouth.

"I can't stand it!" she wailed. Almost wailed; her voice broke in the middle. "General Croft called our business office five minutes ago. He's canceling the air show. Not just for now, but maybe or as long as six months. Between the cyber-attacks and now what happened at Dugway—he said that in the face of a concerted terrorist attack on the industrial-military complex we must exercise prudence and bullshit like that. He kept going on and on about how we had to protect what we have and consider our options."

"Yuina—" began Howard, but she wasn't listening.

"I tried to tell him that we had some solutions, that Shelton Aeronautics was ready to respond to these threats, but he didn't hear me. It was like he was locked into a speech and he couldn't shake loose. I think he's really rattled. I think he's scared because of what happened at Dugway. He's freaked out and now they've canceled the air show. How are we going to get them to listen? It's all ruined! All this work, it's over, it's ruined. The Chinese have—"

"Shut up!" bellowed Howard in a bull voice that struck the weeping scientist into a shocked and sniffling silence. Howard jabbed a finger at her hologram as if it could feel his emphatic pokes. "Listen to me, you silly bitch. We are not beaten and this is definitely not over. Pull yourself together. You're a governor of Majestic Three for Christ's sake. Act like it for a change. So the Chinese outplayed us on this round. We are far from done, honey."

"But . . . I don't understand . . . we are done. They clearly built a working Device and we're years away from that! Our top-of-the-line is Specter 101, and that can't do what that ship did at Dugway . . ."

Howard smiled at her. "It doesn't have to."

She frowned, forgetting her tears for a moment. "What?"

"Trust me," he said.

Chapter Seventy-nine

Elk Neck State Park
Cecil County, Maryland
Sunday, October 20, 12:05 p.m.

I waited behind a tree.

Okay, I lurked behind a tree.

The forest quieted itself out of my consciousness; I focused less on what sounds should be there and more on which sounds shouldn't.

They were pretty stealthy, I'll give them that, but inside my head the Warrior grinned. This is the kind of thing he lives for. It's why he exists at all. Which meant that to some degree I lived for this, too.

The hunt.

The ache to confront and engage and overcome. The desire to prove through the ugly and uncivilized filter of violence that I belonged here, that I deserved to live and to continue. And to an equal degree that they no longer owned the right to survive because they were lesser predators.

This is not the territory of logic, and it's miles and years away from any justification in civilized behavior. This is the lizard brain whispering survival secrets to the most primitive centers of the primate mind. Because they hunted me, because Junie was in my protection, these woods had become mine. The boundaries were marked with blood rather than piss, and the killer within me would defend my territory in any way necessary.

Painted by dappled leaf shadows, I waited. My rapid-release folding knife was open, the blade down at my side where the steel wouldn't catch stray sunlight.

They came in single file and I let them pass.

Three tall men in black BDUs, black boots, black weapons and gear. Pale faces, clean shaven, with buzz-cut hair, square jaws. Powerful men who carried no body fat at all, and who walked with cat grace, eyes tracking left and right, seeing the forest but not seeing me. They were armed. Pistols in belt holsters, knives. Two of them carried M4s, the leader had a combat shotgun with pistol grips on the handle and pump.

These, I knew, were different from the other men. Vastly different from the four men in cars I'd met this morning—God, was it only this morning?—and tougher even than the men who had invaded Junie's cottage. These were prime soldiers. They were the elite. These were the kind of soldiers you could drop into a war zone or a hot LZ or a jungle at night and expect them to get the job done and come back alive. That they were all killers I had no doubt. This wasn't work for missionaries. These were the true Closers, the men sent to shut Junie down and erase any threat she might ever pose. If they had their way, Junie Flynn would disappear off the face of the earth. Her house and all of its contents would be reduced to smoking rubble.

They did not know that I was here.

All they could know is that the ground team had met armed resistance. They knew that someone in the house had fired on them, hitting two, probably killing at least one.

That was not enough knowledge. I knew more about them than they knew about me.

If they knew that I was out here—not me specifically but someone like me—they would be doing this a different way.

That was a mistake. And at this level of the game the rules only allow for one mistake.

As the third man passed I stepped out from my hiding spot and moved behind him very quickly. The technique was one that these men probably knew. The surprise wasn't in the selection of skill but in its application. In the timing.

Three limbs moved at once. My left hand whipped around and clamped over his nose and mouth, pinching everything closed, shutting off breath and sound. At the same time my right foot chopped out, knee and toes pointing outward at an angle as I stepped on the back of his knee. Bending the leg, toppling the weight backward into the inexorable pull of gravity, aided by the pull of the hand clamped over his mouth. My right hand was already in play, already darting forward and around, pressing the wickedly sharp edge of the blade deep into the skin under his left ear. As he fell, I pulled his chin to the left and cut his throat from ear to ear.

All of it in less than a second.

We all know this one fact, that we are only ever one step ahead of the darkness. It can reach out to tap us on the shoulder at any time.

The man died in an instant.

If he had been a sentry the death would have been solitary and unheard. But he was with others and I wanted his death to be heard. Not loud. Just a whisper from the darkness behind.

The second man whirled at the sound and I jerked back on the dead man's head at the moment of my cut so that the hydrostatic pressure of heart hosed outward in a red geyser. The second man took it in the face.

I was already moving, body-checking the dead man into the second Closer. Blind, encumbered by dead weight falling against him, he had no chance, no time, no distance to use his M4. I thrust the knife into his throat, drilling it, giving the blade a half turn as it entered and a half turn to clear the path for a fast withdraw.

Two seconds, two dead men.

The man with the shotgun was the one who had the only real chance.

If he'd jumped forward before he turned, he might have been able to use that chance. That might have given him the time to bring the shotgun barrel to bear, to at least clip me with a blast before I took him. If the darkness was riding copilot for him, he might have been able to blast me back into the shadows.

He did not jump forward.

He merely whirled in place instead.

I leaped over two dead men, my left hand slapping the shotgun barrel down, my right going for the long reach to slash. Biceps, face, chest, wrist. The shotgun fell, I tackled him and bore him to the ground, straddling him, pinning his bleeding arms, pressing my forearm across his throat, stopping the red tip of the knife a millimeter from his eye.

"Shhhh," I said.

Chapter Eighty

The Warehouse
Baltimore, Maryland
Sunday, October 20, 12:06 p.m.

Gus Dietrich banged open the door to Joe Ledger's office without knocking. Church and Rudy Sanchez looked up sharply at him.

"Got to get you out of here, boss," said Gus breathlessly, "and I mean right now. We have every kind of federal agent at the gate right now waving warrants from the attorney general. Can't stop 'em."

"Warrants for what?" demanded Rudy.

"Joe. They have an arrest warrant for him and a search and seizure for his office. Don't know what's up their ass, but they want Joe in the worst way and that warrant is legit."

"This is absurd," said Rudy.

"How much time?" asked Church.

"I can stall them for a couple of minutes. I have your helo smoking on the roof."

Without a word Church closed his laptop and began packing it away. Ledger's laptop was locked in the top drawer of the file cabinet. Church touched a panel on the wall and the file cabinet sank into the floor with a soft hiss of hydraulics. A second file cabinet came down from the ceiling to replace it.

Rudy cocked an eyebrow. "That's very clever."

"Borrowed from a James Bond novel," admitted Church, "but it was a smart idea."

They exited the office and Church handed his laptop to Gus. "Put this in the vault. Cut all lines to MindReader and put the mainframe autodelete on standby. Make sure the staff cooperates in every way possible within the guidelines of their training. Then meet me at the Shop. Transfer all current case notes and records there. That'll be our new war room."

Gus nodded. The Shop was a secondary support location a few blocks away. It was run by Big Bob Faraday, a former Echo Team agent who had been permanently injured on a mission. It was also the home of Mike Harnick's vehicle design department, logistical support, and a few other essential departments.

"What about the warrant?" asked Gus.

"Let them execute it. They are welcome to search Captain Ledger's office."

Rudy said, "What should I do?"

Church smiled. "Come with me, Doctor. No reason for you to be involved in this mess."

"What about Joe? We can't just leave him to the wolves . . ."

"Captain Ledger is a resourceful man, Doctor. I rather think it is the wolves who are in danger."

Chapter Eighty-one

Hadley and Meyers Real Estate

Baltimore, Maryland

Sunday, October 20, 12:09 p.m.

Erasmus Tull stepped out of the office and stood in the quiet of the empty parking lot behind the real estate office. From there he could see the distant corner of the Warehouse several blocks away.

He punched in a phone number that he had not called in a very long time.

It rang so many times that Tull didn't think the other party was going to answer.

Then a voice said, "Hello, Erasmus."

Tull said, "Hello, Deacon."

Chapter Eighty-two

The Warehouse

Baltimore, Maryland

Sunday, October 20, 12:10 p.m.

Mr. Church held up a hand for silence. "I must admit that I'm surprised to hear from you again."

"I know. This is kind of a whim," said Tull. "Are you sorry to hear that I'm alive?"

"You've managed to stay off the radar quite well," said Mr. Church.

"You taught me a lot about caution."

"Apparently."

"I know you looked for me. Hunted me."

"What other option did you leave, Erasmus? You left quite a mess behind you."

Tull sighed. "Story of my life."

"And of mine," agreed Mr. Church. "Some people are born in the storm lands."

"Yes."

"What can I do for you, Erasmus?" asked Church. "Do you want to come in? You know that I can guarantee your safety."

"Until you put a bullet in me."

"It doesn't have to play out that way. You can buy a lot of goodwill by unburdening your soul."

"And if I don't have a soul?"

"I don't have time for poetry, Erasmus. Or philosophical debates. I have a lot going on at the moment."

"I know."

Church paused. "Do you?"

"Yes."

"Is that why you're calling me?"

"In part." Tull paused. "You know, Deacon, you're not as smart as you think you are. You always pretend to know what's going on, but you don't know. You think you know what's going on right now, today—but you don't."

"I make no claims to understanding the current situation, Erasmus. I'll admit to being totally at sea. Does that make you feel better?"

"Actually, it does. I've never heard you admit to being clueless. That's worth a lot."

"Care to tell me what *is* going on? You seem to have all the answers today."

"You have no idea how true that is. I not only know the answers, I *am* the answer."

There was an almost pleading note to that statement. Church filed it away.

"The world you know is about to change, Deacon. After tomorrow it's never going to be the same again."

"You're involved in what's happening today?" asked Church.

"Oh yes."

"Are you looking to make a deal?"

"No," said Tull, and Church thought he heard a note of regret in the man's voice. "I wanted to clear the air about something, Deacon. Remember the conversation we had after the thing in Turkey? After I killed that entire Syrian strike team? You asked me if I needed to step down for a while, you asked if this was getting to be too much for me."

"I remember."

"Do you remember what I said to you?" asked Tull.

"Yes," said Church. "You said that killing didn't hurt you. I tried to explain that it hurts everyone and that we have to address that. But you said that you weren't like everyone else."

"Yes."

"You said that you were a monster and monsters loved to destroy."

"Yes." There was fierce emotion in the man's voice now.

"I tell you now what I told you then, Erasmus," said Church, "no matter how far you've walked under the shadow of darkness you can always turn and go back."

"It's funny that you, of all people, should preach about redemption, Deacon. I may be a monster, but you've spilled an ocean of blood. What does that make you?"

Church looked out the window of the helicopter as it lifted from the roof of the Warehouse. "We both know exactly what I am," he said.

"And we both know exactly what I am," said Tull.

"Erasmus—"

"Goodbye, Deacon. If there is a God, maybe I'll see you on the other side."

There was a sudden white light so brilliant that everything was instantly washed to a blank canvas of nothingness.

The ten pigeon drones exploded at the same moment. Ten tiny versions of the Truman Engine detonating on different parts of the building.

The shock wave blew outward at the speed of sound, blowing out windows ten blocks away. The fireball threw cars and boats a hundred yards into the bay. And the entire Warehouse leaped up into the air atop a fireball of superheated gases that drove upward like the fist of Satan, vaporizing thousands of tons of brick and steel, melting vehicles into pools of slag and splattering them for blocks.

The last thing Mr. Church saw before the blast buffeted his helicopter out of control was the tiny figure of Gus Dietrich on the roof near the helicopter, one hand lifted in a lighthearted salute. Then Gus, and the building, and everyone inside of it were gone.

Gone.

"Dios mío!" cried Rudy Sanchez, seemingly from far away.

Then the helicopter was tilting sideways, spilling the lifting air, sliding into the claws of gravity, and a fireball and the brown water both rushed toward it.

Chapter Eighty-three

Hadley and Meyers Real Estate
Baltimore, Maryland
Sunday, October 20, 12:13 p.m.

The shock wave picked Tull up and flung him against the side of the real estate office. The trees in the parking lot bent over as if weeping, the windows imploded. Hundreds of car alarms began screaming.

Tull collapsed to the ground, dazed, flash-burned, blood pouring from his nose and ears.

And all the time he never stopped laughing.

Chapter Eighty-four

Elk Neck State Park
Cecil County, Maryland
Sunday, October 20, 12:14 p.m.

Even with all of the pain he had to be feeling, the Closer had enough control to understand. He was not being murdered in this moment. His ticket to a longer life was silence.

He clamped his teeth and lips shut to hold back the screams.

I bent close, my lips near his ear. The position, the closeness was an awful parody of intimacy.

"Who sent you?" I whispered.

His mouth remained shut.

I touched the point of the knife to the soft flesh below his eye. "Is it worth dying for?"

Nothing. But he tried to scare me to death with his he-man steely stare.

With the knife in place, I used my free hand to tear open his shirt. He wore the same kind of body armor I'd see on the Closers down in Wolf Trap. I tore open the Velcro straps and pulled it down. No dog tags underneath. In fact he had no ID anywhere.

I bent close and spoke very quietly to him. "Who are you working for? What's your agency? What unit are you with?"

He said nothing.

"Who's your commanding officer?"

Nothing.

"Listen to me, asshole, you're hurt but you're not over the line. We can change that real fast."

Nothing. His eyes were bright with pain but he kept that glare going.

I am not a big fan of torture. Kind of don't ever want to do it, but there are moments when your options are limited. Top calls them "L.A. nuke moments." The logic goes this way: If you know for certain that there is a nuclear device about to detonate in L.A., killing millions of people, and you have in custody a terrorist who knows where that bomb is, which is the better moral choice—to stick by your guns and say "No, America does not believe in torture" or to ruin one guy's day and save millions? It's not a good choice, bad choice thing because they're both bad choices. In that situation, you have to make the right choice, the smart choice, even if it's one you may have trouble living with later.

Add to that the fact that the Warrior was running the show right now.

The man talked.

Not much, but enough.

He confirmed that they were here to collect Junie Flynn. Alive, if possible, but dead was within the mission parameters. He confirmed that I was to be terminated with extreme prejudice. When I asked him why, he said something really funky.

"They told us about you," he said. "They told us that you're trying to tear the whole thing down."

"What thing?"

"Everything. The country, the Project. You're out of control, Ledger, and they will stop you."

"Wait—suddenly I'm the bad guy? You dickheads attacked us. You blew up a freaking lighthouse with missiles. How did I get to be the bad guy?"

He sneered at me. "We did what we had to do to protect the United States. Maybe we don't wear the uniform anymore, but every goddamn one of us would die for this country." Then he gave me a pitying, disgusted look. "They said you used to be a good guy, Ledger. What happened to you? How much did you sell your country for?"

I wanted to drop a flag on the play and sit down to reread the rulebook. He was making my speech. Okay, maybe it was a badly worded and needlessly clichéd version of my speech, but even so.

"They must have sold you a pretty amazing line of shit," I told him. "You actually think I'm the bad guy?"

"We know you are, asshole. You and that crazy UFO broad want to see this country burn. You want to see Chinese troops marching up Pennsylvania Avenue."

"Dude," I said, "you lost me a couple of turns back. What the fuck are you talking about?"

And that's when the silly son of a bitch made his move.

With slashed arms and a killer crouched over him and no genuine options, he went for it. He tried to buck me off while simultaneously twisting his hips and turning his face away.

I killed him for trying it.

It didn't take much. He made his move, and I made mine.

Damn it.

I crouched over him, watching this man die. I don't know if I have ever been more conflicted about killing an enemy combatant before. Inside my head the Modern Man was appalled at what I'd done. The Cop detested me for losing control of the moment and thereby silencing my only information source. The Warrior . . .

Oh, man, the Warrior was howling with red delight. He saw that blood pouring into the dirt and he wanted to roll in it like a dog. Like a werewolf.

This was a very bad place to be, a very dark place. My feet were at the edge of the abyss, and down there things howled up at me in a voice that was far too familiar, far too personal.

I staggered back in both mind and body, and I turned away.

The knife was in my hand. It was red with blood, but strangely there was not even a drop of it on my flesh. As if I had used an innocent hand to pick up a guilty weapon.

What a dreadful illusion that was. And I marveled at how many lies are sewn into the fabric of our awareness.

"I'm sorry," I said, not knowing who it was meant for. The dead men, the people in my life who might suddenly be in danger because of me, Junie? Or was it meant for myself? If you are a sane and moral person, then with every act of violence there is less of you. I know this to be true. I've been aware each time the scalpel of experience pares away a chunk of me. Rudy Sanchez is fond of the expression, "Violence always leaves a mark."

As a therapist and an empathetic man I know he understands that, but Rudy's experience is largely that of an observer. The violence he's seen has been from a distance. Not always, but mostly. When you are ankle deep in blood, however, the truth of that saying is both more profound and horribly understated.

These thoughts shambled through my brain as I quickly searched the pockets of the other dead men. I did not expect to find ID, of course. Instead I found other MPP pistols, knives, hand grenades, and a few small electronic gadgets I did not recognize. I crammed my pockets with the stuff, as much as I could carry. In the front pants pocket of the last man I'd killed I found a compact satellite phone that was no larger than a cell.

I flipped it open. Instead of offering me an open line, it immediately went to autoconnect. It was set to call only one line. Only two seconds passed before a voice said, "Condor One to Six, copy."

I took a gamble.

"Copy, Condor One, go for Six."

"Give me a location and a sit-rep?"

As I spoke I crunched a few dry leaves in my palm. Sounds like crappy reception. Great for disguising your voice. I also dropped parts of words to make it sound like the signal was fluctuating. My buddies and I used to do this at fast-food drive-throughs, too.

"—three klicks no—west of—lighthouse and—"

"We're getting some heavy interference, Six. Adjust your squelch."

I crumpled more leaves. "Negative,—ondor,—phone took—hit—"

"Give me a target status."

"Have engaged—and terminated—hostile."

"Six, I'm reading that you have engaged and terminated one hostile? Confirm."

"—onfirm—d."

There was a pause, then, "Initial or secondary target?"

Junie had to be the initial target. They could only have found out about me within the last few hours.

"Secondary—arget has—neutralized."

"Do you have eyes on initial target?"

I made the fake static worse, but paused long enough to say, "—south-east—"

Then I switched off the phone. With any luck they'd shift their search.

But off in the distance, I heard a dog bark. Ghost.

And more helicopters coming.

To kill Junie and to kill me. And they thought I was the bad guy.

"Christ," I breathed.

And ran.

Chapter Eighty-five

VanMeer Castle
Near Pittsburgh, Pennsylvania
Sunday, October 20, 12:18 p.m.

"Are you sure he's dead?" asked Howard.

"Turn on the news and you tell me," said Tull. He was shouting, still partially deafened from the blast.

"Where are you?"

"Aldo and I are driving, getting away from the blast zone."

Howard closed his eyes for a moment, trying to imagine that blast. The TV would only show the aftereffects and he wished he could have actually seen it. Heard it. Been pushed around by it. His loins twitched at the thought of a blast like that. The blast, and all that it accomplished.

"Field Team Nine is still hunting Ledger and the Flynn woman," said Tull. "Last report said that they've taken some heavy losses but they haven't yet confirmed a kill."

"That doesn't matter," said Howard. "There's enough firepower at Turkey Point to do the job. In the meantime, get out of Baltimore and come here."

"There?"

"Yes, I think you deserve to be with Mr. Bones and me when we make our big announcement."

"When?"

"Come now. We'll make the call first thing in the morning."

Howard disconnected the call.

"That was Tull?"

"Yes. Deacon is dead."

Mr. Bones smiled. "You're joking."

"Let's turn on the news and find out."

They did and the big plasma screen on the wall showed them an aerial view of a blast crater gouged out of the warehouse district in Baltimore. A cargo ship lay on its side in the brown water and other warehouses were blazing. Firefighters aimed dozens of streams of high-pressure water at the buildings, trying to save some. Others, more fully involved, were left to burn. Of the DMS Warehouse, nothing at all remained. Not a stick, not an unbroken stone.

The banner beneath the image read, in huge red letters, TERROR STRIKES BALTIMORE.

"How appropriate," said Howard. "Not terrorism. Terror."

But Mr. Bones did not answer. He stared slack jawed at the devastation.

"Oh my God . . . ," he breathed.

"Tull used ten of the miniature Truman Engines."

"All of that?" breathed Mr. Bones aghast. "Just ten of the little ones?"

"Yes," said Howard, "and I can't imagine anything more wonderful or more perfectly timed."

"But . . . but . . . the air show has been canceled. How does this . . . ?"

Howard dug a cell phone out of his pocket and tossed it to Mr. Bones. "I think it's time we made some phone calls."

Chapter Eighty-six

Elk Neck State Park
Cecil County, Maryland
Sunday, October 20, 12:23 p.m.

The sky got very loud. Craning my head to look up as I ran, I could see both of the unmarked black helicopters up there. But the noise was bigger than that. There were other engine sounds, rotors with a different signature coming hard from the south.

I broke from cover into a clearing that circled a small pond. There was a mound of sandstone rising on one side of the pond and I scrambled up to get the best possible view. The two black helicopters were moving slowly, rising from a low-level search and moving through a climbing turn to face south. It took ten seconds before I could see the other chopper. What I wanted to see—needed to see—was a different kind of black helo. Also black, but with a higher gloss to the paint and the distinctive weapons array that marked it as a DMS bird. I wanted to see thin red lines around the doors and down the tail.

What I saw instead were two helicopters, neither of them Black Hawks, neither of them black. The first was a hulking HH-60J Jayhawk and its companion was a much smaller AgustaWestland AW109. Both were painted with the bright white and blood red of the Coast Guard. Both, I knew, would be armed. M240D belt-fed, gas-operated medium machine guns firing 7.62mm NATO ammunition.

Under any other circumstance, two Coast Guard choppers would be the Horsemen of the Apocalypse to anything troubling the shores of Maryland.

This was a different kind of day.

So far, it wasn't a good day for the good guys.

The Black Hawks could have fought it out with their own machine guns, and they certainly had the edge. Kind of hard to pit the M240D against a minigun. The Guardsmen could spit out nine hundred rounds per minute. The minigun uses the same caliber of ammunition, but it blasts it out at a staggering six thousand rounds per minute.

But the Closers weren't interested in a gunfight, not even with bigger guns.

There was a big, clunky gun mounted on the underbelly of the chopper. The distance was too great for me to make out details, but I knew that it would have four curved prongs instead of an open barrel. There was too much noise for me to hear the *tok* sound, but I saw a brief shimmer in the air as a focused beam of microwaves shot from the Closer's bird and hit the first of the Coast Guard helicopters.

At first I thought that the shot had missed. Then suddenly the lead helo blew apart in a massive ball of intense red flame. It could not have been a full second later that the second helo exploded. It was so fast. So ugly. So thorough. Starbursts of flaming debris flew outward like the petals of some grotesque flower.

I screamed at the sky as the burning wreckage fell in strangely slow motion onto the rifling green treetops below.

I raised the stolen MPP in a foolish, wasteful, suicidal, and pointless attempt to strike back. My finger pulled the trigger. *Tok! Tok!*

And then something happened . . .

Something that seemed completely impossible.

As I fired at the closest Black Hawk—it exploded!

I gaped. It was impossible. At that distance, with the small gun I held—it was impossible. It was so freakishly absurd they wouldn't have put it in a movie. Only as an afterimage did I see the arrow-straight trail of silver-black smoke.

I whirled to follow the back trail of the smoke to its source.

And there it was.

A gleaming black UH-60 Black Hawk helicopter, the body detailed with lines of red the exact same color of blood. Men crowded the open bay door, hunched over the machine gun. I knew those faces. Even from here, I knew them.

I spoke one name.

"Top . . ."

You could almost see the other black helicopter freeze in midair in a WTF moment. Then the closer helo spun toward the DMS bird. Both helicopters were evenly matched for this kind of fight. However, there was a moment that echoed the confrontation between the black helos and the Coast Guard—a moment when this could have turned into a shooting match with machine guns.

But I knew Top. He had to have seen the two Coast Guard birds die. All those brave men, incinerated in an instant. Top's son had been killed in Iraq in the first days of the war. His daughter had lost both legs when her Bradley rolled over an IED. "Fair" was never really part of the kind of war we were fighting. M3 and their killers had opened up on us with no declaration of war, no agreement of rules, no promise of quarter. They'd come like butchers onto the field. The death toll for today was already too high. Hector and the others aboard my chopper, the two Coast Guard crews.

Fair?

Fuck fair.

The DMS Black Hawk blew those sons of bitches out of the sky.

That's fair.

Part Five
The Truman Engine

It was the darndest thing I've ever seen. It was big, it was very bright, it changed colors and it was about the size of the Moon. We watched it for ten minutes, but none of us could figure out what it was. One thing's for sure, I'll never make fun of people who say they've seen unidentified objects in the sky. If I become president, I'll make every piece of information this country has about UFO sightings available to the public and the scientists.

—PRESIDENT JIMMY CARTER

I can assure you that, given they exist, these flying saucers are made by no power on this Earth.

—PRESIDENT HARRY S. TRUMAN, *press conference, April 4, 1950*

Chapter Eighty-seven

Mr. Bones sat and listened in silence while Howard Shelton had a screaming match with Admiral Xiè, the head of the experimental aircraft division of the People's Army. Bones sipped an unsweetened iced tea and listened with total fascination.

The call had started with at least a show of civility. Compliments and respectful acknowledgments. All right and proper, all total horse shit.

Once that was out of the way—and once Howard was convinced that Admiral Xiè was alone—Howard became much more direct.

"I trust your spies have been keeping you up to date on certain events around the world?"

"There have been some reports," agreed Admiral Xiè.

"Like the unfortunate incident in the Taiwan Strait?"

"Like that, yes."

"What about Dugway? Did you hear about that, too?"

Admiral Xiè was quiet. "Why would you ask *me* about that?"

"Why do you think I'd ask you?" replied Howard.

"I do not know, Mr. Shelton. There is a tone in your voice, or is it a quality of a bad connection?"

"Seriously, Admiral? You want to play these kinds of games? Are you going to tell me that you don't know a single thing about what happened at Dugway this afternoon?"

"I—"

"And I suppose you don't know anything about the sightings of a black triangular craft seen buzzing through the skies near Changxing? Right where a certain testing facility is rumored to be located."

Admiral Xiè said, "What can I tell you, Mr. Shelton? What is it you would like to hear?"

"I would like to hear that you aren't invading U.S. fucking airspace and shooting down U.S. fucking stealth jets is what I'd like to fucking hear."

"Are you deranged?" demanded Admiral Xiè. "Running test flights on a prototype craft is one thing, but do you think everyone here has taken total leave of their senses?"

"Don't you goddamn lie to me, Xiè. We had a deal and—"

"And I kept my part of that deal," the admiral fired back. "It is you who cannot be trusted to leave your toys in the toy box rather than succumb to the childish desire to play with them."

The conversation went downhill from there. Mr. Bones spoke good enough Mandarin to appreciate the vulgar acts Admiral Xiè said were common among the female members of the Shelton family. He also liked Howard's replies, which, though not as flowery, hit home just as solidly. He knew for certain that had the two men been in the same room they would be wrestling on the floor, kneeing crotches, spitting in eyes, and probably biting.

Somewhere in the middle of the shouting match, though, there was a bit of a sea change and it took Mr. Bones a couple of minutes to figure it out. The tenor of the conversation shifted from a straight-up mutual defamation competition to something resembling unqualified attack and unflinching defense.

That was very troubling. What he expected to happen—what Howard had predicted would happen—was that the admiral would reach a point where denial was no longer useful, convenient, or fun and then he'd go on the attack. He'd throw the truth in Howard's face and make him eat it uncooked.

So . . . why wasn't that happening?

Chapter Eighty-eight

Elk Neck State Park
Cecil County, Maryland
Sunday, October 20, 12:33 p.m.

I found Junie and Ghost where I'd left them, and I popped a flare for the

Echo Team chopper to pick us up. If there were any Closers left in the forest, they steered clear.

Bunny and Lydia and Pete pulled us into the Black Hawk and we dusted off immediately. Everybody wanted to do a lot of back-slapping, but I growled for some damn quiet so I could yell at the pilot.

"Get us the hell out of range of this damn jammer. Pedal to the metal."

The chopper rose high and turned to the southwest. Ivan and Sam were crouched down behind the two miniguns, the barrels depressed toward the forest.

Nothing and no one shot at us.

We thought we'd come through the fire.

Then we passed out of the jam zone.

I called the Warehouse. And got nothing.

I tapped over to Bug's channel.

He was there.

He was crying.

He told me why.

Everyone was on the team channel. They all heard it.

It punched the air out of my lungs. The interior of the helo began spinning as if we were trapped in the heart of a cyclone.

"What?" I whispered. "What?"

A big sob broke in Bug's chest. This was killing him.

"Bug . . . what about Rudy? What about Church?"

"Oh, Jesus, Joe," he said, his voice breaking with pain, "I don't know. The whole area around the Warehouse is gone . . ."

I spoke to Aunt Sallie, to Dr. Hu. I spoke to several other DMS officials. There was a scramble to get the staff out of every field office. Bomb squads were searching the buildings, inside and out.

No one knew anything.

There was no word about Church and Rudy, or about anyone else who had been at the Warehouse.

Auntie went over everything. Stuff I knew about, stuff I didn't want to hear. It was all bad. The events at Dugway. The Chinese pilot who got shot down trying to make a suicide run at a carrier in the Taiwan Strait. And the thing that had appeared in both places. A massive, triangular craft that destroyed the Locust and shot down the Chinese fighter and

314 | Jonathan Maberry

then vanished at impossible speeds. She told me about sightings of UFOs all over the country. All over the world.

And she told me about the warrant out for my arrest on charges that I was a terrorist.

When I told her that I had Junie Flynn and that she was, for all intents and purposes, a living version of the Majestic Black Book, all Aunt Sallie said was, "Okay."

She ordered me to go to a safe house. I told her that I had one in mind and explained where it was. Then I hung up and went back into the main cabin. We clustered around the computer in the back and listened to the news. Dozens of buildings were on fire, hundreds of people injured. The number of known dead was forty, but the newscasters couldn't have known that the entire staff of the Warehouse had been called into work. All of them. *Two hundred people.*

Gone now.

I felt totally numb.

I looked at Junie, who was huddled in a seat, hugging Ghost to her chest. I looked at the shocked faces and horrified eyes of Top and Bunny and the others.

None of us spoke.

None of us could.

Chapter Eighty-nine

House of Jack Ledger,
Near Robinwood, Maryland
Sunday, October 20, 1:17 p.m.

What do you do when your world is turned upside down?

How do you react when suddenly fate in the form of some madman's will takes a crude scalpel and carves a hole in the skin of your world? What mechanism is there in us that prepares for the moment when dozens of people you know—friends, colleagues, employees, associates—are simply edited out of your day-to-day existence?

We shriek at the sky, demanding how this could happen. Needing to know why it had happened. What was the point?

What did it serve?

Where will it end?

These are unanswerable questions of course. After 9/11, after Haiti and the tsunamis in Thailand and Japan, after hurricanes and tornados, after wars and terrorist bombings, there are millions who have looked up to the sky or inward into personal darkness and demanded those answers. And they, too, were left bereft, adrift, unanswered and afraid.

Junie Flynn came and sat next to me. She took my hand and held it. In many ways she was still a stranger to me, and she knew none of the people at the Warehouse, but her touch was warm and alive. When you are sinking you grab any rope that's offered. Ghost came and snuggled against me, catching the mood aboard the helicopter, whimpering softly, needing reassurance, giving comfort in closeness and with simplicity.

The pilot asked, "Where, Captain?"

I told him. My uncle Jack had a farm near Robinwood, right on the Maryland-Pennsylvania border. I called ahead, told my uncle we were coming. Told him to pack a bag and go visit his daughter in Wildwood, New Jersey. I told him it was a matter of national security. Jack Ledger is a good guy, a retired career cop. I never told him what I do for a living but his brother, my dad, has probably hinted. All he asked me was, "Are you okay, Joey?"

"I'm okay," I lied.

Maybe the biggest lie I ever told.

Rudy Sanchez was my best friend. He was the only person who knew me. The only one who understood the mysteries of my fractured mind. He was closer to me than my brother, Sean.

I had brought him into the DMS. That meant that, however indirectly, I got that good man killed.

And Church?

Church was the ultimate good guy. He was as close to an actual super-hero as this world is ever likely to have. A legendary warrior in a very old and very dirty game. Infinitely dangerous, incredibly smart and wise. If he was dead, then the bad guys had managed to score one of the biggest wins in a long time. Maybe the biggest in my lifetime.

I had nowhere to put all this in my head.

It wasn't made to fit.

We flew on.

The "farm" was that in name only. Once upon a time it had been a dairy farm, but Jack wanted to be a cop like his brother. He and my dad sold half of the thousand acres, split the money, and my dad bought a big house in Baltimore. Jack rented out the farm while he worked as a cop in Hagerstown, and then once he had his twenty-five in, he gave it up and settled down to paint landscapes. He was very much a loner—just him and his dogs, Spartacus and Leonidas.

I sent the address via encoded text to Aunt Sallie and requested information and any tactical support that could be managed.

She texted back this message: "K"

By the time the Black Hawk reached the farm, Jack was long gone.

Where once there had been miles of grasslands for the cattle, now there was a forest of young pines and hardwoods. Beautiful, serene, and excellent cover.

We touched down behind the barn.

Bunny oversaw the removal of all our gear. Junie went into the house with Ghost. Top and I sat down on the porch while I called Aunt Sallie for an update.

"Do we know if anyone got out?" I asked.

"We're still waiting on word," she said. Auntie was an abrasive woman, given to barbed jokes and sarcasm, but not today. Her voice was as subdued as a nun's. I had the irrational desire to give her a big comforting hug.

"Nothing from Church?"

"Nothing."

I reminded her that Junie Flynn had the entire Black Book in her head, so in a way we had possession of it.

"We need to broadcast this on the frequency they gave us in the videos. We have to let them know that they can stop the countdown."

"What's your plan, Ledger? To hand over the woman?"

"Well, no . . . maybe they only need information from the book and . . ."

It sounded lame. It *was* lame. Auntie mumbled something about giving it a try, but we knew that this wasn't going to save the East Coast. Whoever took the president surely wanted the *actual* Black Book. Which we did not have and were no closer to having than we were this morning.

Maybe less so. Without Church, without my whole staff at the Warehouse. Maybe we were nowhere at all.

Auntie ended the call quickly.

Top parked a haunch on the porch rail. "How are you doing?"

I started to snarl at him, to tell him what an incredibly stupid question that was, and then I caught the look on his face. Not a noncom's look. Not a fellow soldier's look. It was a father's look. Grave, aware, composed.

I closed my eyes, exhaling a big lungful of air, feeling the aches in muscle and soul, feeling the weariness that was burning like a plague through my body.

"I don't know how I feel, Top," I said after a while. "If Rudy was there . . . then I lost the best friend I ever had. And everyone at the Warehouse. I—can't wrap my head around it."

"I can see that."

Again I almost barked at him, but he shook his head.

"If this was the regular army, Cap'n," he said, "you'd be able to tell me to shut the fuck up. If we were just friends, you could do that. But this is the DMS and I'm your topkick and we're at war. We don't get to be like regular folks. We waived that right when we joined."

I looked at him.

"You're in shock," he said. "You came straight out of a combat situation into a deep personal loss. You barely said two words on the flight here. You never introduced Miss Flynn to anyone, and most of the time you sat and stared into the middle distance."

"I lost friends down there, damn it."

Top got up, pulled a chair over, and sat down in front of me.

"Yeah, you lost friends down there. So did I. So did Bunny and Lydia. Even the new guys had friends down there. The pilot, Jerry, he had friends down there. But here's the news, Cap'n, you don't own the pink slip on grief. We're all in this together. We're all in it right now. You know what everyone else was doing while we were flying over here? They were watching you. They were looking to you. You are the captain. You are the leader of the team, and more than that, you are the DMS for them. Mr. Church might be dead and gone. Rudy, too, and Gus and a lot of other people who were higher on the ladder than this bunch of shooters. So,

318 | Jonathan Maberry

they look to you." Top gave a soft snort, almost a sigh. "The bad news is that you don't get the luxury of falling apart and you don't get to let this kick your ass. Those soldiers in there have probably never been more scared than they are right now. They need to see you nut up and stand up and yell 'fuck you' to the gods of war."

I stared at him.

"'Cause the war isn't over," he said, then he stood up and walked away.

Chapter Ninety

House of Jack Ledger
Near Robinwood, Maryland
Sunday, October 20, 4:59 p.m.

Before I went inside, I used my cell to make a call. I reached Gunnery Sergeant Brick Anderson at the Shop.

"Cap Ledger!" he cried. "Sweet Jesus I thought you were dead. Holy mother of—"

"Listen, Brick, we don't have much time," I cut in. "First, have you heard from anyone who was at the Warehouse?"

"Gus Dietrich called me a couple minutes before the place blew, said that Dr. Sanchez and the big man were on their way over—but they never got here."

I squeezed my eyes shut, but didn't interrupt.

"Gus sent over all the updated files, though," said Brick. "There's stuff coded for you. Want me to send it?"

"Yes," I growled. "And right goddamn now. I'm running blind here."

"Sending it now. What else can I do?"

"I need Black Bess and at least one other vehicle. I need them loaded with everything you can squeeze in, including a MindReader substation. And I need all of it right now. I'm about an hour and a half from you, up in Robinwood."

I gave him the address.

"Give me ten minutes and then we're on the road." Brick Anderson was a good man who'd lost a leg in combat.

"Brick, this is getting messy out here, so you don't have to bring it yourself."

He hung up on me.

I put the cell back into my pocket and went inside.

They were all in the kitchen, seated around the big table. There was a lot of food on the table but it didn't look like anyone was eating. Junie stood apart, leaning against the counter near a Mr. Coffee that was brewing a fresh pot. No one was looking at anybody, except Top and Junie, who were both looking at me.

"Coffee will be ready soon," she said, then she cleared her throat. "Do you want me to leave?"

"No," I said. "You're welcome to stay, but I have to talk to my team. Then they're going to need to hear what you have to say."

She nodded and pulled a stool over next to the counter and sat on it. Top turned a chair backward and sat down at the far end of the table. I stood by the door.

"We haven't lost," I said.

It took a moment, and one by one they glanced up at me.

"It feels like it. It feels like we got our asses kicked. We lost Hector, Red, and Slick, and that was bad. That would have been the worst day of the week for us. I wish I could say that it would have been the worst day this month, but that wasn't true even before the bomb."

No nods, but they were looking at me.

"We don't know who we're at war with. Not exactly. Maybe it's Majestic Three. Maybe it's someone else. Or maybe we're caught in the middle of something. But no matter how it swings, we're at war."

A few nods.

"People die in war. Sucks to say it, sucks worse to mean it, but people die. Friends die. Family dies. And what really sucks is that this is worse than we think."

Bunny looked up at that. "Worse?" he asked. "Excuse me, boss, but how the fuck can it be worse?"

I told them about Dugway and the dogfight in the Taiwan Strait.

It was Junie who broke the silence. "Wait—Joe, tell me that part again. About what the craft looked like."

I described it exactly as Aunt Sallie had described it to me.

"A black triangle," she said, nodding. Then for the benefit of the others she explained, "They call it a T-craft. Most of the really reliable UFO sightings don't describe a flying saucer—what they see is a T-craft just like this. That's the kind of craft M3 and groups in other countries have been scavenging. When President Truman initiated the Majestic Program, that's the kind of ship he wanted them to either repair or make. The T-craft is powered by a special engine, either one made from original parts or a facsimile—a Truman Engine."

"What are you saying, miss?" asked Sam Imura. "Are these ships aliens? Or are they ships we've built?"

"I don't know. If they're alien, then it would be the first time they've ever attacked us. If this is something we built—the U.S. or another world power—then it will change everything. War, the arms race . . . all of that is going to change."

"Why?" asked Lydia.

"You're soldiers," said Junie, "so let me put it in terms you'd understand—having a working T-craft is the equivalent of bringing a nuclear bomb to a knife fight."

"Bullshit. How the fuck would *you* know?" Lydia's tone was so sharp that Junie jumped.

But Top snapped his fingers as loud as a gunshot. "Secure that shit, Warbride," he snapped. "This lady is a civilian advisor and you will treat her with respect."

"Yes, First Sergeant," barked Lydia, straightening in her chair. To Junie, she said, "Please excuse my tone, ma'am."

Junie shook her head. "No, it's okay. I understand. To you people I'm a nonmilitary UFO freak and probably a severe pain in the ass. I get that, and *I'm* sorry. But Joe and your Mr. Church reached out to me because I understand this stuff. I know about the T-craft and Majestic Three and the secret arms race that's been going on since 1947. And I want to help."

Lydia and the others studied her and then one by one their eyes turned toward me.

I placed my cell phone down on the table. "None of us knows exactly what the fuck is going on. But here's a news flash—each of us knows *something* the others don't, and Brick Anderson just sent me the case notes from Mr. Church. This is everything that Church and our friends at the Warehouse had been able to put together, right up until they died. This is our field intel. This is what we have to go on. That—and what's inside Junie Flynn's head. As of now she is an official liaison to this team and will be afforded every courtesy and access. You think she's an outsider? Think again. These motherfuckers murdered her parents to try and bury this information. That buys her a ticket to our club. That means everyone here has lost a friend or loved one." I leaned on the table. "Does that make you mad? Does that make you want to go out and cut some heads? Good—it damn well ought to. It damn well better. But first we need a name. We need to put somebody in the crosshairs. It's up to us or no one. We go through this material. Everyone works it. Everyone has a voice. I want to hear every theory, every possibility. And once we know who set off that bomb at the Warehouse, then we are going to go after them and show them what hell is really like. Do you hear me?"

Their eyes bored into mine. I saw rage and resentment, anger and bloodlust.

"Hooah," they snarled.

Lydia stood up, grabbed Junie by the sleeve and pulled her—firmly but gently—over to the table. "If you're one of us then you're one of us," she said.

I saw Top silently mouth the word, *Hooah*.

Chapter Ninety-one

The Oval Office, the White House
Sunday, October 20, 5:19 p.m.

Acting president William Collins slammed the door of the Oval Office and wheeled around to glare at Mark Eppenfeld, the attorney general.

"Where do we stand with Ledger and the DMS?"

Eppenfeld stared at him, appalled. "Mr. President . . . surely this matter can wait until a more appropriate time. The DMS is clearly under attack. America itself appears to be under attack. Between Dugway, the cyber-terrorism, and this terrible, terrible incident in Baltimore . . ."

"That's why we need to jump on it. How much more proof do we need that Ledger has gone rogue and is waging a terror campaign against this nation? As soon as we try to execute a warrant to gain access to his office the whole place blows up. Do you want to stand there and tell me that he didn't rig it to blow if somebody started looking too close?"

"That's supposition, Mr. President, and I don't think it's the next natural link in the chain of logic."

"And I'm saying it is," replied the president very sternly. "How many times do I have to say that Ledger is an enemy of the state?"

"Mr. President, the money and stock certificates found at Captain Ledger's apartment are clean. No fingerprints."

"So?"

"Does something need to have leaves and sap before we call it a plant?"

The president sneered at him. "Don't try to get cute, Mark. And let me caution you . . . some people might find your constant defense of a known terrorist like Joe Ledger to be a matter of some concern."

Eppenfeld straightened. "Mr. President . . . are you threatening me? May I remind you that until you relieve me of this office or I choose to resign, I am the attorney general of the United States. Threats made against me are—"

"Oh, for Christ's sake, Mark, get off your high horse," Collins said quickly. "I'm trying to help you make the right choice here."

Eppenfeld's face was a stone. "And what, sir, is the right choice in this matter?"

"The right choice is to prevent this thing from escalating. As long as Joe Ledger—or anyone working with him—has access to MindReader then he will continue to pose a grave threat to national security."

"I already informed you, Mr. President, that we do not have just cause to confiscate that computer system as it is the personal property of Mr. Church. As his body has not been identified we cannot confirm that he is among the victims of the explosion, and therefore his property rights are in force."

"No, Mark, you misunderstand me . . . I'm not saying we should go after the computer. If we can't touch it, then nobody should be able to touch it. I'm saying that we need to shut the Department of Military Sciences down. Shut it all down, and shut it down right now." He leaned forward and smiled, then opened a blue folder on his desk. Inside was a document written on official stationery. "Every field office is on property owned outright or leased by the United States. In the interests of national

security I am issuing an executive order for that purpose, effective immediately."

He handed the document to Eppenfeld, who read it through. The AG's
shoulders slowly sagged.

"The DMS is finished, Mark," said the president. "Done."

Chapter Ninety-two

House of Jack Ledger
Near Robinwood, Maryland
Sunday, October 20, 7:41 p.m.

The October sun was a memory and darkness rose up, immense and absolute. The lingering summer heat vanished, leaving a cold mist that filled
the hollows and valleys of northern Maryland.

We downloaded the case files to the laptop and began going through
them. Junie sat at the other end of the table, between Top and Lydia, but
she kept darting covert glances my way. I only caught them with my pe-
ripheral vision and by the time I looked up each time, she'd already
looked away or bent over the material again. I wasn't sure what kind of
message she was trying to send me.

One of the first things I found were Rudy Sanchez's notes from a series
of phone calls he'd made to friends of Mr. Church—and friends of their
friends. A lot of it confirmed things that Junie had already told me.
T-craft. Alien-human hybrids. The Majestic Project. M3. And a long list
of suspected members of that mysterious group. I took special note of the
names that kept coming up most often. Then I looked at the reports on the
cyber-attacks.

"Time to put all of our cards on the table and play twenty questions so
we can all see what we know," I said. "Let's start with this: Do we believe
this or not? Are we, a group of rational adults and trained special operators, going to sit here and say yes, we believe in aliens, and crashed
UFOs, and all of it? Show of hands."

I waited. Junie chewed her lip.

The first hand that went up was the one I thought would be last.

Top.

Everyone looked at him, startled. Top was a hard sell on a lot of edgy issues, and a lot of the times his doubt proved to be a steadying and sobering reality check.

Top said, "I'm not saying I buy all of it. Lot of it seems like science-fiction bullshit to me, but . . . there's a sense to it. These cocksuckers are throwing a lot of assets at us to keep us out of this, and all of that started as soon as we started looking for the Black Book. If the book is some made-up shit, then why bring down all this heat?"

It was a soldier's response, an operator's response.

Pete Dobbs nodded. "I've pretty much been on board since I heard about the president. I know some guys in the Secret Service and they keep their shit tight. And we all talked about it some," he said, indicating the rest of Echo. "We came up with four or five good ways to snatch the president, but none of them would leave zero traces."

"Plus there's that crop circle thing," said Ivan, nodding. "That's some freaky shit right there. No way you're going to tell me that a couple of jerkoffs with flat boards and string faked that thing on the White House lawn right when the Secret Service was crashing the building. So . . . count me in."

The next hand to go up was Sam Imura's. "Not a big believer in anything up there or out there," he said. "But . . . somebody's building flying saucers." He cut a look at Junie. "Sorry, T-craft. If it's us, then we've suddenly gotten a lot smarter. Those things are way past anything we have that I've ever seen, and one of the upsides to working for Mr. Church is you get to see next year's stuff this year. I don't know what year that stuff belongs to."

He'd used Mr. Church's name so casually, and it chilled the air in the kitchen.

"The big man always loved having the best toys," said Bunny softly. "Damn, I still can't believe—"

Lydia suddenly turned in her seat and punched him in the chest.

"Hey!" she snapped. "We're on a mission clock, *pendejo*. Go to the funeral later."

He blinked at her in surprise, then his eyes hardened and he nodded. "Yeah, shit, sorry."

"Where do you stand, Staff Sergeant?" I asked.

"I'm with the team on this, boss," said Bunny. "If this is aliens and stuff, then it's aliens and stuff."

Everyone else agreed.

"Does any of this answer the question of who took the president? Is that M3? Is it the Chinese or the Russians? Or is it the aliens?"

Top, Junie, and I all said it at the same time: "Aliens."

"Okay," said Pete, "but why?"

"I think that's pretty obvious," said Top.

Junie and I nodded.

The others looked perplexed.

"If these aliens are here," Top said, "then you got to ask yourself why they didn't scavenge their own stuff. If these D-type components are so damned valuable and dangerous, then it seems foolish to let 'em lie around where we can pick 'em up. Maybe that's the point. Not to belittle the human race, but there's also the possibility that we're part of a controlled experiment. Give the monkeys a bunch of Legos and see what happens. Maybe for most of the last sixty years we've been shoving those Legos up our asses, but now we're building a set of stairs that we can use to climb out of our cage. We might have crossed that line from 'oh, isn't it cute that the humans are flying those quaint little airplanes' to 'holy fuck, they're actually building T-craft.'"

"Or maybe they left that stuff there as an alarm," said Junie. "As long as we play with the toys then they know we're no threat. But now we're figured out how *their* science works. Maybe that's what triggered the response."

I nodded again. "Might even be as simple as the aliens not knowing who was doing this research. They're high tech, but that doesn't mean they can see through walls. On a planet this big—and with the kind of communication gaps there have to be between them and us—maybe they needed us to step out of the shadows and announce ourselves."

"Like flying a T-craft?" asked Bunny.

"Like flying one—and doing shit like trying to provoke a war in the Taiwan Strait and shooting down stealth aircraft. That looks the same from every angle: Someone has built a T-craft and is trying to use it to start a war. *That* might be the kind of alarm that might make them take steps. Like nabbing the president, like threatening big-ticket destruction. And maybe worse." I looked around. "I think maybe the aliens have decided that they want their toys back."

Chapter Ninety-three

House of Jack Ledger

Near Robinwood, Maryland

Sunday, October 20, 8:19 p.m.

Headlights flashed through the windows and suddenly everyone was instantly on their feet, weapons in hand. Ghost ran growling to the door.

"Ivan," I said, "take Junie into the basement. Stay there until you hear one of us tell you it's safe to come out. Everyone else, on the team channel."

Junie did not argue. She nodded and let Ivan escort her through the cellar door, however she paused in the doorway and gave me a brief, encouraging, radiant smile.

I smiled back, but as I turned away Top was right there. He didn't say a word. He didn't need to.

"Head's in the game," I said quietly.

He said, "Hooah," just as quietly.

We darkened the lights. Pete and Lydia took up shooters' positions inside the living room and Sam ran upstairs with his sniper rifle. Top faded back and vanished through the back door. Bunny walked out onto the porch with me, weapons low and out of sight. Just a couple of farm guys coming out to see who was being neighborly. Ghost sat in the shadows behind one of the chairs, invisible and totally alert.

There were three vehicles coming along the road, but I couldn't see anything past the headlights. Two of them were trucks, but I couldn't tell much through the glare. As the lead truck reached the entrance to the big turnaround in front of the house, the driver flashed his brights at me. Once, twice, three times. Then the truck turned and I saw what it was.

I heard Bunny say, "Well kiss my ass."

He was grinning as he stood up.

The lead vehicle was a big, white Mister Softee truck, but I knew that it wasn't here to sell ice cream to kids. I caught a glimpse of the massive form behind the wheel. The second vehicle was a Ford Explorer—not mine, which would have been destroyed along with everything else at the Warehouse—but one very much like it. There were several figures behind the smoked glass.

When Bunny saw the third vehicle, he nodded and said, "Fuck yeah."

It was Echo Team's tactical vehicle, Black Bess.

The door to the Mister Softee truck opened and I saw a mechanical leg step out first. Sleek and alien-looking, but it was definitely local manufacture. It was attached to the formidable figure of Gunnery Sergeant Brick Anderson. Brick looked like the actor Ving Rhames, except for the metal leg and a network of shrapnel scars on his face.

The man who stepped out of Black Bess was Brian Bird—Birddog to everyone. Also tall, but not as overwhelmingly massive as Brick. Few people are. Some rhinos, maybe.

"Oh look, Gunny," said Birddog, "I believe that's Captain Ledger, a wanted felon."

"No doubt, no doubt," agreed Brick. "We should make sure we lock these here vehicles because we wouldn't want dangerous firearms and high explosives to fall into the hands of such an enemy of decent society."

"You two," I said, "are invited to kiss my ass."

I reached up to tap my earbud to tell everyone to stand down, then the doors of the Explorer opened. The driver was a man I didn't know, and he was dressed in a black suit, white shirt, black tie.

The man who stepped out of the passenger side of the vehicle. Yeah, I knew him.

He was big and blocky, with bandages on his face and one arm strapped to his body.

Ghost leaped to his feet and began barking.

In my earbud I heard Top gasp. Bunny said, "Jesus Christ."

The big man looked up at the house. He could not see my shooters at every window, but he had to know they were there.

"Good evening, Captain Ledger," said Mr. Church. "I'm delighted to see that you're safe and sound."

I rushed down off the porch, delighted to see him alive, but with every step I became more intensely worried about the fact that there was no sign at all of Rudy.

Church waited for me. He looked awful. Covered in cuts and scrapes, stitches and bandages. Pain and loss aged him. As I slowed to a walk, he caught my eye, saw me looking past him.

"Dr. Sanchez is alive," he said.

I stopped dead in my tracks.

Alive.

"How is he?" I demanded. "*Where* is he?"

"The Wilmer Eye Institute at Johns Hopkins."

"What?"

"We were in a helicopter about fifty feet above the building at the time of the explosion. The pilot lost control of the bird and we went into the bay. The pilot was killed, as were two of the crewmen. Dr. Sanchez was unconscious when we made it to shore. Shrapnel from the blast and structural debris on impact with the water. He sustained some head trauma and a deep laceration across his face. The doctors are optimistic they can save his left eye. The right . . . well . . ." Church shook his head.

"God."

"He has some fractures, cuts, and burns, of course, but they're secondary."

I felt stunned. It was like being kicked in the face. On one hand I was overjoyed that Rudy was still alive; but then to hear about him being so savagely injured.

"Will he live?"

"I believe so. It's too soon to evaluate brain function."

I closed my eyes.

Church pitched his voice to a confidential one. "I . . . have not contacted Circe yet. However, Aunt Sallie has agents en route to pick her up and bring her to Johns Hopkins."

"Did anyone else get out?"

"No. The estimated body count is one hundred and sixty-nine DMS personnel. Seven of the eight FBI agents who came to serve a warrant on you, Captain. Two NSA agents who were with them. Sixteen civilians from the surrounding buildings."

"Gus?" asked Top.

Church's face was wooden. "No."

"Ah, jeez . . ."

Gus Dietrich had been with Church for years. He was the big man's personal assistant, bodyguard, aide, and friend. A good friend of mine, too.

"I'm sorry," I said. "Gus was a good man."

Church's eyes were black metal orbs. "Gus was family."

"Yes."

"They were all family."

"Yes."

"And we are going to hunt down the people responsible for this," he said softly. "We will hunt every last one of them down and we will kill them."

Chapter Ninety-four

House of Jack Ledger
Sunday, October 20, 8:43 p.m.

We gathered in my uncle's den. Echo Team, Junie, Ghost, and Church. Brick and Birddog stood like tall bookends at either side of the fireplace. Church sat very straight and very carefully in an overstuffed chair. I later learned that he had two broken fingers, a separated shoulder, dozens of small cuts and over forty stitches. The bandage wrapped around his forehead hid a deep gash made by the same piece of broken metal that had nearly blinded Rudy. His tinted sunglasses were gone and I got my first real look at his eyes. They were so dark a brown that they looked black, and there was no mercy at all in them. He had to be in tremendous pain, but he endured it with grim stoicism.

"What about Mr. Bug?" asked Junie. "And the other man who was on the video conference. Dr. Hu?"

"They're in New York," said Church. "I've ordered all field offices evacuated. Staff has been moved to secondary locations while bomb teams are doing thorough inspections."

"Why didn't Auntie or Bug tell me you and Rudy were alive?" I asked.

"For the same reason I did not call ahead to tell you I was on my way. Given the timing with everything that's happened today, I think it's a safe bet that one or more of the DMS communication channels has been hacked. The very fact that a team was sent after you quickly enough to have arrived within a half an hour of you reaching the lighthouse makes that much clearer. The DMS is radio silent for now. I had Birddog bring one of the new prototype mike systems for you. You'll swap that for your old stuff."

Birddog used the toe of his boot to tap the equipment case on the floor. "Got you covered," boss.

"What about the bomb?" asked Lydia. "What kind of explosive did they use?"

"Unknown. Detective Spencer and his team are coordinating with state and federal investigators to answer that question. There is a curious lack of residue. No nitrites, no radiation. No chemical signature of any kind that they have so far been able to detect. It may be that this is a new form of explosive."

Church told us what happened. His voice was flat, dispassionate.

"Sir," began Bunny, "do we know anything of substance?"

That question ignited a spark in Church's eye. A small, cold flame. "We do not yet know who ordered the hit, though I suspect we are close to a name," he said, "but we know who set off that bomb."

Everyone came to point, eyes narrowing, mouths drawing tight into feral lines of undisguised hate.

"Who?" I said in a fierce whisper.

"He used to be a field agent," said Church. "One of mine. One of the very best. He was already highly trained when I recruited him into a group I was running prior to the formation of the DMS. We brought him to a higher level of skill, but that statement doesn't do him justice. He quickly became the go-to operator for any operation that required unparalleled combat and technical skills. Had things gone another way I have no doubt that he would have become a senior team leader. I would almost certainly have given him leadership of Echo Team during the *seif al din* matter . . . but he was gone by then."

"What happened?"

"You cannot serve two masters," said Church. "I think it's safe to say that he was steered in my direction with the goal of my providing him with more advanced training than his true masters had been able to provide. It's likely that he became a trainer himself."

"Let me guess," I said, "the Closers?"

"It would be my guess. Tull called me directly before triggering the bomb and—"

"Wait," interrupted Junie. "What did you say? What was his name?"

"Tull," said Church. "His name is Erasmus Tull."

Junie made a sound. It was almost a gasp, but there was more to it than that. It was as if everything she was suddenly tried to jerk backward out of the moment. Everyone turned to her. Junie's face was as white as paste. Her eyes were wide disks filled with an impossible amount of naked fear.

"Tull . . . ," she breathed. "Oh my God."

She slid out of her chair and thumped to the floor, half unconscious from shock. I was up and across the room in a shot. I knelt beside her and took her by the shoulders.

It took effort. It cost her in ways I couldn't immediately understand. She raised her face and looked at me, then at the others in the room, and finally at Rudy and Church. Tears gathered in the corners of her eyes and then broke, rolling down her cheeks.

"He's my older brother," she whispered.

Chapter Ninety-five

VanMeer Castle
Near Pittsburgh, Pennsylvania
Sunday, October 20, 8:46 p.m.

Howard Shelton grinned like a happy uncle and held his arms wide as Erasmus Tull came through the door. There was a lot of laugher and back-slapping. Aldo drifted along in Tull's wake, and Mr. Bones stood politely to one side.

"My boy," Howard kept saying. "Well done, my boy."

Then Howard turned and offered his hand to Aldo.

"And well done to you to, Mr. Castelletti. Fine work."

"Thank you, sir," said Aldo, a bit awed. He had met Howard Shelton once before, but the man intimidated the hell out of him. It was like meeting Donald Trump. "It was Tully's call. I was there to tote barges and lift bales."

"Aldo pulled his own weight," said Tull generously. "Don't let him tell you different."

"It's a shame that the teams sent to retrieve Junie Flynn and dispose of Captain Ledger were less successful."

"'Less successful'?" snorted Mr. Bones. "Ledger damn near wiped them out." He cocked his head at Tull. "You trained that team, I believe."

Tull gave him a long, unsmiling look. "What about it?"

"This must come as a crushing blow. The fruits of your labors being so easily stepped on. What was the total body count? Seventeen men and two helicopters? Only three survivors?"

"If you have a point, Mr. Bones, go ahead and make it," said Tull.

"All right, all right," growled Howard, "everybody stop pissing on each other and put your dicks away. Who gives a damn if Ledger is alive? The point was to keep the DMS occupied and on the run until we were ready to make our move. Done that, Mr. Bones, wouldn't you say?"

Bones said nothing, but he wore a totally false smile.

"The DMS isn't a factor now. It's going to take them weeks or months to recover from losing the Deacon. We have a new set of challenges facing us."

The other three men turned to face him.

"What challenges?" asked Tull. "The air show is tomorrow and—"

"The air show is canceled. That's done."

"What about Specter 101? All the work you've put into it? Is that all scrapped now?"

Mr. Bones said, "My dear Tull, you are horribly out of the loop. I think it's fair to say that the world has changed since you woke up this morning."

Chapter Ninety-six

House of Jack Ledger
Near Robinwood, Pennsylvania
Sunday, October 20, 8:49 p.m.

"Erasmus Tull is your *brother*?"

"Yes," said Junie. "And . . . no. It's complicated."

Top Sims leaned forward and put his forearms on his knees. "Miss, I would appreciate it if you would *un*complicate it for us. That man killed a couple of hundred people that I used to know."

The room was dead silent. Junie looked around at everyone. At me. I hoped that the things I was feeling in my heart weren't showing in my eyes. I knew the Killer was watching her.

"We were a year apart, but in the same orphanage," she said, and immediately Church raised his good hand.

"Miss Flynn," he said calmly, "credit us with some intelligence. We researched your history. You were never in an orphanage. Not in this country, and not under that name."

Junie swallowed.

"That's . . . only partly true," she said. "I was in an orphanage until I was six years old, in Group Eight. Erasmus Tull was in Group Seven."

" 'Group'?" said Bunny. "What kind of orphanage are you talking about, lady?"

Junie looked deeply frightened. I think that if there was a way out of that room she would have bolted and run. Instead, she took a big breath, forced herself to make direct eye contact with Mr. Church, and said, "I belong to a very specific group of children who were born and partially raised at a facility in Nevada. The site has no official name. The building I lived in was called Hive Two. There were ninety-six children in that facility, and there were at least ten facilities exactly like it."

"Um . . . ," said Bunny, "are we talking clones?"

"No, of course not," said Junie with a trace of a smile.

"Good, because I—"

"I'm pretty sure I'm an alien-human hybrid," she said. "Just like Erasmus Tull."

Chapter Ninety-seven

House of Jack Ledger
Near Robinwood, Maryland
Sunday, October 20, 8:51 p.m.

Bunch of people, mostly killers, sitting in a room.

Looking at the pretty lady, the civilian.

Who just said that she might be related to the man who killed the entire staff at the Warehouse.

Who said that she might be part alien.

All of us, sitting there with that painted on the air in front of us.

"That's it," Bunny said. "I quit. I'm going home."

Mr. Church nodded to Junie. "I know."

You could actually hear the sound of every head in the room whipping around from staring at Junie to gaping at Church.

"*What?*" I croaked. "You *knew?*"

Church nodded. Pain flickered on his stern face. "I read through all of Dr. Sanchez's interview notes on the way here. Several of the experts mentioned the alien-human hybrid initiative, indicating that without an acceptable biological interface these T-craft cannot fly. A certain percentage of alien DNA is necessary, and so to ensure the success of their vehicle-design program, Majestic Three would have had to be ready with pilots who had that DNA signature. Hybrids." Junie nodded, and he continued. "Among those persons who claim to be hybrids or who are suspected of being such, there is a high percentage of savantism. In some cases it is prodigious savantism, with deep memory and awareness of multiple areas. Math and numbers are common, but there are other areas as well. Many of these people have exceptional hand-eye coordination. And there is the issue if having both eidetic memory and hyperthymesia. The instances of that are so rare in the general population that to find it in any contained population suggestions a connection. I know for a fact that Erasmus Tull has those qualities. It's part of what made him such an exceptional operator. Show him a building blueprint or let him read a mission case file and he has it all stored. Expose him to a language, a combination, a cypher, and it's stored in his head."

"Just like the Majestic Black Book," I said.

"Yes," said Junie.

"Holy mother of shit," said Lydia.

"Wait, wait," said Pete, "can we go back to the part where you two are related?"

"It's an ugly thing," said Junie. She took a tissue out of her sweater pocket and wiped her nose. "You've heard about all of those alien abductions? You know, people taken out of their beds and subjected to all sorts of tests? Well, as far as I know most or all of that is faked. It's M3 using hallucinogenic compounds and some mind-control tech they developed. They implant a false memory using drug-enforced hypnosis."

"That sounds military," said Ivan. "I mean . . . I know guys in psi-ops who do that sort of thing."

"Yes," said Church.

"After the people are abducted," continued Junie, "they are used as part of a breeding program. Early on they tried to get the abductees to mate. They even used date-rape drugs like Rohypnol, gamma-hydroxybutyrate, Ketamine, and even Ambien—because it had both sedative and amnesiac properties. But there were too many behavior problems associated with forced sex, and because it required the time and expense of monitoring the pregnancy after the abductees were returned. And, of course, kidnapping the child if he or she demonstrates useful qualities. There are some real horror stories associated with that, and the program began tripping over itself. So they changed tack and decided to harvest eggs and sperm instead. That way they can cut the parents totally out of the picture and raise the babies under controlled conditions."

"Like the facility in Nevada?" asked Mr. Church.

"Yes. That was my home as a baby. There were nearly a hundred of us. We weren't clones or anything like that. Each of us came from a human egg and sperm via in vitro fertilization. I was in the eighth batch of viable fetuses. Group Eight." She paused and a shadow passed across her face. "There were problems with the previous batches. The first few were awful. I saw photographs. Birth defects of the most horrible kinds. That's when they were trying to determine how much alien DNA to introduce, and at which point of fetal development."

"Christ," whispered Top. He was the only member of Echo Team with kids. His eyes were filled with sickness and anger. "What happened to those kids? The ones with the birth defects?"

Junie shook her head. "They were considered failed experiments. The same with the next batches. It wasn't until the batch before mine, Group Seven, that they began getting an acceptable yield. There were still some problems, but they . . . allowed most of them to grow up."

"Erasmus Tull was in Group Seven?" I asked.

"Yes."

"Did he have any 'problems'?"

She nodded. "Behavior problems. He was brilliant and he had all the qualities they needed for the pilot program—enhanced coordination, perfect memory, total calm in high-pressure situations. But—he was hard to control at first. He was very violent, but in a strange way. He never picked a fight, but if someone else started one, his reactions were way over the top. Once a little boy shoved him in the playroom. Erasmus got up, walked over to the toy box, picked up a heavy net bag of building blocks, walked back over to the other boy and started beating him with it. By the time the staff heard the screams and came in, the other boy was dead and Erasmus was completely covered in blood." She paused. "Erasmus was four years old."

My mouth went dry.

"They put him through a battery of psychological tests, and he passed every one. After a while they determined that it was an aberration, a one-time event. Until it happened again. Seven months later two boys tried to beat Erasmus up because they were afraid of him. They caught him in the boys' bathroom."

"What happened?" asked Birddog, whose face had gone as pale as everyone else's.

"He killed them both."

"So," said Bunny, working it through, "are you saying that he was born without a conscience? Or he is too alien to understand right and wrong?"

"I really don't know. I'm not sure if the people at M3 know either. However, they must have learned something from all the tests they did on him, because he wasn't terminated for having birth defects. Erasmus and a few others who were a lot like him were removed from the program shortly after the incident in the bathroom. Actually a lot of us were taken out of the program and assigned to families."

"Like Jericho and Amanda Flynn?" suggested Church.

"Yes."

"Did they know where you came from?"

Junie gave me a brief guilty look. "Yes."

"So, all that stuff you told me about your father was bullshit? Winning those science fairs, getting hired by DARPA . . . that was all crap?"

"No," she said quickly and reached out to touch my arm. "Most of it's the absolute truth, but . . ."

I pulled my arm away. "How about the *whole* truth? How about you stop fucking with my head?"

She nodded as tears rolled down her face. "What I said about my father was true. He didn't know about any of this until long after he was working inside the Project. Even then he still thought he was working on a DARPA-sanctioned project. It's where he met my mother. She was a developmental psychologist and . . . she was a key member of M3's breeding program. She helped tie my father to the program. Did she ever really love him? I don't know. Maybe, toward the end. I don't know. But she *grew* me in a lab, Joe. All the adoption papers were handled by her. My father was in love and he was work-obsessed, so he believed everything his wife told him." She paused and dabbed at the tears on her cheeks. "He was a good man, Joe. I think maybe he had some issues of his own. Asperger's, perhaps. He was always focused on work and never really that connected to other people. He didn't know where I came from or what I was. He tried to be a good father to me, but when it was clear that I didn't want to follow his career path, we drifted. That's when I started acting out. I tried to tell him about the 'orphanage,' but he wouldn't listen. He thought they were silly stories. Until I told him about a kid I knew named Erasmus Tull."

"Why did that change things?" I asked.

"Because Dad knew Erasmus Tull," she said. "By the time I was in college, Erasmus was around the lab all the time. He'd become part of the team that was searching for new components, and he was apparently very successful at it. He kept getting promotions even though he was so young. Hearing about Erasmus—someone I could not possibly know—seemed to do something to Dad. That's when he began making copies of everything related to the Project."

"Including the Black Book," said Church quietly.

"Yes. Dad had been such a company man that they never thought he'd betray them. But loyalty has to cut both ways, and when he realized that the Project was built on lies, he turned against them. Dad was a patriot, Joe. When they found out that he'd copied the Black Book, they had him killed."

"But your mother was killed in the same rigged accident," I said. "Why? Whose side was she on?"

"My mother was still very much with the company . . . and there's a pretty good chance she's the one who turned Dad in."

"So why'd they kill her?" asked Lydia.

Junie gave her a long, hard look. "You should ask Erasmus Tull that question. Maybe it was easier to manage the hit that way. Or maybe he was running out of time."

"I have one last question," said Church. "When you began your podcast and published your books on M3 and the Black Book, those people had to suspect that your father told you crucial secrets. Why didn't they come after you?"

"They did, once. A car bombing in Egypt that was blamed on terrorists. And a close call with what the police called a 'failed abduction-rape.' It failed because half the football team came stumbling out of a bar just as two men in black clothes tried to pull me into a van."

"No," said Sam, "those were close calls, but someone like this guy Tull could have taken you out with a bullet or one of those microwave pistols. And you've been living all alone at that lighthouse for how long? Not to offend you, miss, but you should be dead a hundred times over."

"Which means they don't want you dead," said Top. "Now why would that be?"

"I think it's obvious," I said. "For whatever reason, the governors of M3 want the world to know about the Majestic Black Book. Maybe they're planning a big event, a reveal, and this is part of a plan to pave the way."

"That sounds thin," said Pete.

"It's not," countered Church. "Our government does that all the time. We leaked information on the stealth program before we rolled the first ships out. It cut down on wild speculation from eyewitnesses who thought they were seeing UFOs. This is a standard policy, like a valve that lets off steam. It makes the reveal less of a staggering drama."

"Iran did that with their nuclear program," I said, and he nodded. "Which means that Junie's podcasts and books could be part of a limited and very selective disclosure process."

"I think you're right," she confessed. "Besides, before last night they probably thought I only knew bits and pieces of the book. After all . . . I sat on the information for years. I was afraid to do anything with it. My life hasn't exactly taught me to trust anyone. Family, governments . . . you wonder why I write about conspiracies? My whole life has been in the heart of one of the biggest conspiracies of the last century, and that's *not* a theory."

"And last night you told the whole damn world that you had the Black Book and were going to share it with everyone," said Bunny. "No offense, but . . . why not just paint a bull's-eye on yourself? You had to know they'd move heaven and earth to pop a cap in you."

She shrugged. "I guess it doesn't seem to matter anymore."

"Why not?"

She was a long time answering. Ghost caught something, some emotion, and he whimpered and leaned against her. Junie bent and wrapped her arms around him, burying her cheek against the soft white fur on the top of his head.

"Gene therapy is still largely experimental. There are always unexpected side effects," she said, her eyes distant and her voice very soft. Then, she took a long, ragged breath, reached up, entwined her fingers in her wild blond hair . . . and pulled it off. Beneath the wig she was totally bald, her smooth skull unmarked except for the small blue tattoos the radiology techs put there to mark the spot where the tumor is. Then she looked up, looked at each of us.

"They don't need to kill me," she said. "They already have."

Chapter Ninety-eight

VanMeer Castle
Near Pittsburgh, Pennsylvania
Sunday, October 20, 8:59 p.m.

They stood in a row, staring through the glass at the massive vehicle.

"Well," said Aldo quietly, "now there's something you don't see every day."

"Actually . . . ," said Howard, but let the rest hang.

"And it works?" breathed Aldo.

"Yes indeed."

"But I thought there were all sorts of problems . . ."

"Ah," said Howard, "you've been in the field too long, my boy. We are no longer throwing all of our efforts into *trying* to build a Device or a Truman Engine. We *have* built it. You see, we were doing things backward. We kept trying to assemble the ten components of the engine first and that always led to disaster. It didn't appear to make sense. Then we stepped back and reevaluated the process of sympathetic gravity. When certain conditions are maintained the ten D-type components remain inert; but when they're allowed to enter into close proximity, the engine assembles itself. It's wonderful, almost magical if you didn't know that it was science."

"Right, but then it blows up."

"Yes and no," said Howard. "It only blows up if there is nothing to balance the energetic discharge at the precise moment when the components form the complete engine. We kept trying to do only that. Then we realized that this isn't how the original builders of these craft did it. They clearly kept at least one part in stasis—much like you and Tull did with the miniatures today. Those parts needed to stay in stasis until the *eleventh* component was in place. Or . . . perhaps we should more appropriately say that we were aware of components one through nine and component eleven, but we never realized that there was a component missing from the complete engine. We kept trying to build it without that crucial tenth piece."

Tull got it first, and he nodded.

"The pilot," he said. "The pilot has to be in place before the engine can be allowed to complete itself."

"Clever boy!" Howard cried out in delight and patted Tull on the cheek. "You were always the smartest one in your group. Yes, that is exactly what needs to happen. Once the pilot was in place, he could then allow the eleventh piece to slide into place, thus completing a true biomechanical engine."

"Son of a bitch . . . ," Aldo said with real admiration. He grinned from ear to ear. His joy was so infectious that even Mr. Bones smiled. "So it doesn't take a full alien to run these things."

"We didn't know that at first," said Mr. Bones. "At first all we could determine is that a dead alien wouldn't work. We tried that once and got the same big bang. That's what really kicked the hybrid program into top gear. After some very costly and very, um, unfortunate tests, we managed to quantify how much of the organic material needs to be alien DNA and how much can be ordinary human. Turns out it's not a lot—eighteen percent—but it has to be the right eighteen percent. That was thirty years' worth of disasters, lab accidents, and collateral damage before we figured that out."

"How many pilots do you guys have?"

"Oh, there are plenty," said Howard, "but 'pilot' really isn't the right word. Any hybrid can form the basis of the biomechanical engine matrix. That person does not have to be the one to fly the ship. So, in a pinch any hybrid will do, as long as there is a way for us to control the ship. Remote-control science is booming—the entire military drone program is a side effect of our research into remote control over these ships. And as for the hybrids . . . and there's no shortage of the hybrids out there. We seeded them into the general population in the hopes that they'll breed. The more the merrier, because we keep track and we can always grab what we need. They can't really hide—they're all too exceptional for that."

Mr. Bones smirked. "The folks in the New Age community call them 'indigo children,' they think that the human race has suddenly taken an unexpected evolutionary jump. There are thousands of them out there now. Almost half a percent of all the children adopted in the United States since 1985 are hybrids. We know which ones are from which batch. Just as we know which ones are *specials*. Like our dear Erasmus Tull. Twenty-two percent of his brain is alien. Makes him special in a lot of ways. His IQ in unchartable, and he has so many nifty gifts."

Tull glanced at him. "Do I know any of the real pilots?"

"Some. There are a few from your group, but most come from Group Eight."

Tull made a face. He did not approve of the candidates from the groups that came after his. They were too emotional. Many of them were so unsuited to the Project that they were kept on the periphery, allowed to live because they were useful breeding stock, but kept in the dark about who they were or that they were part of anything besides a foster family. With Group Nine and beyond, the kids were raised in facilities that more closely approximated orphanages. Easier to cycle them into foster families that way. Fewer questions.

Technicians crawled all over the triangular machine, making adjustments, checking the fuselage for the tiniest imperfections.

"There are still openings in the pilot program," mused Howard. "Not too late."

"Don't start that again."

Aldo looked at him. "Really? You telling me you had a chance to fly one of these things and you *passed*? Are you out of your fucking mind? I'd give my left nut to fly one."

"Tull washed out of the program," said Mr. Bones cattily.

"You're shitting me," said Aldo.

"Not at all. He was in one of the first groups of pilot candidates, but our Mr. Tull had a problem with the commitment to the program."

"What's that supposed to mean?"

Tull shook his head. "He's screwing with me, Aldo. I quit the program because in order to fly the ship you have to let the ship do most of the work. It . . . reads you. It does all the work. You sit there like meat in a chair."

"It's more complicated than that," said Howard. "The biomechanical interface requires—"

"Hey," snapped Tull, "can we just drop it? I don't want to be a pilot, not like that. We all know where I belong in the Majestic Project. I think I proved that this afternoon."

Howard chuckled and patted him on the back. "Yes, you did, my boy, and I couldn't be prouder of you."

"And yet Junie Flynn is still out there with a complete copy of the Majestic Black Book," said Mr. Bones dryly. "Probably memorized, considering her talents. Yes, your fellows killed a lot of the bad guys, but let's not forget that the destruction of the DMS was intended as a distraction. I believe that prioritizing that over killing Junie Flynn was a poor strategic choice."

Tull turned to him and smiled a killer's smile. "You know, Bonesy, you've always been kind of a dick. Are you aware of that?"

"Hey now," warned Howard. "Mr. Bones is a governor of—"

"I know exactly what he is, Howard," said Tull. "He's a toadie. Without you, he'd be nothing."

"Attacking me doesn't change the fact that you let Junie Flynn slip away," said Mr. Bones, unperturbed.

"Did I?" He fished in his pocket and removed a small tracking device that was part of the Ghost Box unit. "I know exactly where she is."

"What?" said Mr. Bones, startled.

"As soon as I took charge of this mission I sent a whole flock of the pigeon drones to Turkey Point. When Ledger's team picked Junie and Ledger up, the drones clamped on to their Black Hawk. I've been getting continuous feeds all day. Right now they're at a farm in Robinwood, Maryland. Guess who owns that farm?" Tull did not wait for them to reply. "John Allen Ledger, aka Jack Ledger, our boy's uncle. And, according to satellite photos, the Black Hawk is parked behind the barn and there are three vehicles at the place. I think Ledger's using the farm as a bolt-hole, gathering anyone we didn't clip at the Warehouse. I'll bet you Aldo's *right* nut that Junie Flynn is right there. Safe, sound, and in our crosshairs any time we want her."

Chapter Ninety-nine

House of Jack Ledger
Near Robinwood, Maryland
Sunday, October 20, 9:06 p.m.

I was floored. I felt like the biggest horse's ass in the world. And I felt a stabbing sadness that drove its wicked point all the way through me.

"Junie, I—"

She put her fingertips to my mouth.

"Please," she said. "There's not a lot to say. I've been over the shock of it for weeks. I've made my peace and I know that once I transition out of here then a lot of things will be better for me. No more pain. No more fear." Her eyes were bright with tears, and with calm dignity, Junie put her wig back on and adjusted it. She gave me a small smile. "It's really my hair," she said. "I had it cut off and made into a wig before I started the radiation. Vain, I know, but we all have our flaws."

"There are no medical records . . ." Church began.

"I know. I have friends all over. One of the perks of being a player in the conspiracy theory field is you get to meet a lot of people who know how to keep a secret. I pay cash for all of my treatments and there's a place in Philadelphia where I can get those treatments without using my real name."

I closed my fingers around her hand, pulled it away from my mouth but didn't let it go. She allowed me to hold her hand, and even gave me a small reassuring squeeze. That nearly broke my heart. She, this woman with a horrible past and no future at all, giving *me* reassurance.

Into the staggering silence, Mr. Church's phone rang. He looked down at the display. "Linden Brierly," he said. No one spoke. Church said very little, thanked Brierly, and disconnected. Then he placed a call to Aunt Sallie. "Auntie, Brierly said he already called you, so you know where we stand," he told her. "I'm initiating Protocol Seventeen."

He disconnected and placed the phone on the table next to his chair.

We waited in silence while he gathered himself. I'll bet he was aching for a vanilla wafer.

Mr. Church said, "By executive order, as of oh-eight-thirty Eastern Time the president of the United States has officially revoked the charter of the Department of Military Sciences. All field offices are to be closed immediately. We are to cease all activities, abandon all cases, and vacate all premises associated with the DMS. We are to return all weapons, equipment, and credentials provided by same. All personnel are hereby suspended with pay from government service pending notification of status."

We stared at him, totally dumbfounded.

"The executive order further states that anyone acting contrary to the letter or the spirit of this order should be considered a threat to national security and an enemy of the state."

Mr. Church picked up his teacup and sipped it.

"Well," said Top, "at least they're still paying us."

There were a few smiles. No real laughs.

Bunny looked down at the papers spread out on the table. "So, basically if we keep trying to save the country and maybe the world from a bunch of murderous assholes with outer space weapons, then *we're* the bad guys?"

"In a nutshell," said Mr. Church.

Bunny looked around the room, then shrugged his big shoulders. "Then, hey . . . let's be bad guys."

Chapter One Hundred

VanMeer Castle

Near Pittsburgh, Pennsylvania

Sunday, October 20, 9:15 p.m.

"You knew all of this and you're content to just *leave* them there?" demanded Mr. Bones.

"Not exactly," said Erasmus Tull. "I didn't come here to get a pat on the head as a good dog, Bones. I wanted to talk this over with Mr. Shelton. And, yes, with you. I know you guys used Junie to seed the ground for the eventual reveal of Specter 101 and that whole generation of superspeed aircraft, but if she really has memorized the Black Book, why not bring her in and—I don't know—*file her away* somewhere. Great reference book."

"Nice looking, too," agreed Aldo.

"She'd never cooperate with something like that," said Mr. Bones.

"'Cooperate'?" said Tull, amused. "You really don't get out of the lab much, do you? If we want her to 'cooperate' then we just apply the right pressure."

Howard pursed his lips. "That's not bad. Her use as a free agent is pretty much done. Let's bring her in."

Mr. Bones snorted. "She's with Joe Ledger. Are you going to send more of your Closers in to do the pickup? How many are you willing to waste on that little project?"

"No," said Tull. "I'll do it."

Howard shook his head. "I want you here. We have important guests coming in the morning. You don't want to miss the demonstration."

"When?"

"Eight thirty. I convinced certain key members of the DoD, including some very important generals that Shelton Aeronautics has something in late-stage development that might provide a response to the attack at Dugway. Everyone I called is *very* interested. So, instead of a big reveal at the air show, which is moot anyway, we're going to have a private screening, so to speak."

"Eighty thirty." Tull looked at his watch. "Robinwood's about four hours from here. It'll be tight, but we'll be back before the show. Even have time to take a shower and put on a tie."

Chapter One Hundred One

House of Jack Ledger
Near Robinwood, Maryland
Sunday, October 20, 9:16 p.m.

"Great plan," I said to Bunny, "and what exactly is our band of 'bad guys' supposed to do? Who should we go and rough up?"

"Um," said Bunny. "yeah . . . there's that."

"Do you have a suggestion, Captain?" asked Church.

"Maybe," I said. "There's one name that keeps coming up in this. In the cyber-attacks, in the field of radical weapons and technology . . . and on the list of possible M3 members Junie put together. Well, guess what, Rudy made a bunch of calls today to UFO experts and one question he asked everyone was who is most likely to be a member of M3. People threw a lot of names around, but there's one name that appeared on over eighty percent of the lists. Anyone want to take a guess?"

It was Junie who answered.

"Howard Shelton."

Mr. Church nodded.

"Howard Shelton," I agreed. "He was even there when your father—or whatever he was—was winning the prizes that got him recruited by DARPA."

"Wait," said Ivan, "how could it be Shelton? Those cyber-attacks slammed him. All those dead people at Wolf Trap? The attacks on his computers . . ."

"If we were discussing someone who was well balanced," said Mr. Church, "I would be inclined to agree that Mr. Shelton is an unlikely candidate. But I can see where Captain Ledger is going with this. Shelton could be making himself bleed in order to prove that he is a victim and not the attacker. There are a lot of cases of that kind of pathology."

"Pretty elaborate way to establish an alibi," said Ivan.

"And pretty effective," I said. "Especially if the areas taking the cyber-hits were important—but not important to his plans with M3 and the T-craft."

"Hold on," said Pete, "I don't know a lot about Shelton. Who is he?"

Bunny tapped some keys on the MindReader substation and a picture of a man's face appeared. "Meet Howard Shelton, grade-A scum-sucker."

The face on the screen was a professional portrait of a sixty-something man with warm brown eyes, silver hair, strong jaw, straight nose, and perfect teeth. He looked like the kind of actor who played the older, wiser doctor on soap operas. He exuded warmth and confidence. The photographer even contrived to suggest the barest hint of a twinkle in his eyes.

"Run him down for us, Junie," I said. "Why's he at the top of our list?"

"He's a billionaire from Pennsylvania," she said. "Mostly old money, but a lot of it. His family's been tied to politics since Teddy Roosevelt but none of the Sheltons have ever held office. Shelton's companies hold defense contracts to the tune of sixteen billion."

Mr. Church said, "Shelton is also a principal stockholder in Blue Diamond Security."

"Okay," asked Pete, "but how does that tie Shelton to UFOs and stuff?"

Junie recapped for the team what she'd said during the video conference, about companies that made fortunes off unexpected and radical design leaps. "If you look at companies that have made more unusual and varied breakthroughs, and you trace outright ownership or significant stock ownership, then again you have a short list of names, and Shelton's name is always on the list."

"How much of this do you know," I asked, "and how much is guesswork?"

"It's all guesswork," she said. "No, let me correct that—the financial picture based on radical patents is real. The connection to the DoD and DARPA is real. The connection to every new generation of stealth technology is real. The guesswork is that he's tapping alien tech as the source. And that he's a member of M3."

"The kicker for me," I said, "is the controlling interest in Blue Diamond. I think if we scratched the surface of these Closers we'd find that most or all of them work for Blue Diamond."

Pete made a face. "I don't know if I buy it. I mean, when it comes to big business, how can you tell the difference between someone who really believes in doing what's right for the common good and someone who does it to make a profit? A lot of industrialists have profited off every war, that doesn't make them bad guys. And not to sound corny or anything, but there's still that whole Constitution thing."

"There is one more factor," said Church. "Something that Bug found, but it's not really proof. More a lack of proof. There is no official record of Howard Shelton ever being investigated. Not by a congressional committee, not by the FBI or the DEA. You know that when MindReader exits a system it erases its tracks? Most computers can't do that at all, and even the very best ones leave a bit of a twitch in the software. Like a scar. However, when Bug looked for any trace of official investigations into Howard Shelton, all he could find were scars in those places where case files or even case numbers should be."

"So he's managed to expunge his record?" asked Junie.

"Expunge it and clean it up so well that all anyone—even MindReader—can do is find smudged fingerprints. That has Bug very worried. No known system should be able to do that, which means that there is an unknown system out there. Something that operates very much like MindReader."

I snapped my fingers. "And that's how they're doing the cyber-attacks!"

"That would be my guess," agreed Church. "With a system like that it would be relatively easy to shift blame toward the DMS. Bug tells me that the system may, in fact, be so harmonious that it's allowed them to hack MindReader."

We all turned to stare at the computer.

"Frightening, isn't it?" said Church.

I reached over to turn the computer off.

"That won't be necessary, Captain," said Church. "Bug has introduced some aggressive new software into the anti-intrusion system. He believes that MindReader is protected now."

"Believes or knows?"

Church merely smiled.

Junie looked around the room. "What happens now?"

I stood up. "We get some rack time, and then by dawn's early light we go and pay a call on Howard Shelton."

"How? Do you just bust in?"

"Sadly, no. Pete's right, there's a constitutional issue. If there's even the slightest chance Shelton is innocent, then I'm not willing to destroy him because I made a bad call. No, we'll go in and ask some questions. Like . . . are you a member of M3? Do you have the Black Book? And did you just kill two hundred of my friends? Questions like that."

"God, whether he's innocent or guilty he'll throw you out."

"He is welcome to try."

Chapter One Hundred Two

House of Jack Ledger
Near Robinwood, Maryland
Sunday, October, 20, 9:43 p.m.

The meeting broke up.

There were two full bathrooms at Uncle Jack's, so the showers were in constant use. As was the kitchen. Bunny and Lydia volunteered to "walk the perimeter." Right. Brick and Birddog were out there, too, but they were actually working, transferring gear from the Mister Softee truck—which was a rolling arsenal—to Black Bess and the Explorer.

I tried to catch a moment alone with Junie, but she slipped away, vanishing upstairs.

Eventually the only ones left in the den were Church, Ghost, and I.

I dragged a chair over and sat next to him.

"How are you?"

He ignored the question. Instead he nodded toward the chair where Junie had sat. "That is a remarkable young woman."

"Yes," I said.

"Some people suffer adversity and become victims of it for life," he said. "It colors everything they do. In a sense it pollutes their potential."

I said nothing.

"While others refuse to break. They never allow themselves to be defined by their hurt. Those people are rare and they are precious."

"She's dying."

Church shook his head. "She has cancer," he said. "But I have seldom met someone more truly alive than her."

I looked at him.

"Unless I am very much mistaken, Captain, you are acutely aware of that."

He rose and moved over to the couch, kicked off his shoes, laid down, and appeared to go to sleep. Ghost went and sprawled on the floor in front of the couch. When he looked at me for approval, I gave him a wink.

Chapter One Hundred Three

House of Jack Ledger
Near Robinwood, Maryland
Sunday, October, 20, 10:11 p.m.

I found her upstairs in a small bedroom on the third floor. It had a single bed and big windows that looked out over trees. Pale moonlight painted the room in blue-white softness. She sat on the window seat, knees pulled up against her chest, arms wrapped around her legs. I knocked gently on the door frame.

She didn't turn to see who was there. She made no specific move and yet there was a feeling of invitation. Or, at least I seemed to sense that. I came in and stood by the window. Moonlight has a way of making everything, no matter how ordinary, seem charged with magical potential—a forest doubly so.

"I love the world," she said, a propos of nothing.

I sat down on the edge of the window seat.

"No matter what's happening there's always something beautiful. I don't know when I became aware of it, but the first time it really struck me was in Egypt, after the bomb went off. I was hurt, dazed, bleeding pretty badly, and I thought I was dying. I was on my back and all I could see was the sky above me. There was a bird up there, way high, coasting on the thermal currents, hovering almost perfectly. It looked so peaceful, so in tune with what it was and in harmony with its place in the universe. I mean, I knew that it was probably a vulture looking for a dead animal, but that's part of life, too. Everything dies. If nothing died, then the world would never be renewed, so death is part of a continually unfolding of beauty."

"Junie, I—"

She leaned against me. Maybe it was an unconscious act, a primal need for closeness deep in the night of an ongoing war. Or maybe it was a very conscious choice. Either way, her body was a solid warmth against mine. I knew she was dying, but the reality of her was so vital. So alive.

I put my around her and she made a small sound of acceptance, or allowing, of pleasure.

"I'm sorry I lied to you," she said.

"No," I said. "You had no reason to trust me. After all that you've been through, I'm kind of surprised you can trust anyone."

We watched the moonlight.

After a long time I asked, "Are you afraid?"

"Of dying?" Her voice was a pale whisper. When I looked at her I saw tears glittering like jewels on her lovely face. "No. There's always a light in the darkness."

She turned to me then, and took my face in her hands and kissed my lips.

"I'm cold, Joe," she said in that whisper of a voice. "Keep me warm."

I stood up and drew Junie to her feet and we kissed. It was the softest, sweetest kiss I'd ever experienced. Then we undressed each other with sudden urgency, stripping away the stained and ragged clothes and all their proofs that a harsh world existed. Her body was ripe and lithe and ghostly pale. I drew her into the warm circle of my arms and we stood there and kissed by moonlight for a few scalding moments, and then we were in the small bed. Our bodies moved together with a familiarity and comfort as if we had known each other for years, yielding and receiving, offering and taking, sharing and plunging into that river of sweetness that has flowed since the dawn of time and will flow on until the stars are dark cinders. She buried her mouth against the hollow of my neck to muffle a scream of delight that was not the little death but an affirmation of life. I cried out, too, both of us wordless but articulate in the message we shared, in a statement that we are still alive. For now, in this moment, we are still alive.

Part Six
Terminal Velocity

Everyone is a moon, and has a dark side which he never shows to anybody.

—MARK TWAIN

Seven blunders of the world that lead to violence: wealth without work, pleasure without conscience, knowledge without character, commerce without morality, science without humanity, worship without sacrifice, politics without principle.

—MAHATMA GANDHI

Chapter One Hundred Four

We left my uncle's farm at four in the morning. I was in the Explorer with Ghost and Junie. Top and Bunny were in the backseat.

The rest of Echo Team was in Black Bess. I left Church in the care of Brick and Birddog.

"Whoa, whoa now," said Brick. "How is it that the young miss gets to go on this raid and we have to sit here and play with our dicks?"

"That's not how it is, Gunny. Junie volunteered to go. She knows Tull, she understands the science, and she has to be close for us to use the team channel because the other stuff is tapped. She has to come. You don't."

"Listen, boss," protested Brick, "maybe I don't have a left foot but I can pull a trigger and fire an RPG."

"What he said, Cap," agreed Birddog. "They were my friends at the Warehouse, too."

"Look," I told them, "I appreciate the offers, but this isn't a frontal assault. We don't even know if Shelton is our bad guy. I need you guys to make sure Mr. Church gets to the Hangar safely. The DMS is on the run and we can't trust our radios. You need to get him to Aunt Sallie and then go to ground. We don't know what else Tull and these Closers have planned, but hear me on this: If anyone takes a run at Church I want you to give them the worst day of their lives. Understood?"

"Hooah," they growled.

Church walked us out. "Good hunting," he said.

He had created the DMS and over the years he'd seen hundreds of his people fall defending the country and the world. Now a fool of a president and a group of maniacs were trying to tear it all down. Even battered and pushed to the edge, I did not believe for one second that Church was going to accept defeat. Not him. Not after everything that had happened. As I climbed into my Explorer I met his eye.

"Good hunting to you, too," I said to him. He measured out a frozen millimeter of a smile.

The drive to Pittsburgh took a little over three hours. I dented a few traffic laws. Sue me. World in the balance, yada yada yada.

It was also one of the most awkward drives.

We talked about friends who had died in Baltimore.

We talked about Shelton, building our case against him.

We talked about aliens and UFOs, and the fact that we were having the conversation at all. When Junie reminded us that she had alien DNA it shut us up for almost twenty miles. I mean, really, go ahead and story-top that.

When the conversational button reset, we talked about all the things we each wanted to do to Erasmus Tull. I doubt Junie enjoyed that part of the trip. I did, but I was of two minds. Half of me wanted to take about forty minutes and use every second beating the son of a bitch to a finely textured pulp. The Warrior inside my head cheered that decision.

The rest of me wanted to give him the Indiana Jones treatment the second I saw him. If you ever saw *Raiders of the Lost Ark* you'll know the scene. Indy is suddenly confronted by this Arab warrior who's like seven feet tall, packed with muscles and swinging a scimitar. The crowd clears out, leaving a market square empty for what will be the fight scene of the century. But Indiana Jones just pulls his pistol and shoots the guy in the world's best "oh, fuck you" moment. Turns out, the actor, Harrison Ford, had dysentery and really wasn't up to filming the elaborate fight scene that had been choreographed. Spielberg loved it so much he kept that version of the scene in the movie. Every soldier I've ever met agrees that it's the smartest fight scene in the history of film.

Tull was a hybrid who was supposed to be faster, stronger, and more ruthless than anyone. Thing is, I've both been there and done that. Genetically enhanced mercenaries amped up with ape DNA. People infected with a prion disease that turned them into zombies. Soldiers who had undergone gene therapy with insect DNA. And last year . . . the Upierczi. Actual vampires. Okay, they weren't supernatural or anything like that, but they were easily twice as strong and three times as fast as me. So . . . I've done the whole fight the impossible fight thing and it's getting old. I'm only in my early thirties and my body is crisscrossed with scar tissue. I've had more broken bones than I can remember. There was a time in my life when I thought I needed to prove to myself that I couldn't be defeated, that I was strong, that the bad guys could never hurt another innocent because I wasn't tough enough to stop them. But, you know, me and the guys have saved the world. The actual world. A couple of times now. I don't need to prove anything to anyone, and Rudy has been trying to tell me for fifteen years that I *never* had to prove anything.

So, my game plan, should I see Erasmus Tull, was to put him down like a dog and call it a day.

I liked that plan.

We drove on toward the dawn.

And the one thing we did not talk about—Junie and me, that is—was what happened last night. That was the thing I wanted most to talk about. Something that wasn't tainted by madness and murder, by terrorist agendas and political corruption. By blood and death.

But as we drove, Junie Flynn took my hand and held it. She didn't care if the two hulking thugs in the back saw it. Neither did I.

Chapter One Hundred Five

Near VanMeer Castle

Pennsylvania

Monday, October 21, 7:22 a.m.

Ten miles from Shelton's castle there was a distinctive *bing-bong* in my ear and I heard Bug say, "Bug to Cowboy, do you copy?"

"Bug," I said tightly, "this line has been compromised."

"Not anymore," he said with a laugh.

"What?"

"We found a whole bunch of these weird little transmitter things stuck to the outside of the Hangar and the other offices. That's how they hacked our system. Well, that kind of pissed me off, so I took a laptop up to the roof, cut one of the little bastards open and uploaded a whole bunch of really fun viruses, kicked them off the satellite and long story short—we have a clear com channel. If they hack it, they get a feedback screech at one hundred and eighty decibels. Anyone listening in is going to be saying, 'Huh?' a thousand times a day for the rest of their lives. So, booyah!"

I laughed. "Bug, I could kiss you."

"Um, dude . . . no. Just . . . no."

"Where are you, though?" I asked. "I thought they shut the Hangar down."

"Well . . . yeah, they have us surrounded and all that, but Aunt Sallie initiated Protocol Seventeen. We sealed the upper levels and we're down in the bunker. They, um, probably don't know we *have* a bunker."

"Nice."

"Where are you?" he asked, and I gave him as much of the story as I could.

"Shelton, huh? Yeah, maybe. I'm going to put all of this new stuff into MindReader and see what she says. Last time I ran him, we only got a sixty-eight percent confidence that he's the bad guy."

"I need more than that or I really am going to jail."

"Speaking of which, before that . . . stuff down in Baltimore . . . Mr. Church called a bunch of his lawyer friends. Jesus, Cowboy, you wouldn't believe who he has on our legal team. Three of them are former U.S. attorney generals. Three. And other guys. It's like the Justice League of America without the spandex. They're putting together your defense right now."

"Nice."

"Tell you one thing, man," said Bug, "if this is a frame up and the acting president is involved in *any* way . . . this will take him down."

"I'm going to block out some time later on to cry about that," I said. "But right now we're pulling up to Shelton's place."

"And I got your back."

I stopped on a rise a mile from the estate. Top and Bunny leaned forward and peered through the windshield. Bunny whistled. Ghost made a corresponding *whuff.* He was impressed, too. Though, I'm not really sure whether we were really impressed or simply appalled. The Shelton house was a castle. An actual castle. One of those old world fairy-tale castles brought over from Europe and reassembled stone by stone here in the States. Bug told us that it had two hundred plus rooms. Plus. Like they have so many rooms they lose track. The room count didn't include the bathrooms. Made me want to piss in as many of them as I could and leave all the seats up.

The castle had spires and turrets and wings sticking out at improbable angles. Smoke curled from several chimneys. I didn't even bother trying to count the windows just on the side I could see. My math skills don't extend into abstract numbers.

"Wonder if Count Dracula rents a room from him," said Bunny.

"Time to go," I said.

Without another word, Top and Bunny exited the car. The plan was to have them close on the property through the thick pine forest that lined the right side of the road. They took heavy equipment bags out of the back. They left the door open for Junie.

"Are you sure you don't want me to come with you?" asked Junie.

"Not a chance," I said. "Stay with Top and Bunny and make sure you keep your communicator turned on. You'll be able to hear what I hear, and I've got a lapel camera that will let you see what I see. Feed me any intel you can. People, weird science stuff, anything. But whatever you do, stay away from the house. If we're right about Shelton, then things could get very nasty in there and you are not a soldier."

"I can handle a gun," she said.

"Since when?"

"Lydia showed me this morning. Loading, gun safety, as much as she could, and you know I can't forget what I learned." Her eyes met mine. "Or what I experience."

It was suddenly three hundred degrees too hot in the car.

"Um . . . listen," I began, but before I could embarrass myself, she bent forward and kissed me.

And then she was gone. Top, Bunny, and Junie vanished into the woods.

Ghost looked at me with a pitying expression.

"Oh, and like you're a class act," I said. "You sniff dog asses."

I took my foot off the brake and rolled down the long hill.

Chapter One Hundred Six

VanMeer Castle
Near Pittsburgh, Pennsylvania
Monday, October 21, 7:27 a.m.

As I drove that last mile, Bug gave me more background on the man I was going to meet.

Howard Shelton was the third richest man in Pennsylvania. Yeah, I know that doesn't sound like much if you don't know Pennsylvania. The coal mines and steelworks aren't completely gone, and there are a lot of moneymaking industries in the Keystone State. Corn, oat, soybean, and mushroom farming is massive. As is mining for iron, portland cement, lime, and various kinds of stone. Plus there are major electronics manufacturers and some of the biggest pharmaceutical companies. Shelton had fingers in all those pies, which is where his family's old money came from. Old Abner Shelton, Howard's great-grandfather, was a crony of Teddy Roosevelt. Abner's brother, Humphrey, had the stateroom next to the Astors on the *Titanic.*

The newer money—say from the thirties on up—was in defense contracts and military research and development. Every time a bomb drops Shelton puts a couple of bucks in his pocket. Even if those bombs don't have the American flag stenciled on their cowling.

I idled outside a wrought-iron gate that was wider than my apartment and designed with all sorts of animals and oak leaves and birds. Between the gate and the house was a winding half mile of road that snaked between sculpted gardens, marble fountains, and rows of oaks and beeches and elms. The garage stood apart from the house and was nicer than my dad's mayoral minimansion in Baltimore. There was a Bentley parked outside and a Lamborghini getting a hand polish from a man in driver's livery.

"Y'know, pal," I said to Ghost, "there's rich and there's rich and then there's fuck you."

He flopped down on the seat and began licking his balls. Clearly he agreed.

I tapped my earbud. "Cowboy to Ronin."

"Ronin here," came the immediate reply. Sam Imura. We'd timed things to allow Black Bess to take up a position on the far side of the estate with Ivan behind the wheel. Sam and Pete were supposed to break the perimeter and find useful places to loiter.

"I'm at the front gate," I said. "What's your twenty?"

"Finished the first circuit and sitting in an apple tree on your three o'clock. Damn, boss, this place is bigger than Rhode Island."

"Hold there," I said. "But don't be a wallflower if the party starts hopping."

"Copy that," said Imura.

"Prankster," I said, "you in the game?"

Prankster—Pete Dobbs—confirmed that he was on the grounds, way over on the east side.

I got right up to the gate and tooted the horn and waited while a guard came out of the booth. He'd been there since I pulled up but apparently didn't give much of a fuck about a guy in a Ford Explorer. Maybe if I'd rolled up in a Land Rover or a Lexus LX he'd have at least pretended to notice my existence.

Jeez, even the help was snobby around here.

Ghost glanced at the guard, went back to his hobby, then changed his mind and sat up. At first glance the guard was a big slab of white meat in a polyester jacket, but that was all deception. His jacket was a little too loose, his pants cut baggy in the crotch, and he had black sneakers on his feet. If I wasn't in a sneaky profession I might have dismissed him. But the jacket was a little too baggy, and it was unbuttoned.

"What do you figure?" I asked Ghost. "Uzi or MAC-Ten?"

Ghost offered no opinion.

"MAC-Ten," I decided. Though it could easily be a microwave pulse pistol if these guys were Closers.

The pants? Cut baggy in the crotch to allow the man to kick. So, some martial arts, too. The sneakers? They were thin-soled. Not running shoes—these were fighting shoes. The thicker the sole the more potentially damaging torque to the knees when kicking or pivoting on one leg. I'd guess almost no tread, too. Tread binds. This guy was a serious fighter and was dressed for it.

As the guy opened the small access door in the gate, I double-tapped my earbud. "Bug, get me a rundown on the security staff here. Tell me who this is." There was a control panel on the steering wheel that allowed me to activate a set of high-def cameras mounted discreetly around the car. A holographic display appeared on the upper left of my windshield—invisible from outside. I zoomed in on the guard's face. Immediately a series of white dots appeared on the image as the facial recognition package began identifying and cataloging unique points on his face and taking approximate measurements.

MindReader pinged before the guy could walk to where I'd stopped.

"Name's Henry Sullivan," said Bug. "Thirty-three years old. U.S. Special Forces, retired. Worked six years as an 'advisor' for Blue Diamond Security."

"Bingo," I said. "Martial arts?"

"Muay Thai kickboxing," said Bug, "and boxing. Golden Gloves in Detroit where he grew up."

"Swell," I said. That put him in a better class than some of his MMA buddies. "Criminal record?"

"Nothing stateside, however there were some disciplinary notes in his army jacket. Doesn't bond well with people of color. Got into several fights with black soldiers. While he was with Blue Diamond in Afghanistan he was one of four men suspected in the rape of two fifteen-year-old girls. No charges filed. Looks like the company paid off the families. Overall," concluded Bug, "he's a total dick."

"Charming," I said, and wondered if it would be out of line if I accidentally ran him over a few times.

The guard twirled his finger for me to lower my window.

I did, considering the best way to play this. I fished in my jacket pocket for NSA credentials. According to the card I was Special Agent David Paul Leonhard.

Dave Leonhard pitched for the Orioles in the late sixties.

"State your business," said Sullivan, his voice flat and disinterested.

"I'm here to see Mr. Shelton."

"Do you have an appointment?"

"No."

"Sorry, you'll have to make an appointment."

I badged him. "National Security, please open the gate and stand back." Sullivan gave me a four-second appraisal. "Wait here."

He turned and walked away. Not to his guard booth, but far enough so he could make a call on a cell without me overhearing. Dumbass. I hit a locate-and-trace on the steering column and MindReader picked up his signal, kicked open a door on the right satellite, and fed the conversation in my earbud. Sometimes I think Mr. Church writes his Christmas wish list based on stuff he sees in *Mission: Impossible* films . . . but that means his field agents always have the best toys.

"*. . . asshole here flashing an NSA ID.*" He walked around back and read my license plate number. I didn't have one of those James Bond license plate flipper thingies, but I did have a great set of fake tags. Government plates, legitimate number, and when they ran them they'd come up with a Ford Explorer belonging to the NSA. While Sullivan waited for a come-back on the number, I relaxed and scratched Ghost's head. He usually likes that, but right now he kept craning around to study all of the potential juicy places where he could bite Sullivan. Ghost is a very smart dog.

A voice on the other end of Sullivan's call came back with the expected information. "*Let him through.*"

Sullivan closed his phone and came back to the window. "Drive up to the side entrance. Turn off your engine and leave your keys in the ignition. Someone will meet you. You'll be escorted inside."

"Thanks, sport," I said. People hate to be called "sport." Ghost gave him an "I'll eat you later" look, but Sullivan managed not to keel over from fear. Instead the guard gave us another quick two-count stare, then gave a single nod and walked away. What was he doing? Remembering my face in case we ever met again? Probably. Which was fine with me, because if we did meet again, and if that encounter was less civil than this, I wanted him to know me.

I drove through the gate and up to the house, parked where I was sup-posed to park, and was met by four goons dressed similarly to Sullivan. I'd switched the facial recognition from the car to the left lens of my mirrored sunglasses, and MindReader began pulling their info out of cyberspace. They were all cut from the same cloth. All ex-military—though one of them was a Brit, a former SAS shooter—and all formerly employed by Blue Diamond Security. According to Bug, their most recent tax returns listed their employer as Shelton Aeronautics.

Big surprise.

The lead guard was a thug named Burke who had a lantern jaw and shoulders you could suspend a bridge from. Bug gave me his background, and it made Sullivan look like a saint. A very violent man who wasn't on death row because his most heinous acts were perpetrated on foreign soil in countries no one gives enough of a political shit about.

I can't tell you how badly I wanted to take Burke behind the woodshed and explain karma to him.

He gave me a stony look and demanded to see my ID.

I showed it to him.

"Hand them to me please," he said, pitching it as an order.

I've been working for the DMS long enough to have developed a useful set of government-standard expressions. One of them is the polite "go fuck yourself" not quite a sneer that's so highly prized by the FBI and NSA.

"Now," Burke said, snapping his fingers in my face.

I folded my ID case and tucked it inside my jacket.

"I'm here to see Mr. Shelton," I said. "And you're wasting my time."

Burke stepped a little closer to me. "Here's a news flash, asshole. You're on private property and you haven't produced a warrant. Hand over your credentials or hit the road."

I shook my head. "I have a document in my pocket that says I can go wherever I want and see whomever I want, so I advise you to desist in this obfuscation and conduct me to your employer."

I'm good at Scrabble and I liked seeing the eyes of goons like this glaze over as they tried to sort out what I'd just said.

"Yeah?" said Burke in what was for him probably a class-A comeback. "Let's see the warrant."

I didn't have anything to show him. Instead I said, "You are aware, I assume, of the terrorist attack in Baltimore yesterday. And the cyber-warfare that has been targeting your employer and other key companies. Do you really want to hamper my investigation?"

"I said, show me some paperwork or turn around and drive out of here."

Ghost didn't like Burke's tone and was giving him half an inch of fang in a silent snarl.

"You better keep a short leash on that mutt," said Burke. The other three men shifted slightly to form a tighter circle. They probably thought it gave them a tactical advantage. They were mistaken.

I got up in Burke's face. "You're about to make a major career mistake, Mr. Burke. Push it and see what happens. Now—take me to Shelton."

Burke grinned. "Let's see . . . oh, how about kiss my—"

And his cell phone rang.

Special ring tone, two strident notes on a rising scale.

The goon squad froze. Burke stepped back from me and removed his cell phone with the speed you'd expect from someone scrambling to get a scorpion out of his boxers.

"Yes, Mr. Shelton?" he said, almost snapping to attention even though this was a phone call. Made me wonder how many cameras were on us right now.

I kept my face bland and used a subtle finger signal to prep Ghost for attack. The dog didn't need any incentive—he had his eyes on Burke's crotch and the hair on his back was rippling like the spine of a ridgeback.

"Right away, Mr. Shelton," said Burke. Then he looked at me and I could actually see the guy's blood pressure go up about twenty points. "Of course, Mr. Shelton."

He lowered the phone, glanced at his crew, all of whom were staring into the middle distance like they were waiting for a bus. None of them looked at Burke as he took a ragged breath to steady the witches' brew of emotions that was boiling inside his chest.

"Agent Leonhard," he said to me, "I apologize for my rude behavior. It was wrong and I hope you can forgive my childish attitude and ill-chosen words."

The syntax was all wrong for him, so I figured he was repeating verbatim what Shelton had told him to say. Usually I'm sympathetic with a guy who gets a two-by-four kicked up his ass by his boss; but, Burke was a total piece of shit, so fuck it.

"Well," I said in my best officious-government-prick voice, "when you are done eating crow perhaps you'll conduct me to your employer's office."

In my ear I heard Bug say, "Oh, *snap!*"

I swear to god Ghost snickered.

Burke's blood pressure looked like it could blow bolts out of plate steel.

"This way, sir," he said in a strangled voice.

Chapter One Hundred Seven

VanMeer Castle

Near Pittsburgh, Pennsylvania

Monday, October 21, 7:32 a.m.

Burke stepped back and held out an arm to indicate an electric golf cart. I got in the passenger side, Ghost jumped on the back. Burke hesitated for a moment before climbing behind the wheel. I saw him make brief eye contact with the other men and one of them snapped a glance toward my Explorer and back. It was clear that Burke was telling them to search my car. I smiled. Let them look. They'll have a certain kind of fun. Or not.

Burke climbed in and we drove away.

Neither of us spoke. It wasn't really a bonding experience. Ghost sat up and stared at the back of Burke's neck. Every once in a while he licked his lips with a big, juicy *glup*.

It was full dark now but there were enough lights on the grounds and on the exterior of the house to film a movie. We passed several guard patrols, fixed and walking. Two of the guards had dogs. Dobermans. They gave Ghost the evil eye but Ghost sneered at them. Ghost is well over a hundred pounds of solid muscle, and he was trained by the best military dog trainers in the business. The DMS trainer, Zan Rosin, put him through a few extra courses, and I'd worked with Ghost for a year and a half, teaching him every dirty trick I could think of. Ghost loved a good tussle, and if he couldn't kick the asses of a couple of pussy Dobermans I'd trade him in for a hamster.

At the back of the castle was a ramp hidden by decorative shrubs. We rolled past them and into an arched entrance that was probably built for horses and wagons once upon a time. Beyond the arch was a large concrete room built to look like the mead hall of a Viking longhouse. Shields and crossed axes on the walls, half an authentic-looking dragon-headed longship thrust out from one wall. Rich tapestries depicting Viking raids on small villages, complete with slaughter and rapine. At the far end was a row of rough tables fashioned from dark wood, and set into the walls were doorways that I guess would probably lead to staff quarters. Almost certainly where the guards—Shelton's Viking horde—bivouacked.

I'm a manly man and all that, but I felt like I was going to drown in a river of testosterone.

Burke parked the golf cart in a slot that had his name stenciled on it. As I got out I made sure to look completely around the room knowing that whatever I saw was being seen by my team and Bug. The mirrored glasses I wore had a superb high-def spycam built into one of the temple pieces. You could already buy this year's version of that camera, but we had next year's. A gift from one of Church's friends in the industry.

I had a whole bunch of toys with me. As I followed Burke across the mess hall, I kept my hands in my pockets, unobtrusively peeling back the film on a sticky little bug. As Burke led me through a doorway into the east wing of the castle, I paused with my hand briefly on the frame, planting the little doodad. It was small and designed to gradually absorb the colors of whatever it touched. Within five seconds it would invisible. Nice.

As I followed Burke, I continued to record the layout with my glasses. We already had a schematic of the place based on the original design of the castle—which was a matter of public record from when the Sheltons bought it from a bankrupted Austrian count—but we didn't know what modifications had been made since. The video feeds would be used to create a 3-D model for every part of the building I visited. Sure, this was still a castle and I wasn't going to see much of it, but intel was intel. Every little bit helps.

This wing was clearly dedicated for servants and operations. There were small brass plaques on doors marked: ELECTRICAL, SECURITY, GROUNDS-KEEPING, and others. One really caught my eye: WRANGLERS. When my gaze lingered on it for an extra second, Bug explained it.

"Shelton collects animals," he said. "He has a zoo somewhere on the grounds, and he buys rare critters for a game ranch he keeps in Texas. Brings in stuff from all over and lets his rich buddies shoot them. Axis bucks, scimitar bulls, waterbucks, Ibex, Russian boar hogs, rams—who needs to stalk a sheep? I mean, I'm cool with hunting and all . . . but sheep? Seriously? How's that a sport unless you like . . . I don't know . . . kickbox it to death or something."

I flexed my jaw muscles to send a tiny burst of squelch. One flex for "yes," though right now it was a general acknowledgment. I don't have any serious objection to hunting, and I don't mind entertaining the trout every once in a while, but somehow a bunch of rich assholes in camouflage with high-power scopes and state-of-the-art rifles didn't exactly fit my image of "sportsmen."

Bug said, "I'll find out what else he has on-site. Wouldn't want you to walk into a jaguar, right?"

Two flexes. No.

We went through a series of winding halls, sharp turns, staircases, crossed an entrance hallway that you could have parked a line of F-15s in, and finally entered a wing that was clearly the domain of the master of this feudal estate. I was mildly surprised not to see the staff here dressed in doublets. Every once in a while I touched a wall, a doorframe, a bannister rail, and each time I left another of the chameleon devices. Burke never saw a thing.

I was pretty sure that there was a more direct route to Shelton's office, but this was probably Burke's passive-aggressive way of screwing with me. As a bit of revenge it walked with a limp. Burke was a weasel.

Bug came on and whispered to me again. "Hey, I've been doing more background checks on Shelton's security team. Holy moly, these are some bad mamba-jambas. Some serious mixed martial arts competitors. That guy Burke? He was tied to an illegal cage-fight circuit in Central and South America. Crazy stuff like you see in the movies. People actually getting killed."

I flexed my jaw once to acknowledge that I understood.

"Don't let Burke get on your blindside. Shelton's bought his way out of a lot of charges that should have put him in jail. His psych profile reads like Stephen King wrote it."

Another flex.

"Last thing," said Bug, "see if you can get to Shelton's laptop. Not sure if he'll have anything useful, but it's our best shot. If nothing else, we might be able to hack his e-mails."

A flex. The line went quiet after that.

We stopped at a secretary's desk behind which was an almost completely artificial woman. Poufy hair that was too perfect a shade of honey blond, blue-within-blue contact lenses, Botox lips, a severe nose job that could not have been the best choice in the catalog, and huge boobs that had no parallel in human genetics. She stared at me from under a battery of stiff black lashes.

"Mr. Shelton will see you now," she said in a Paris accent that was as real as the "French" in French fries. "However, your dog must wait outside."

I said, *"Je ne quitterai jamais mon chien ici avec vous. Il a peur des robots."*

She gave me a blank stare. No clue what I'd just said.

I breezed past her with Ghost at my heels.

Beyond her desk was a set of massive oak doors that stood ajar, allowing us peons to enter. Like everything else in this place, the message was simple: *I'm rich, you're not; learn your place.*

Beyond the doors was the largest office I'd ever seen. It was absurd. I mean, truly absurd. A full-scale replica of the *Kitty Hawk* hung from the ceiling and it didn't begin to crowd the room. High ceilings, tall stained-glass windows, ranks of suits of armor, framed art with a bent toward portraits of pinched-faced scowling men who I assumed were ancient Sheltons, and a desk that you could cut down to make the deck of an aircraft carrier. The tall bank of windows behind the desk were all in ornate stained glass. If you looked up the word "ostentatious" in the dictionary, there would be a note directing you to the special signed-and-numbered limited edition, and Shelton's picture would be in that.

Howard Shelton sat behind the desk on—I kid you not—a hand-carved wooden throne. Inlaid with gold and silver. He rose as I approached and I wondered if I was supposed to shake his hand, bow, or knuckle my forelock.

Burke followed me in, but there were already two similarly dressed guards in the office. They stood to either side of Shelton's desk, glowering like Visigoths. Their faces were lumpy, with broken noses and cauliflower ears. Brawlers for sure. The smallest of the three was maybe two-twenty, all of it in his arms and shoulders.

At a nod from Burke, the two guards walked around the desk, each of them sizing me up the way a Brooklyn butcher sizes up a side of beef. They and Burke formed a semicircle around me.

Ghost fidgeted. He wanted me to let him out to play. It was a tempting thought, but that wasn't why we were here.

Shelton was even better looking in person. He radiated warmth and health.

"Good evening," he said. "Special Agent Leonhard is it?"

"Yes, sir," I said. "Thank you for seeing me on such short notice."

Shelton's eyes twinkled. "Should I call you Special Agent?" he asked.

"I—"

"Or would you prefer 'Captain Ledger'?"

Nobody was smiling except Shelton.

I said, "Ah, crap."

Chapter One Hundred Eight

House of Jack Ledger
Near Robinwood, Maryland
Monday, October 21, three hours ago

"What do you think?" asked Aldo, handing the field glasses back to Tull.

They lay side by side on a grassy knoll overlooking the Ledger farmhouse. There were no vehicles parked in the turnaround in front of the house.

"Did we miss them?"

Tull studied the house with narrowed eyes. There were several lights on and in one downstairs room the blue-white flicker of a TV. Tull tapped the wire mike he wore.

"Snake, what are you seeing out back?"

The team sergeant, Snake, came on the line at once. "The Black Hawk is tied down. Engine's cold."

"You do a thermal scan on the house?" asked Tull.

"Copy that. We have four heat signatures in the house. Nothing in the barn or other buildings."

"Roger that."

Tull turned to Aldo. "I don't like it. I don't think Ledger or the girl are here."

"Shit."

Tull wormed his way back from the top of the knoll, then he rolled over and stood up. He tapped his mike again. "Snake, we think the birds have flown. Aldo and I are going to run the back trail. We'll get an eye in the sky to find them. They might be heading to another safe house."

"Yes, sir . . . What about the four inside?"

Tull didn't even hesitate. "Kill them."

He clicked off the channel and ran for his car with Aldo at his heels.

Chapter One Hundred Nine

VanMeer Castle
Near Pittsburgh, Pennsylvania
Monday, October 21, 7:41 a.m.

I said something clever like, "Um . . . what?"

Shelton smiled.

Then everybody was pulling guns. The three guards, me. Ghost crouched, waiting for my command to hit.

Shelton's smile turned into a belly laugh.

"Oh, for Christ's sake," he said with a rough guffaw, "put your damn guns down. There's expensive stuff in here."

You could taste the compassion for my physical well-being.

I didn't put my gun down. I pointed it at Shelton's head.

"Them first or you first, take your pick," I said.

He shook his head, really enjoying this. He even gave me a couple of seconds of slow, ironic applause. "Nice tough guy line. I dig it."

The moment still burned around us. Shelton flicked a glance at Burke. "You heard me. Put them away."

It wasn't a suggestion.

The three guards immediately lowered their pistols, peeled back their jacket flaps and reholstered. Burke was about a half second slower than the others. Making a point, I suppose. It was lost on Shelton, who clearly didn't give a shit. I filed it away, though, adding it to Burke's tab.

I still had my gun out but I was beginning to feel like the kid who wore a costume on the day the Halloween party was canceled.

"Do you mind?" asked Shelton. He settled into the cushions of his leather chair and picked up a delicate china teacup, sipped it, and looked at me over the rim.

I lowered my piece. "Ghost," I said, "ease down."

Ghost laid down in his sphinx posture, ready to rise and leap at a moment's notice.

Shelton cocked an eye at my gun. "You going to put that thing away?"

"Let's wait and see," I said.

"Whatever. Have a seat, or do you want to stand, too?"

One of the guards—not Burke—pushed over a guest chair that cost more than my car. Rich red leather that was soft as butter when I sat down. I laid my Beretta on my thigh.

"So," said Shelton, "why am I so fortunate as to have the famous Captain Joseph Edwin Ledger here on a chilly October morning?"

"Publishers Clearing House sent me. You may be a winner."

We smiled at each other. The guards glared at me. Ghost glared at them.

"Aren't you going to ask how I know who you are?" asked Shelton.

"Why bother? You caught me on at least fifty cameras between the front gate and here and I'm pretty sure you can afford a facial recognition software package."

"I own the patent on the one the FBI uses," he said.

"So there you go."

"It doesn't bother you that I know who you are?"

"Actually it does," I said. "And I have a slot open between nine and nine-oh-five this morning during which I plan to faint."

"Funny," he said.

"Not really."

"Want to tell me why you're here?"

"Depends on how much of your business is open to a public forum."

He considered. "These guys have been with me for years."

"That's your call, but I wonder if you spelled their names right in your little black book."

It was all about those last two words. That wiped the shit-eating grin off Shelton's face faster than a good slap. He stared at me for a heavy three count, then without looking at his guys or changing the tone of his voice he said, "Get out. Close the door behind you and make sure nobody bothers me."

"Mr. Shelton," began Burke, "I don't think that's a good—"

Shelton's eyes swiveled toward Burke. "Get the fuck out. Now."

This time there was a different tone.

The three men headed for the door without another word. I turned to watch them go. Burke shot me a look that would have burned holes in sheet metal. I pointed my right index finger at him and used my thumb to drop the hammer. He lingered long enough to respond with a single nod.

Yeah, I'd be seeing Burke around the playground.

When we were alone, Shelton appraised me. "The question," he said, "is whether you know something or if you're on a fishing expedition."

I said nothing.

He really seemed to be enjoying this. "Those sunglasses . . . they wired? Is this going to be on YouTube or some shit?"

I took them off, folded the earpieces and tucked them into an inner pocket. In my ear, Bug said, "Hey!"

I ignored him. I still had my lapel cam, though the image was crappy.

"Happy now?" I asked Shelton.

"No," he said. "And I don't trust you for shit."

He opened his desk drawer, being very slow and careful about it so as not to alarm the big scary guy with the gun and the dog. He removed a device that looked like a small TV remote, but wasn't. He showed it to me, then pressed a button and set it down on the desk.

"Jammer?" I asked.

"Jammer," he said. "And don't worry—I don't have cameras in my office. I watch people, they don't watch me. It's just you and me."

"Good. Can we stop fucking around now?"

Shelton nodded and sipped his tea. "I know your file. Army Rangers for four years, during which you didn't do squat."

"At the time," I said, "there was no squat that needed doing."

"Then you were a cop in Baltimore. Baltimore? Seriously? That shit-hole?"

"Says the guy from Pittsburgh."

"Hey, Pittsburgh's come a long way in the last twenty years. Used to be a dump but now it's a center for the arts. Watch your mouth."

"Baltimore . . . has an aquarium," I riposted.

He grinned at that.

"Okay. Getting back to who the fuck you are. You were a uniform, then you were a detective and after 9/11 they put you on some dinky Homeland taskforce, and then you went away. The official story is that you went to Quantico and are doing something for the FBI, but that's horse shit. You somehow got onto the radar of that psychopath Deacon—what's he calling himself these days? Mr. Church?—and for the last couple of years you've been indulging your own inner psychosis by shooting everyone you don't like. All in the interests of national security and Mom's apple pie."

"That's a nice profile. Can I put that on my Facebook page?"

"And according to everyone you think you're funnier than balls."

"Balls are pretty funny," I admitted. "But I am funnier, yes."

"And now you're here throwing around the wrong words. Why is that?"

"You tell me."

He made a face like innocence abused. "Me? What do I know?"

"You nearly popped a vein when I mentioned the Black Book."

Shelton tried to smile through that, but there was a little tic in his left eye. "What black book would that be?"

"Really? We're all alone and you want to get cute?"

He chuckled. If I wasn't sure that he was who he was, I might have bought it. The crinkles at the corners of his eyes, that legendary twinkle. Teeth so bright I could shave by them.

"The thing is," he said, "I don't know what you know. We haven't actually confirmed whether you're here fishing for something or if you know something."

"That's pretty much a two-way street," I admitted. "I don't know if you're a remarkably well-informed innocent bystander, a supporting character in someone else's mad scientist dream, or if you're the supervillain I've been longing to meet."

"Not knowing what goes on your head, Ledger, I have no idea how to answer that. What is this supervillain of yours supposed to have done?"

"Blown up a lot of people in Baltimore."

"Ah, yeah . . . I saw that on the news. So sad."

I held up a finger. "Some things we joke about," I said. "Some things get you hurt."

"Fair enough. But give me something more than vague threats and we'll see if we can have a conversation."

"This isn't a conversation?" I asked.

"No. We're kind of jerking each other off here. I don't mean that in a gay way, you understand. It's a figure of speech."

I had to admit that, even though he was a piece of pond scum, he was charming. He hid his silver-spoon upbringing with just the right amount of trash talk. Some of it was almost certainly cribbed from old *Sopranos* DVDs. I kept expecting him to call me a "chamoke," but Shelton was pure WASP going back to forever. When the Mayflower landed, his ancestors were there at the rock selling deeds to swampland.

"What would you like to know?" I asked.

He shrugged. "Oh, I don't know. Something that you couldn't have gotten off the Internet. Oh, what, you look surprised? You don't think my name comes up when you search for the Black Book?"

I said nothing.

On the floor, Ghost gave me a look like he was losing confidence in who was the actual pack leader here.

I could see his point.

"Let's try this," I said. "Ever heard of Junie Flynn?"

"Sure. I watch TV. I even listen to her podcast. According to what she said the other night, either she has the Black Book or she *is* the Black Book. Works out the same either way."

"You read the Cliffs Notes version of this, haven't you?"

Shelton looked at his watch. "I have a busy day, Captain. Can we speed this along a little faster?"

"Sure," I said. Using the same slow care that he'd used, I opened my jacket and snugged my pistol back into the shoulder rig. Then I removed a small device from my pocket and showed it to him. It was about the same size as the unit he'd taken from his desk.

"What's that? Another jammer? I already told you, no one can hear us in here. Room's soundproof and—"

"Good," I said as I pointed the device at him and pressed a button. A compressed gas charge shot a tiny glass dart at him at six hundred feet per second. Not as fast as a bullet, but much faster than a middle-aged scumbag could dodge. He got a hand up, but the dart stung his palm.

He gave a single, small cry and then fell face forward onto his desk.

Chapter One Hundred Ten

VanMeer Castle

Near Pittsburgh, Pennsylvania

Monday, October 21, 7:45 a.m.

First thing I did was make sure the door was locked. I put my ear to the wood, but there was no sound at all from outside. Soundproof indeed.

"Ghost," I called, and he snapped to attention. "Scout."

Instantly he began casing the room, sniffing for anything that could be a problem. Ghost is heavily cross-trained to find people, bombs, blood, and hidden things—like concealed doorways. Electronics will take you a good long way, but nothing beats the nose of an inquisitive dog.

There was a heavy chest against one wall—dense wood banded with studded iron strips—so I shoved that against the jamb. A determined group of men could break in, but nobody was going to sneak up on me. Then I checked to make sure Shelton was still breathing.

He was.

The juice in the dart I'd shot him with was a fast-acting but mild tranquilizer. One that Dr. Hu insisted wouldn't trigger Shelton's next heart attack. I had a syrette in my pocket with a stimulant that would bring him back up to the surface, but before I did that I swept everything off of Shelton's desk and hauled him onto it. Then I fished out a coil of silk cord from my jacket and lashed his ankles together and then stretched his arms out wide so the hands dangled off the edges. I ran the silk cord under the desk. I wanted his hands exposed. The silk was thin but he wasn't going to break it. Then I removed a small roll of duct tape, tore off long strips and ran them from one edge of the desk to the other so that they effectively anchored Shelton's head in place. He could open his eyes and mouth but would not be able to turn his head at all.

I snapped my fingers and tapped the desk. Ghost came rushing over and jumped up, then stood glaring down at Shelton. Two fat droplets of drool fell from Ghost's mouth onto Shelton's shirt.

"Hey," I said, "he's not a breakfast entrée."

Ghost gave me a withering stare.

I tapped my earbud for Bug and got nothing. So I picked up the jammer and played with the buttons until I found one that switched it off.

When I tried Bug again he was right there and he sounded like he was having kittens.

"Cowboy! Are you okay?"

"It's okay," I said. "There was a jammer, but it's off now. Ready for a little smash and grab?"

"Always, man, you know me."

Shelton's laptop was on a small table beside the desk. It was a style I'd never seen before. I removed a MindReader uplink and plugged it into the USB port. The little device flashed with green lights to let me know that it was happily gobbling up all Shelton's files. Encrypted or not.

"Getting the feeds now," said Bug. "Whoa . . . what kind of system is this?"

I bent and peered at the display on the side of the uplink. "The readout here says this stuff is heavily encrypted. How bad is that going to hurt us?"

Bug chuckled. "Silly mortal. I laugh at encryption. Ha! Ha, I say."

"Yeah, yeah, yeah, just tell me how long will it take you to—"

"My whole team's locked in the bunker with me," he cut in. "You have the undivided attention of twenty-six world-class computer rock gods. It's just . . . oh shit, man . . . You know what this is? This is that Chinese Ghost Box. The *actual* fucking Ghost Box. I am so getting wood here, man. This is soooo sexy."

"Bug, you're scaring me."

"No, hey, *this* is how they've been screwing with us."

"What the hell is a Ghost Box? Sounds like some kind of weird porno."

"No, no, no, man, this is all over the rumor mill. A super-computer system designed not to be noticed. It was built to be invisible to other systems. Long technical explanation that would make your head hurt. Short version is that without an actual hardline connection, we could never interpret that system."

"Does my five-dollar USB cable count as an actual hardline?"

"Oh, hell yes. Achilles' heel, man. Direct cable connection. Nothing beats it. And if the Chinese geeks who built this ever find out that they were punked by something you can get at RadioShack, they'll kill themselves."

"Well . . . that's . . . ," I fished for a word along the lines of "lucky," but it had been so long since any word like that actual fit that I let the sentence hang. "Just tell me you can crack the encryption."

"Not in the next minute, no, but eventually? Yeah. This is huge, man. Really huge."

"I like huge. Okay, as soon as you get *anything* that puts Shelton in my crosshairs I want to know about it."

"You got it."

"Outstanding." I switched to the team channel. "Prankster, Ronin? Give me a sit-rep."

"Prankster here, boss," came Pete's immediate reply. "I'm in the building, hunkered down in a little bit of nowhere till you're done with your business. Ready to entertain the tourists."

"Copy that, Prankster. Sit tight until I give the word," I said. "Ronin, how's the view?"

"Clear and bright," said Sam. He was a superb sniper—cold, precise, and patient. I would not want to be out on the grounds tonight. Not unless I was wearing an Abrams tank. "Found myself a nice spot for a high angle."

"Excellent," I said. "But the show doesn't start until I give the word."

"Hooah," they said.

"And, Ronin . . . nobody dies unless I give a kill order. Copy?"

"Copy that, boss."

I looked around the office Most of the rear wall of the office was taken up with towering stained glass depicting the Wild Hunt from Celtic folklore, but there were louvered panels near the bottom. I cranked one up and peered out. All quiet on the western front. Or, in this case, the eastern lawn.

Shelton groaned and I checked his vitals. So far, so good. I busied myself creeping the room and planting all sorts of chameleon bugs in useful places. Some were active units that would allow Bug to tap into the house's computer-controlled alarm systems. Others were passive units that would remain inert for now but which would come to life with a signal sent from a satellite. Those were for later.

I gave Bug all of three minutes and then tapped my earbud. "Talk to me, man. Tell me you found *anything*. Unpaid parking tickets, kiddie porn . . . give me something I can use on this asshole."

"Damn, Cowboy," said Bug, "you weren't joking when you said this stuff was encrypted. I mean . . . we're having to fight through multiple levels of very weird protection. I'm kind of impressed. If I didn't have MindReader but *knew* about it, I might build something like this."

"Cut to the chase. Can you hack it? Do we have anything?"

"Give me a little credit. I said that it was tough, I didn't say that it was tougher than me."

Sometimes it's hard to tell whether Bug is referring to himself or to MindReader. Or if he knew that there was a difference.

"We're in now, but it's going to take us a lot of time to evaluate this stuff. And the Ghost Box system keeps trying to counterattack with all sorts of viruses. I tell you, Cowboy, I might need to bitch slap this thing to keep it in line."

"Meaning?"

"We have some seriously fucked-up viruses that would turn their whole network into Chernobyl. If Ghost Box keeps trying to counterhack us I'm going to have to clone MindReader's command protocols onto—"

I cut him off. "Do whatever you have to do, Bug. Put a leash on it, but don't ruin anything until you're sure you have all the goodies. What about that drive?"

"Ah," he said, "there's really a lot of crazy stuff on that puppy, and it's ringing ten kinds of bells. We got eyes-only stuff from Department of Defense, Homeland, NASA, jeez . . . there's so much good shit here."

"Hey," I growled, "stop drooling and let me know the second you find anything illegal, or anything classified that we can—"

"Cowboy, you're not listening to me. *All* of this stuff is classified. This is deep, deep shit here. I'm seeing stuff that even with black budget clearance codes the president doesn't get to see. We got missile defense systems, we got HAARP stuff, spy satellite stuff, black ops sanctions . . . jeez-oh-man."

I straightened and looked at Shelton. "Whoa, back up, Bug, and tell me that you're not kidding here. Tell me that we hit actual pay dirt on the first try."

"Well . . . it's not the Black Book or anything, but there's no way Shelton has legal clearance for this stuff. No way in hell. His official clearance level is in the basement compared to this stuff."

"Who does have this level of clearance?"

"I . . . don't know, man. God? This is weird, weird shit. I need Deacon to look at this, but I'm telling you that if we leaked even a little of this to a congressional oversight committee we could put Shelton away for two or three thousand years. But . . . and I'm not joking around here, we could tear down half of Washington, too. You should see some of the names that I'm finding here." He paused and there was a *click* that changed the audio signal. "Look, I cut everyone out of this conversation, okay?"

"Okay. Talk to me."

"Cowboy . . . this is actually scaring me. This is stuff they kill people over. This is actual black budget stuff."

"On a laptop? You cracked it in a couple of minutes."

"That's it, man," he said, "only a system like MindReader *could* crack this. You know that, there's nothing else—and I mean *nothing* else—that could decrypt this stuff. We found and neutralized six separate erase programs. That's one of the first thing MindReader looks for—self-destruct and hard-dump programs. If anyone else had hacked this that whole laptop would be smoking slag by now."

"Okay."

"The stuff we're finding, though, is making my paranoia-o-meter go haywire. Deacon is going to freak when he sees this. This is . . . well, jeez, man, this is scaring the shit out of me."

I knew Bug well enough to know when he was joking or exaggerating. He wasn't.

"But . . . Cowboy, so far I don't see anything that links him to what happened at Dugway or the Warehouse. Or M3. Not yet."

"Find it for me, Bug. I'm on thin ice here."

"Working on it."

"Contact Aunt Sallie and Deacon on scramble and cycle them into this."

Bug rang off. The lights on the uplink told me that the file transfer was complete. I knew it also meant that MindReader had done the other part of its job: rewriting the software on the laptop to eradicate every possible trace of intrusion. Smiling, I pulled the uplink and dropped it into my pocket, then I closed the Ghost Box and repositioned it exactly as I found it.

The clock in my head was ticking as loud as gunfire.

I turned to Shelton. Now for the next phase of this insane little game.

"So," I said to his comatose form, "whatever else you are, you're really part of an illegal shadow government. Like right out of one of the Bourne movies. Until now I was going to cut you some slack, but—oops, you're an actual bad guy. What a damn shame for you."

Ghost looked from me to Shelton and uttered a low growl. I knew that he couldn't understand everything I said, but he reads emotion very well. Or, maybe he reads me very well. The look he gave Shelton was probably every bit as cold and unsympathetic as mine.

I removed a small leather case from a pocket, unzipped it, and began removing some toys Dr. Hu had provided for me.

"Well hell, guys," I said as I pulled the syrette out of my pocket and jabbed it into Shelton's throat, "guess it's time to play Truth or Consequences."

It took four seconds for the stimulant to counteract the tranquilizer. It took another five seconds for Shelton to wake up completely. After that it took less than one second for him to realize how deep in the shit he was.

I leaned close to him and smiled. The three aspects of myself were all clamoring for dominance. The Civilized Man wanted to have a reasonable conversation, to appeal to Shelton's better nature. The Cop wanted to throw the Constitution at him and use threats of prison and disgrace. The Killer wanted to wire him up and play bad games. I felt my control slipping.

That seldom ends well for anyone.

When Howard Shelton opened his eyes and looked up into my face, guess which face I showed him?

Chapter One Hundred Eleven

VanMeer Castle
Near Pittsburgh, Pennsylvania
Monday, October 21, 7:50 a.m.

"What the hell are you doing?" croaked Shelton. He tried to yell but between the aftereffects of the drugs and what he saw on my face, his words came out cracked and crumbling. He jerked against the silk cord, which accomplished nothing beyond tightening the knots; and when he tried to turn his head, the duct tape kept him from moving at all. He was trapped and totally helpless, and he knew it.

Terror blossomed in his eyes.

"I'm going to keep it simple," I said. "You have the Majestic Black Book. I *want* the book. This will only get as messy as you want to make it."

"You're insane."

"Yesterday's news."

"I mean it," he growled. "You're crazy."

I leaned a few inches closer. "Want to see how much?"

"This is an illegal search and seizure. This is assault and battery. It's—"

"Blah blah blah," I cut in. "I'm a wanted felon, a terrorist, and an enemy of the state. Two hundred of my friends were blown to atoms yesterday. And either you or aliens abducted the president and are threatening to destroy the entire eastern seaboard if I don't get the Black Book. So . . . yeah, I guess you could say I'm a bit over the edge."

Ghost made a faint whuffing sound. It was a strangely hungry sound, and Shelton gave him a frightened look.

"Dog's a little troubled, too," I said. "Dementia by association."

Shelton jerked against the silk cord. "Listen to me, shitbag," he snarled, "you're making the worst mistake of your life. Right now it's just you and me, so if you want to take your head out of your ass and untie me then we can let this drop. I promise no repercussions."

I smiled at him.

"Don't be stupid," Shelton said. "Even if I gave you the book—which I don't *have*—there's no way you'd ever get out of this house. I have a goddamn army of men here—"

"You have fifty-four men," I corrected. "And six dogs. Not counting the secretarial and housekeeping staff."

"Those are *my* people, dickhead. They'll tear you apart and feed you to my dogs. And that includes your mutt."

I reached down out of his line of vision and punched a button on the device inside the little leather case. Shelton tried to see what I was doing, but the tape prevented him. Then I touched the little finger of his left hand.

"Here's how we're going to play this," I said as I removed a pair of sturdy wire cutters from my pocket. "I'm going to ask you where the Black Book is. If you say something I don't want to hear, I'll cut off one of your fingers."

He went as pale as old milk.

"I'll fucking kill you and everyone you love," he seethed.

I reached down with the cutters. He tried to see what I was doing, but I wanted him to just feel it.

The cutters went *SNIP!*

His scream was immediate and enormous.

It was so loud it hurt my ears.

Ghost howled.

I grinned.

"That would be an example of something I don't want to hear," I said when he stopped to gulp in some air. "You have nine more fingers."

"Fuck you . . . ," he said in a weak voice. "Fuck you . . ."

SNIP!

He screamed again.

"Eight left. Oh, and you're going to need to get your carpet cleaned."

"Oh . . . *Christ! God sweet Jesus. . . . ahhhhhhhhh!*"

His terror was like a great dark beast crouching over both of us.

"I can cut them clean or I can get creative," I said. "And by creative I mean I can feed them to my dog while they're still attached. This is your call."

I gave him one second to think about it.

SNIP!

His shriek was ultrasonic.

"Jesus Christ, what are you doing? Oh shit, motherfucker. My hand! What are you doing? I didn't say anything!"

"I'm double-parked," I said, "and you're wasting my time."

"Oh . . . *God . . . it fucking hurts . . .*"

"God isn't here," I said, leaning closer still. "It's you and me and my dog and what's left of your hand."

Tears boiled from the corners of his eyes.

"I . . . *can't* . . . ," he blubbered. "I can't . . ."

A moment later he was shrieking again. Ghost's howls rose like spikes of sound.

"You can save your thumb," I whispered. "Or would you rather we go to the challenge round? Should I get out the bolt cutters and go right to your wrist?"

"No . . . *NO!* Oh god, please, no . . ."

"Howard . . . ," I coaxed in a lazy singsong voice. "You're being naughty."

"They'll *kill* me! God . . . they'll kill me if I say anything."

I bent closer still, and now my face was an inch from his. "Listen to me," I said softly. "You're still on this side of a bad line. If you make me take you over that line there won't be enough of you left to put in a wheelchair. Is that what you want? Is that where you're making me take this? I can leave you blind and ruined. If you're really lucky I'll leave you enough of a mouth so you can scream. But I can't even promise that unless you talk to me."

Shelton was weeping openly, tears and snot running in lines down the sides of his face. His face was beet red and I wondered what kind of a window I had before his heart burst or he stroked out. There was aspirin and other goodies in the stimulant, and that would help, but I was definitely pushing the envelope here.

"They'll kill me," he said one more time, but as he said it his eyes shifted away from me toward a wall on which was hung a portrait of Harry S. Truman.

I followed his eyes and then looked back at him. "Is it in there?"

His voice was tiny. "Y—yes . . ." He closed his eyes. "Oh, God . . ."

"Ghost—watch," I said and hopped off the desk. There was a small electronics detector in another pocket and I ran it along the edges of the painting. All the little lights pinged. I strolled back to Shelton and patted his cheek. Maybe a little too hard. "Nice try. It's wired six ways from Sunday, which means that if I sneeze on it your goon squad will be in here in ten seconds." I leaned very close so that my breath was hot on his cheeks and eyes. "The first thing they'll see is you die in ways that will give them nightmares the rest of their lives."

Tears rolled from his eyes.

"Tell me how to bypass the security or what they'll bury won't even look like a man." I bent closer still and described exactly what I'd do.

He screamed without me having to actually do anything.

And then he broke.

Like that.

"Okay, okay, please God, okay . . . don't hurt me anymore . . ."

There was a lot of stuff like that. I had to coax him through the procedures to disarm the security measures on the safe. Some of them involved the same remote Shelton had used to activate the jammers. Others involved more complicated codes that I had to enter on a keypad that was hidden behind a carefully crafted panel on his desk. Lucky for him there was no retina scanner. I told him as much. He sobbed some more.

I left Ghost there to watch him while I made sure there were no passive alarms or tripwires. Dr. Hu's little scanner was very efficient.

After five minutes I felt confident enough to swing the painting aside on its concealed hinges and enter the last set of codes on a second keypad. I've been to viral research labs and I don't know that I'd ever seen an entry procedure as complicated as this. Fourteen separate steps. The safe set into the wall was a dummy. It was filled with stock certificates, bearer bonds, two jewelry cases, and at least five hundred thousand dollars in paper-wrapped bundles. I dropped it all on the floor. Once the safe was clear, Shelton talked me through the steps to access the hidden compartment behind the back wall.

The fake metal wall slid up with a hiss to reveal a space that was ten inches wide and a foot tall. There were three things in the compartment. A small metal cylinder the approximate size and shape of a cigar tube, a jagged piece of metal wrapped in bubble wrap, and a book wrapped in thick velvet.

The book was a little larger than a paperback novel and thicker than the Bible. Thousands of tissue-thin pages.

And, yes, it was black. I flipped through it. Lots of sketches of mechanical devices that I didn't recognize. Page after page of notes written in a neat, cramped hand.

Bingo.

I tapped my earbud. "Package acquired."

Bug made a strange series of falsetto noises and said, "I think I just came in my pants."

"Never remind me of this conversation," I told him.

Another voice cut in. Auntie. "Cowboy, confirm mission status."

"Package acquired," I repeated. "I have the Majestic Black Book."

There was a sudden burst of static so sharp and loud that I almost tore the earbud off, but then it was gone.

"What the hell was that?" I demanded.

"I—don't know," said Auntie. "For a second everything lit up like a Christmas tree."

"Well, whatever it was, don't let it happen again. Near blew my head off. Cowboy out."

Then I turned back to Shelton, who stared at the book in my hand. His eyes were wild.

"They'll kill me for this," he said. His face was greasy with agonized sweat.

"Who will?"

"Them!" he snapped.

"Who? Are we talking little green men?"

"No, you maniac . . . the others in the Project. They'll kill me and now they'll kill you."

"Not a chance," I said, smiling a smug little smile. "They won't even know I was here. Give me some names," I suggested.

He looked at me like I'd suddenly suggested we both dress up in dinner clothes and waltz through the halls.

"Give me some names," I repeated, "and I'll make sure that you get full protection."

"You can't offer any goddamn protection. The DMS is done, it's gone. God, you're really an idiot aren't you?" he said.

Okay, that hurt, coming from a guy I had strapped to a desk.

"Do you think there's any place you can hide me that they can't find?" He was wheezing with pain and terror.

"Yes, I do," I said, not at all sure if I was telling a lie.

"They'll find me and kill me and then they'll find you and every-one—"

"Yeah, yeah, they'll kill everyone I love. My family, my dog, blah blah blah. You watch too many Scorsese films. They won't find out about this unless you tell them."

"Wrong, shithead," he panted, "they'll find out as soon as my people take me to the hospital. They probably have a spy here . . ."

I parked a haunch on the edge of the desk. "Why would anyone take you to the hospital?"

He stared at me, caught in a terrible moment of indecision. Was I making a joke? Or did my question carry an even worse threat.

"You're going to kill me," he said hollowly.

"Actually," I said, "no. I'm not going to hurt a hair on your head."

"But . . . but . . . I don't . . ."

I reached across him, out of his line of sight and twisted my hand again.

The agonized expression on his face immediately changed.

"W—what . . . ?" he stammered. "What . . . ?"

I reached down and removed the tiny metal needles I'd inserted into nerve clusters on each of his fingers. They were like acupuncture needles, with wires trailing away to the small device in the leather case. I held it up for Shelton to see.

"Ta-da!" I said quietly. "Electric nerve stimulators. You can set these things to send all kinds of signals. I could make it feel like you just gave birth to a ten-pound baby, so severed fingers were easy as pie. All the fun of torture without the mess. Order now and you get a free at-home water-boarding kit. Fun for the whole family."

He gaped at me, totally unable to speak.

Ghost dripped more slobber on Shelton's shirt.

I bent close and tapped Shelton with the book.

"Now listen close, asshole," I said. "I have the book and you have the thanks of a grateful nation and all that. Except that nation is going to put you in jail until three days after the end of the world."

Shelton mustered enough of his wits and focus to say, "Fuck you."

Tried to spit in my face, too, but I dodged it.

I laid the book on his chest. "Understand something, friend," I said, "just because I faked you out doesn't mean that I'm incapable of playing rough. It would be a real mistake to think that."

"Go to hell," he said.

Suddenly fists began pounding on the door outside. Not knocking. Pounding.

Then the door shuddered as something slammed into it. It wasn't anyone trying to kick it in. This sounded like one of those heavy-duty breaching tools—a steel weight swung by a couple of big guys. Shelton's guards were breaking in. Ghost began barking furiously.

On the desk, Shelton laughed. "Guess you're not the only one who can play a hole card, you sick bastard. As soon as you opened that last panel a signal went out to my whole team. They're going to come in here and tear you apart, Ledger, and I'm going to piss on your bones."

The heavy oak door began to splinter.

Chapter One Hundred Twelve

VanMeer Castle
Near Pittsburgh, Pennsylvania
Monday, October 21, 7:54 a.m.

There was another huge *whump* on the door. The stout wood panels were cracking. It wouldn't take them long to break in. Shit.

I tapped my earbud. "Cowboy to Bug, do you copy?"

"Right with you, boss. We're finding some crazy, crazy stuff on that—"

"Save it," I said, "the big bad wolf is at the door. I'm going to have to get creative here."

"Copy that," he said, and there was a nasty little laugh in his voice.

I grinned, too, though there were still a lot of ways this could go south on me. Events already seemed to be spinning that way.

Whump!

I grabbed the right cuff of my jacket and yanked. The sleeve tore away easily. Velcro, baby. Then I tore off the left sleeve. When the Velcro fastenings ripped it exposed small strips of adhesive. There were similar strips inside the cuffs. With all four exposed I pressed them across the big crack that was forming in the door, affixing half to the oak and half to the heavy frame. I made sure to leave a lot of slack, though. I wanted the door to open, at least part of the way.

The adhesive was great stuff. In seconds it would bond with the wall and even Bunny couldn't pull it off. Fun with chemistry. That would mean that all the bursting strength of the door would have to tear the material apart.

Ghost barked at me while I worked, but I whistled a happy tune.

Then I returned to Shelton. His face was gray and streaked with sweat. I felt his pulse and it sounded like machine gun fire. His skin was cold, though. He was going into shock.

Shit.

"Okay, sparky, here's the thing," I said amiably. "There are two ways this can play out—"

"Kiss my ass. In ten seconds my guys are going to—"

"I know, I know, tear me apart so you can piss on my bones. Yesterday's news. No, what we need to focus on is what happens *before* they break in. They can find you alive and unharmed, or they can find you dead, and believe me when I tell you that I don't need ten whole seconds to change your life. Or end it. If I'm going to hell, then you'll be driving the cab, *capiche?*"

He opened his mouth to say something smartass or threatening, but didn't. Instead I saw pain flicker across his face.

Uh-oh.

Whump!

Splinters flew into the room. Ghost stood wide legged and growled at the noise. He was fierce and he'd definitely get the first man through the door, but I had no illusions about our survival if things kept sliding downhill. Even so, I kept those concerns off my face.

I drew my piece and screwed the barrel into the soft underside of Shelton's jaw. "No more jokes. I know you rigged the cyber-attacks and even killed your own people to make the authorities look elsewhere. I know you framed me and somehow got the president to shut down the DMS. I know you're a governor of Majestic Three. I know you've been breeding alien-human hybrids, and I know that you're building spaceships."

His jaw went slack as I rattled all that off.

"Yeah, we're smart, too. We know all that. We also now have *two* copies of the Black Book. The original and the pretty blond copy."

His mouth worked like a silent gasping fish.

"But I really need to know what the end game is here. It's not just to sell a new stealth fighter. You could have done that without all this bullshit. You didn't need to frame me or kill my friends to accomplish that."

Whump!

Whoever was hitting the door was serious about it.

Shelton found his voice and sneered at me. "You fucking idiot. You think you know a lot but you don't know shit, but you don't know what I've done to protect this country. You think *I'm* the bad guy? The fucking Chinese blew up the Locust bomber. They're the ones who have a working T-craft. Not us. We're years away."

He sold it so well that for a moment I almost bought it.

Almost.

He was stalling, feeding me another lie, but why? He had things to bargain with.

Suddenly Shelton's body stiffened and he arched his back as if I'd just Tasered him. His eyes rolled up in their sockets and he gave a single strangled cry. Then he collapsed back onto the desk. His breath rattled in his throat.

I felt for his pulse.

And didn't find one.

Goddamn it.

"Bug," I said as I dug into my pocket for another hypo, "we have a problem. Shelton's coding on me."

I jabbed Shelton with the needle and then started CPR.

Whump!

Shelton twitched and gasped, dragging in a ragged lungful of air.

Ghost's bark jumped up a notch and I turned to see the door crack from top to bottom. The shattered wood bowed into the room, caught against the sleeves I'd affixed across the door, pressed them to their ripping point, and tore them apart.

I flung myself off the desk, hooked my arm around Ghost and dove for cover.

The wires inside the sleeves snapped, triggering the detonators in the cuff buttons, sending tiny electrical impulses into the chemicals that saturated the fabric.

The explosion was spectacular.

The force picked me up and threw me all the way across the room. It destroyed the massive door, turning the heavy wood into a death storm of jagged splinters that tore into Shelton's men. Arms and legs flew everywhere; blood sprayed the walls and ceiling.

The screams were terrible.

Some of those screams were mine.

Chapter One Hundred Thirteen

House of Jack Ledger, three hours ago

Near Robinwood, Maryland

Monday, October 21, three hours ago

Snake Harris ran down through a gulley that was still bathed in shadows. Six men ran behind him, each of them with automatic weapons aimed toward the house. Snake was the only one carrying a handgun. It was boxy and awkward looking, with four prongs instead of a barrel; however, Snake had used that pistol several times. The last time was at Wolf Trap in Virginia while working a job under the name Henckhouser. He and his partner had painted the walls using those guns. Snake loved the effect.

He ran with the pistol in a two-hand grip, his eyes focused on the back porch door. The telemetry from the satellite told him that the four heat signatures inside were stationary. Probably asleep.

That was okay. If they wanted to take it lying down, then that was just fine.

As his team reached the end of the gulley he looked across the lawn and saw the second team move into position beside the front porch. Another six men. And a third six-man team was in the attached garage, ready to kick the door that led into the cellar. Eighteen men and himself, ready to close around this place like a fist.

The primary mission objective was simple. Secure Junie Flynn. If she was there. Everyone else dies.

There was a burst of very faint squelch in his earbud, the signal that the garage team was in place.

Snake whispered a single word.

"Go."

The teams rushed their objectives. Snake's sergeant, a hulking man, passed him and kicked the door. Almost in the same second Snake heard the front door bang in. And then they were pouring into the house, rushing from darkness into lighted rooms, weapons up and out, searching out the four lives whose time on earth had come to an end.

The closest heat signature was the den and Snake burst inside, his gun already firing.

Tok!

The curled form under a blanket on the couch exploded as the microwave pulse burned into it. There was a flash of colored blanket shreds and then the air was filled with feathers. In the confusion, his men opened up and tore the form, the couch, and the whole side of the room apart. Splinters flew from the floor, plaster leaped from the walls, glass disintegrated out into the side yard.

There were shouts upstairs, more gunfire.

"Hold your fire!" Snake yelled. "Hold your fire."

The chatter of automatic gunfire dwindled down to silence, the last of the brass tinkled onto the ground.

Feathers floated on the smoke and mingled with plaster dust.

The couch was torn apart. So were the two thick pillows that had been positioned under the blanket.

"Where's the target?" growled Snake.

"Thermals are saying it's here," insisted his sergeant.

Snake whipped left and right, his team kicked over chairs, tore open closets.

They found the heat source.

It was under the couch. A device about the size of a TV remote.

"It's a signal relay," said the sergeant. "These fuckers are getting cute. They've forwarded a thermal signature here to draw us away from where they are. Christ, boss, they could be anywhere."

Which is when the house blew up.

IN THE BARN, seated on a folding chair next to stacked boxes of Jack Ledger's personal possessions, Gunnery Sergeant Brick Anderson tossed the detonator onto the floor.

"That's for Baltimore," he said.

Outside he heard a few sporadic shots. Birddog, cleaning up the leavings.

Brick switched off the jammer that hid the true thermal signatures. He stood up and walked to the barn door. The house was a burning pile of sticks.

"Joe's not going to be happy about that," he said.

A man moved out of the shadows.

"He'll get over it," said Mr. Church.

Chapter One Hundred Fourteen

VanMeer Castle
Near Pittsburgh, Pennsylvania
Monday, October 21, 7:57 a.m.

I landed on my side with Ghost cradled against my chest; the impetus of my dive sent us sliding fifteen feet across the polished floor. The shock wave kept us going until my shoulders slammed into a table on which was a huge bouquet of flowers. The blast flattened the table, withered the flowers and splattered us with splinters and chunks of masonry.

The aftershock of the explosion echoed away from me, rolling down the halls. The screams of the maimed mercenaries filled the air. Ghost staggered to his feet, barked once, and then fell over on his side. It was only then that I saw the blood smeared on the left side of his head. A piece of debris had struck him, ripping open the flesh.

I lunged over to him, touching his chest, and my heart almost stopped while I searched for his. Found the beat. Rapid, thin. But there.

He was alive, but he was out cold. Maybe crippled. Maybe dying.

I tapped my earbud.

"Cowboy to Echo Team, I have the package. I need extraction and backup right now."

Nobody answered me.

Across the room, Howard Shelton laughed weakly.

I turned to him.

"You dumb fuck," he said.

I heard a sound behind me. There was nothing but empty wall, but as I spun around, something hit me. I had a vague image of light coming through a doorway that shouldn't be there. There were figures in the light. Men. One small man with glasses. Several very big men.

I saw the stock of a rifle swing toward me and then blackness screamed in my head.

Chapter One Hundred Fifteen

VanMeer Castle
Near Pittsburgh, Pennsylvania
Monday, October 21, 7:59 a.m.

I never really went out.

Out would have felt better.

Instead I floated in a haze of sick disorientation. I was floating. Not in a good way. There were hands under my armpits, holding me almost off the ground. The toes of my shoes scraped along as they carried me for about a million miles. At one point they threw me into the back of a vehicle. A golf cart, I think. I may have drifted off for a while. They woke me by dragging me out of the golf cart and hustling me down another hall.

By the time we got where we were going, they were grunting and wheezing. And I was not quite as out of it as I was at the start of our journey.

I made damn sure not to let them know that.

When they dumped me onto the floor, I collapsed in a suitably boneless heap and didn't move.

There were voices.

Shelton. Weak, but getting stronger. And a lot of people fussing over him. I heard him gasp and curse when someone gave him an injection. I heard the *puff-puff-hiss* of a blood pressure cuff. Lots of technical medical terms. Lots of cursing. Mostly Shelton, telling everyone that he was okay, ordering them to leave him alone.

One voice was consistent throughout. Male, fussy, nasal. I think I heard Shelton call him Mr. Bones.

Minutes passed and the room settled.

Then I heard footsteps coming toward me. Slow at first and then speeding up with the unmistakable gait of someone about to punt the ball into the end zone, and I had no doubt at all what that ball was.

So I stopped faking it and rolled into the kicker, jamming the kick short as I looped a punch up and over and into something that squished like a bag of figs.

I pried my eyes open to see a medium-size man with a bow tie and round glasses stagger back from me, hands cupped around his balls, eyes absolutely bugged wide, mouth locked into an *O* of indescribable pain.

And one second later there were gun barrels screwed into both of my temples.

The little guy I'd punched was turning an interesting shade of puce. He dropped to his knees and it was clear he was trying his level best not to cry.

A dozen feet away, Howard Shelton sat in an expensive leather chair, his shirt unbuttoned, his color bad but better than it had been upstairs. I saw his Ghost Box laptop on a wheeled table next to him. The Majestic Black Book lay on his lap. A second Ghost Box rested on a table by a low couch. "Bones . . . get off the damn floor. You're embarrassing yourself."

Bones shot him a look of pure hatred. I don't think it was particularly directed at Shelton, but he had to fire off at someone. "Kill that son of a bitch." He spat the words at the guards, but nobody pulled a trigger.

Shelton nodded past me. "Burke, help him up."

I turned to see that there were other guards there. My friend Burke was there. He didn't look like he was enjoying the day. He walked past me to help the man called Mr. Bones. As he passed me, Burke whispered, "I'm going to cut your balls off."

So, fuck it, I swung a nice one into his nutsack, too.

Hey, these guys had me dead to rights. I had no illusions about getting out of there alive. Might as well enjoy myself.

Burke's eyes flared wide in genuine surprise. Guess he figured a guy on his knees with guns to his head wouldn't try it. Wrong guess. He tried to twist out of the way, but I caught him good. He dropped down right next to Bones.

The guards reversed their guns and beat the shit out of me.

So, there were three of us down on the floor.

"Enough," snapped Shelton and the hammering stopped.

Blood leaked out of my ear.

Guards helped Mr. Bones up. I saw that the front of his pants were wet and dark. Not the first guy to piss himself after a good punch to the balls. Burke's pants were dry, and he was getting to his feet all by himself. His face was as red as a ripe tomato and if I thought he hated me before, I'm pretty sure he'd found a new definition for murderous rage. That was okay. It's not the enraged ones you have to worry about. It's the calm ones.

"You're quite something," said Shelton. He drummed his fingers on the cover of the Black Book. "I very nearly like you, Ledger."

I didn't say anything.

"No, really," he said. "You're a breath of fresh air. You're a reality check. I ought to give you a consultant's fee for quality control. Here we are thinking we're the toughest, scariest sons of bitches in the world. You know, super-rich industrialist and his henchmen, right here in my own castle surrounded by a million dollars' worth of security and my own private army, and you roll up in a fucking Ford Explorer, torture the shit out of me—well, okay, mind-fuck me—and make me give up the most important single document since the ten fucking commandments. You blow five of my guys to Swedish meatballs, and you punch the nuts off my fellow governor and my chief of security. This is all very important to know, considering what I have going on, and with the guests we have coming." He chuckled. "But I got to tell you, Ledger, you are a lot of fun."

"Give me a chance to catch my breath," I said, "and I'll be happy to entertain you some more."

He pretended to think about it. "Nah. Attractive as that offer is. I think I'll pass. What do you think, Mr. Bones?"

Bones had crawled to the low sofa and pulled his legs up to hide the stains on the front of his pants. "He's a piece of shit. Kill him."

"Burke? What about you?"

Burke had to clear his throat to find a voice that didn't sound like the soprano section of the church choir. "I apologize for any deficiencies in the security. I'd like to thank Captain Ledger for all his help. I think making him eat his own dick is a start."

"Yes," hissed Bones.

"Jesus, you guys are brutal," said Shelton. "But it's an interesting thought. Let's keep it on the table."

"I should have cut your fingers off for real," I said.

"Yeah, well, that's why you're who you are and why I'm who I am."

I struggled to get to my knees, which was as far as they were going to give me.

"Tell me something, Shelton," I said. "When you kept blubbering that they were going to kill you . . . who exactly are 'they'?"

Howard laughed. "Nobody. Just screwing with your head."

"You thought I was cutting your fingers off and you were *screwing* with me."

He shrugged. "I was in the moment. And it worked, too. You bought it. You tried to bargain with me. Nice."

I shook my head. "Shit."

In his chair, Mr. Bones made a sound like a tiny, hysterical giggle.

"I wasn't joking when I said that you helped us out. We shouldn't be vulnerable here. And you should never have gotten your hands on the book."

"I'm clever as all get-out," I said. "Ought to have my own reality show. *Joe Ledger Pisses You Off.*"

"I'd watch it."

"So, tell me, Howard—what the *fuck* are you doing? I mean. I get why you're reverse-engineering flying saucers. Big bucks in patents for new technologies, and you get to feed shiny new toys to the military market. That's a sustainable market, and I don't really give much of a cold crap about it."

He nodded. "It pays the light bill."

"Sure. But I'm pretty sure you're behind what's been going on these last few weeks. The cyber-attacks . . . ? That was misdirection, right? Hiding among other victims?"

"Sure."

"Killing the staff at Wolf Trap?"

"Dual purpose," he said. "That way I become the main victim, and poor me, everyone rushing to send me flowers and condolences. But we suspected there was a leak at Wolf Trap. Didn't know who, so . . ."

"Sixty people to plug a leak?"

Howard smiled. "People don't mean shit to me. Or, haven't you figured that out yet?" He tapped his forehead. "I'm brilliant but most of what's up here is a bag of cats."

"Don't bait him, Howard," said Mr. Bones. "He's crazier than you are."

"Um," I said, "not really looking forward to a contest on that point. Though being framed as a terrorist kind of rattled my marbles. That was you, too, right?"

"Don't complain," said Mr. Bones, "we made you a very rich man."

"I'm public enemy number one."

"You want us to apologize?" asked Mr. Bones. "Really, go ahead and kiss my ass."

"Yeah, yeah, okay. But what about the ship?" I said. "Big black triangle. That's yours, right?"

"Kind of."

"'Kind of'?"

"We're not the only ones with a T-craft."

"But that was you buzzing the Seventh Fleet, right?"

"Nope. That was China out there making a point. And I think they made a pretty solid point. They used what we perceived was their state-of-the-art fighter, a J-22, to lure the American Hornets into a game of chicken, knowing that the Hornets would take them apart. But . . . the J-22 was the warm-up act and it exited stage right so the real star of the show could make an appearance."

"The T-craft."

"Yup. And it flew right through the heart of the fleet at Mach twenty. Ripped past them in a way that said *You can't catch me and you don't have anything that can shoot me down.* It was a damn bold statement and I bet it left skid marks in the drawers of everyone from admiral to mess hall cook. It told the fleet and our government that China just won the arms race."

"Unless we *also* have a T-craft," I said. "I mean, that's what the Majestic Project is all about. It's what you've been working on since the forties."

"Well . . . ," Howard said, drawing it out. He stood up, holding the Black Book to his chest with the reverence of a priest holding a Bible. "Yes and no. You see, M3 has been working on this, 'round the clock, since Harry Truman cracked the whip. The three governors have over-seen that project with great diligence and dedication. But . . . that's not the only game in town. Mr. Bones and I, being two of the three current governors, think the M3 project has spent way too much time spinning its wheels. I mean, okay, we made an ungodly amount of money, but it began to occur to us that building a spaceship as a weapon of war was a damn poor way to win the arms race."

I frowned. "But you just said that's essentially what the Chinese just did?"

"Not exactly," he said with a dark smile. "Bones, you want to show him?"

"Not really," complained Bones, but he got up anyway, looked down at his soiled pants, glared acid lava death at me, and limped to the big cur-tained wall that formed one side of the room. He touched a button and the curtains whisked back. From where I sat on the floor all I could see through the revealed windows was the rocky ceiling of a cavern. I hadn't realized how deep we'd gone. When Bones saw that I was still on the floor, he snapped, "Well, come on."

Under the watchful eye of the guards, I climbed slowly my feet. The room took a sickening sideways lurch and I staggered toward the win-dows, catching myself on the sill. Then I forgot about bruises, an aching head, or a sick stomach.

Beyond the glass was a massive natural limestone cavern. Longer and wider than a football field. Maybe eight times that big. Dozens of techni-cians in white coveralls crawled all over the skin of a massive black trian-gular ship.

But even that wasn't what kicked me solidly in the gut.

Beyond that ship squatted another. And beyond that, another. And more of them, filling the entire cavern.

Shelton and Mr. Bones had an entire fleet of T-craft.

"Surprise," said Mr. Bones. "Now you know why we risked every-thing. Now you know why we couldn't allow anything to get in our way. China launched the first T-craft. They threw down the gauntlet. This is going to be our response."

I licked my lips. "You're going to start a war with China?"

Shelton and Mr. Bones laughed.

"You're a very small picture guy, Captain Ledger," said Shelton as he came to stand with us by the window. "We have no interest in *fighting* a war with a nation of one-point-four billion people. That would be nuts. That would be suicide."

"Then what . . . ?"

Howard looked at his watch. "Our guests should be arriving in a few minutes. They probably have exactly the same thoughts about this that you do. Small thinking."

He placed one palm flat on the glass as if he could touch the row of T-craft.

"We do not want to fight a war with China," he said again, his voice softer now, almost distant. "Why fight a war when you can just simply *win it*. No, Captain Ledger, in a little over two hours we will blow the People's Republic of China off the map."

Chapter One Hundred Sixteen

VanMeer Castle
Near Pittsburgh, Pennsylvania
Monday, October 21, 8:06 a.m

Top Sims tapped his earbud. "Sergeant Rock to Cowboy, copy?"

It was the fifth time he'd repeated the call.

"Damn, Top," whispered Bunny.

"Is Joe all right?" asked Junie. She knelt between the two soldiers, a small, pale figure in the night, bracketed by hulking shapes in black combat gear.

Top touched a finger to his lips and nodded as a car came rolling over the hill and stopped at the main gate. The guard waved him in. Top watched the car all the way to where it parked by the side of the castle. As the two passengers got out he handed the binoculars to Junie.

"New arrivals," he said. "Do you recognize either of them?"

She looked—and gasped. "The driver, that's Erasmus."

Top nodded and tapped his earbud again. "Sergeant Rock to Deacon, do you copy?"

"Go for Deacon," said Mr. Church, his voice as clear as if he was standing right there.

"Bookworm confirms visual on Erasmus Tull at Shelton Castle."

Junie looked at him. "'Bookworm'?" she echoed.

Bunny leaned close. "It was that or 'Stargirl.'"

"God."

Mr. Church said, "Sergeant Rock, I cannot impress upon you strongly enough how important it is for this sighting to be without question. How high is your confidence in the target?"

Junie said, "It's him. There's no doubt about it."

There was the slightest of pauses. "Thank you," said Mr. Church. "That information is our lifeline."

Then there was a subtle change in the white noise on the line.

"This is the Deacon. I am alerting all stations and all commands. We have high confidence in our target. Echo Team go to full alert. Backup, put the pedal down. It's carnival time."

Bunny chuckled. "Hoo-fucking-ah."

Chapter One Hundred Seventeen

VanMeer Castle

Near Pittsburgh, Pennsylvania

Monday, October 21, 8:09 a.m.

"Oh my God . . . ," I breathed, *"why?"*

"Why destroy China?" Shelton slapped me on the shoulder. "Why end the rising threat that is China? Is that a serious question, Captain? Would you rather have them continue to cut our balls off by making us slaves to their money? Would you like to see us slip farther down the financial tower? China has become the number-one economy and they hold the mortgage to the United States. At the same time they steal ideas, they pirate everything that we have, they've built themselves into the number-one global superpower by exploiting our weakness. Our *laziness*. They have a working T-craft now. They can strike us any time they want. That bit of theater in the Taiwan Strait—that was a demonstration of their power. That was them telling us that the Seventh Fleet—the most powerful armada of ships this world has ever known—will no longer be the defining power in global politics. That was them telling us that the arms race is over, Captain Ledger, and they won."

He got up in my face. "Unless . . ."

"Unless what?" I demanded. "You start a war with them?"

"No . . . like I said, this wouldn't be a war. As of now 'war' is no longer a relevant term. It's archaic, old world. No, what we're going to do will be a single, decisive stroke that would result in total victory. They have one T-craft, Captain. Granted, it's a true Device because they got lucky and found most of the right parts, and then begged, borrowed, and stole the rest. We tried to play that game and came up short. We had to build a synthesized engine, a Truman Engine. And here's a funny thing—although the Chinese have a true Device, they haven't cracked the synthesis process for making artificial components. That's our science, and it's our trump card. They can use that T-craft to threaten us, to do us great harm, but they *need that ship*. That one ship *is* their fleet. But . . . oh, Captain, we are not building a fleet of ships. We don't want to get into dogfights or struggle for the supremacy of the skies. Or even of near space. Captain . . . M3 did not build the Truman Engines for that."

Shelton touched a button on a control panel mounted into the sill. "T-six you are cleared for departure."

The T-craft closest to the window suddenly pulsed with white light. It was like a throb, like the first dramatic beat of a heart. Arcs of electricity danced along its skin like white snakes.

"You see that?" asked Mr. Bones. "That's what is supposed to happen when a Truman Engine fires properly. The energetic discharge is contained and channeled into all shipboard systems. No explosion."

"It's a pilot thing," said Shelton, nodding. "The energy is regulated by the biomechanical matrix. Wicked science, and even though we built these things, we don't understand where the energy burst comes from. Our other governor, Dr. Hoshino, thinks that the process of firing opens a dimensional gateway to a source of dark matter. She might be right, that part's more her field than mine. All that matters to me is that Mr. Bones and I figured out how to harness that force. How to use it to fly the T-craft, and how to use these ships as the greatest weapons mankind has ever seen."

The craft lifted without a tremble. There were no visible engines and none of the struggle against gravity you see with the vertical takeoff-

and-landing jets. The craft simply moved upward in a dreadful silence. As it rose above the level of the windows I could see the three round lights near each point of the triangle and a larger central light. It pulsed again, and then the craft began moving away from us, flying over the other T-craft. Men in white jumpsuits cheered and waved at it. As if this was something to celebrate.

"Where's it going?" I asked, though I already knew.

"China," said Mr. Bones. "And it will be there right around the time our guests arrive."

"Guests?"

"Generals and a few congressmen who were convinced that this would be a better use of their time than vying for photo ops in Baltimore."

"Do they know what you intend to do?"

Shelton smiled. "Not yet."

"Tell me why you're doing this."

"Sure. Sure, I'll tell you 'cause I've read your file and I know that you're an actual psycho killer, so you'll appreciate this," said Shelton.

The bastard was really enjoying this. He slapped both palms on the glass.

"What you see here, all these ships . . . these aren't ships, Ledger. These aren't our fleet. They're our arsenal. They are *bombs*."

"Bombs? You're going to use these things to drop nukes?"

"Nukes?" laughed Shelton. "Shit, that's another archaic concept. Nukes are messy. They're as dangerous to the user as they are to the target. No, Ledger, think bigger. Think 'clean energy' as applied to warfare. You see, every single one of these T-craft can deliver a Truman Engine to any point on Earth at twenty times the speed of sound. And then I can remote detonate them by *removing* life support for the pilot. It's easy enough. It's a small sacrifice, but it works. Don't believe me . . . ask the kamikaze. Ask the suicide bombers who strap on a vest. They know that the sacrifice of a single life can make a profound impact on the whole world. Now, magnify that by the power of the Truman Engine. If China wants to fight us, let them use their craft to blow up an aircraft carrier or shoot down a few fighter jets. It's seven thousand miles from here to Beijing and any of these T-craft can be there in less than an hour. An airburst over Beijing will reduce the entire city to dust in a millisecond. Twenty million people will cease to exist that fast. *Bang!*" As he said that he slapped his palm flat against the cover of the Black Book.

"And they'll launch every nuke they have right back at you."

"Will they? Before they can hit the launch codes I'll blow Shanghai into orbit. Twenty-five million people. *Bang!* Gone! Guangzhou? Thirteen million. *Bang!* Shenzen, Tainjin, Dongguan. *Bang! Bang! Bang!*" He kept slapping the cover of the Black Book. "With half a dozen ships—with only six pilots—we can burn away over one hundred and seventy million of our enemy's people. How long do you think they will want to fight that war? And . . . even if they decide to throw away their own ship in a suicide run at us, they can take New York or Washington. But only one. It'll hurt us, but we will be poised to strike back and the American people will demand that we do. In less than a day China will become a wasteland. I have forty completed Truman Engines. We have nineteen craft built, and thirty more in production. How many do you think we'll really need to conquer *all* of our enemies? After China burns, do you think Russia will attack us? Or those bumblers in North Korea?"

"Those generals—your 'guests'—they'll stop you."

"Not a chance," said Mr. Bones. "We will be giving them a practical demonstration. Before any debate starts they'll see the destruction of Beijing. It will be a fact of life, Captain Ledger. That page of history will have already been written. Which means they will have to decide what to do next."

"Then our own allies will—"

"Will *what*, Captain?" laughed Shelton. "Name one country that will stand up and take a swing at us once they've seen what we can do. What they *know* we can do. Name one country with the balls to stand up to this fleet."

"America," I said.

He stared at me, half smiling, waiting for the punch line.

So I gave it to him.

I touched my earbud.

"Did you get all that?"

Mr. Church said, "Every word."

His voice boomed from the speakers of Howard Shelton's Ghost Box.

And then all the lights went out.

Chapter One Hundred Eighteen

The White House
Monday, October 21, 8:12 a.m.

"Did you get all that?" asked Joe Ledger, his voice mildly distorted by static.

"Every word," answered Mr. Church. His voice was clear as a bell.

President William Collins glared at the open laptop on his desk. He felt the stares of the two men standing in front of his desk. Attorney General Mark Eppenfeld and Secret Service Director Linden Brierly.

Collins licked his lips.

"It could be faked," he said. "Deacon and Ledger could be faking this whole thing."

"Bill," said Eppenfeld gently, "for god's sake . . ."

Bill Collins got up and turned to the big windows. Few things were more beautiful than the Rose Garden seen by dawn's light. The other men stood there, watching him, saying nothing.

"What do you want me to do?" asked Collins.

Chapter One Hundred Nineteen

VanMeer Castle
Near Pittsburgh, Pennsylvania
Monday, October 21, 8:13 a.m.

Carpe diem.

Seize the day. Useful phrase. Didn't really apply to the moment.

I seized the gun of the guard next to me.

I didn't need lights to find him. I pivoted, whipped my hands out, found him, adjusted my angle so that I had one hand on the rifle and used the other to chop him across the throat. That's a trick they teach to blind fighters or anyone fighting in the dark. If you can find any part of your enemy you can instantly estimate where the rest of him is. A body is a body, and we all know where the parts are.

I tore the gun out of his hands, dropped into a squat, and hosed the room.

In the muzzle flash I saw two guards spinning around, punched into a ragged dance by the rounds. I saw Bones hook an arm around Shelton and pull him down to the floor. I saw the Black Book fly from Shelton's hands and go slithering across the floor. I saw Burke dive behind the couch.

Then the magazine was empty.

In the sudden darkness I moved, cutting low and left, crabbing toward one of the guards, but I misjudged my distance and couldn't find them. I flung the empty rifle away and the instant it struck a wall there were three quick shots from Burke. The muzzle flashes gave me the snapshot of the room that I need.

I rolled right and slid in the blood of one of the dead guards, then crawled over him, feeling for rifle and magazines, praying I had time before the emergency lights came on.

The lights came on right then.

"There he is!" screeched Bones, and I saw Burke swing his barrel toward me. But at the same time one of the guards tried to lunge at me. Burke's first round tore off the back of the man's head. I dove under his body and rolled hard against the sofa, slamming it back against Burke. It caught him solidly in the thighs. His pistol dropped onto a cushion and then bounced on the floor. As I swung the rifle up, Burke threw himself over the back of the couch and tried to smash me flat. Bug's warning about him echoed in my head. Burke was a cage fighter from a circuit where people actually died.

I'm actually fine with that.

I had some issues that I wanted to work out.

As Burke landed on me, he wrapped his thighs around my torso, parried my right arm with his left, and used that mounted position to try and punch my face into junk. This sort of thing works really well in cage fights where the other guy fights the same way. It works when you're fighting the kind of martial artists who are really sportsmen—the board-breaking, tournament-trophy crowd—and it even works sometimes when they're fighting a barroom brawler.

The reason you don't see a lot of these guys get their asses handed to them is that the guys who study hand-to-hand combat *as* combat tend to use their skills to kill people. They don't compete and they don't need to prop up their egos by winning trophies. In real combat, when bullets are flying and people are dying, you don't see the real fighters try to wrestle their opponents down into a floor pin.

Here's why.

I swept my elbow into the path of his punch. Not as a block—I *hit* his fist with my elbow. Big elbow bones trump much smaller hand bones every time. His fist exploded. Then I reached my right hand up, hooked two fingers in his mouth between teeth and cheek, and tore the front of his face off. Before he could even scream, I shot my hips up and twisted, toppling him hard and fast. I rose up ten inches and then dropped elbow-first into his nuts. To do that right, you aim past the balls and try to break the pelvic bones. Which I did.

As I rose I ran over his body and stepped down hard on his throat.

Combat isn't a fucking sport.

I turned to find Shelton and Bones, but I caught only a glimpse of them, flanked by the remaining guards, scurrying through an emergency door. Shelton had the damn Black Book in his hand. I snatched up Burke's gun and began firing as I ran. I thought I heard a single scream of pain as the door slammed shut.

Tried the handle. Tried to kick it. Even tried to shoot it. The door stayed shut.

Ivan started yelling in my earbud.

"Hellboy to Cowboy, Hellboy to Cowboy, you will not believe what just flew past me."

"What's the status on the craft?"

"Tried to take it down with an RPG but no joy. T-craft took off heading west like a bat out of hell."

Another voice cut in. "Deacon for Cowboy. Fighter squadrons have been scrambled from here to the Taiwan Strait. All planes have been ordered to destroy that craft."

"Good luck. Any of them firing missiles that can match Mach twenty speed?"

"No. The Air Force hopes to intercept the T-craft in a head-on encounter."

"Definitely good luck. I hope someone's on the phone to Beijing."

"That call is being made," said Church. "What is the status of the Black Book?"

"Shelton has it. I need to get out of this damn room so I can get it back."

"Bug has your transponder signal. Prankster and Warbride are on the way to your twenty."

"Already here," cut in Lydia. "We're outside looking at an airlock."

"You bring party favors, Warbride?" I asked.

"Finest kind, Cowboy. You got any cover?"

"Give me ten seconds."

I shoved the couch and heavy leather chair into a corner and dove behind it, then curled into as compact a ball as I could manage. *"Go!"*

The airlock door weighed somewhere around four tons, but Dr. Hu's lab provides us with some interesting goodies. Each member of Echo Team carries two large self-adhesive explosive charges called "blaster-plasters." I don't know the chemistry, but cutting off a two-inch square will blast a deadbolt lock out of a solid oak door with sufficient explosive force to drive it like a nail into the first interior wall it hits. I'm pretty sure Lydia used all four of the heavy-grade blaster-plasters she and Prankster were carrying.

"Fire in the hole!" she bellowed.

The airlock muffled most of the bang on my side, but the whole frame around the airlock leapt heavily into the room, struck the floor with a resounding *karang*, pirouetted once and fell right on top of Burke's corpse. The shock slammed the couch backward and nearly flattened me against the wall, and blew the heavy-grade windows out of the observation room and into the big cavern below.

I peered over the edge of the couch and saw the red lines of laser sights cutting back and forth as two black-clad figures moved in, Colt M4A1 carbines held high and tight, heads bent, elbows out.

"Echo! Echo!" I yelled. "Cowboy on your eleven o'clock."

"Come out," said Lydia.

I rose from my hiding place and pointed at the door Shelton had used. "Open that door."

"Last plaster," said Prankster as he knelt by the lock, stripped the plastic off of the adhesive and pressed it into place. While he did that I took weapons and ammunition from the dead guards. We ducked into the hall and Prankster triggered the blast.

The last plaster was more than enough. The explosion destroyed the lock and the door swung wide, revealing a stone corridor that was splashed with blood.

"You hit somebody, Cowboy."

We ran into the passage and followed it around a curve and down multiple sets of zigzag stone steps. It was clear that we were heading to the cavern. The blood was steady and heavy. Either one person had taken a bad one and was going to bleed out soon, or I'd hit a couple of targets.

When we rounded the curve we found out which.

Mr. Bones sat in the corridor, his back to the wall, legs stretched out in front of him. He had a pistol in one hand and as we slowed to a cautious walk he tried to raise it. Not at us. He tried to eat the barrel. Prankster reached him in two long strides and kicked the gun out of his hand.

I touched Warbride and pointed down the hall. "Check the tunnel."

She and Prankster moved off, leaving me with the dying governor.

I squatted down and he raised glassy eyes toward me. He was past the point of fear. All he had left was pain and despair.

He tried to smile. His teeth were slick with blood and spit.

"You . . . can't stop . . . us . . . ," he said, wheezing out the words, using up what was left of him to try and turn a dial on me.

"Yeah? What does it matter to you? You're dead. And here's a news flash for you, sparky, no matter what happens, no matter how all this plays out, no matter what becomes of everything you and all the other members of the Majestic Project have spent your lives to accomplish . . . you're not going to be there to see any of it. You'll never know. That must suck."

"It doesn't matter," he said in a way that clearly meant that it did.

I stood up. His eyes followed me, looking from the gun in my hand to my eyes and back again.

"Go on . . . end it."

I smiled.

"Fuck you," I said. "Lay there and bleed."

I ran to find my team.

Chapter One Hundred Twenty

VanMeer Castle
Near Pittsburgh, Pennsylvania
Monday, October 21, 8:18 a.m.

I rounded the next bend and saw Warbride and Prankster hunkered down by the entrance to the cavern. As I moved up behind them I could see that things were going into the crapper very quickly.

Hatches on all of the T-craft were open and pilots in orange jumpsuits were climbing up as techs disconnected hoses and cables. I wondered how many of the pilots knew that they were flying suicide missions. Not many, I guessed. Easier to fool people than to try and manage a large number of highly intelligent, highly trained pilots who had to go kill themselves. The kamikaze had Shinto going for them. I didn't see Shelton as a spiritual leader who could make realistic promises about a glorious afterlife.

I tapped my earbud.

"Cowboy to Deacon."

"Go for Deacon."

"Where are we with stopping that T-craft."

"Nowhere. It has eluded all attempts so far."

"Well, here's more bad news. I'm looking at a fleet of these frigging things that are going to be lifting off in the next few minutes. We need a play here."

"Open to suggestions, Cowboy. I'm off-site."

I opened the call to the whole team. "Who has eyes on the exit from this cavern? Did anyone see the first one launch?"

"Ronin to Cowboy," said Sam Imura. "It came out from behind the second hill north of the castle, call it four o'clock using the castle. It's private forestland back there."

"Shit. I need that hole closed and I need it closed right now."

There were three seconds of agonizing silence on the line. Then Bunny said, "Cowboy, Sergeant Rock and I can get over there, but all we have are blaster-plasters. They'll have to be rigged high in order to block an entrance that big. That's going to take time."

"We don't have time," I said.

It was Top who answered. "Buy us what you can."

I looked at Lydia and Pete. The hard looks on their faces gave me an answer before I asked the question.

"Copy that, Sergeant Rock. Warbride, Prankster, and I will make as much mischief as we can."

"Good hunting," said Top.

I knew that Bunny would have wanted to say something to Lydia, and she to him, but there was no time left. No privacy left. All that was left to us was the killing and the dying.

Somewhere out there was a sleek, dark craft that had no business being in the skies of our world. An impossible machine flying at impossible speeds to fulfill the dark dreams of a greedy and murderous madman. Would our fighters knock it down? *Could* they?

And if they didn't, what would happen to the world?

If the Truman Engine detonated over Beijing, how could we ever convince a shocked and grieving Chinese people that this was not an act of war? How could they ever hear our explanations through the roar of their own hurt and outrage? They would attack us because that is what countries do. We are a warlike people, but beneath the technology and the machines and the sophistication of our weapons we have that primitive imperative to lash out when struck. To hit back, even if our blows land on the wrong flesh.

Shelton thought that this would lead to the end of war, to a kind of peace through conquest. And how wonderful it would be to live in a world where we could lay down our arms and never again fire a shot in anger. How idyllic.

The price tag was the thing, though. If the deaths of tens of millions was the cost of a future without war, how could we actually call that peace?

These thoughts hammered in my head as Lydia Ruiz, Pete Dobbs, and I prepared to rush into the cavern.

And a twisted little voice whispered to me as I checked my ammunition and adjusted my gear. It said, *If the bomb goes off over Beijing and the Chinese retaliate, won't we need these other ships? Even if it's a war we don't choose to start, how can justify taking away our best hope of surviving the inevitable retaliation?*

Man . . . those were ugly, ugly questions.

Questions for which I had no answers.

Chapter One Hundred Twenty-one

The Situation Room
The White House
Monday, October 21, 8:22 a.m.

President William Collins sat at the head of the table, with the Joint Chiefs on his right, the national security advisor and chief of staff on his left.

On a large OLED screen, a real-time satellite showed a white dot moving at incredible speeds toward the Pacific Ocean. The satellite tracked scores of other dots, some in front of the fast one, some behind, all of them moving many times slower.

"It reached Mach sixteen over Ohio," said General Croft. "We're currently clocking it at Mach nineteen point four."

"What are our options for shooting it down?" demanded Collins. Hands were clutched together on the tabletop, fidgeting like frightened mice.

The generals and admirals and secretaries looked at each other and away.

"Come on, what are our options?"

"Mr. President," said Croft, "we don't have anything that can catch it."

"We have prototypes, we have experimental ships that go that fast."

"None of them are in the air, sir. None of them have successfully cleared the test phase."

"I don't care," Collins exploded. "Get them in the air."

"They aren't armed yet, sir. It would take a few weeks to—"

"Then what the hell do we do?"

"Mr. President," said Admiral James, "everything that has wings and a gun is in the air. We've got seventy jets converging on it from three points and we'll fill the air with missiles and rockets."

"Good," said Collins, jumping on that, clutching the thread of hope it offered. "When? How soon before they shoot it down?"

"Six minutes until contact." James paused. "Mr. President, at this speed we're going to get one shot. Just one."

Chapter One Hundred Twenty-two

VanMeer Castle
Near Pittsburgh, Pennsylvania
Monday, October 21, 8:28 a.m.

"What's the game plan, *jefe*?" asked Warbride.

"It's real simple," I said. "Kill anything in a jumpsuit. Put a bullet in anything that looks like a computer. Don't die."

"Hell," said Prankster, "even I can remember that."

I held up my fist. They bumped it.

Corny, I know. Juvenile, sure.

If you're one second away from running into hell—actual hell—you can do whatever you damn well please.

We turned, set, closed everything out but the mission.

"Go," I snapped.

We burst from the hallway and split, Warbride went wide and left, Prankster cut right and I ran dead up the middle, all of us firing, firing, firing.

Rounds hammered into pilots and technicians, into Blue Diamond guards and machines. People screamed, men and women.

We did not discriminate, we didn't pick targets. We killed everyone we saw. It was butchery.

Men fell from ladders that were hooked onto the sides of T-craft. Men sprawled over computer consoles, their blood soaking into the machines and shorting them out. Men toppled screaming from catwalks.

Return fire was confused. There were so many techs, so much valuable equipment that the Blue Diamond guards had to pick and choose their targets. We did not.

Prankster paused under a T-craft, plucked a grenade from his vest, pulled the pin and hurled it high overhead. It hit the top of the machine and exploded. If that did any damage, I couldn't see it.

"The struts," I yelled, hoping he could hear me through the din.

A moment later I saw a grenade go rolling and bouncing beneath the same T-craft. It rolled to a stop at the base of one of the steel struts. The blast bent the strut inward at a forty-five-degree angle.

That was enough. It was too much for the ponderous weight of the massive vehicle. The black ship canted toward its crippled leg and in its fall smashed a whole row of important-looking computers.

Then I saw Shelton. He was surrounded by a cadre of guards, two of whom had to help him limp along. I must have clipped him when I'd shot Mr. Bones. They were hustling toward a big industrial elevator. I broke into a run. I don't think I've ever run that fast in my life, firing the weapon I'd taken from a dead guard. Emptying one magazine from a hundred feet away, dropping two of the guards. Hitting Shelton at least once in the arm. I dropped the magazine and swapped in a fresh one, fired, fired.

As the elevator doors shut.

I sprayed the narrowing gap, throwing as much death as I could into the metal box.

It closed.

There was a second elevator waiting right there. Give chase or stay with my team.

I tapped my earbud. "Warbride, Prankster, Shelton's in the freight elevator."

"Go get the fucker," screamed Warbride. "We got this."

It was the only choice I could make. I dove into the elevator. There were three buttons.

GARAGE

HOUSE

HELIPAD

I knew where Shelton was going and stabbed the top button. As the doors swung shut I looked out at the carnage. Two of the best and the bravest against a cavern full of people.

As the door closed I saw something that absolutely horrified me. Two of the T-craft suddenly pulsed with brilliant white light. Truman Engines were firing. Some of the craft were going to escape.

The world was going to burn.

Chapter One Hundred Twenty-three

The Situation Room

The White House

Monday, October 21, 8:33 a.m.

President Collins leaned forward, hands balled into fists, as the phalanx of slow dots moved toward the single light that tore across the Pacific. Suddenly the screen was littered with hundreds of smaller lights that erupted from the oncoming jets.

"All missiles have been fired," said Admiral James. "Ten seconds to impact."

The missiles flew in a converging line, like a net being drawn tight around a fish.

"Come on, come on," breathed Collins. The room crackled with tension.

And then the white dot changed direction. It was a shockingly fast eighty-degree turn. The direction and altitude meter for the craft ripped through a new sequence of numbers.

"It's turning," cried James. "God, it's climbing."

"It's accelerating," said General Croft.

The T-craft shot over the line of missiles at Mach 23.6.

The missiles still flew toward where it was.

But it wasn't there anymore.

Every second it was closer to China.

Chapter One Hundred Twenty-four

VanMeer Castle
Near Pittsburgh, Pennsylvania
Monday, October 21, 8:36 a.m.

Yeah, there's nothing like a slow elevator ride in the middle of a wild and crazy firefight. Very relaxing. The frigging thing lumbered upward. Should have been playing some silly damn piece of music. "The Girl from Ipanema."

I reloaded and took up a defensive position to one side of the door in case they ambushed me.

The doors opened.

They ambushed me.

Two shooters opened up with automatic weapons from ten feet.

Didn't do them much good though, because as soon as there was a crack in the door I lobbed out a fragmentation grenade. Maybe they were too sure they had me. Maybe they didn't see the grenade fly out as I dove to the corner. Didn't matter. They capped off about a third of a magazine each before the grenade blew them apart.

I ran over the pieces.

I expected the helipad to be on the roof, but it wasn't. We were on a flat pad to the east side of the castle. All the fighting seemed to be on the other side of the building.

Damn.

I opened up with the machine gun, dodging out and left in the smoke. I caught a third guard across the thighs and he fell, his weapon punching rounds into the asphalt on the helicopter deck.

I saw six men trying to squeeze into a business helicopter built for five. I helped with the problem by firing into the crowd. Shelton shoved one man straight into the path of the bullets and the man danced backed and knocked his boss into the chopper.

"Kill him," shrieked Shelton. There was blood on his face and he held one arm tight across his belly. I realized the man next to him was Sullivan, the guard from the front gate.

They were trying to fight while trying to climb into the helicopter. All I wanted to do was kill them.

In combat, sometimes it's about the choices you make.

I emptied the magazine into them. Dropped the rifle, pulled a block, fired and fired.

From over the edge of the roof I heard a lot of gunfire. More of it over the mike, inside the house. Lot of people were dying. In all the confusion I thought—just for a moment—that I heard a dog barking. Was it the Dobermans or was it Ghost? Was my dog even alive? Was any of my team still alive?

My slide locked back and I reached for a fresh magazine.

Which I did not have. All I had left was one grenade, but Sullivan and the remaining guards opened up on me. I threw myself into a dive roll and came up behind the housing of a huge air-conditioning unit. Bullets whanged and pinged off its skin, but the internal workings blocked any penetrating shots. I pulled the pin on the grenade, said a prayer to Saint Jude and tossed it.

He's the saint of lost causes. I figured, what the hell?

The grenade exploded in the air. Someone screamed.

I peered around the corner and saw the last guard down with no face, and Sullivan sitting on his ass trying to hold the outside of his head on. He looked at me with an expression of profound confusion, as if there was no way on earth that something like this could possibly happen to him.

And then he fell over.

I came out from behind the air conditioner. I had no bullets and no grenades, but nobody seemed to be moving. Only the helo's rotors were moving, spinning with desultory slowness. *Whup, whup, whup.*

I ran low and fast to the machine, bending on the way to scoop up Sullivan's fallen pistol. I peered inside the bird. The pilot was slumped over, his face full of shrapnel.

Howard Shelton was curled into a ball. With one bloody hand he clutched the Majestic Black Book to his chest. There were red bullet holes above and below the book.

I took it away from him.

He stared at me with eyes that were filled with such pure hatred that I felt my skin grow hot. I tapped my earbud. "Cowboy to Deacon, Cowboy to Deacon."

"Go for Deacon."

"I have the package. Repeat, I have the package. Transmit the message, we have the Majestic Black Book."

"Thank you, Captain." He disconnected to make perhaps the most important radio message in history.

Would they be listening?

Was it too late for that to even matter?

I had few illusions about it. The T-craft was going to be in China soon. We were almost out of time.

"Damn you," whispered Shelton. I turned to him.

He had a little .25 belly gun in the same hand that had held the book just a moment before. It wobbled in his grip. Tears of sweat ran down his face. His skin was gray.

"Shelton, listen to me," I said. "There's still time to climb down off this ledge. Tell me what I need to know to recall that ship."

He gave a single slow shake of his head. When he tried to speak he blew a big pink bubble that burst and dottled his face with tiny red dots.

"We can work something out," I said. "We can step back from the brink. You don't have to do this. This isn't how you save America."

His face contorted. I thought he was trying to smile, but his mangled lips curled into a sneer of total contempt.

"Fuck America," he said.

And the son of a bitch shot me.

Chapter One Hundred Twenty-five

The Situation Room

The White House

Monday, October 21, 8:41 a.m.

On the screen, the T-craft flew over the North Pacific Ocean at Mach 25. It flew straight along the Tropic of Cancer and then at Marcus Island changed course on a flight path that would take it directly over the city of Hiroshima on its way to mainland China. It would pass over Pusan in South Korea, fly above the Yellow Sea, and hit the mainland at Dalian.

President Collins and his executives sat in stunned silence as they watched doomsday approach. No one said a word. Everything had already been said. Everything had already been done.

Now all that was left was to watch the horror unfold.

Chapter One Hundred Twenty-six

VanMeer Castle

Near Pittsburgh, Pennsylvania

Monday, October 21, 8:42 a.m.

Junie Flynn crouched behind a tree and watched hell unfold before her.

Top and Bunny had left her there because the fight on the grounds was going south. Blue Diamond guards were everywhere. Murderous Dobermans raced along inside the fence, hunting for Ivan and Sam.

From this distance, even with the binoculars Top had left her, she couldn't make out who was who.

The air flashed and popped with gunfire as the Blue Diamond men tried to hunt down the kill team on the grounds. And somewhere down there was Erasmus Tull.

A hybrid, like her.

A monster.

She listened through the din, trying to make sense of it all. Listening for Joe.

He was such a strange man. Incredibly savage and yet capable of more tenderness that any man she'd ever been with. She could recall everything about last night. The heat of that first kiss. The way his hands had been as he undressed her—urgent and yet never rough, never a sense of *taking*. She remembered the lean hardness of his body. The many scars, old and new. The sensation of oneness as he entered her. His muffled cry as he buried his face against her throat as he came.

"Joe," she whispered to the night, then immediately clamped a hand over her mouth.

God, was the microphone on?

There was movement over to the left, far away from all the action. Junie raised the binoculars and focused them, saw a helicopter and several men. Then flash after flash as they fired at each other.

And there he was.

Joe.

She saw him throw a grenade, and that seemed to end the fight. Then he leaned in through the open door of the helicopter.

A few seconds later there was a single flash and Joe staggered backward, reeling awkwardly, turning, dropping.

She screamed his name, and before she knew what she was doing, Junie Flynn was up and running. The binoculars in one hand, a microwave pistol in the other.

Chapter One Hundred Twenty-seven

VanMeer Castle
Near Pittsburgh, Pennsylvania
Monday, October 21, 8:46 a.m.

I staggered back, my chest on fire. I heard another *pop* and another as Shelton continued to fire at me. A second round punched me in the gut. A third hit somewhere near my hip and spun me half around. His aim sucked, but I'd made it easy for him with that first shot. I'd leaned right into the helicopter.

I reeled away from him, hiding behind the front end of the chopper as he squeezed off shot after shot.

The microfiber Kevlar I had on kept those bullets from killing me, but the foot-pounds of impact, even from a small-caliber gun, smashed me. When I took a breath, two ends of a broken rib grated together in an internal shriek of white hot agony. I clamped a hand to my mouth to stifle a scream—and tasted blood.

I stared at my hand, at my arm. And down at my chest.

The Kevlar was completely intact. But there was a neat round hole one inch to the right of the arm hole. As I lifted the arm I could feel the wrongness of torn muscle and shredded flesh. Suddenly my legs buckled and I dropped to my knees. Somehow I kept hold of the pistol, but I felt like the effort of lifting it was going to take more than I had to spend.

Shit.

"Did I kill you, you son of a bitch?" yelled Shelton.

"No," I growled back, "but thanks for trying, ass-hat."

He actually laughed.

Weirdly, so did I.

I wasn't entirely sure he hadn't killed me. With each breath my lungs felt worse, wrong. Wet.

"Don't worry about it, Mr. Shelton," said a voice behind me. "I'll be happy to take care of this piece of shit."

I turned slowly. Turning fast wasn't happening. The bullet had gone in but it hadn't come out. Low-caliber round, must have hit bone and taken a detour deeper into my chest cavity.

Two men stood by a gate that led from the helipad to a parking area. One was tall and broad and very Italian. The other looked a little like me. Big, ropy muscles, blond hair and blue eyes. His hair was curly, though.

I sagged down, dropping my butt onto my heels, fighting my body's desire to simply collapse.

They towered over me. Both of them held guns, barrels pointed casually down at their sides. Both of them were smiling. This was going to be easy for them and they knew it.

I looked up at Blondie.

"Erasmus Tull?" I asked.

"Yeah. Ledger?"

"Yeah."

He smiled. "I've been looking forward to this."

I sighed. "I figured."

"You have a lot of friends at the Warehouse?"

"Yeah."

He nodded.

"Time to join—"

I shot him in the face.

Hey, fuck it.

Tull stayed on his feet for one full second, his eyes wide with astonishment. Then he fell backward in a boneless sprawl. Maybe I didn't have dysentery like Harrison Ford, but seeing Tull definitely made me sick to my stomach. I figured Indiana Jones would be proud.

Tull's friend yelled in shock, his face splashed with blood. He brought his gun up.

I could have taken him, too. In that moment of astonishment.

Except after that single shot the slide locked back on Sullivan's gun.

The Italian guy raised his piece. He was screaming something. But I wasn't tracking very well. The empty gun toppled from my hand.

And then the Italian exploded.

As an after echo I heard a single dry *tok!*

It was all very messy and immediate and for a moment the air was stained with a lingering pink mist. But as it cleared I saw Junie Flynn standing there, legs wide, both hands wrapped around a microwave pulse pistol.

"Junie," I said.

She rushed through the gate and ran right to me and damn near bowled me over, but when she saw the blood she skidded to a stop and fell to her knees in front of me.

"Joe, oh my god, Joe . . . you've been shot."

Her hands were everywhere, probing, touching. She pulled her sweater off and gently stuffed it inside my vest and pushed my arm down to hold it in place.

In my earbud I heard Mr. Church. "Cowboy—give me a sit-rep. Is the package still in hand?"

The package lay on the ground, covered in blood. I used my good hand to pick it up. There was a bullet drilled three quarters of the way through it. I remembered the shot that had hit my hip.

"Confirmed," I said. "The package is in hand."

Then I remembered the cavern.

"Listen to me, Deacon, that cavern is still open and they're firing up the T-craft. You have to—"

"Captain," interrupted Church, "I am channeling in a visitor."

"Who am I on the line with?" I demanded.

There was a burst of squelch, then an unfamiliar voice said, "Captain Andrew Murray, sir, Pennsylvania Air National Guard. Requesting permission to join the party."

Junie's grave face blossomed into a smile.

"I hope you brought more to this pig roast than a beer bong, Captain."

"If you have any use for a six-pack of A-10 Thunderbolts, then we're forty miles out, coming hard, locked and loaded."

I had to laugh. "Guess we ain't the left-handed stepchildren no more."

"We are acting on orders of the commander-in-chief," said Murray.

"Captain," I said. "There is a cavern opening on the north side of this property." I gave the coordinates to Murray. "If *anything*—any craft of any kind—gets out of that cavern we are going to be at war with China before lunchtime. That is not a joke. Confirm."

"Advise on location of your personnel, Cowboy."

I thought of Warbride and Prankster. One old friend, one new. Both family, born as children of war.

My heart wanted to break.

"There's no time left on the shot clock, Captain," I said. "Pull the trigger."

"Understood, Cowboy. Go with God and let the devil take the rest."

Then I tapped my earbud. "Warbride, Prankster . . . Evac now. Repeat—evac now!"

There was no answer.

Junie touched my face. "Joe," she said.

And then the sky was full of missiles and fire rained from heaven.

Chapter One Hundred Twenty-eight

The Situation Room
The White House
Monday, October 21, 8:54 a.m.

The white dot—so puny and absurd a representation of what it was—crossed over into Chinese airspace.

Bill Collins got up from his seat and walked down the row of generals and officials until he stood in front of the screen. His face was a mask of shock.

He had been president for just over twenty-four hours.

If there was a country left after this was all over, he would be remembered as the president who could not stop an unwinnable war from killing millions. He would be reviled. The captain of the ship always takes the blame.

Distantly, vaguely, he wondered how this all might have played out if he hadn't done everything he could to remove the DMS and cripple their power. Even now reports were coming in from a terrible firefight in Pennsylvania. Collins had reluctantly agreed—in light of Shelton's confession—to send air support to Ledger's assault on VanMeer Castle. A second, small screen showed the impact of missiles from six fighters. It was too soon to tell if any more of the T-craft had escaped.

"The message about the Black Book," he said, "was it sent?"

The question was not directed to anyone in particular.

A second white dot appeared on the screen. Collins knew from Mr. Church's intelligence that this was probably China's T-craft, scrambled to confront the enemy. The Chinese craft was on the far side of the country, though. It could never intercept Shelton's craft in time.

On the screen the white dot was one second away from Beijing.

"God help us all," Collins said, but for a moment he thought he saw a third white dot. One that blipped in out of nowhere right beside Shelton's craft.

Then there was a huge white burst on the screen. Intensely white, too bright to look at.

Collins shielded his eyes with his hand for a moment. He cried out like a terrified child.

Silence.

When Collins dared to open his eyes he saw that only one white dot was still there. The other one—or perhaps two—were gone. The last dot had stopped, though, and it hovered directly over Beijing.

And, against all sense, Beijing itself was still there.

Then the dot began moving. It headed out to sea. And then the altimeter began rolling madly, insisting that the craft was moving upward.

Upward.

Upward.

Until it passed within miles of the satellite tracking it and passed beyond its observational range.

Everyone at the table stared in total, stunned silence.

Then a voice behind him said, "The message was sent and received, Bill."

Collins whirled around. Everyone turned.

A man sat at the head of the table. In Collins's seat. In the seat reserved for the president.

Collins's mouth worked and worked.

And then he screamed.

The man at the head of the table leaned forward wearily. He looked worn and thin. His color was bad. But he smiled.

"Gentlemen, the message was received," said the president of the United States.

Epilogue

(1)

"We're losing him!"

I've been a cop, I've been a soldier. I've heard people say that. EMTs working on an accident victim by the side of the road as a family SUV incinerated their vacation dreams. ER docs with blood smeared to the elbows as they massage the failing heart of a gunshot victim. Trauma surgeons charging the paddles for the fourth time while a rookie cop slides down into the big black.

I've heard it ten times. Twenty. More.

"Put pressure there . . . no, *there*, damn it!"

Familiar words. A routine of haste and desperation that seldom ends well.

"BP is falling. Sixty over forty."

You stand by and watch. You have faith in the pros, in what they can do. You've seen them pull off Hail Marys with two seconds on the clock, or drop sixty-foot jumpers at the buzzer. Not always, but enough times so you don't lose all your hope.

"He's flatlining!"

I've heard it, seen it.

"Charging, charging . . ."

"We're losing him."

I've heard it all so many times.

But never when it was me down there. Not when I was the one losing the blood, not when I was the one feeling the black ice creeping in through the pores, listening to the doctors and nurses, hanging on every word, hoping to catch a lifeline.

"Joe!" I heard her voice. Junie Flynn. Calling my name from a thousand miles away.

I tried to answer.

But I had no breath left.

(2)

When I woke up, she was there.

Junie Flynn.

No makeup, rumpled clothes, circles under her eyes. Absolutely beautiful.

It took me a while to realize that I was awake. And another few minutes to grasp the fact that I was alive. I remembered being dead.

I think.

She held my hand and looked into the middle distance, thinking thoughts that were her own, and for a long time she didn't notice that my eyes were open.

Then she did, and a great, slow smile blossomed over her face. It shed years and weariness from her.

"Joe," she said.

"Junie." My voice was nothing, a rasp over dry wood. She gave me a sip of water.

"I hate hospitals," I said.

"From what your friends told me I thought you loved them. You're in them all the time."

"Nope. Hate 'em."

She rose and bent and kissed me. Her long hair brushed my face, and I did not care one little bit that it was a wig.

But thinking about that made me think of her.

"How are you?" I asked.

She smiled, a sad little smile. "I'll live."

And I wished with all my heart that it was true.

I raised my head and looked around.

"Where am I? And . . . *when* am I?"

"It's Friday. You've been here since Monday. We're in Johns Hopkins."

I looked around the room. I guess I am becoming a connoisseur of hospitals. "Nice wallpaper."

You couldn't see the wallpaper for all the bouquets of flowers. It looked like a tropical jungle. There were huge color photos of Ghost, clearly taken at my apartment. They'd shaved all the fur off his head so they could stitch him up. Someone had tied a wildly colorful scarf around his neck. He looked thoroughly disgusted, but I suspected it was an act. Someone had used a Sharpie to scrawl on the photo: "Ouch, Ouch, Arf, Arf." It was signed with a paw print.

"Isn't that adorable?" asked Junie.

"So cute I want to throw up."

She laughed and gave me more water.

Then I asked the first of a series of very hard questions. Questions I needed the answers to but that I did not want to hear.

"My team. Lydia . . . Pete . . ."

She hesitated.

"God," I began, but she touched my chest.

"No, they're alive. They're hurt . . . but they're alive."

"How bad?"

"Lydia will be okay. Concussion and some burns."

"And Pete?"

"He was shot, too. I heard Bunny tell the others that Pete won't be able to be a soldier anymore. Too much damage. But the doctors say he'll probably walk again. With time."

"Jesus. Was it worth it?"

"Yes," she said. "Oh definitely. The T-craft was destroyed and—"

"Wait . . . how? Who shot it down?"

She frowned. "Don't you remember? Mr. Church told you about it in the ambulance."

"I don't remember an ambulance. C'mon, Junie, what happened?"

"The message got through. About the Black Book. It got through."

"And . . . ?"

"And they blew the other ship up. Both ships, actually."

"Junie, what the hell are you talking about. Who blew up the ships?"

She smiled at me. "The aliens," she said. "Right after the message was delivered, they destroyed the T-craft Howard Shelton sent, and then they destroyed the Chinese T-craft. The jet fighters destroyed the ones in the cavern. They're all gone. And Mr. Church is working with governments in eleven countries to expose groups like M3. All D-type components are being collected and destroyed. NATO is overseeing it, and because of all the secrecy in the past there's a lot of transparency."

"The public knows?"

Her smile ebbed. "Well, transparency in certain quarters. The story they're feeding the press is that a group of multinational extremists hijacked some experimental stealth craft and used them to commit acts of terrorism. It's nonsense of course, but that's the stance they're taking."

"What about the Black Book?"

"I—don't know what they did with it. Mr. Church said that it's been handled. Some arrangement he made with the president."

"With Collins? That jackass couldn't—"

"God, Joe, you really did forget everything." She got up and brought over one of the loveliest of the floral arrangements and held it so I could read the card.

With the thanks of a grateful nation,
And the personal thanks of a fellow citizen of this world.

It was hand-signed by the president.

The president.

I made Junie tell me the whole story over again from the beginning.

(3)

The next day they let me see Rudy.

His head was swathed in bandages and one dark eye stared out at me. It was surrounded by bruised flesh.

I sat in my wheelchair. He lay in his bed.

Everyone left us alone.

I think we sat that way for an hour before either of us said anything.

Finally, it was Rudy who spoke.

"Aliens," he said.

"Aliens," I agreed.

Then Circe came in and kicked me out. She closed the door and Junie wheeled me back to my room.

(4)

The warmth that had lingered all through October blew away in early November. With temperatures drifting toward freezing even under a noonday sun, I leaned against the fender of my Explorer, staring at the rubble of what used to be the Warehouse. The whole area was still quarantined, no public allowed. The cops passed me through when I badged them. I forget what badge I grabbed out of the truck. Didn't matter, really.

Ghost sat on the ground, staring at the nothing where so many of our friends died. He whined quietly. I scratched his head, careful to avoid the long scar. I felt like whining, too.

Or, maybe crying.

The cold wind made my chest hurt. I was supposed to be wearing a sling, but I added that to the list of other things that I was supposed to do and chose not to.

"Coffee?" said a voice and I turned to see Mr. Church standing there. I hadn't heard him approach. Nor had Ghost. We never did. Church is a spooky bastard.

He had a venti Starbucks in one hand and a bottle of water in the other. Church was wearing a topcoat that cost more than my education and looked totally unruffled. He held the coffee out to me and I took it; then he fished in his pocket and removed a blueberry scone wrapped in a paper napkin. He gave the scone to Ghost.

I noticed Church wasn't wearing his sling either. He had a new pair of tinted glasses. Except for the healing cuts on his face you couldn't tell that he'd been hurt. I suspect that this was something he had practiced over the years. Me, too, I guess.

Church leaned on the Explorer's door next to me. Ghost ate his scone in the slow, delicate way he does. When he was done, Church poured water into his palm and let Ghost lick it up. He wiped residual dog slobber with the paper napkin.

A strange man. I don't think I'll ever understand him.

I cut him a look. "You haven't done anything to Junie."

"You sound surprised. What do you think I would want to 'do' to her?"

"Lock her away and test her."

"She is a friendly, Captain."

"She's more than that," I said.

He nodded. "We're all rather fond of Junie Flynn. I asked if she would agree to a few tests, and she said she would once you were back on your feet. She will be admitted to a testing facility as a Jane Doe, and afforded DMS protection. The final reports will be sealed and marked 'DMS eyes only.'" He paused. "No one else will know who she is, or . . . anything about her 'unique' family history."

"What happens if the tests show that she really is a hybrid?"

He smiled faintly. "I rather doubt that anything we discover about her will surprise me. No matter what genes are anchored to her DNA, at the end of the day she's one of us."

I nodded. "Yes she is."

But for how long? I wondered.

As if he could read my thoughts, Church said, "I convinced Miss Flynn to allow me to share her medical records with a few friends of mine in the industry. Top oncologists in the U.S. and elsewhere. After reviewing her test results, the doctors are saying some very encouraging things."

I stared at him.

"Miss Flynn has already scheduled new tests with some of these doctors."

"I—"

"We can't save everyone, Captain," he said, cutting me off before I could thank him. "But sometimes new doors of opportunity open."

We sipped our coffee, and looked at the hole in the world where the warehouse should have been.

"Dr. Sanchez tells me that it's your intention to try and visit every family," said Church.

I said nothing.

"One hundred and sixty-nine families in seventeen states. It's a logistical improbability."

"Maybe."

"And it isn't practical."

I turned to stare at him. "They were my friends," I growled.

He nodded. "They were my friends, too."

"They were my family."

"I understand. But what are you trying to accomplish? No one blames you."

"That's not the point—"

"No. No one expects you to be there in that way, either."

"Yes, they do."

"No, Captain, they do not. The families of the dead expect the government to do something, and I have made sure that is happening without red tape or delays. Officers of the appropriate military branches were present at every funeral. Every service was paid for."

"How? That would cost—"

"I have friends in the industry."

I gave that a bitter laugh. "What, you have friends in the death industry?"

Behind his tinted lenses, Church's eyes looked old and sad. "Why would that surprise you?"

I turned away.

He said, "Everything that should be done for the families of the fallen is being done, make no mistake. We will have a memorial service for all our friends, and that is where you need to be. There are a lot of people in the DMS who will be looking to you for leadership, for strength."

A line of dump trucks rumbled past, heading through the security checkpoint, driving into the ruins to begin the process of carting away all traces of this place.

"So many . . . ," I said.

"Yes," he agreed. "So many."

I drank the rest of my coffee and tossed the empty cup into a metal barrel that was half filled with burned debris. Church bent and ran his hand along Ghost's back, smoothing the hair.

Without looking at me, he said, "There are a lot of empty warehouses in Baltimore."

"No," I said. "It wouldn't be the same."

"Of course not."

"It can't be the same."

Church straightened and faced me. "It's not supposed to be the same, Captain. This station is gone. Most of the staff is gone. The war, however, continues. It will not pause to let us grieve, and it does not care if we are weary from our struggles. As a martial artist I would guess you're familiar with the Japanese proverb *'Nanakorobi yaoki'*?"

"'Fall seven times and stand up eight,'" I translated.

"The war requires us to stand up again, Captain."

He patted me on the shoulder and walked away. A block away I saw Brick standing by the open door of Church's car. Where Gus Dietrich should have stood. Someone else had risen to take that post. Brick saw me watching and gave me a single, slow nod. One survivor to another in a war that leaves no one unmarked.

I sighed.

(5)

The abduction of the President never made it to the public record. It was being handled internally and a brand new agency was being chartered that would oversee all aspects of that matter as well as anything that once fell under the Majestic umbrella. M3 was gone. The last remaining governor of M3, Yuina Hoshino, was now in custody and had been offered a very simple choice: talk or vanish into the system as a terrorist and traitor. When her lawyers trotted out the Majestic Charter signed by President Harry Truman, it complicated things in ways that will keep the Attorney General and the congressional committee formed to investigate the matter busy for decades to come. A lot of heads will roll, and a big, ugly cancer in the flesh of the American government is feeling the bite of a scalpel. Church's hand is on that scalpel. He was never the person to screw with at the best of times, but since the destruction of the Warehouse . . . well, let's just say that given a choice between being a suspected heretic during the days of the Inquisition and being any part of the Majestic program, the heretics had a much happier time of things.

The two T-craft—Shelton's and the Chinese model—were gone, blown to atoms in the skies above Beijing. No one will go on record to state who shot them down. At least, not on any record the public will ever get to see. I've seen the confidential reports. They'll be sealed and buried.

There have been no further sightings of T-craft anywhere. Not in months . . . but we're watching the skies. All of us, every nation on earth, are watching the skies.

The president claims to have no memory at all of anything that happened to him after going to bed that night. We've played poker—before and since—and I know when he's bluffing about a hole card. I just don't pretend to know what card he's going to play. Time will tell.

After the fight at Shelton's place, Mr. Church brought in four full DMS teams and locked everything down. This was suddenly and unexpectedly backed by a sternly written Executive Order. Dr. Hu—skeptic that he is—has been spending a lot of time there. I've heard that he's taken to drinking.

The real open question is China. We can't prove that it was their T-craft that destroyed the Locust bomber. At least, I don't think we can prove it. Oddly, diplomatic relations with China have never been more cordial and cooperative.

By special Executive Order Mr. Church has been given complete authority over the disposition of all materials and research scavenged from M3 and VanMeer castle. That includes the Black Book. The official word is that it was destroyed in the explosion when the cavern was destroyed. Knowing Church as I do, all of that stuff will be either destroyed or locked away. Or, perhaps given back to the rightful owners, though how that could be arranged was something Church never shared with me.

And . . . who were those owners? We still don't know.

They're out there somewhere, watching us to see if we keep our grubby fingers off their toys. Sure, that's an assumption, but in this case I don't think that it makes an ass of you or me.

Oh, yeah . . . and all the cats down at NASA are delighted to suddenly have their budget tripled. Imagine that.

(6)

On the first day of the New Year, as a soft veil of snow fell across the eastern seaboard, I stood next to Rudy Sanchez as he said all the right words to Circe O'Tree and she said the right words to him. They smiled at each other as if the world had never teetered on the edge of the abyss. They kissed like there would be an uncounted number of tomorrows. It did not matter to them or anyone that he wore a black eye patch or that he walked with a noticeable limp.

As they turned to greet the thunderous applause of soldiers and scientists, humanitarians and stone killers, close friends and foreign dignitaries, I looked for a few familiar faces in the crowd. I saw Mr. Church seated near the back. He was smiling. It may have been the only genuine and uncomplicated smile I'd ever seen on his face. But of course, no one but me was looking. Maybe Circe, but she was too practiced at pretending not to be his daughter to let her eyes linger there. I wonder what that smile did for her heart.

Rudy would see it, too. But maybe of all of us he was the one person who could have predicted that this cold, strange man could smile with such joy.

Then I turned my head away from Church and found another smiling face. Another joyful face. A face framed by masses of wavy blond hair, a face dusted by sun freckles. A face with eyes the color of a summer sky. She stood between the improbable bookends of Top and Bunny. They were all applauding.

Those blue eyes sought me out and there was a subtle transformation in her smile. What had been a smile of sheer happiness for Rudy and Circe now became something else, something private.

A smile meant for me.

A smile filled with love.

And I knew that when she looked at my face, that's what she saw.

The war might still be there, it might always be there, but at moments like this I could take a deep breath and remember what it was we fought to preserve.

And if our world was larger, and if we were not alone in the glittering vastness of the universe, I found that I was no longer afraid of that.

I found that it gave me hope.

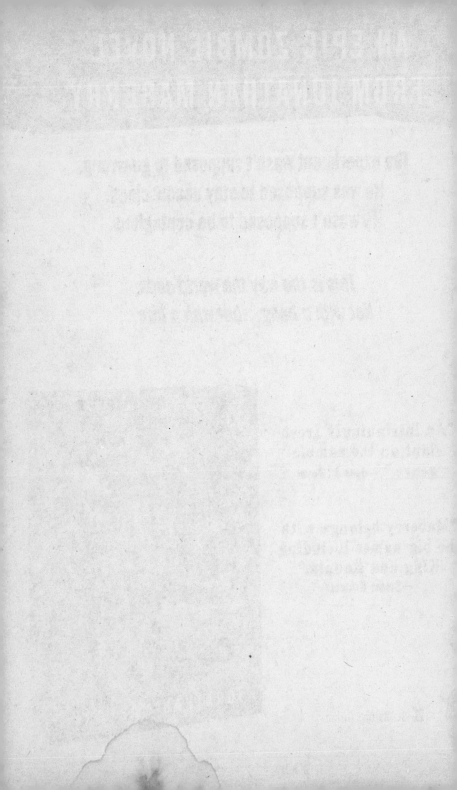